THIS MAN WAS MEANT TO CHANGE HER LIFE FOR ALL TIME.

He smiled down at her before he lurched to his feet and, using their still-joined hands, yanked her up out of the mud. He pulled until she slammed into his huge body, wet sticking to wet, the soaked silk of her dress completely useless and rendering her practically naked as it clung to every chilled curve of her body, outlining the shaped satin and lace of her bra and panties as she shivered like a drowned rat against him.

He held their joined hands between their bodies, their mingling blood running wet with the icy water and the mud sluicing down their forearms. His opposite arm, still bearing the blade in hand, wrapped around her waist and drew her very tightly against him.

"Now we will see what we will see, Tatyana Petrova," he said in a low, rough tone of voice. The remark was ominous at best, but Tatyana was surprisingly unafraid within the circle of his secure arms. She looked up at him, her body shaking and her teeth chattering, and when she met those mystically bright eyes, she realized that her life had just changed irrevocably. . . .

Other Books by Jacquelyn Frank

The Nightwalkers
Jacob
Gideon
Elijah
Damien
Noah
Adam

The Shadowdwellers
Ecstasy
Rapture
Pleasure

The Gatherers
Hunting Julian
Stealing Kathryn

Drink of Me

Published by Kensington Publishing Corporation

HUNTER

JACQUELYN FRANK

Writing As

JAX

ZEBRA BOOKS
KENSINGTON PUBLISHING CORP.
http://www.kensingtonbooks.com

First Zebra Books Mass-Market Paperback Printing: February 2014
ISBN-13: 978-1-4201-3444-5
ISBN-10: 1-4201-3444-2

First eKensington Electronic Edition: May 2013
First Zebra Books Electronic Edition: February 2014
eISBN-13: 978-1-4201-3543-5
eISBN-10: 1-4201-3543-0

10 9 8 7 6 5 4 3 2 1

Prologue

It had been ten years.

He turned his face up toward the night sky, feeling the sharp cold of winter across his skin, seeking the kiss of the moon as its thin light shone through the veil of clouds skimming its surface. Frost coated the hardened ground; every step he took crunching into dormant grasses and autumn's discarded leaves as he moved deeper into the woodlands. There was no snow, neither fresh nor old. Not unheard of, but rare for this time of year. He wondered if it had snowed at all this season yet.

He didn't guard his steps, the feeling of being on home soil relaxing his normal vigilance. The vibration of his power and presence brought nature to awareness, rippling through it in some ways, meshing with it in others; as foreign to it as it was familiar.

At last, he spied the breach between the two slanted oaks that marked the clearing. When he stepped between the thick trunks of these two old sentries, he saw the lone willow in the center of the uneven terrain of the clearing, and he felt his heartbeat quicken in anticipation. After all, it had been a decade since he'd last seen the Blessing Tree. A decade too long.

Oh, how he had missed this place!

The magnificent old tree whispered of its ancient power, tantalizing him with its hum of familiarity and homecoming. This was the center of his world. It had been since he was only seventeen. His blood stained the bark of the old willow, and so did the blood of his family. He had roamed very far from this core place, but distance had never changed the fact that his roots were here, just as much as the old willow's were.

It had been the agony within his family, caused by his very presence, which had driven him to abandon his home. He had been in pain, blinded by anger and guilt. All of the turbulent emotions young men are prone to succumbing to. Those feelings had spurred his decision to leave. Even now, years later, the hurt still lingered in his slightly tarnished spirit.

He moved closer to the old tree, the ground lumpy now with the running of its massive root system. Its gnarled trunk shone silvery luminescent in the frail moonlight, even through the curtain of thin, naked branches. He passed through them and headed farther in.

When he reached the base of the Blessing Tree, he carefully stepped up the steep knots of inclining roots. He touched the light gray of the bark, watching the weak moonlight dance with dappled patterns over the back of his hand. His palm warmed and prickled, the energy of the tree flowing through him. He couldn't help the deep sigh that rushed out of him as he was infused through every cell with the blessing and wisdom of the august tree. It swept away all the remnants of poorly managed emotions, lingering bitterness, and the disappointments of the past, giving much needed succor. His mind and heart cleared, his pulse pounded with joy.

He was home at last.

Chapter One

Tatyana Petrova bent her head forward and banged her forehead on the upper rim of her steering wheel.

"This isn't happening to me," she announced to the quickly chilling interior of her car. "This is the sort of thing that happens to stupid, unprepared women. You see," she explained, "I'm neither stupid nor unprepared. Therefore, logic dictates that this isn't happening to me."

She reached for her key, confident that her speech would make all the difference in the world. It turned in the ignition . . . and a nifty little click echoed into the car. This was followed by immediate, deafening, highly discouraging silence. Tatyana growled with disgust and yanked the useless key from the ignition of what had always been the most incredibly reliable automotive companion she had ever owned. She loved her car. From its multi-disc CD player to its in-dash hands-free cell phone, and even its cup holder that fit perfectly around her favorite cup.

"I have triple A. I have a cell phone. I even know how to change a damn tire!" She made an exaggerated sound of frustration. "But of course I can't get a cell signal in the middle of nowhere because I'm surrounded by mountains, and I don't *have* a flat tire!"

Tatyana sighed, laying her head back on the headrest. She cast a mean look at the cell phone on the passenger seat, and then decided it was time to end her temper tantrum. She was a modern gal and she could handle any crisis. It was just that she needed about five minutes of woe-is-me, PMS-worthy despair before she took action. Scooping up the phone and shoving it in her bag, she swung herself out of the car and marched back to the trunk. After popping it open, she rummaged around in her gym bag until she found her sneakers. She traded her heels for them, sliding her stocking feet easily into the Nikes. Granted, it didn't make a fashion statement when she was wearing a designer silk dress in shocking red that sparkled with a light dusting of glitter, but she wasn't about to trek up and down mountain roads in spiky leather stilettos just because they looked good. It was bad enough she had chosen a fringed shawl for a wrap and was likely to freeze her butt off by the time she found a working phone.

And that wasn't even the worst of it.

No, the worst of it was that her best friend, her confidant, the man she adored and loved most in the world . . . was going to kill her. Possibly even literally. She sighed as she slammed the trunk shut, then shivered.

"Happy freakin' New Year!" she cheered to herself, watching her breath cloud ominously in the air.

She was supposed to be in Manhattan at one of the swankiest New Year's parties in town. The firm she worked for was notorious for going all out, reserving the entire Panorama Grill, the restaurant at the top of the building she worked in. There was also the minor technicality that it was considered very bad form by your bosses if you didn't show up at the year-end party. Promotions could be gained or lost at this event based solely on appearances.

But was she making a fabulous impression on her bosses like she was supposed to? *Nooo*. Of course not. Here she was, her car broken down in the back of beyond with her unhappily freezing her cha-chas off, all for the sake of a be-loved brother who was going to murder her for the effort.

"Dimitre, I love you very much and I know you are worth this, but why in hell did you have to move to this scene straight out of *Deliverance*? God, I can't see a single light anywhere." She turned herself in a complete circle, to no avail. If the skyline around her was any indication, she was currently in a valley and the Catskills surrounded her with their sparsely populated mountain faces. "Well, at least the roads are paved and I don't hear any banjos in the distance," she quipped to herself as she shouldered her purse and began to trek off in the direction she'd been headed.

It was really her only choice. Tatyana was closer to where her brother lived than the nearest town, so it just made sense to keep going.

"And *someone* should have warned me about the sucky cell phone reception out here. I can't believe that, with what I pay for this phone, I can't even get a signal in an emergency. Now, here I am, a stranded woman marching down a spooky, remote road with no one to hear me scream. I'm in a damned plot for a B horror flick!"

Tatyana kept marching down said remote road at full steam, promising an ignorant Dimitre that he would be very sorry if his sister met a gruesome death by chainsaw. Of course, at the rate she was talking to herself, and considering her present frame of mind, maybe she'd be picking up her own chain-saw.

If she could only find a hardware store.

"Annali, love, what *are* you doing?"

Annali waved off the taunting query with a graceful hand, the filmy material of her blouse fluttering like the petals of a lavender orchid around her wrist. The romantic cuffs at the ends of the snug sleeves made for an incongruous picture as

she leaned over a massive worktable, one that was cluttered
to the very edges with a hundred or more labeled bottles and
pouches filled with all manner of curiosities. Adjoining tables held burners, sinks, a heavy mortar and pestle of marble,
and a network of beakers, flasks, and distillery equipment.
She toiled over all of these while dressed in an outfit spun of
the finest silk, yet she hadn't even bothered to don an apron
to protect her blouse or skirt.

She was clearly in the middle of something complex. Her
right hand was toying with a strand of pearls at her throat in
a rapid, absent gesture, while the notebook she was scrawl-
ing in was filled nearly corner to corner with notations by
her left hand.

Only half of her hair, a myriad sandy blond tones, remained swept up into its original coiffure; the other half was
a tumble of wayward curls that bounced happily on her
shoulders at their parole from the severe upsweep. She was
missing one of her shoes, her bare foot swinging in tempo to
some internal beat only she could hear. She had a smudge of
ink on her cheek that had an eerie Rorschach effect when
stared at too long.

"Stop hovering, Ryce," she scolded as she continued to
write furious notes without even bothering to look up.

"How long have you been closeted away here, Annali?"
Ryce persisted, looking for clues. There was a half-drunk
cup of tea on the table behind her, but he knew it was long
cold. There were no indications as to whether or not she'd
eaten. It was par for the course when she worked in a fever
like this that she'd always forget to eat.

"What day is it?" she countered.

"Friday."

"I've been here since Thursday."

Ryce was not misled.

"Of what bloody week?" he shot back.

She made a little moue with her pretty lips and finally
looked up at him so she could give him a full-on pout. "Please

stop pestering me. I'm a grown woman and I'm quite capable of caring for myself."

"That remains to be seen," Ryce said dryly, reaching out to sweep one of her slender hands in his, drawing it to his lips in a flutter of soft, lavender ruffles. He kissed the back of her wrist. "You know, Dimitre would never forgive me if I allowed you to starve to death. Come on, let me take you to dinner. Once I've fed you, I promise to leave you be."

"In the middle of all this?" she demanded, clearly aghast at the suggestion as she swept her free hand over the large work area, the pen in her fingers almost being flung away in her enthusiasm. "Ryce, you know very well I can't just get up and abandon things mid-experiment."

"It's nice to know that some things never change."

Annali gasped even as Ryce pivoted around sharply on the ball of his foot to face the new voice. The familiar newcomer had entered via the exterior conservatory doors, by way of the outlying gardens, and held the knobs, one in each hand, as he grinned at their gaping expressions.

"Hunter!"

Leave it to Annali to recover herself the quickest, Ryce thought with humor as she whipped her hand out of his grasp and flew at the fresh arrival like a beautiful lavender flamingo, all slim, delicate-looking arms and legs. She coiled her wrists behind Hunter's neck and drew him down for an enthusiastic welcome home kiss as he caught her around the ribs. Hunter flushed as her kisses moved to his cheeks with repeated enthusiasm. He flicked up brilliant blue eyes to see Ryce smirking at him, enjoying this display of Annali's affections. Hunter grinned and gave him a rude hand gesture behind her back as he bent to kiss her supple cheek affectionately.

"Blessed be. It's good to see you, Annali," he said warmly when she finally settled back onto her heels.

"Well it's *not* good to see you," she declared in contradiction, her Southern accent exaggerated by pique as she reached

out to slap him smartly on his shoulder in true Scarlett
O'Hara style. All she was missing was a hoopskirt and a fan.
"You are such a fiend, staying away so long!"

"Anna," Ryce scolded her from the worktables.

"Well, it's true," Annali said, whipping out one of her in-
famous pouts. There was a collective sigh from the men. It
was very hard to resist Annali's adorably perfect little pouts.

"I had my reasons, Annie," Hunter said simply, putting
her a little farther away from himself, trying to ease the discomfort of her little guilt trip.

"I know. But, in the name of the Lady, Hunter, this is the
information age! You could have written. A few lousy e-mails
here and there to let us know you were still alive wouldn't
have killed you."

Hunter glanced up at Ryce in a silent plea. Ryce gave him
a meaningful look and shook his head. Both men knew Annali had never, and would never, fully understand the reasons behind Hunter's departure so long ago. Neither would
she understand why Hunter had cut himself off from all contact with his friends. It had been difficult for Ryce to comprehend as well; but though he didn't agree with all of Hunter's
reasons, he respected them. For ten years he'd left Hunter to
his own devices, never contacting him, as per his wishes.

Until now.

It was painfully good to see him, Ryce thought as he
clasped his arms behind his back in a casual movement that
belied the emotions he was feeling, taking the opportunity to
look over Hunter. His old friend had changed in many ways.
He was as vigorous and sturdy a man as he'd ever been, in a
physical sense, but time had matured his body, making him
seem far more at ease within the roped musculature of his
build. It took discipline to maintain such a physique. Ryce
wondered if it was still Hunter's passions for Thoroughbreds
and martial arts that kept him fit and motivated. A person
could change a great deal in one decade, but Ryce doubted

that those essentials had altered. Hunter was born to ride and fight. His seat on a horse was a phenomenal thing to behold, poetry between man and beast. His hand-to-hand reactions, the ease of his uncanny reflexes, and his succinct choices in the heat of a fight made him unbelievably valuable at one's back.

Hunter had also cut his hair. That was a sharp difference. He'd previously kept the pitch-colored locks long enough to touch his shoulders, sweeping them into a tail as Ryce himself did. Now his hair was severely shortened, cropped to a perfectly manicured line over the back of his neck, with only the front and top showing a slightly rakish length that hung in curving spears over his forehead. His eyes, the remarkable cerulean blue that leapt out at anyone he glanced at, were notably less shadowed by pain and grief, and Ryce was glad to see it. As for the rest, he could only guess at this juncture. Who knew how time had treated Hunter? It had treated them all so differently. In fact, it was time that had compelled Ryce to draw Hunter home at last, back into their fold where he truly belonged.

Time and danger.

"Well, anyway," Annali said breezily, "I forgive you. But only because I have so much to tell you and I need to hear absolutely everything about you as well."

"Since Ryce is intent on feeding you, pet, why don't we all go out to eat?" Hunter suggested. "I'm starved, as well as jet-lagged, and I think dinner and a fresh bed would make all the difference."

"I don't doubt it," Ryce said at last. "Annali, go and change for dinner. Hunter and I will be waiting for you in the front parlor when you're ready."

"Ryce," Annali used his name as a gentle scold, her fair lavender blue eyes holding a world of admonishment. "Hunter's only just come through the door. I don't want you harping on him already, okay?" She spoke with lightness, but knowing her so well, Ryce knew there was a little bit of an irrational fear that if he upset the apple cart, Hunter would just walk off again and this time he wouldn't come back for good.

"I'm curious over her definition of harping," Hunter chuckled, an ungentlemanly reminder that she'd just been harassing him herself.

Annali turned a speaking glance on Hunter that announced her pique that he should make fun at her expense. "I mean it," she sniffed, her tone like a mother scolding young boys. "Both of you behave and be nice."

"Go change, Anna," Ryce persisted, giving her a gentle shove in the direction of the conservatory exit.

As she left, Hunter turned to close the exterior doors against the winter cold before it destroyed the hothouse atmosphere and endangered some of Annali's precious plants. By the time he turned around, Ryce had done the same with the hallway doors. The two men crossed the room, meeting in the middle with an enthusiastic handshake and hug.

"It's good to see you, my friend. Blessed be to you," Ryce greeted with an eagerness no less keen than Annali's before he stepped back.

"And you as well," Hunter said with a grin. "Ryce, Annali is beautiful. And happy. It's hard to reconcile the woman I just saw with the haunted seventeen-year-old she was when I left. Well done, my friend."

"Annali deserves all the credit," Ryce said dismissively. "I see you've picked up a fair bit of Romany in your inflections." He noted this as a first clue to Hunter's whereabouts all these years.

"No doubt," Hunter chuckled. "Among others. Whereas the Queen's English is sounding surprisingly bastardized from your tongue. Too much time in New York, I'm thinking." Hunter released Ryce's hand and clasped his shoulder briefly. "You look very well. I hope the others are all in good health, too?"

"As well as ever. As you can see"—he gestured to the

workstations sprawled in the center of the conservatory— "Annali is a thriving biochemist and is still the obsessive botanist. With much success, I might add."

"I'm not surprised at Annali succeeding at anything," Hunter remarked, with a visibly strong streak of pride.

"Agreed," Ryce said, taking great comfort in the signs he saw in Hunter that told him he'd made the right choice by summoning him home. The only thing he would ever regret was that he hadn't done so much sooner. "Kaia is buried knee deep in work at the local hospital, as well as a free clinic. She's presently on a short lecture circuit. Dimitre, the new witch I told you about, is with her."

"You mean Annali's new love?"

"New and only. Besides you, there was never anyone else."

Hunter smiled at that, a whimsical tilting of his lips. "She had a young girl's crush back then. Hero-worship. It lasted only as long as those things do. She's thought of me as a big brother ever since, just as she does you." He raised a brow of inquisition. "I assume you're going to tell me why Annali's mate is off with Kaia?"

"In time," Ryce agreed. He watched as Hunter turned to inspect some of Annali's potion bottles. "Lennox is well, but Gracelynne is recovering from a riding accident," he said casually.

That brought Hunter's attention fully back to Ryce, his handsome face folding into concern and consternation. "A riding accident?" Ryce knew there was no getting around the sharp questions in those intuitive eyes. "Forgive me, Ryce, but I am trying to wrap my mind around the concept of Gracie having a riding accident. She's nearly as good as I am on horseback."

"Of course she is. You can just imagine her embarrassment. A spirited horse and a low branch was all it took," the Englishman said dismissively. "She landed on her rear good and hard, but she's got nothing worse than a bruised coccyx and a broken wrist to show for it. After dinner we will discuss it in more detail. Annali was unusually disturbed seeing Gracelynne brought down like that, and I'd prefer we not thrash it out in front of her. You know how she can be when someone she loves is hurt. Brings up bad memories."

Hunter frowned and nodded. He knew very well why Annali was sensitive to those things. Her parents had been murdered right before her eyes eleven years earlier.

"In the meantime, I suggest you shower and change for dinner yourself," Ryce went on to say. "You're looking a bit the worse for wear from your flight."

"I feel worse for wear. Thanks for pointing it out." Hunter stopped and went still, his mind clicking. He narrowed severe eyes on his friend. "You didn't mention Asher."

Ryce tried not to visibly wince, but there was no avoiding the instant tension that rushed through him at the mention of Asher's name.

"Ryce, don't you dare tell me I've been called back because of him." Hunter's good humor and congeniality vanished instantly. His entire body coiled tight as he narrowed a cutting indigo stare on Ryce, giving the other man a chill because of the sheer intensity that was put into the look. Ryce was a potent man in his own right, the High Priest of this notoriously powerful coven, but if there was one man he knew not to cross, it was Hunter Finn.

Hunter was Sentinel of Willow Coven, Spellcaster witch and defender of all his brethren in the coven. Ryce's personal assassin, if necessary. Or at least he had been at one time. But the whole point of Hunter's return was to resume that role, and it was almost comforting to see the coldness in him that assured Ryce the man still had the edge it took to be a killer. He would need it before long.

"Hunter, you don't understand," he said at last, releasing a regretful sigh. "You've been away a long time and, as requested, I kept from contacting you. Even now I would have honored the request and handled this on my own, but . . ."

Ryce's strong hands curled into fists. "Things have changed. I can't explain everything to you now, and I beg you not to bring anything up at dinner. Please"—Ryce held out a placating palm—"just trust me. We will enjoy a good meal with good friends, and after Annali and the others have retired, you and I will talk."

"It isn't like you to do things behind their backs. This isn't the way I remember us doing things. Haven't we always made choices as a united group? Or has that changed since I've been gone?"

"It hasn't changed as a general rule," Ryce assured him, his tone a little impatient that Hunter would even ask the question. "But it can't be that way this time, Hunter. Please, I beg you not to ask any more questions until later."

Hunter scowled at his friend for a long moment, and then nodded curtly in agreement. He had sense enough to know how serious things were when Ryce started keeping secrets from the others. The other man had been the leader of this group for as long as Hunter could remember. There were reasons for that, not the least of which was that Ryce was one of the world's most powerful white witches.

It was on that merit alone that Hunter acquiesced to his High Priest. After all, it was because of Ryce's personal request that he'd rousted himself out of his self-imposed exile in the first place . . .

Finally returning to the coven he had once called home.

Hunter had every intention of respecting Ryce's request to wait for explanations, but he had no desire to wait to see Gracelynne. After he'd showered and dressed for dinner, he left his suite in the west wing and crossed the mansion to the east wing, where Gracie's rooms were housed. Willow House, a grand estate in the Catskill Mountains of New York, boggled the mind with its sheer size and appointments. Ryce had even larger holdings in England, but this manse had been built with all the luxuries of modern architecture and convenience.

Ryce's taste was everywhere. The mansion was a melding of the modern with timeless classics. He'd pulled it off quite well. The most thoughtful concept the Englishman had incorporated into the design was that each of the members of Willow Coven had his or her own complete living suite, including a sitting room, private bath, and kitchenette along with a bedroom.

Regardless of these conveniences, household custom dictated that, if one was present in the house, cocktails and dinner were shared together at set times. However, with private kitchenettes, there was always the option for one to be a little anti-social if the mood struck. Hunter suspected that Ryce still took tea at four o'clock every day as well, and since half the household was native to England, it would be a communal affair, too.

You could take the Brit out of Britain . . .

That made him smile. He had missed Willow House. He'd missed his companions and their familiar ways. It was an almost surreal feeling to be walking these halls again after such a great gap in time. So much was the same, the basic layout and shapes of the halls and rooms, but furnishings and colors had changed dramatically over time. Familiar paintings had shifted positions or even rooms. Floors once carpeted were now polished wood or marble. This was all Ryce's doing, he knew. Willow Coven's leader was a closet decorator. He had a wonderful eye, making it grand and beautiful without tawdriness or ostentatiousness, a distinction that was only made by a fine line at times.

Witchcraft was a full-time art, and each of them had his specialty, but there was such a thing as over-devotion when it came to magic. It was important for them to find and enjoy pursuits outside of their work. One could only excel at the Craft if one took enjoyment in it. It was sad when witches labored hard at their magic without ever truly learning to enjoy it. Without taking pleasure in magic, witches would never reached their fullest power and potential.

This truth had been a strong motivator in Hunter's departure from the coven so many years ago. At the time he'd known he would take no joy in his magic so long as he was weighed down by the sorrow he was feeling. Indeed, he'd thought to forsake his gifts completely for the remainder of his life. It had never once occurred to him that his place wouldn't be filled in his absence, or that the others would be waiting for his return. He was still trying to wrap his thoughts around the concept even as he reacted emotionally to being home again.

When he reached Gracelynne's suite, Hunter didn't bother to knock. He entered the sitting room, expecting to see her sitting by the fire working on one project or another. He stopped in his tracks when he saw the darkness of the room, and then laughed softly under his breath, reminding himself that not everything would be exactly as he remembered it.

He crossed to the doors of her bedroom and here he paused to knock gently.

"Bugger off, Rochelle, I don't want to eat," came Gracelynne's rather petulant reply from within.

Hunter's expression altered to bemusement. Gracie, it seemed, was feeling a little cranky and taking it out on their chef. He stifled a grin and knocked again.

"I said bugger off, goddamn it! Now quit pestering me, you bloody twit!"

Hunter's amusement faded under the onslaught of the viciously spoken remark. Surely he'd heard wrong, because the Gracelynne he knew would never be abusive to anyone who didn't truly deserve it. He reached for the door and pushed it open, ignoring privacy now as a frown marred his features. The bedroom was equally as dark as the sitting room, and with a snap of his fingers, Hunter brought the bedside lamp to life, spilling light into the room.

Illumination flooded over the woman who awkwardly
flung herself up into a sitting position and whipped around
to glare at the intruder through a tangled mop of jaw-length,
ginger curls. A pair of dull, earthen brown eyes bored into
him angrily for several long seconds before recognition occurred. Her small, pointed chin dropped down as her mouth
opened in shock.

"Hunter," she whispered.

And then she burst into tears. She covered her mouth and
tried to turn away from him, but he was already sitting on
her bed and dragging her close into his embrace. He held her
securely, rocking her softly as she wept hard and wild, her
angry hands fisting around the fabric of his shirt at his
shoulders; her body shaking with her emotion. All the while,
Hunter was swallowing back fury and shock.

Beneath the curtain of corkscrew curls, Gracelynne's face
and neck were covered in livid bruises that showed the clear
mark of fingerprints. One of her hands was wrapped from
palm to elbow in the rough but colorful purple of a fiberglass
cast. He thought a hasty detection spell within his mind, allowing him to sense the stiffness in her entire body posture,
the soreness in her belly and legs, and the distinctive bruising on the sides of both her hips. There was hardly a spot on
her body that hadn't been abused in some fashion.

"Gracie," he murmured softly to her, closing his eyes and
concentrating on purging himself of the fury rushing wildly
through him. She didn't need him to be uncontrolled in his
emotions right now. She needed his strength and as much
comforting peace as he could manage.

"Oh, Hunter. The Lady has blessed us. You've come home
to us!" she sobbed, her hands creeping deep into his hair and
holding him as if she had no intention of releasing him ever
again. It made him smile against her soft cheek and he shifted
the smile into a gentle kiss against her bruises.

"I missed you, Gracie," he told her on a fierce whisper,

but he didn't squeeze her in hugs as he had Annali, knowing she was too sore to bear such enthusiasm.

And all the while, all he could think of was that Ryce had lied to him.

There was no way in hell Gracelynne had gotten her injuries in a riding accident. He'd known it the very instant the light had touched her. As an avid equestrian, he knew what happened when one fell from a horse, or even got swept from horseback by a tree limb, as Ryce had suggested. No. Trees and animals didn't cause wounds like these.

Men did.

A human being had caused these injuries, both interior and exterior. He could feel the damage ran deeper than bruises and broken bones. He didn't need the wrenching heartache of her tears to sense that, although every salty drop sent the knowledge home all the more. It wasn't Grace he would be questioning about this, though. Oh no. She wasn't handling the aftermath of whatever had happened well at all; sitting in the dark, refusing food, and the Goddess only knew what other manifestations of grief and anger she suffered.

Annali's sensitivities or no, he wasn't going to rest until Ryce explained himself. As Willow Coven's High Priest, Ryce was ultimately responsible for the safety of those who lived within his protection. Plainly he had failed Gracelynne when it came to this duty. Hunter would have him answer for it before the end of the hour, dinner be damned.

"I'm home now, honey," he soothed her softly. "And I'm so happy to see you."

"So long," she sniffled, swiping her undamaged hand over her cheeks. "You've been gone so long. It hasn't been the same without you. So much has changed . . ." She pulled away with that remark, shivering as she turned her body slightly. "I know you felt you had to go. I always understood your reasons. I don't mean to lay a guilt trip on you."

"I know that," he scolded gently, touching her chin to

make her look back into his eyes directly. He wouldn't have her afraid to speak her mind to him with the boldness she had always used before. "Just as I know it was you who had to pick up the slack I left behind me when I went. I heard no complaints, though. You've done extremely well in my absence, and Willow Coven has been blessed to have you. The house is clearly safe and secure, and all, except yourself at the moment, are in extraordinarily good health from what I've seen.

"As for guilt trips, you and Annali are loving in your reproaches. Ryce was a bit more petulant when . . ." Hunter hesitated, not wanting her to think he'd been called back because of her, even though he now suspected the attack she'd suffered had something to do with it. "Well, you know how he loves to give stern lectures about duty and honor and yaddayaddayadda . . ." He rolled his eyes, making her laugh through her tears.

"Right. That's our Ryce," she agreed, reaching to rub his arm, as if she couldn't believe he was real and solid and *there*. "Well, you look very handsome and well turned out. Not travel clothes, I'll warrant. Going out so soon?"

"Yes. Ryce and Annie are taking me out to dinner. It sounds like you haven't eaten yet," he said with a pointed look of reproof for her earlier petulance when he'd knocked on her door. "Why don't you come with us, honey? A quick shower to get this mop-top under control," he said, tousling her curls roughly until she laughed and slapped him away, "and you'll be good as gold."

"Cheeky bugger," she scolded him. "I can't possibly go out in public looking this way," she argued, touching her face self-consciously.

"Suit yourself," he said easily, pausing to kiss her on both of her cheeks very slowly and pointedly. "You *will* eat, however. I'm sending Rochelle up with a tray of your favorites, and I don't want to hear that you turned it away. I'll take it as a personal insult."

"No, I won't," she agreed with a full smile. "I've an appetite now that I've seen you. I'm so happy you've come home!"

"And I'm happy to be home. I'll come see you as soon as we get back, okay?"

"Brilliant," she agreed, giving him as huge a hug as she could manage.

Chapter Two

"You know what I need?" Tatyana asked the frigid night rather sarcastically. "I need a nice snow shower. No, better yet, a thunderstorm. With some icy rain running down the back of my dress. Now that would make this perfect."

She sighed through severely chattering teeth and kept walking. She'd traded walking with jogging to warm herself up, but she was at the end of a really long day, which was the end to a really long week, and she was too tired to run anymore. She simply could not understand how she could have gotten into so much trouble so damn quickly. Clouds obscured a great deal of the sky, and she had no stars to guide her, but it wasn't as though she were trekking the Himalayas. It was the freaking *Catskills*! How could she not have passed a single house? Farm? Shack!

The world was conspiring against her. She wasn't a fatalistic person normally, firmly believing that each person made his or her own providence, but this was really too much after the week she'd had.

First her lovesick assistant had quit, without any notice, to get married, leaving Tatyana in the lurch when she'd needed to prepare a presentation to her newest clients. That was Monday. Tuesday, her brother Sergei, the private investigator, had shown up at her office. He had been a veritable font of evil information on her already and definitively *ex* boyfriend, just so he could reiterate more strongly how badly in need of a beating the rotten bastard was. Her overprotective sibling had taken up half her morning with his gossip until she'd been forced to throw him out. Wednesday had been the beginning of a three-day office campaign to drive her completely bats about this lousy New Year's party she didn't have a date for, thank you very much.

Then, today, her ex-boyfriend had been lurking by her car when she had left the office, with a fresh new rose and an old, greasy charm. He'd tried to cajole her into inviting him to be her date. She had said yes, so long as he promised to bring his wife, whom he had neglected to mention to her during their dating. The jerk had not taken her suggestion well at all, hurling the rose and various insults at her.

Her only consolation, she had reminded herself, was that she'd never slept with the loser. The thought actually warmed her as she picked up her pace. In fact, she was so focused on her brisk stride that it took her several minutes to note the lights suddenly appearing over the rise in the road she was climbing. When she finally did, she stopped dead in her tracks and exhaled a happy cloud of relieved breath. It was a house. A very freaking big house by the look of it.

"Holy shit," she gasped. "I've found it!" Dimitre had said the place was huge. A compound, he'd said. It looked more like a resort! "Ooo, chimneys! Fire. Me like fire."

The only problem? There were about twenty acres of land between said house and one popsicle redhead standing stupidly on the side of the road. On the plus side, it seemed to be a mostly cleared field. On the boo-hiss side, it was all uphill from there.

She abandoned the road and began to trek across the field.

*   *   *

Hunter waylaid Ryce just as he was about to enter the parlor. He sensed Annali was still upstairs, so he dragged Ryce into the privacy of the room and slammed the door shut. He instantly turned on his old friend.

"I just saw Gracie," he snapped.

He really didn't need to say more and Ryce knew it.

"Hunter, I asked you to . . ."

"I refuse to wait for an explanation as to why you lied to me," he interrupted harshly. "It's absolutely unacceptable, Ryce. Our precious Annali isn't here for you to hide behind, and knowing her, she'll be late, which gives you plenty of time to explain to me what the *hell* is going on here! I have all my senses, and I have my intelligence, Ryce! I can damn well tell the difference between a woman who fell from a horse and a woman who has been abused at someone's hands." Hunter paused to draw a furious breath, trying to force his emotions under control. "Now, you will explain yourself, whether or not you think I have the right to demand it."

"I didn't withhold full explanation to punish you for abandoning the coven, Hunter," Ryce retorted sharply. "I am not so petty, and you bloody well should know it. I've been patient and accepting of your choices for ten years and that hasn't changed just because I was compelled to call you back."

Hunter watched as the High Priest of his coven bent his dark head and collected his thoughts for a moment. They were both taking slow, measured breaths in order to cool their roiling tempers. It would do neither of them any good to begin fighting, and it certainly wouldn't benefit the coven.

"Gracelynne was attacked a few days ago," Ryce continued abruptly. "She says she doesn't remember the fight or the attacker, and if you had seen her directly after you'd understand why she can't . . . or won't. She was out riding, alone. A few hours later her horse returned to the stable, saddle empty. Lennox and I went and found her." Ryce shook his head slowly as he reviewed the horrible memory. "The entire area for an acre around where we found her looked like a war zone. She put up a hell of a fight. You knew her best when she was more of a scrapper, when her enthusiasm in a firefight got her through more than anything. But she's changed, Hunter. Gracelynne's become a true warrior. She's extraordinarily skilled and manages her Elemental magic with style and control. Wait until you see it," he said, his voice flooded with pride. "When you do, you'll understand what it took for Gracie to be defeated. It was no easy task for her enemy, I assure you."

"Nox analyzed the spell remains left around the area in an attempt to understand what had happened. It's a very useful skill he's developed," Ryce explained, "that allows him to study the forensics of magical residue. Whoever it was, the bastard was clever. Gracie's attacker magically dampened the entire area so she couldn't cast a call for help, while simultaneously masking all of our natural connections as a coven. I don't need to tell you how powerful a spell like that would have to be, Hunter. A warlock would drain a great deal of resources for that spell alone, never mind battling with someone of Gracie's skill afterward."

"Are you certain it was a warlock, then? Not a rogue?" It was usual for dark warlocks and white witches to mix, but there were also non-aligned witches, rogues who were without a coven, who sometimes got it in their heads to cause trouble.

"Nothing is certain, but I do have suspicions and I will explain them in a moment. I estimate Gracie's conflict had to have lasted at least an hour in order to leave her so weak. Once she was isolated from the rest of us, all her enemy had to do was beat her back until she exhausted her magic. It's hard to imagine any single warlock having the power to take on Grace in such a manner, but Nox swears he could find only two magical signatures. Hers and her enemy's." Ryce's teeth made a sharp sound as they clenched together. "Once he had her exhausted and at his mercy, he went for the old-fashioned joy of putting his hands on her."

"A male," Hunter hissed. "I can see you are as certain of it as I am. Was she raped, Ryce? She had handprints buried into the flesh of her hips, but she didn't cringe from my touch. Does she even know?" he demanded.

"We had no choice but to bring Gracelynne to hospital, since Kaia wasn't here. They did a kit, but the nurse said she didn't see any tearing or bruising. No sign of . . . biological evidence. But you and I both know a warlock can use magic to make a victim compliant, and it doesn't take magic to use a condom. No one will know for certain but Gracelynne, and right now . . ."

"She can't remember."

"I suspect her attacker got a kick out of threatening her with rape at the very least. She was naked and insensate when we found her, staked out on the ground like some kind of twisted sacrifice. But there was no track of the enemy, even though I could feel he'd been there moments before we arrived."

Hunter took in a low, steady breath, trying to keep himself from feeling the sharp bile of guilt in his throat. A few days. Only a few days earlier and he might have been there. To help, maybe. To track, definitely.

The only comfort was that vengeance was still waiting for him. Unfortunately, it would be of little comfort to Gracelynne. It was no wonder Annali had been freaked out after they had discovered Grace in such a state. Annali had spent a nightmarish pair of weeks being violated by a psychotic warlock named Evan when she'd been only sixteen years old. This after she'd watched him kill her family. Only Hunter and Ryce's fortuitous rescue had spared her from a continuing life worse than death.

"Just who is it you think did this?" he asked, his tone heavy with disgust for the twisted behaviors of his own sex.

"If I had to make a guess? It's a dark coven in Pennsylvania, not far across the border between the states," Ryce informed him. "Hunter, they are by far the most massive collection of warlocks I have ever seen in my lifetime. I've read about only a few other cult covens like this, bursting at the seams with dark witches. Someone is hoping to eradicate Willow coven by sheer force of numbers. They tried once in November, attacking us on an outing when all of us were together in one place. Twelve to seven odds, and they had the element of surprise. We almost lost Annali's new lover, Dimitre. We might have lost more than that if not for him. He's a Tempus witch. He can control time."

"No fucking way," Hunter exclaimed. "Damn, Ryce, I've been all over this world this past decade, and I've run into covens from here to Shanghai. I have met only one Tempus witch in my experience, and her coven had to bind her powers because she went insane from memory jumping. She couldn't control it."

A witch's magic, or Craft, was usually focused on a singular school of power. There were well over a dozen disciplines, but the Tempus school was rare for a reason. It was also unbelievably potent if it could be mastered. Of all the schools of witchcraft, Spellcasters were among the most powerful. It was common for this discipline to produce witches who became either Sentinel or High Priest in white covens. Willow Coven had two Spellcasters: Ryce, and now again Hunter. Although they shared the same school, their skills had forked off into two very different directions over the years. Ryce enjoyed delving into the magic of the Egyptians and even more ancient Craft. Hunter had begun there, but leaving the coven had sent him veering into more modern mysticism. However, while their sources of magic now seemed so different, the punch they packed was equally impressive.

"Right. His power is a bit twitchy," Ryce agreed, "but Dimitre has a handle on it, though it's all a bit new. Still, it was enough to save us that day. We may have finished the warlocks off easily, thanks to him, but I promise you, they were bloody powerful. They would have kicked our asses into the corner. Willow Coven would have survived, but not intact. I'm convinced I would have lost a witch that day."

Hunter knew Ryce didn't exaggerate for drama.

"I take it they've been raising hell elsewhere?" Hunter asked.

"Yes. Ever since they tipped their hand to us. They knew we would track them, so it's as though it's bloody Christmas morning for them now. They're doing some terrible damage in the civilian world and they need to be checked." Ryce looked at him with grim determination in his eyes. "The Great Mother only knows how many familiars a coven that size is holding captive. The very thought shreds my soul.

"I realized right away that this was going to be an undertaking far more massive than we're used to. You understand? Granted, we *are* the most powerful white coven on the Eastern Seaboard, Hunter, even without our Sentinel." There was no reproach in his pointed look. "But it was clear that this would take us all working at the top of our talents in order for us to succeed. And you as well." Ryce turned his head aside, staring off into nothingness for a long beat. "But before we could get you here to help, they struck again.

"They went for the women first, Hunter. Annali was attacked the same day Gracelynne was. I suspect if Kaia hadn't left the night before with Dimitre, she would have met with a similar ambush."

"What happened to Annali?" Hunter demanded through his teeth.

"Some cuts, some bruises . . . scared the hell out of her. But she's resourceful, our Annie. She got the better of the three who cornered her."

"Sweet Lady, three to one?"

"Unfortunately for the warlocks, they underestimated our girl's powers. Annali dispatched them quickly. She thought it was a random ambush by rogues until everyone met up at

Gracie's bedside and exchanged notes. We're lucky they misjudged Annie or she'd be in a bed beside Grace and I'd be answering to one hell of a pissed-off Tempus."

"Did they?" Hunter asked suddenly, giving Ryce a dark look. "Or are you being led to believe that? Maybe they didn't fail, Ryce. Maybe they succeeded at exactly what they wanted to."

Ryce's brows lifted in surprise. "What are you saying?"

"Besides you and me, Gracelynne is the most powerful member of the coven. She has the experience, the temerity to fight to the death, and the skill. You said it yourself. She's a force to contend with. They don't know about me. No one knew you'd summoned me back. So next to you, she was the second strongest threat in a pitched battle. Taking her out severely weakens your position, Ryce. What better way to get to you than to take out your biggest gun?"

"Bloody hell," Ryce swore on a soft breath.

"It's the nature of the attack that gets me. Whoever it was made certain to screw with Grace's mind. Sure, they took her out physically, but that's temporary. People heal. Messing with her head will last longer. And maybe it isn't a coincidence this happened when our Healer witch is off on a lecture. And this thing with Annali," Hunter went on, "is just odd. Three to one for Annali. One to one for Grace? Failure with Anna, but success with Grace. Something isn't right."

Ryce agreed. But with Hunter back, he felt more secure. Ryce's faith in the future safety of his coven solidified just a bit more. He'd been afraid for some time now that he was going to lose one of his beloved witches, that he wouldn't be strong enough to protect them. When Gracie had been found so horribly injured, it had devastated him as a leader and protector.

Hunter reached out to lay a strong, steady hand on Ryce's shoulder. A decade could change much, but he knew it would never change the fact that the well-being of the Willow Coven meant everything to Ryce. Anything that happened to them would hit straight at his heart. These attacks had taken a great toll on his confidence, and Hunter could see it even if no one else would. Ryce wouldn't allow his shaken self-assurance to be visible to those who depended on him for his strength. As High Priest, he would reveal his starkest fears only to his Sentinel, who was his advisor and confidant as well as his in-pocket warrior. The leader of Willow Coven had gone too long without this crucial support system. Hunter wasn't responsible for Ryce never having replaced him in all these years, but he would take back the mantle of Sentinel with pride and full commitment, bringing peace to his old and trusted friend.

Ryce was a born leader. He was a natural mediator and guide. His power and his ability to stand strong in truth and grounded in the morals of their coven were legendary. Hunter was a guardian. A rock. He'd always performed best as the strength behind the leader. He had the unflagging loyalty necessary to be Ryce's champion and protector, while being malleable enough to take orders with ease. But he also had the strength to question his commander when necessary, to keep Ryce's emotions in check, just as he was doing now.

Ryce and the coven had survived for a long time without him. They had even thrived. Nevertheless, it was clear that he was needed now, and Ryce had proven his wisdom as a leader by recognizing that.

Even though it had meant breaking a ten-year-long promise.

"I see now why you summoned me, Ryce."

"We need your power, Hunter," he said. "For starters, Gracie needs justice. Your type of justice. We're all in need of protection that only you are capable of giving us. You are Sentinel," he said firmly, meeting the bold blue of his friend's gaze, speaking so much more with that look than with his words. "We've always needed you."

"I don't understand why you didn't replace me," Hunter said in an unexpectedly quiet voice, his brows drawing together deeply in a frown. "The coven has needed a Sentinel for ten years, and you never thought to fill my place? It has made you weaker than you could've been. This dark coven might not have attacked you if you'd had a Sentinel."

"It comes to this," Ryce said, his hands resting on his hips and his legs braced apart. "With all due respect to Gracie and the others, there will never be a witch on this planet who could fill your shoes. You've always been, and will always be, the most competent witch I know. Everyone else pales beside you. Besides"—he shrugged and gave Hunter a crooked little smile—"you're family, Hunter. The bond of the coven is stronger than blood, and we're all brothers and sisters here. Losing you was like losing a critical limb, and not just because of your power and protection, my friend. You left holes in the hearts of your family, even though we loved you enough to let you go. So long as you were alive there could be no other Sentinel for us. Surely you know that?"

Hunter lowered his eyes, but a corner of his mouth curled in a smile.

"It was a pleasant surprise to hear from you, Ryce. I didn't react at all the way I thought I would whenever I imagined you breaking your silence to call me. When your scry came through and you made the request, I suddenly realized that I was ready. More than ready. That it was long overdue. I was good in this place. I was whole, powerful, and loved, and I really wanted that back."

"Then we're even. We really wanted you back. For a variety of selfish reasons. However, I've only one use for you at the moment."

"First line of defense?"

"More like a harbinger. Annali is coming, so we'll talk more about it later, but I mean to send you into the serpents' nest with a message for those sons of bitches who thought to lay hands on our sister witches." Ryce's smile turned positively wicked. "I can't wait until they get a taste of you, mate."

"As it turns out, neither can I," Hunter agreed as he turned to face the opening door.

Annali swept into the room, all silk and sparkling smile, ink smudges left behind. She instantly drifted into Hunter's embrace, unable to resist hugging him again. He chuckled at her easy affection, the warmth of it shedding the darkness of his conversation with Ryce, and turning him back to the task of settling back in with his family. He looked down into her light eyes, the nearly lavender color enhanced by her dark violet dress. Her hair, the warm blond of beach sand, was coiffed to perfection once more, all but a few soft curls near her ears.

"Well, aren't you a picture," Hunter praised her. "Come on. I'm starving, and I hear someone has a new love to tell me all about."

"Ryce! You told? I wanted to tell him." Annali made a face at her High Priest. "You spoiled my surprise."

"Regardless of who mentioned it, I haven't got any of the juicy details. Let's get going and I promise to hang on your every word."

Hunter laid a hand on her waist and guided her out of the parlor to the front door. Ryce helped Anna into a beautiful sable faux, making sure she was snug against the cold night, and Hunter grasped the handle of the large, ornately carved oak door.

He pulled it open, thoroughly surprised when a woman stumbled into him.

Chapter Three

Tatyana had braced a hand on the door just for a moment in order to pull a painful twig from the instep of her sneaker when it gave way under her weight. Since she'd tested it for sturdiness beforehand, she was taken completely by surprise. She stumbled backward over the threshold, crashing into something solid and blessedly warm. The contrast in temperatures caused a violent series of shivers to set in straight away. She was so numb from cold she was frankly startled to find her body able to react at all.

Then again, she wasn't so numb that she couldn't feel a pair of very strong, very large hands grasping her by her breasts as she was caught up against that cozy physical warmth. Male warmth, she realized, to go with male hands cradling her intimately. Intimate enough to make her blush and scuffle in a quick effort to get her feet under her. He helped her with a firm, decisive resettling of her weight and his hands slid down to the more neutral territory of her waist, where they stayed to steady her.

Flustered and embarrassed, she whipped around in a nearly military about-face, the action doing nothing to shed the hands that simply slid around the silk of her cocktail dress. By the time she was looking up into his face, she was quite snugly held in his hands and very nearly against his body.

Tatyana opened her mouth to excuse herself, but the words all died pitiful little deaths in the back of her throat, a tragic mass suicide of vowels and consonants from which she might never recover. All of this because she'd looked up into the very bluest and most outrageously beautiful eyes she'd ever seen. Skies and oceans were never this perfectly blue, she marveled in awe. Only an artist's tube of brilliant cerulean could ever come close. Fringed by blacker than black lashes and rakish spikes of pitch colored hair hanging around them here and there, those eyes were far too perfect for actual words.

It went downhill from there. Or was it uphill? More likely the whole damn roller coaster, she thought. Suntanned and windburned skin that dashed ruggedness onto what otherwise would have been boyishly handsome features, and a squared-off jaw that would have done Superman proud. Incongruous with the bravado of rough good looks, there was the lightest splash of freckles over the bridge of his nose, no doubt a result of all the wind and sun he clearly spent time in. However, the sight was enough to break her silence, and she finally managed to make sounds.

Giggles.

Oh, wow, now there's something to be remembered for, she thought with an agonized internal groan. There he was, Mr. Hotter-Than-Hot and she . . .

Giggling, shivering, and swept up in the embrace of a striking male stranger, Tatyana officially brought a close to her dreadful week by appearing as a loony bin escapee to Mr. HTH and all the rest of the family of her brother's girl-friend. Or at least she assumed they were her family. Hella-tion, she hoped she'd stumbled into the right house.

You know what, I'm just going to work on that theory and go from there, she thought decisively. The truth was, she knew nothing about her brother's new 'family' as he was wont to call it. Could be because she didn't listen very well after he made remarks like that, her head buzzing jealously and her mental foot stamping on the ground as she whined internally. She was his family. She and his cornucopia of other siblings. Their parents. Their aunts and uncles. What the heck did he need a new one for?

She always got over it within a minute or two. Mainly because he sounded so damn happy. That and she'd spoken to Annali on the phone a couple of times and had found it super hard to hate her guts. Especially since she was making Dimitre deliriously happier than Tatyana had heard him sound in a long time. Plus, Annali had to go and be all sweet and kind and, according to report, owned three pairs of the cutest Christian Louboutin shoes ever sold.

Hunter watched with amazement and fascination as the half-frozen redhead slapped a hand over her mouth to stop herself from giggling. She was only partially successful; the giggles escaped her nose in short little snorts of mirth. She was also shaking harder by the second. Her eyes, a pale, pale jade that reminded him of a cat's, were wide with shock and mortification. Her skin was starkly white from the cold, but embarrassment appeared in a pair of pink spots on her cheeks.

In spite of this less-than-stellar face-to-face introduction, Hunter was astonished by how exceedingly attractive she was. Her dark, deep red hair had highlights of copper and mahogany, the length undetermined because it was tightly knotted into an intricate coiffure. She had huge eyes with fringes of red-brown lashes; perfect porcelain skin with drifts of freckles sweeping back like light, spotted angel's wings over the rises of her cheeks. Her swept-back hair revealed the cutest ears to go with an equally adorable nose and chin. In contradiction, her sophistication came from outstanding cheekbones, a wide forehead with its distinctive

widow's peak hairline, and a stunning mouth he'd noted before she'd hidden it away, with plush, berry-red lips that
begged for all kinds of kissing.

Damned if that wasn't the most outrageous thought he'd
ever had in his life, Hunter mused as he finally galvanized
himself into action. Reaching down, he swept up the
stranger in both arms, using his foot to kick the door shut.
Ryce and Annali were already following him as he tried to
remember where he'd seen a fire.

"Main front parlor," Ryce reminded him.

Hunter turned to go, aware that Annali was hurrying away
toward the conservatory. Meanwhile, he and Ryce rushed
the freezing woman into the parlor. Hunter didn't bother
with furniture. He took a knee right in front of the fire and
settled her down on the rug while Ryce went to work stoking
the blaze good and hot. He reached to yank a blanket from a
nearby basket and covered her with it from the waist down,
wrapping up her mostly bare legs as snugly as he could.
Then he reached for her icy hands and began to rub them
vigorously one at a time. When Ryce was done at the fire, he
left to fetch more blankets and anything else he could think
of to help.

"You're frozen half through," Hunter murmured. "I don't
know how you even found this house, sweetheart, but you're
damn lucky you did."

"I-I s-saw t-t-t-the l-lights . . ." she managed to stutter
through chattering teeth.

Tatyana watched the stranger frown with puzzlement at
that, and she couldn't make sense of his reaction. She decided to just be grateful that she was finally beneath a roof
and getting warm. It felt as though warmth would take forever, but it was nice to know it was on its way. Just then the
door to the room opened and a striking woman in violet
came in bearing a small silver tray. With the ease of a serv-
ing geisha, she knelt smoothly beside Tatyana without so

much as tilting the tray she held. A good thing, too, because there was a steaming cup in its center.

"Some tea," she offered, perpetuating the geisha-like image by picking up the cup in both hands and offering it to her as if it held blessings within it.

Tatyana laughed off the strange poetic bent of her thoughts. She'd been indulging in a lot of fancy since she'd stumbled into this house. She put it down to exposure-induced hallucinations and sat up to accept the cup with the help of a strong male hand at her back.

"Sip carefully, but make sure to drink it all," he urged her in a gentle tenor that was both coaxing and soothing. The woman in violet smiled in easy agreement.

His free hand closed over Tatyana's, helping her steady the cup in her trembling hand. Her heart, which had been racing ever since she'd realized her car wasn't going to be-have itself, finally began to ease as she looked at the kind and concerned faces of these strangers. Yes, she told herself. This most certainly had to be her brother's new family. He'd spoken of them with nothing but respect and praise.

The second male returned when she was halfway through her cup of tea, draping a luxurious comforter of down over her lap and a warmer shawl over her back.

"Thank you," she said when she was certain she could speak without her teeth chattering. "You're all very kind."

"But of course," the male with a distinct British accent said magnanimously.

"You poor thing, you must've been walking out in that cold a very long time! And in nothing but silk and lace. They make us beautiful, sugar, but they're about as effective against the cold as huddling over a burnt match."

The pretty blonde tsked under her tongue. Her Southern accent lilted gracefully in her speech, and Tatyana instantly knew that she was Annali Templeton. This beautiful stranger, with her pansy colored eyes and the highly refined features and manners of a perfect lady, was the woman her brother was in love with. Tatyana was astounded as she glanced around the room and took in the furnishings and artwork, realizing that this was a very wealthy household. All three of them were dressed elegantly, a casual sophistication that un- mistakably came easily to them. It wasn't that her brother wouldn't belong in this type of environment; after all, he was a university professor with intelligence and sophistication of his own. It was just that Dimitre had never seemed the type to go for a cool, blond socialite. But then again, Tatyana needed to reconcile this sophisticate with the warm, bright personality she had made contact with over the phone those few, brief times. The concern and sympathy radiating from her was quite genuine. It would be just like Dimi to see be- yond the surface to something special.

"I'm so sorry to be inconveniencing you all," she said, suddenly feeling embarrassed by all of their attention and the way they were putting themselves out for her benefit. She hadn't even introduced herself and she wasn't really even supposed to be there. Dimitre was going to pitch a fit as it was. Tatyana moved to get to her feet, but hands reached out from everywhere to keep her seated on the floor and to keep the cup of tea in her hands.

"You're no inconvenience," said the male who had ini- tially caught her, his warm fingers reaching out to sweep an errant strand of her hair from her cheek. He gave her a smile that was just as warm and comforting as his touch, making her feel as though he were wrapping his goodwill around her. A strange sense of protection and security shimmered through her awareness. She shivered, but this time it was be- cause of the odd sensation of sanctuary this stranger seemed to settle over her, not because of the cold.

"I'm Annali Templeton," Annali introduced herself as she urged Tatyana to drink more tea. "This is Hunter Finn and behind you is Ryce Champion. You couldn't have found your way to a safer place, I assure you. Now drink. Relax. When you are well-warmed you'll join us for dinner."

"Oh, but I—"

"Ah, but you see, our Annali doesn't hear arguments," Ryce teased. "She is quite stubborn and will have her way. The hour is late and surely you're hungry after your chilly adventures tonight. So there's no sense arguing, really."

"What my pushy friends are trying to say is that they are used to getting their way in things and won't take 'no' for an answer," Hunter explained gently in her ear. "For that matter, neither will I."

Tatyana caught her breath as she looked into those vivid blue eyes. He was so near to her now she could feel the gentle waves of his breaths against her cheek, bathing her in warmth and the scent of mint, as though he'd recently brushed his teeth. She flushed, feeling her cheeks turn rosy with heat, but she couldn't make herself look away from that bold gaze no matter how much she thought she needed to. If he kept looking at her like that, all hot and gorgeous as he was, she'd be saying yes to all kinds of things he wasn't even asking. What woman in her right mind could ever say no to Hunter Finn, he of the devastating eyes?

Certainly not her.

"I'm Tatyana Petrova," she said at last, her name rushing out breathily.

Chapter Four

"Tatyana!"

"Did she say Petrova?" Ryce asked quickly. Apparently needlessly as well, if the look on Annali's face was anything to judge from. The female witch had gone extraordinarily pale.

"Yes, I did," Tatyana said quietly but firmly. "And if you don't mind, I would like to see my brother. I am very sorry to intrude on your New Year's, and I won't keep you any longer. If you could just call Dimitre here . . ."

Annali's heart was pounding violently with anxiety. She was suddenly in the presence of Dimitre's most-beloved sibling out of a total of twelve brothers and sisters. He and his youngest sister were best friends, as she had heard it, confidants who adored one another. Despite brief phone conversations, Annali was essentially meeting Tatyana for the first time. Tatyana was, in fact, the very first family member of Dimitre's she had ever met. Dimitre and Annali had known each other only two months, and it had taken only a little over a week for the couple to realize they were destined to love one another. However, until now, they had remained isolated from Dimitre's family. For Annali, meeting Tatyana was the equivalent of meeting the President of the United States. She absolutely, positively could not screw up.

But of course, this encounter was already a disaster in the making. Annali knew full well Dimitre was going to be furious when he found out Tatyana was there. He had purposely tried to keep her away for her own protection. But how was Tatyana supposed to know that? She didn't know her brother was a witch! She didn't know his coven was under threat from evil. Hell, his sister didn't even know there was any such thing as magic.

To make matters worse, Dimitre wasn't even at Willow House. He had gone away and had seen no reason to call Tatyana and tell her. Annali had admonished him for it because it was out of character for him not to share that kind of information with Tatyana, but he simply had not wanted to deal with the hassle of explaining who their fellow witch Kaia was and why he would need to attend a doctor's lectures with her. He couldn't out-and-out lie to Tatyana, after all.

And that was the final problem.

Annali was keeping a sworn secret from her High Priest and coven mates. Dimitre had pleaded with her for silence, and out of love for him, she had promised it . . . on a conditional basis. She had sworn to give him time to come clean about Tatyana with Ryce when he was ready. More importantly, he needed to come clean with Tatyana . . . for a multitude of reasons.

It was an untenable position to be in, and she was furious with Dimitre for it, but she had made her choices and would have to bear up to the responsibility of them. Not now, but as soon as she could, she would have to tell Ryce and Hunter about Tatyana. But first, she needed to deal with Tatyana.

"Actually," she spoke up at last, trying to clear out the uneasiness in her throat, "Dimitre isn't here. One of our housemates had some traveling to do and he accompanied her last minute to help her out."

"He isn't . . . ?" There was a pause as she digested the information. "But he would have called me." Everyone could hear the blatant mistrust in her voice and could see it in the dangerous narrowing of her eyes. She would much rather believe them up to no good than to believe her best friend had not confided in her. "I don't believe you," she bit out sharply.

There was something quite beautiful to Hunter about Tatyana getting her back up. The vitality. The life . . . and something more. Something he couldn't put his finger on exactly. She just about took his breath away. It was obvious to him that the newest addition to Willow Coven was very close to this sister of his. She clearly expected him to tell her if he was going out of town. He was forced to wonder why Dimitre would step out of routine like that. Why wouldn't Dimitre tell his sister about a simple trip?

Hunter turned to look at Ryce, his eyes narrowing slightly on the High Priest. Snatches of little factoids suddenly began to fall together in his mind like connecting pieces of a puzzle. Keeping silent for the moment, Hunter would bide his time before confronting Ryce with his suspicions. There were more important issues to deal with for the moment. Mainly, a pretty redhead's bruised feelings.

"Sugar," Annali said gently, "I assure you it's the truth. And I'm equally sure he didn't mean to be rude to you and not tell you. It's a short trip and he'll be back soon. He has his cell with him and probably figured he'd tell you if you called." She smiled even as she said meaningfully, "I'm sure he had no idea you were planning to come here or he would have been here to meet you. He would never forget something like a visit from you. He knows I would have killed him if he didn't give me time to make everything perfect for his favorite sister."

Tatyana blushed a pretty, bright pink under her light freckles.

"Well, it was . . . kinda spur of the totally bipolar manic moment. Oh boy," she groaned, dropping her head forward and covering her face with her hands. "This is such a major screw-up. I am so sorry. And you're all going out, I can see." She started to get up again. "All I need is a phone. I'll catch a cab and I can stay in—"

"The guest room upstairs," Annali said hastily. "I won't take no for an answer, remember? Dimitre would have our heads if we didn't show you every courtesy. Starting with supper tonight. You will eat with us."

Annali knew Hunter and Ryce were looking at her as if she had lost her mind, but she wouldn't look up at them. She kept Tatyana's full attention instead.

"But weren't you going out?" Tatyana nodded her head at their mode of dress.

"We have a stellar chef here at Willow House. In or out makes little difference to us," Annali said carelessly. "Besides, I already asked our chef Rochelle to prepare a meal when I realized we'd be staying home."

"Willow House?" she asked.

"A privilege of having a home this big," Ryce injected, "is being entitled to the snobbery of calling it by a name of some sort."

"And you all live here . . . but you aren't related?" Tatyana looked confused. "I thought Dimitre said you lived with your family, Annali."

"She does," Hunter said softly, his eyes perfectly tender as he looked over at Annali. "We are her family. We're all connected by things even more important than blood."

"Oh! I see. Great, Tat. Way to trivialize your brother's girlfriend's relationships," she said wryly.

"Oh, don't worry, honey. You didn't." Annali brushed it off with a wave. "We know very well how unusual we are.

People find it hard to imagine that so many vastly different people can live under one roof and actually get along."

"Usually," Ryce amended.

"Mostly," Annali countered.

"Isn't that what usually means?" Ryce asked Hunter archly.

"Well, one is a quantifier, the other more qualitative," Hunter mused.

"I'm not sure I agree with that," Ryce argued.

"Finish your tea and ignore them, sugar," Annali whispered beneath their speculations. "Whatever you do, don't encourage them. Once they start talking language . . ." She shuddered dramatically. "These arguments have been known to have a narcotic effect."

Tatyana giggled into her cup, sipping tea and quietly listening to Hunter and Ryce bicker over what she realized amounted to nothing, a mark of the familiarity bred between the oldest of friends. She felt the tension and chill bleeding out of her body as she swallowed down the last of the flavorful tea. As minor disasters went, this one was beginning to take an unexpected turn for the better.

Though she was finished with her tea, she kept the cup against her lips a moment and used it to hide a covert peek at the man called Hunter Finn. Though Ryce was what she would call more classically dashing and aristocratically handsome, Hunter's features and physique appealed to her much more. He had the kind of body that made women lick their lips in anticipation of total yumminess. If she hadn't had a cup between her lips, she would definitely be lip-licking. Broad shoulders, perfect for laying one's head on, and a well-defined chest and belly that she already knew felt like heated riverbed rocks, all smooth, hard, and bumpy in the right places. Then there were her personal favorites, his long legs and awesomely sexy thighs, which were just as fit as the rest of him and high on her scale of appreciation.

All of which would mean a big zero if he hadn't also been incredibly chivalrous and brilliantly charming since the moment she'd fallen into his big, capable hands. Mix in a smile that blinded and a sense of humor he was displaying at Ryce's expense, and he had an overall drool factor that went off the charts.

Tatyana lowered her cup and her eyes, licking her lips covertly to check for any possible drool. She knew nothing about him, she reminded herself. Men this fine were always married with kids. Or gay. She glanced quickly between Hunter and Ryce.

Nah. She barely had any straight friends, so she had an inner radar about these things. Then again, it would be just her luck with the week she was having. She looked at them again, narrowing her eyes as if it would help determine their sexual preferences.

She gave up on the examination quickly. What did it matter? They lived in the back of beyond and she lived in Queens. She worked in Manhattan and had everything she could ever need all within a block where cell phones always worked and everybody delivered and she could raise her pinkie finger and find a cab magically by her side.

They had cows. Lots of cows, unmarked roads, *everything* was on a hill, and the nearest neighbors were the Hatfields and the McCoys. Not to mention it was fifty degrees colder than the rest of the civilized world. Well, okay, maybe ten degrees, she relented reasonably, but that made all the difference to her hands and feet and other far more precious body parts that'd nearly been frozen off.

Hunter Finn turned one of those heart-stopping smiles on her and reached out to run a pair of fingers from her temple to her chin. It was a friendly little touch, no big deal really. Except, he left a path of tingles in his wake that popped, sparkled, and rushed down the side of her neck, hitting her nervous system in a shiver she couldn't repress.

Horrified that he'd possibly see the juvenile fluttering for what it was, Tatyana pulled away and abruptly surged to her feet while giving her unruly libido a mental kick in its ass. It was one thing to ogle the good-looking man covertly, and quite another to get all weak-kneed and quivery where the good-looking man might see it. Once they knew you were attracted, they were all ego and preening peacocks. She'd drunk her fill of egos and arrogance, with their idiocy chasers. Now if she could just remember that, things were bound to get better before the week was over.

Tatyana realized she was babbling to herself and gave her head a shake to stop herself. She always babbled when she was nervous. In her mind or out loud. Taking a deep breath, she managed a smile for the three people looking at her with curiosity in their eyes.

"There. All better now," she said brightly, as she brushed her dress into place and touched her hair self-consciously. "Thank you so much. Annali, that tea worked wonderfully."

"You can stop thanking us," Hunter said. "You've done so enough."

"Now on that issue Hunter and I can finally agree," Ryce mused, reaching to take her arm and helping her step over discarded blankets. He escorted her out of the room.

Hunter turned to give Annali a crooked grin. "Care to share what was in the tea?" he asked.

"Oh, a little of this and a little of that," she said, the reliability of the stock answer warming his soul with that sense of home. On impulse he reached out and seized her in a tight hug. She gasped in surprise, and then laughed.

"Well it did the trick," he remarked. "Though you should be careful. You can look at her and see that she isn't a stupid woman. Don't do anything she will question."

"Hunter, really," she scolded as she wriggled out of his arms to settle onto her own feet. "I've been doing this for eleven years now. I know what I'm doing and I know how to conceal my tricks. Honestly," she ended with exasperation.

"You're right," he relented quickly, holding up a peaceable hand. "I'm sorry. Old habits die hard. I think it will always be my instinct to protect you. The whole lot of you."

"That's because it's your job. You are Sentinel after all," she reminded him. "You were born to be a defender."

"On that note, do you have any idea how dangerous it is to have a civilian in the house right now? I mean, we can refrain from magic, but only if nothing comes up."

"That's why I wanted us to eat in. We are protected here. And you know I couldn't let her go off to some hotel. She can see we have the room, and if I didn't offer she would think we didn't want her here even more than she already does. Dimitre has been putting her off until he could get settled and in control of his life and craft. She was very hurt by that as it is. Then this thing with the trip and not telling her?" Annali sighed and brushed away a stray strand of hair. "Poor thing. I couldn't let her feel any more rejected."

"Of course not. You're right, Annie." Hunter smiled and touched a fond finger to her forehead, taking a long moment to simply absorb the woman she had become. "Sometimes I focus so much on being a witch that I forget how to be human."

"That's because you didn't have us to remind you. But that will all change now."

"Lidija . . ."

"Dimitre is going to kill you. You are so asking for it."

"I'll cross that sword when I come to it," Tatyana sighed into the phone to her sister. Ryce had shown her to a strange library of some sort and was letting her use a phone to first call for a tow and now to let Lidija know she had arrived safe and sound. Lidija hadn't known where she was off to when Tatyana had called her before leaving the party. Lidija had cared only that she got there safely on the most notoriously dangerous night for driving in the state of New York.

But now that she did know where Tatyana had run off to, she was quite eager to point out all the flaws in her plan so she could get in some hearty I-told-you-so's.

"Stop scolding me like a child. I'm a grown woman and I'm free to make my own choices." She paused for a beat, picking invisible lint from the skirt of her dress. "I just needed to see him, Lidija. I miss him. I've been worried. I've been feeling so shut out and it's never been like that between us, ever. I understand he's in love with this woman, but I won't let him just push me aside like I'm some . . . some old girlfriend instead of his sister."

"I'm not scolding," Lidija said with a pout in her tone. "Or at least I don't mean to be. I know he's been acting weird lately. It really was wrong that he didn't even come to Christmas after he missed Thanksgiving. Mama was beside herself. Someone had to do something, and it may as well be you. I'm glad you're safe. What do you think of these people he is living with? Are they axe murderers? A cult maybe? Alien worshippers or something weird like that?"

"Hmm, they do have a lot of weapons on the walls," she mused, glancing at the shields and mounted arsenal between the bookcases.

"Tatyana Danica Petrova, that isn't funny!" Lidija lambasted her in hot Russian. "I worry about him, too, you know! And you as well! Tell me you were kidding, Tat. I mean it."

"*Dushenka*," Tatyana soothed gently in their parents' tongue. "I was teasing. These are good people. You know I've a sense for such things."

"Are you sure? Tell me you're sure so I can be very convincing when everyone starts going crazy over what you've done."

"I'm positive. Stop worrying. The only danger was of freezing my ass off and stepping in a cow pie. Both of those dangers have been eliminated, and I'm fine now. Better than fine. You'd drop dead on the spot if you could see this place. Donald Trump would be jealous."

"You know, as much as you've been bitching about your week, you have the damndest luck," Lidija said enviously. "I bet those two guys you were telling me about are gorgeous and single, as well as rich. I just know it."

"Believe me, men this good-looking and living together are very probably gay," Tatyana laughed.

"Don't try to make me feel better. Go eat dinner. Call me when Dimitre comes home. Remember, if you want, any one of us can be there in a couple of hours to back you up."

"That isn't necessary. Lidija, tell everyone not to worry. I'll get to the bottom of all of this and live to tell the tale. You're right, you know. Someone had to do something, and I did. Now everyone can relax while I scope out the deal here."

"Relax? This family?" Lidija said with a snort.

"Good-bye, *dushenka*."

"Good night."

Tatyana hung up the phone, shaking her head and smiling to herself. When she had headed up to the Catskills, she hadn't even told her father or brothers she was going. No 'why' or 'where,' knowing if she did they would try to talk her out of it. Even though they were as eaten up with worry and concern as she was, they would have reminded her that Dimitre was a grown man living an adult life.

But it wasn't like that between her and Dimitre. They were . . . special. She and Dimitre had always had a very special 'sense' for one another. Call it being psychic, or 'the sight' as her Old World family did, but of the many siblings they were singularly connected. Ever since she was born, Dimitre had always known when she needed him. He always knew when she was in trouble or hurt. As she had grown older, the ability became reciprocal. Her sight had been narrowed in on Dimitre for weeks now, bringing her confusing and sometimes terrifying images. She had even begun to have wild dreams, occasionally nightmares, in which Dimitre was under a constant cloud of danger. How the hell was she supposed to ignore that? She also couldn't tell anyone else about it. They knew how accurate her sight was and it would have freaked her family out. It was better that she find out for herself what exactly was going on in this house with these people. On the surface everything seemed copacetic, and so far her psychic sense wasn't even so much as twitching a warning to her. Hopefully she was just being neurotic and overprotective.

"You don't have a hint of an accent."

Tatyana jumped in her own skin and pivoted quickly to face one of her hosts.

Hunter Finn.

"I beg your pardon?"

"Your Russian is flawless. Your heritage is obvious in your name, of course, but you speak like a native without any hint of accent. Are you second-generation American or first?"

"First, actually," she said slowly. "My parents came over after my first three siblings were born. You speak Russian?"

"I spent a few years in Russia and far longer in Romania. My Russian is passable, my Romanian and Romany are much better."

"Romanian and Romany? There is a difference?"

"Yes. Mostly dialect." He shrugged as if it weren't so remarkable that he should know this. "I didn't mean to eavesdrop on your conversation. I only wanted to let you know we were going to relax with something to drink before dinner, in the front parlor, when you're ready. And"—he paused, his eyes taking on a beautiful illumination that took her breath away—"I'm not, you know."

"Not?" she asked dumbly. "I don't . . ."

"Gay," he clarified. And in case she was in doubt of it, he let those brilliant blue eyes of his slowly drop down over her, let them reach out and connect to her in an almost physical touch. Tatyana felt her skin turn bright and white hot everywhere that assured masculine gaze touched. It was so fast and so sharp it was as if he'd set fire to flash paper, a dazzling burst of flame dancing to life. Then he winked at her and left the room, leaving her speechless and gaping in his wake.

"Passable Russian, my eye," she muttered as she pressed cool hands to her flaming cheeks. The dirty rat. It was incredibly bad form to tease her about a private conversation he'd had no business listening in on in the first place. It wasn't as though that had been the last thing she'd said, either. He'd been standing there a minute or two at least.

Tatyana looked at the empty doorway thoughtfully. It wasn't lost on her how incongruous it was to encounter such educated and obviously worldly people in such a remote setting. They were a strange mix, these three. A Southern belle, an Englishman, and . . . she wasn't exactly sure where Hunter Finn originated from. She heard the occasional lilt of the Slavic in his speech; he was darkly colored in a very eastern European way, and yet there was something very American in his manner. Still, how was she to conclude anything on an acquaintance that must not even total an hour as yet?

Tatyana shook herself mentally and turned to search for a reflective surface. She wasn't about to go looking for a bathroom in this monstrous house. With her luck she'd get lost. She found a highly polished steel shield and looked herself over. Her cheeks were windburned and her lips a bit chapped from her journey in the cold, but otherwise she deemed herself presentable. She was suddenly grateful for the expensive silk dress with its bold red color and soft glimmer of sparkles. It had done squat for her in the cold, but for sitting down to drinks and dinner it was just the thing. At least she would be off to a good start as she tried not to embarrass her absent brother.

"Good God," she sighed, "when did I become so insecure?"

She wasn't the type to feel outclassed no matter where she went or whom she met, but for some unknown reason she felt terribly like a fish out of water tonight. As though, instinctually, she felt that these people surpassed her in some way beyond her comprehension.

She shook the alien feeling off and headed out of the library.

Chapter Five

"If you want my opinion as Sentinel, of course I'm going to say we have to get rid of her," Hunter said flatly. "The looming danger of the dark coven hunting us makes this no place for an ignorant civilian."

"My thoughts exactly. Annali, what in the world were you thinking?"

"Oh, come now, Ryce. You're overreacting!" Anna declared. "You're just being paranoid."

"After what happened to Gracelynne?" Ryce snapped. "Not bloody likely!"

"Ryce has good reason to be concerned," Hunter interceded, "but when I step away from the role of Sentinel, I have to agree with Annali."

"Thank you," Anna said, pulling her shoulders back with triumph.

"We aren't just witches, Ryce. We are human beings. This woman is family to our fellow witch. That makes her family to us by association."

"Blast." Ryce sighed, knowing Hunter was right. "I'm always the one trying to remind everyone how important it is to live our lives as humans as well as witches, and here I am being reminded by the two of you."

"You're concerned for her safety. We all are. But frankly, I'd rather have her in here with us. The second she walked into this house she became associated with the coven," Hunter pointed out. "If any warlocks are out there watching, they might go after her just to see what she is worth. Hell, knowing them they'd do it just because she is beautiful. Then they'd take what they want just like they always do."

The idea was sobering to the trio. They had each seen up close the twisted ways dark witches had of taking what didn't belong to them, never caring if it destroyed someone's soul in the process. That was the very definition of dark witchery. Take. Get. Grab. Selfishness and greediness backed by monumental powers and corrupted magic.

"We'll keep her in the house until Dimitre returns," Ryce said gravely. "We'll do our best to keep our magic hidden until he decides what to tell her. We cannot let her go unprotected. You are so right, Hunter. The moment she walked over that threshold, everything changed."

More than either of them know, Annali thought apprehensively. She was nearly shuddering with relief that they were focused on protecting Tatyana so closely. If they only knew just how much of a target to warlocks Dimitre's sister truly was . . .

The dark beasts would literally kill to have her. And once they got her . . .

Annali did shudder this time, unwanted memories rushing over her. Hunter chuckled abruptly, missing her reaction to her dark thoughts. He grinned at Ryce. "You know, Ryce, she actually thought you and I might be lovers."

Annali made a high-pitched and very unladylike sound of shock. She was jolted out of her private thoughts and sent into wild giggles. Ryce's jaw dropped open with shock.

"Me? *Me? You* I can understand," Ryce provoked him, "but me? I'm the picture of heterosexual virility."

"I always said you were too pretty for your own good,

Ryce," Annali guffawed, grabbing her side as tears welled up in her eyes.

"Shut the bloody hell up, Annali," Ryce groused.

"Shh, Anna," Hunter chuckled. "She's coming."

Anna struggled to compose herself just as Tatyana cautiously entered the room. She looked terribly self-conscious as she smoothed hands down over her short skirt. The gesture drew Hunter's attention to her legs and his smile grew out of his control. She was tall for a woman, at least 5'10", and clearly the majority of that length was in her legs. The long, shapely limbs began with smooth, rounded hips, which then blended marvelously into firm thighs, showcased by the rustling twitch of her flirtatious skirt. They were as sexy as they were long, even if they did end abruptly in a pair of white Nikes. Hunter could easily imagine what a nice pair of heels could do for her; not to mention what legs that lengthy and shapely would feel like wrapping encouragingly around him.

The unexpected thought sent frissons of shocking excitement shooting around under Hunter's skin, like a hormonal pinball machine that was hitting on all his key bumpers and racking up bonus points. He felt his breath hitching hard over a sudden constriction in his chest. He was hardly an angel, his brain being naturally wired with testosterone just like any other man's, but Hunter could honestly look at his own thoughts with astonishment. He reminded himself that it was probably just his penchant for redheads, combined with the fact that it had been a while since he'd enjoyed the company of a woman in any capacity outside of simple friendship. When one lived with the Romany Gypsies, hospitality was cut sharply short if one got involved in the sexual politics of the clans. It had been best to focus on what he'd wanted to learn and to leave recreation out of it.

However, his reaction to the exquisite woman moving slowly into the room wasn't quelled by his logic. It wasn't

even quelled by the fact that she was the sister of a fellow in-
coven witch. He hadn't met many natural Russian redheads,
so he wondered about her coloring briefly. Then he quickly
brushed the curiosity aside when he found himself considering a surefire way of finding out. Down that road of thoughts
lay any number of untoward bodily reactions he'd just as
soon keep under control at present. Hunter satisfied himself
simply with a guess that the color was far too unique in its
darkness and diffused highlights to be contrived. Tatyana's
eyes, that sheer jade that leapt out of her lovely features, settled on him. Hunter had to stifle a reflexive groan as her gaze
drifted with open contemplation down the length of his
body. The tip of her tongue made a teasing appearance between her lips, giving them a meditative lick that just about
fried his impulse control. Then, as if realizing what she was
doing, her eyes snapped back to his and her face blossomed
in a blush of delicate pink.

Untoward bodily reactions abounded.

If she'd made just as studied a return trip up his body,
she'd have proof positive he was as heterosexual as they
came. Hunter quickly took a seat, figuring it would be a really good idea to do so before their guest actually did take
notice. He felt her gaze on him like a warm weight and he
found himself looking back up into her boldly appraising
eyes and an encore of the peeking pink tongue. She flushed
and looked away, quickly crossing her arms over her breasts
and rubbing her hands over her upper arms as if she'd caught
a chill, but Hunter had a sudden insight that made him smile
a bit wolfishly. This fence, he realized, very definitely had
two sides to it, and suddenly he didn't feel so ignoble.
Enough so that he allowed himself to contemplate what kind
of reaction she was hiding beneath those crossed arms.

Annali sensed the unexpected shift in tension in the
room. Pressing her lips together to control an amused smile,
she glanced at Hunter from beneath her lashes. Each witch
in the coven could sense all of the other witches living there:

where they were, sometimes what they were doing, and they could even feel some of what they were feeling if the emotions were strong enough.

Hunter had always been an unexpected mix of personality, his emotions fluctuating between a deeply serious sense of nobility, honor, and loyalty . . . and an equally intense animal drive for hardcore killing and ruthlessness in achieving his goals. Of all the males in the Willow Coven, Hunter was known to be the least likely to lack impulse control.

Well, at present, impulses were definitely being indulged. Hunter was captivated by Dimitre's lovely younger sister. And the feeling was apparently mutual. Annali didn't need a magical connection to figure that out, only a feminine one. Tatyana Petrova was acting like a woman who was trying hard not to look too long at someone when she very much wanted to do exactly that. Tatyana turned her back toward Hunter, but her chin kept dipping toward her shoulder as if she wanted to glance over it. Annali was impressed whenever the other woman caught herself in time to keep from looking back at him.

Annali slid over on her love seat and patted the vacancy she'd made next to herself. "Tatyana, come and sit. Let Ryce get you a cocktail."

"Thank you," she said as she came to take a seat, "but I don't really drink."

"Don't be shy," Ryce said warmly, obviously already forgiving her for casting aspersions on his manhood. "I'm quite the bartender," he assured her, moving to the wet bar in a corner of the room. "Annali, vodka cranberry?"

She nodded, smiling at him. He raised a brow at Tatyana.

"Same, please," she relented. A drink suddenly sounded like heaven. She was still feeling an unshakable chill in her bones in spite of being physically warmed . . . not to mentioned scorched by the contemplative looks of one Hunter Finn.

When Ryce came to Hunter he raised a brow. It was such

a simple gesture, but Tatyana read a wealth of information in it. Why was it that he knew Annali's tastes so well, but not Hunter's?

"My tastes haven't changed, Ryce."

"Vodka, neat," Ryce announced.

Tatyana narrowed curious jade eyes on Hunter and then Ryce. If they lived together as closely as she'd been led to believe, why would Hunter have to make that strange distinction?

"So tell us about yourself," Annali invited her pleasantly, reaching with a warm hand to cover one of hers where it rested on her thigh. "Dimitre has been very stingy with details about your family. I think all we really know is that there are thirteen children and that your parents are still alive."

"Yes, but are they sane?" Hunter countered, shaking his head in awe. "Thirteen kids. That's astounding."

"I want to know how the bedroom to bathroom quotient worked," Ryce chuckled.

"Well, we definitely could have used this house," Tatyana remarked. "But we did well enough. There's really not much to tell. I'm an architect. I work out of Manhattan. I live in Queens with only two roommates." She made the distinction with a grin and an excited dance of two fingers as though having only two roommates was the best thing since the electric lightbulb.

"Why aren't you out at a party somewhere?" Hunter asked. "You look like you're dressed for it."

"Oh, I'm not much of a party girl really. I'm either a homebody or a workaholic. I swing both ways," she said with a slow, broad wink at Hunter that made him fall back against the cushions of his chair and bark out a laugh of stunned amusement.

The little minx took her drink from Ryce and quickly hid a mischievous grin against the rim of the glass. She didn't realize he'd shared her speculations on his sexual orientation, so she turned sharply when Annali nearly choked to death on a poorly timed sip of her drink. Tatyana spared him a dirty look when she comprehended that she'd been ratted out. She began to pound Annali on her back firmly but gently. "And what about you, Hunter?" she asked with pointed wickedness and a smile innocent enough to sell angel's wings. "Which way do you swing?"

"Yes, do tell," Ryce encouraged with a troublesome grin as he handed Hunter his glass, then took a seat for himself.

"I'd say Hunter is a workaholic." Annali rescued him with a wheeze of recovering breath. "Only recently has he rediscovered the values of home and hearth."

Tatyana's merry jade eyes danced with mischief as they met Hunter's. "And where do your talents lie? What can you do?" she asked, her voice a low suggestion that, to Hunter, was just shy of a rich purr. There was no mistaking the taunting double entendre to what she said. So much for those girlish blushes, Hunter thought, his gaze narrowing on her darkly. Tatyana Petrova was hiding a vixen beneath that delicious auburn hair and those innocent freckles.

Smoldering. That was the perfect word to describe the look Hunter Finn was drilling into her. Tatyana had no idea why she was being so openly flirtatious and daring with someone she barely knew. One of her brother's housemates no less. But with pure feminine power and satisfaction, she noted that the look Hunter was giving her practically sizzled. She rather liked the idea of the blatant thoughts that must be going through his head. The man was crammed full of natural sensuality. His eyes packed the most devastating punch, but it could also be seen in his every effortless movement, from his easy stride to the turn of his head. It could be felt in the lightest of his touches. Shivers skipped over the back of her scalp as she recalled the drift of his fingertips against her cheek . . . her temple. Brushing back her hair so simply.

As their eyes met and held across the width of the room, Tatyana was suddenly sure he knew everything she was thinking, and how it was making her feel. Her bravado failed her and color flooded her cheeks. She lowered her eyes to the liquid in her glass.

"I'm an anthropologist," Hunter responded to her query, a sly smile tugging at one corner of his lips as he watched a myriad thoughts and emotions skim across her expressive face. She'd make a terrible poker player, he thought as he kept his eyes firmly on her. He marveled at how brave and sassy she was one moment, and then shy and colored with blushes the next. "I study living human cultures. Most recently that of the—"

"Romany," she finished for him suddenly, looking up at him once more as her eyes lit with a bright spark of fascination. "That's why you have that cadence in your speech. Very like my parents' accents when they speak English, only much more muted."

"A little different," he stipulated, "but similar enough."

"You must have spent years there for it to alter your natural speech," she noted.

"Nearly eight years in the eastern European countries. I followed many tribes all over Europe, but mostly the *Rom* clans in and around Romania." Hunter paused briefly to watch the clear alcohol in his glass as he swirled it around. The life of the Romany was a hard one. One full of mysticism and tradition and a sense of family that had made him increasingly miss what he'd left behind in the States. All the while wars had swept around them, close and closer still, depending on where Hunter had been at the time. There'd been times when the only thing that had saved himself and his friends from certain death was magic. Not just his. The Romany had taught him things he'd never thought possible. Beautiful spells that had nothing to do with defense or offense. Powerful ways of amplifying magic when it was necessary. How to discern the difference between needing to use magic . . . and only wanting to use it.

"It wasn't the amount of time, so much as the intensity of

my immersion into the Romany culture," he told her, only mildly aware that he had Ryce and Annali's full attention as well. "When you meet the Romany, one of two things will happen. Either you will corrupt them, or they will corrupt you. And corruption in that case isn't necessarily a negative thing. I only mean that the culture is so powerful and so beautiful that it draws you into it until you begin to feel like you don't know how you ever lived any other way. You start to wonder how so many people live together in this world, and yet they never truly understand what it means to be a part of a community. An entire village will raise, love, and protect every child within a Romany clan, the elderly are respected and revered. The devotion is . . . breathtaking."

"And the other corruption," Tatyana prompted, her voice barely above a whisper as her nerves tingled right to their roots from the passion of his words. A passion that glowed deeply in his cobalt eyes.

"The same corruption that happens to African tribes who have never seen anything of civilization, and then Westerners come with their conveniences and religions and ruin the sanctity of the tribe. The Romany can be taken over just as easily as they can take you over. I see romance and beauty in the way they live, and just as assuredly, they see it in the way we live. The life of a Gypsy is a hard one. It's easy to see how Western ways and comforts can be alluring. But it's a case of the grass being greener. Neither knows what they will be missing by walking in the other's shoes until they are already halfway into the journey."

There was nothing any of them could say to that. Tatyana couldn't imagine what life would be like without her enormous family. Extended family aside, just the gathering of her siblings and parents made for a full and boisterous experience. Perhaps it was because her parents had come from such poverty that they had learned how to appreciate every moment of life, to celebrate it, and to thrive on traditions. Each of the thirteen Petrova children had been instilled with the sense of loyalty to family that Hunter spoke of. That was what had driven her here, despite her brother's ridiculous wishes otherwise.

Tatyana realized then, as her gaze remained locked to Hunter's eyes, that this stranger wasn't so strange after all. In the span of a single conversation she understood that in this key matter they were kindred spirits. His yearning was palpable. His need for the unwavering devotion of familial allegiance could be felt like an actual weight hanging on her heart. There was unbelievable loneliness in the depths of his eyes. She saw it and felt it so keenly that she imagined for a moment she could actually read his emotions with utter precision. The sadness of his solitude took her breath away and her hands curled tightly around the glass in her hands.

"You've been away from home for a long time," she said softly, barely realizing the uncensored words were passing her lips until she heard Annali make a low sound of agreement . . . or scolding . . . Tatyana wasn't certain which.

"Actually, I've only just returned. This very night."

How strange, Tatyana thought. And how fortunate. That meant that Dimitre had never even met this man. There was a feeling of kismet to her being in this room with him, she realized. How many things had to go exactly right, or in her case exactly wrong, for them to have come to this point, this room, in this very moment? A chill walked up her spine, an excited sensation of anticipation. Fate was playing a very specific hand, and Tatyana had best be paying attention.

Tatyana had always had an unusual sense of fate and the future. Her instincts had been called uncanny by some. Whether it was ESP or psychic ability or whatever term was preferred, she and Dimitre had learned long ago not to ignore it. For Tatyana, it always seemed to creep up on her in increments, letting itself be known little by little. Her brother was just the opposite. His visions hit with power, sometimes bordering on violence. As a child, he'd been diagnosed as an epileptic. When he'd become older, he had learned that what he experienced wasn't seizures, even though they mimicked them in outward appearance. Dimitre didn't ignore his visions, but he had come to despise them. They weakened and embarrassed him, the seizures even threatening his life at times as they attacked his brain.

Tatyana had dealt with a different sort of difficulty. It had taken experience to learn that not everyone could see things before they happened. She would make offhand observations that then came to pass, or her expression and eyes would be blank for minutes at a time, leaving the real world behind while she dwelled in the past or future in her mind. It had been when the children in school began to call her a witch and a freak that she'd learned to keep silent about certain things, and to filter what she said. It was a habit that, to this very day, she had never quite broken free of. She always censored what she said with extraordinary care. What she thought in her mind very rarely found voice. Only she and Dimitre were fully honest with each other about their ability and visions, as well as everything else.

She looked at Hunter thoughtfully and wondered how far his open mind and fascination with the differences in people would extend. As an anthropologist actively traveling the world and immersing himself in obscure cultures, surely he'd seen more than his share of odd things. Maybe he'd even met others like Dimitre and herself. She would never think of asking, of course, but it was nice to wonder and imagine just the same. Invariably, when she did confide in the rare outsider, they wanted her to perform some feat as proof. They never understood that hers was an unreliable gift at best, an ironic one at worst. For instance, she hadn't been given a clue about all that would happen to her tonight. Then again, it was rare for her sight to turn onto herself. It was usually others who benefited.

Tatyana wondered then if her insight into Hunter was a prelude to something yet to come. The uncanny sharpness of senses and empathy with another sometimes preceded her sight. She was feeling the connection between Hunter and herself keenly even now. She nervously licked her lips, hoping the vision wouldn't be anything too dramatic or worrisome. She didn't know these people well enough for her usual tricks of dropping helpful suggestions to be of any use.

Hunter watched their guest far more closely than was appropriate, no doubt, but she was fascinating to observe as emotions and thoughts flew like birds over her features. She had locked gazes with him, so he could look even more deeply into her than when she'd kept her eyes busy elsewhere. There was something quite unusual going on in her thoughts, of that he was positive. What could she possibly be thinking while she stared so openly at him?

Tatyana suddenly broke contact with him and released a strangled gasp a moment before her glass slipped out of her hands. Hunter had to resist the impulse to use a spell, an impulse that came from living for so many years with those who freely used magic. He was in the Western world now, and these things weren't at all accepted as the norm. If he'd used telekinesis to keep the glass from falling, as instinct had dictated, he would no doubt have shocked the hell out of their guest. So he let the glass fall and shatter, though he did prevent the resulting shards from coming anywhere near her exposed legs. Annali reacted, jumping instantly to her feet, already uttering the usual things a hostess would say to put a guest at ease about an act of clumsiness, but Hunter didn't hear her any more than Tatyana seemed to. Her large, pale-green eyes suddenly flew back to his, the growing emotion in them propelling him to the edge of his seat.

Fear filled her gaze and her empty hands were shaking.

"There's something . . ." she whispered.

And that was when Hunter felt the shadow that skimmed swift and dark over the house.

Thunder snapped and rolled in the skies above Willow

House, the force of it sending vibrations through the strong walls and deep down into the foundation. The storm that had been gathering over the moon finally broke and the room filled with the clackety sound of tiny pellets of icy rain bouncing onto the roof and tinkling and tapping against the glass of the windows.

Hunter surged out of his chair and stepped across the room in two swift seconds. He snatched up Tatyana's hand and swept her out of her seat and high into his arms until he'd stepped back over the spray of glass on the floor. He swung her back onto her feet nearly at the threshold of the door leading into the parlor and turned to the others in the room even as he was steadying her.

"Annali, take her up to Gracelynne's suite and remain there until either Ryce or I come for you. Don't argue," he emphasized before even knowing if she was going to do so. She wasn't. She and Ryce had felt that oppressive shadow just as he had. "Where's Nox?" he asked Ryce with sharp demand.

"Upstairs."

"And Asher?" Hunter persisted.

"I've no idea," Ryce told him grimly.

Annali swept like a breeze across the room and slid her arm through Tatyana's, instantly guiding her into the grand hallway, heading for the sweeping staircases that would lead them to the upper stories.

Tatyana resisted after a few moments of compliant shock, trying to turn back toward the men, who were leaving in the opposite direction, drawing open the main doors and plunging out into the dark and frigid weather. "No! They can't go!" she protested. "It isn't safe!"

"They know," Anna assured her while firmly keeping her going in the right direction. "Believe me, Tatyana, they can take very good care of themselves. As for you and I, we have someone we must protect if need be."

"Someone . . . ?" she asked dumbly, letting Annali lead her once again.

"Gracelynne. She lives here as well and is recovering from an accident. She is weak and we need to watch over her."

"But what can we do?"

"What all women do. Surprisingly more than is ever expected of us," Anna said assuredly. "If it even comes to that. Ryce and Hunter will hardly allow a threat to come into the house."

Tatyana was trying to catch her breath, and it had nothing to do with the stairs she was climbing. Something was very wrong in this place. There was an oppressive presence outside. A presence she couldn't define in any way except to know that it was terrible and dangerous.

And Hunter was going to confront it.

She knew this as well. And not just because Hunter and Ryce were currently outdoors. Because she'd seen it. She had felt and seen the shadow falling over Hunter's handsome face, wrapping overpoweringly around his vital body, literally compressing the life from him. She saw it even now as she was being pulled in the wrong direction.

Yes. Wrong. It was wrong for her to be moving away from Hunter. Rarely had she known something with such utter conviction. She had something, something important that Hunter needed, though she didn't understand what. She didn't even know what was out there in the night. Imagery and impressions like these could mean anything, but she was clear about one thing. She wasn't the only one aware of the danger. Hunter, Ryce, and Annali had felt it just as keenly as she had. Had they seen something or heard a noise that she hadn't? Had they seen the same shadow and thought there was a prowler on the grounds?

It didn't matter. Tatyana stopped short on the stairs, pitching all of her weight into ripping her arm free of Annali's while she turned and fled at the same time. In her sneakers she quickly gained several seconds of advantage over Annali. She had almost reached the door before Annali's protesting shouts reached her. She flung the heavy portal wide and cast herself out into the icy night.

Chapter Six

As soon as the door closed behind them, Hunter and Ryce stretched their arms out wide and reached for power. Hunter drew up his memories of the Romany, tapping into that vein of magic that he was now so familiar with. He spoke rapid, bold Romany and was suddenly launching himself from the ground and into the chill sky. He kept track of Ryce's similar efforts as an afterthought, his concentration fully on the list of spells at his disposal. Romany poured from his lips and a shield of pearly gray light shimmered across his body. Then he was above the line of the roof and could look all around the house and property.

And he could see the shadow.

It was skimming fast over soil and brush, running away from the house.

Toward the Blessing Tree.

Hunter was in pursuit in a heartbeat, even though he knew it was a tactic meant to draw him out and mislead him. Corrupted witches hardly ever dared to target the source of a coven's protective power. Mainly because these sources could protect themselves, and the willow had the potential to destroy her enemies in the process of guarding her life.

Hunter felt Ryce approaching an instant before he tore

past him, his greater power allowing him to outstrip the Sentinel in speed. Hunter spoke a Word and immediately he and Ryce were connected in their thoughts.

Your plan? he demanded of his High Priest.

To win, of course. Watch your back. Protect the house. Don't let them lead you away, Ryce warned.

Hunter pulled up short and understood the warning just as he saw the enormous shadow pull apart into five separate sections and run flying in all directions around them.

Circling back to the house.

Spitting out a curse, Hunter flung himself back the way he had come, vaulting the roof just as one of the menacing shades took form in the air above the eastern side. It may have been a while since he'd engaged a member of a dark coven, but there was no mistaking the look of one. Dressed in poetic black, with gothic accents of piercings and accessories, skin pale from corrupting magic for personal gain and personal power: these were key visual cues.

Otherwise, he might have found the warlock beautiful. She was tall and shapely, her dramatic clothing whipped back into snapping banners by the turbulent weather. Her short cap of slick black hair lay in a crown of wet wisps that rested against her temples and nape. Her ruby and black painted lips looked unbelievably thick and ripe. The fact that she reeked of poisoned magic from the little marcasite cross piercing her left nostril to the black polish on her bare little toes, however, had a way of making even the more pleasant traits seem black and spoiled.

Shifting from shadow to flesh while airborne was no small feat, so he knew this was no neophyte he faced. She was an adept at the least.

"So, little warlock," he greeted her loudly through the rushing wash of icy rain, "think you that you are ready to face Willow Coven's Sentinel? Tell me the name of your coven so I may politely send your body parts back for burial."

"Willow Coven has no Sentinel," she retorted, her voice

bursting with honest arrogance and confidence. She had conviction in her abilities. That made her a little more dangerous.

"It does now," he shot back, equally confident. Softly, beneath his breath, he drew out a string of Romany. She, too, began to whisper the words of a spell. Hunter finished first, throwing out his hands and letting lightning fly from his extended palms. The warlock was struck and went flying back over the chimneys, arcing down toward the ground. He didn't see where she went; however he did sense her striking the muddied ground with a bone-breaking impact.

Beneath Hunter there was a sudden flare of light as the front door was thrown open. Then darkness again as it slammed shut. He knew who had come out, simply by virtue of the fact that he couldn't sense any of his brethren witches below him.

Tatyana.

The distraction was ill timed. A second shadow had come over the roof and taken the form of a warlock, this one a male of significant power and sneering confidence as he caught his target unawares. The blow of the enormous ball of fire blindsided Hunter. The projectile exploded against him, throwing flames and molten lava across his body. Only the shield he'd erected saved him from being viciously burned. What he couldn't counteract, however, was the propulsion from the force of the strike. He arced through the air and flew toward the ground rushing up to greet him.

Chapter Seven

Tatyana had run into the rain blindly and was swiping ice off of her face in an attempt to see. She heard a strange sound, like the sharpest rushing of air, and something flew over her head and crashed into the ground, plowing up a furrow of soil and mud until it stopped in a smoldering heap.

And rolled over with a groan.

"Hunter!" Tatyana gasped, shocked and horrified as she whipped around to look over her shoulder, trying to figure out where he'd fallen from. She fell to her knees and used cold, clumsy hands to turn him from his facedown position in the smothering mud. "Hunter!"

His eyes flew open in his mud-smeared face, the hue of them so vibrant and dramatic in the grim darkness that her breath caught with a stunned choke. His irises were literally glowing, a radioactive sapphire. But Tatyana had no time in which to digest this development. Hunter's muscular arm shot out and whipped around her trim waist. He jerked her down onto his wet, muddy body and rolled her over onto her back in the sludge of ice and dirt until she was fully beneath him. He was muttering an unintelligible string of words as his thighs and ankles locked down her legs and the weight of his hips and torso crushed her. Tatyana gasped for breath as her lung capacity was compromised in the compression between an amazingly solid male body and the unforgiving press of the earth.

"Get off of me!" Tatyana yelled, her hands pushing against his stone-hard chest. She might as well have not even been moving for all the good her struggles were achieving. She couldn't breathe, though, so she cursed sharply in Russian and tried to kick her way out.

The impulse froze on its way from her brain, however, as those eerie eyes bore down into her with their unbelievable luminosity, just before a sheeting red aura limned his entire body in a ripple from his head on down until it reached his toes.

Not a half second later Hunter was struck full in the back by an explosive force. Tatyana screamed as fire and showering sparks burst wildly around them. She felt the fierce impact drive into his body and radiate hard into her own, pushing her deeper into the mud beneath her. In spite of the force and fire, nothing burned her. Hunter covered her protectively from head to toe, even his head lowering until his nose and lips almost touched hers, his wet hair falling against her forehead, and his arms wrapped protectively around her head. Tatyana gasped at the sheer brunt of the brutal force he absorbed, but he was whispering a soft assurance in her ear a moment afterward. He was fine and he was there to protect her.

Hunter pulled back after the rain of fiery pellets had stopped and his comforting demeanor vanished completely as he looked down at her sharply, grabbing her chin and forcing her to look into his commanding eyes. His rain-slicked hair hung in long, gleaming black spikes over his forehead, just touching the tops of his lashes and dripping water onto her face and throat. Rising up as he was, backed by the roiling violence of the black and green storm clouds in the night sky behind him, he was all at once glorious and elemental, dangerous and untamed. Lightning flashed, blazing across the harsh planes of his incredible features, making him look like the mythological god of a turbulent world of tempests and fiery rain spit from a consecrated forge.

"Tatyana! When I get up, you run for the house and, damn it, you stay there with Annali, do you hear me?"

She wanted to. More than anything she didn't want to be here, where impossible happenings were assaulting her senses in ways she wasn't equipped to comprehend. Self-preservation was tearing her soul in half. Her logical, practical mind told Tatyana to obey him and run for her very life.

But the other half of her mind was screaming that just as essential to her survival was being here in this moment and doing anything she possibly could to see to the continued existence of this man. It was just as real to her as holding a rock in her hand, just as solid and inescapable a reality.

"I can't!" She gasped out the denial even as she shook with terror and the frigid cold. "I have to stay or you could die! I know things sometimes. I saw it. I don't know how to explain it, but I feel this. I know I have to stay. Please believe me!"

He had no time to respond before another fireball crashed into his back. Hunter was slammed down onto her once more, even as the sucking mud was forced to accept and give way to the additional weight of their combined bodies under impact. Even if he did get up now, Tatyana could never extricate herself from the adhesive mud trap on her own.

Hunter was bearing the painful brunt of the strikes. Even though the newer shield was designed to repel heat and flame, it wasn't nearly as effective against force. But it was the only shield he had that he could extend over another person, and he had to protect Tatyana. She was an innocent being, and for a white witch like he was, that made her life precious, to be protected above all other things. While Hunter was focusing on holding the power of his shield, he had to comprehend what Tatyana was saying to him.

I know things . . . I saw it.

Images flashed like a rapid slideshow in his consciousness. He remembered the glass and the expression on her face just as she dropped it. He remembered what she had said just as the shadow had threatened the coven.

"You're a psychic," he said, the statement calm and keen as he looked down at her once more.

Tatyana had been acting on impulse up until then, but it was something else entirely to admit to a stranger what her bizarre ability was. A combination of shock and bad experience made her hesitate even though instinct warned her now wasn't the time to hold back. In the end it was the calmness of his tone that made her treat the admission just as matter-of-factly.

"Yes. And I'm never wrong about what I see," she told him firmly.

Hunter nodded once resolutely and quickly reached down toward his ankle. There was a flash of silver metal in the dark as he straightened just in time for the next fireball. He cursed as it broke over them, coughing under the impact a moment before the woman crushed beneath him squeaked out a grunt from her compressed lungs. Her hands were clutching his shirt between their bodies, her knuckles pressing into his flesh as she shuddered with emotion and cold.

Ryce! I'm pinned down! he called to the High Priest.

I'm engaged with two warlocks. I can't help you, I'm sorry!

Hunter cursed again, as he tried to think.

You are losing your touch, Sentinel. The wry voice connecting to the open channel was Nox's, and Hunter had never been so relieved to hear his friend's blithe cockney accent in all of his life. *I'm about to engage and draw fire. Better get ready to move,* the other witch warned.

Hunter surged half up on his knees and grabbed Tatyana's hand. The blade of a knife gleamed in his other hand and Tatyana could see a distorted image of herself in the polished surface as he held it poised over her. Her heart was pounding madly as she met riveting azure eyes filled with eerie light and magic.

"Trust me?" he asked shortly, time too vital and short for him to pretty it up with reassurances and arguments in his favor.

Trust him? A virtual stranger who had thrown himself over her and blocked an outpouring of hellfire from inciner- ating her? "Hell yes!" she cried as if he were crazy for even asking.

And just like that the blade sang through the air and bit into the skin of her hand as he held it palm up. Then with a flip he tossed the blade over and caught the sharp dual edges in his palm, squeezing until they pierced through his skin. In a flash he snatched her bloodied hand up with his, clasping their bleeding palms together so the blood mixed.

"Oh God, I hope you've had all your shots," she blurted out. It was a crazy, ludicrous thing to say in such a wildly perilous moment. He smiled down at her, though, before he lurched to his feet and, using their still joined hands, yanked her up out of the mud. He pulled until she slammed into his huge body, wet sticking to wet, the soaked silk of her dress completely useless and rendering her practically naked as it clung to every chilled curve of her body, outlining the shaped satin and lace of her bra and panties as she shivered like a drowned rat against him.

He held her hands between their bodies, their mingling blood running wet with the icy water and the mud sluicing down their forearms. His opposite arm, still bearing the blade in hand, wrapped around her waist and drew her very tightly against him.

"Now we will see what we will see, Tatyana Petrova," he said in a low, rough tone of voice. The remark was ominous at best, but Tatyana was surprisingly unafraid within the circle of his secure arms. She looked up at him, her body shaking and her teeth chattering, and when she met those mystically bright eyes, she realized that her life had just

changed irrevocably. Perhaps it had even happened the
minute she'd fallen through his door and into his hands, and
she just hadn't realized it.

This man was meant to change her life for all time. That
was why she couldn't let any harm come to him. That was
why she'd run out into obvious danger. Fate had demanded it,
and she was merely there to fulfill. Otherwise she would've
been denying herself something incredibly important, and
she could never have brought herself to do that.

An explosive shower of sparks from above and to the
right of them drew their attention. Tatyana blinked up into
the dark of the ominous storm for a long moment, trying to
comprehend what her eyes were seeing. Was that really a
man flying through the air? No. Two men! And one was
preparing to throw an enormous ball of fire that even now
was forming between his spreading hands.

A gentle finger touched the bottom of her chin, softly
pushing up until her gaping mouth closed with a click of her
teeth. Her wide, shocked eyes turned up to Hunter's and she
suddenly understood why his eyes looked as if they held the
supernatural in them.

Because they did.

Hunter's dark head lowered until his lips were brushing
against her ear, the contact eliciting a totally different kind
of shiver inside of her. "No one will hurt you as long as I'm
alive, Tatyana. If you can believe nothing else, believe that."
He drew back, his finely sculpted lips trailing along her
cheek until he was able to look into her eyes. "I have to help
my friend, angel. I've your strength to bring with me now,"
he said, squeezing her hands once tightly. "Find shelter and
stay there where I can see you're safe while we dispatch this
threat. Promise me you'll do that and stay out of danger."

"I w-will," she chattered with a nod.

He pushed her away suddenly, breaking the link of their
hands as he moved off. The moment their palms parted,
Tatyana was overwhelmed by a rapid sensation of loss and

weakness. She staggered as her heart throbbed painfully in her breast, as if every cell of her body demanded she throw herself back into his arms, soak up his heat, and thrive on his energy. He was watching her, saw the impulse in her eyes and body language, and raised a staying hand to hold her at bay.

"GO! Now!"

And just like that she was obeying him, running away from the house and toward an enormous oak tree, flinging herself behind the sturdy trunk. Heart pounding in the vicinity of her throat, she dared to peek around the shield of the tree. She needed to see and to know what was happening to Hunter. She held out her cut hand, staring down at it for a second, somehow understanding that the overpowering compulsions she felt had something to do with whatever magic it was he had worked on their bleeding palms.

Magic.

Had she truly ever known the real meaning of the word? Tatyana doubted that very heartily as she watched events unfolding before her with the horrifying clarity of crossing out of one world, and into another. It was like the first time one's eyes were opened to the nature of people, love, or the world. It was both agonizing and distressing as well as enlightening and empowering. She watched it all with wide eyes, not feeling the icy sleet clinging to her unblinking lashes.

Hunter flew up from the ground with mighty propulsion fueled by his anger and outrage. At the same time his mind was working hard on all that he'd seen and all that he knew. There had been five parts to that shadow when it had separated. He'd dispatched one female and he doubted she'd recover too quickly. Nox was engaging the male that had been battering him and Tatyana with fireballs. Ryce had said that two others were in combat with him. That left one unaccounted for, and that one, he was certain, was by far the most dangerous of them all. Hunter was also certain there was a specific goal for this attack, and he needed to figure out exactly what it was before it succeeded and weakened Willow Coven even further than it already was without Gracelynne and the others to fight with them.

The enemy had attacked when Kaia wasn't there. They were attacking when Asher was unaccounted for. The timing gave them the advantage of numbers, of course, but there had to be more to it than that. There had to be a definite objective to their artful battle tactics. It was clear their intelligence was dated since they didn't know that Willow Coven's powerful Sentinel had returned to the fold, so whatever they'd planned for this night had nothing to do with himself. With Gracelynne out of the picture for now, the most powerful target would be Ryce, but it was still highly unlikely they would seek out Ryce before knocking out all his support. No. They would target the next most powerful after Gracelynne.

Annali.

That would require drawing her out. The house was bespelled and warded. It would be much too difficult to breach the coven defenses embedded permanently in the walls of Willow House. The attackers would know that. So how to draw out Annali?

The Blessing Tree.

Hunter flung himself around in the air to look toward the coven's living power center. He saw Ryce embattled with two warlocks in his path, being kept too busy to prevent what would come next. Hunter could feel it, the impending action and threat. The warning rang through him, a cry from the tree herself as she realized she was in dire threat from an enemy. It was a cry that would sing sharpest to Annali. Anna's spirit was connected to all the plants of the earth. She felt them all on a soulful level, shared their lives and experiences as if they were hundreds of thousands of little pets so precious to her. The Blessing Tree was the progenitor of all of Willow Coven, but to Annali she was the mentor goddess, beloved mother, and most precious child all in one.

The cry of the grand willow ricocheted through every single member of Willow Coven, disrupting precious concentration and sending pain rippling through each of their bodies. It was a reflex, part of the Blessing Tree's defense system, but it didn't mean the tree was in danger of destruction. That didn't stop each of them from being forced to fight for recovery. To keep themselves on task rather than rushing to do the old willow's bidding as her protectors.

All save Annali.

Hunter heard the crash of glass as Annali burst out of the window of Gracelynne's suite in full, beautiful fury. Her hair flew wildly in the storm winds, the wet causing her fallen curls to separate from one another until she looked like a stunning gorgon in her vengeance, with snakes of curls and fury-filled eyes of burning bright lavender, fierce enough to turn any enemy to stone should they dare to cross her. Once she was free of the wards of the house, she cast her best traveling spell, burning precious energy. Annali wasn't a spell-casting witch as a rule. She was an Alchemist. Bottles of concoctions carefully cooked and measured, burnt herbs, and crushed powders were her forte, and in this she was a witch without compare. She had latent powers, of course. They all did. However each had a specialty in the coven and potions were hers. So when she cast her teleportation spell, she was effectively using almost all of her latent power at once.

Hunter swore aloud. He needed to go after her, but he couldn't leave Tatyana and Gracelynne unprotected either. He had to chance it, though. The house wards would have to suffice to protect Gracie. As for Tatyana . . .

He swung back to see her peeping up at him with awe and shock written clearly across her features.

He'd gone too far to shy away from the path now.

"Come!" he commanded, his voice like a clap of thunder in the night as he reached out both hands toward her. He uttered the accompanying spell and a tether of bright blue energy, exactly the color of his eyes in that moment, whipped out to lash around her unsuspecting body. He heard her cry out in surprise, but his senses were steadily being filled by her spirit and emotions, and he realized she felt no real terror at this frightening world she suddenly found herself plunged into. Fascinated, awestruck, and filled with understandable trepidation, but no true fear. He was almost infuriated by her lack of self-preservation. This was no amusement park ride she was catching thrills on. She should be showing a proper respect for the danger she was in.

The tether he'd strung between them retracted toward him, plucking her up off the ground and flinging her quickly into his waiting arms. He caught her against himself with a grunt from the impact. It wasn't the most ideal spell when one was in flight, but it cost little energy and was effective enough to get the job done. She exclaimed on the rush of her forced exhalation, her hands whipping out to clasp him about his shoulders. Tatyana clung to him for dear life, realizing that he was the only thing keeping her in the air. He was satisfied to see she had that much sense at least. But he couldn't fault her too much. At least she wasn't screeching hysterically and crying with feminine fear. To be honest, there were probably very few human *men* who wouldn't be weeping for their makers by this point. Tatyana Petrova was either very brave or incredibly foolhardy.

"Hold on to me very tightly. Whatever you do, don't let go until I say it's okay. Do you understand?"

She nodded vigorously, her clutch around his shoulders tightening dramatically, one of her long legs even going so far as to snake around one of his. The enthusiastic clasp brought them intimately close. She unwittingly drew his thigh between her own. Despite all of his concentration on the dire task at hand, there was no way on earth he could ignore that intimacy. They were both bathed in frigid water, yet there, in that space, she was all supremely natural heat. The contrast demanded his attention, tugged at the chemistry between them, stirred a dark hunger within him that was purely masculine, though not purely human.

Hunter didn't have the time to relish the power of that delightful stimulation, but it was an excellent resource he immediately drew on. The sexual energy sparking through him and between them powered his next spell. It consisted of a single word, coupled with a firm image in his mind of his destination. In a flash of nauseating colors and a distortion of the visual space around them, they left the air above the manse and appeared ankle-deep in a frozen puddle just to the left of the Blessing Tree. The sudden biting cold soaking into Tatyana's sneakers made her surge up against him reflexively and Hunter felt his body explode with heated need. It was so raw and unrefined, so unexpected under the circumstances, that he stumbled back awkwardly under the onslaught. His instinct for self-preservation made him pry her off of himself, even though totally opposing instincts only wanted to draw her closer.

"Go!"

He shoved her, probably too forcefully if her staggering attempt to recover her balance and the surprise on her face were any indication. He tore his gaze from that baffling female, though, and searched for another one entirely.

Annali was thrown full in front of the Blessing Tree, using her physical body as a shield, her hand raised high, gripping a small glass potion bottle. The enemy hovered dark and ominous before her, the dominance of him singeing across Hunter's tastebuds and creeping along the back of his scalp. The physical presence of the male warlock alone intimidated. He was several inches over six feet, taller even than Hunter's 6'2". He had a shadowed, rugged visage; menacing with its dark, slashing brows over glittering obsidian eyes that glared with the black light of his magic. His chiseled lips were sculpted into the cruel lines of a confident sneer. A scar cut diagonally over his upper right cheek, starting at the edge of his right nostril and arcing up to his right temple. His black hair, colored like a moonless night sky, was plastered all around his head and neck and shoulders.

Hunter knew him instantly.

He should. He had been the one to give him that distinctive scar.

However, that had little to do with his recognition. He had known him since the day he'd been born.

"Braen."

The announced name got the warlock's sudden attention, alerting him to Hunter's appearance. Those sinister eyes widened with obvious surprise for just a moment before narrowing with ominous contemplation on him.

"Well, well . . . the prodigal son returns," Braen mocked him, adding a derisive laugh to the observation. "You've impeccable timing as usual, Brother. How remarkable. Only just arrived, are you?"

"As you see," Hunter said shortly, his feet bracing apart aggressively and his hands curling into anticipatory fists.

"I must say I'm disappointed in Ryce. One little attack and he runs crying for his Sentinel to come home? My coven must be more intimidating than even I supposed," the warlock mused.

"*Your* coven." Hunter barked out a laugh of distaste and contempt. "I should have guessed it. You and yours have been a thorn in Willow Coven's side for far too long, Braen. What are we calling ourselves nowadays? What source of poisoned power are we using this time?"

"You may call us Belladonna Coven," Braen invited silkily.

"*Belladonna Coven* has never been anything but a stain on the face of this otherwise beautiful planet!" Annali spat angrily, her hand with the potion in it still raised aggressively. Her grip was almost tight enough to crush the glass,

Hunter observed. He'd never seen her so incensed before. Then again, it had been a very long time since someone had dared to attack the Blessing Tree. And for the threat to be Braen of all people, the brother he'd turned his back on and the one who had . . .

"Really?" Braen mused softly; his smile for her was almost handsome with its sudden flash of white teeth. His easy charm was shining through now that he was scaling back the influence he had been using to cast a pall of intimidation against Annali. "We've hardly crossed paths at all this past decade, Annali. How do you presume to know anything about Belladonna Coven after all this time?" The smile turned in shape ever so slightly, but there was no mistaking its cruelty. "Unless you are feeling a little homesick for the days when we were known as Hawthorn Coven, my tasty little sweet?" Braen licked his lips with obviously lewd intentions.

"I'm not your sweet, you prick bastard!" Annali spat with fury, her face turning a mottled red with the heat of her rage. Hunter had to fly with all speed to catch her arm before she threw her weapon down at Braen's feet. The warlock was baiting her purposely for a reason and Hunter wasn't going to let her find out what it was the hard way. Not so long as he was there to prevent it.

"Easy, honey," he soothed softly, his thumb flicking gently over her roaring pulse as he tried to communicate the need to keep her head. "We all know where your true home is, Annie. Nothing he says will ever change that."

"And what of you, Hunter? Where is your home these days? Will you be staying?" Those merciless black eyes drifted over Hunter's tense posture, then slowly slipped away and traveled to the woman who hadn't been able to move beyond a few steps away from the drama unfolding before her. Hunter knew it wasn't just idle curiosity that held Tatyana there. Now he saw the fear she'd lacked earlier. It was what had locked her into place. "Ah . . ." Braen mused with speculation. "With such pretty lures, perhaps even I would leap out of my stream to flop around on deck."

"Hunter . . ." she whispered hoarsely, her voice inaudible over the slushy fall of ice from the sky.

It was her terror that spoke to him, seeking solace and assurances that he didn't have. He hadn't come up against Braen in a decade, and he had no idea how far his enemy's powers had advanced in that time. Hunter had no way of reassuring Tatyana that he could protect her and Annali at the same time, never mind himself as well. There was something he was missing. He was sure of it. Braen was far too calm. Too complacent. The one thing that would never change; Braen would always display his arrogance and egotistical satisfaction when he felt victory was at hand.

What is it, damn it? What am I missing?

"Not to worry, Sentinel of Willow Coven," Braen laughed with dark amusement. "I didn't come prepared to face you this night. I'm not so foolish as to risk myself without a better plan. Even now the other members of my coven are withdrawing from their battles. The night is yours. Savor your victory, for it will not last or be repeated."

"You'll forgive me if I don't take your word for it," Hunter bit out as he searched for telepathic confirmation from the others. There was apparent truth to the High Cleric of Belladonna Coven's statements. Ryce and Nox were pursuing their enemies to the edges of the property.

Braen merely shrugged, his smile sly and full of lies.

"If it will make you feel better . . ."

Braen spoke a Word as he lifted his wide hands, his palms thrown out toward Hunter and Annali. The Word was very old and Hunter didn't recognize it. He tensed, unable to prepare for the unknown assault with anything other than a hastily erected shield he hoped was barrier enough to protect himself and Annali.

Tatyana saw a blue bolt of static electricity snap through

the suddenly visible wall of energy protecting Hunter and
Annali from the warlock, and every psychic alarm she had
suddenly rang out. She saw Braen's hands cock at the wrists
and face downward toward the ground at the last possible
second. Tatyana suddenly *knew* with a strange clarity she'd
never really known before. There was no doubt. No shock.
In spite of all the overwhelming input assaulting her untried
senses and her natural human resistance, she simply accepted the facts of the moment and reacted to them.

A Russian phrase her mother had always used to tease her
leapt to the front of her mind. Before she could reconsider
the impulse, she spoke the words with a strong conviction of
purpose. She felt an influx of energy run through her from
the ground up, her body locking under the shock of it as her
virgin experience with the call for power rocketed through
her and flew through the conduit of her nervous system before seeking her targets.

Hunter felt power sizzle over the fine hairs at the base of
his neck, then the slam of undeniable connection biting
through his body, entering through the cut of invitation across
his palm and demanding his full attention. Even as blinding
sparks of black lightning erupted from Braen's hands, Hunter
and Annali were ripped away from the anchor of the ground
and sent tumbling awkwardly into the air away from the Blessing Tree and all of her saturated branches.

The black electricity hit the ground with an earthquake of
impact and immediately picked a thousand sheeting paths
over the ice-covered soil, the water conducting the deadly
energy flawlessly in an enormous circle. The corrupted
power blasted up over the Blessing Tree, into her every last
branch and root through the easy circuit of the water and ice.
To the great tree it was no different from being struck by
lightning, a violence she had survived many times in her
centuries-long existence. This too passed over her, not
through her, and only minimal power was required to protect
herself.

Her children, the two witches of her coven who were
spilled awkwardly into the air, had been broken away from
the ground, the tree, and all the sheets of icy puddles they'd
been standing in. Braen's plan to electrocute them with his
shocking poison, an attack that would have slipped easily
beneath and around Hunter's fallible shield, was foiled by
this detachment from all conductors.

All Tatyana could do, however, was watch as the black
energy skipped and glided toward her, flying faster than she
could draw breath. When it struck her, she was completely
unprepared for the pain of impact and possession. It rippled
up from her feet, gripping her every muscle from heels to
scalp and forcing them to contort and flex with all their natural strength and beyond. Her teeth slammed shut, her jaw
clenched so tight that tendons popped in protest. Her arms
and head were flung back, her chest thrusting up into the wet
darkness as the vital organs within were assaulted, delicate
electrical balances among nerves thrown severely out of
syncopation, and synapses frying with excruciating finality.
She had never known such agony could exist. It went on forever, like a cresting labor pain that contracted and contracted
and refused to give birth.

And then merciful darkness claimed her at last.

As soon as Tatyana lost consciousness, her spell dis-
solved into nothingness. But by then Hunter was prepared
and aware, and he cast a quick levitation spell to keep himself and Annali from touching the ground. They were both
righted and facing their enemy. Anna drew up the skirt of her
dress, revealing a flat canvas holder about six inches long
against her thigh, fastened by Velcro, and holding just about
a dozen of the smallest of her potion bottles, each bottle held
securely by an individual pouch of elastic. Only she knew
what was in each bottle. The witch switched potions with a
flick of her wrist and flung the new bottle at the High Cleric.

It broke against the side of his face, making him cry out with an enraged shout. His electrical attack broke off with his shattered concentration as his emotion got the best of him. By then, Annali's potion was exploding its spell all over her enemy.

Ivy, fresh and green and growing thicker by the second, burst from the ground around Braen's feet. The potion splattered over Braen's face and head was what Annali liked to call 'ivy aphrodisiac.' The vines, a magical enhancement that came with the potion, would want to do everything in their power to cling to the liquid, wrapping around and around it and covering every inch of it like a lover's embrace. Of course if you happened to be in the center of all this affection, you found yourself tied fast with the breath being viciously squeezed out of you. It gave the term 'plant lover' a whole new meaning. To Annali, it was the ultimate justice to use nature against the evil of Braen.

Braen snapped free of the first vines easily, laughing derisively at Anna.

"I remember this piddling spell, sweetheart. I'm insulted you would even use it on me—"

Braen was distracted from his insult when new and far larger vines surged up to whip around him. Before he could tear free of even one, he was nearly covered with a dozen others twice as strong.

Annali's smile was bitter and triumphant. "I guess my piddling spell has merit after all, *sweetheart*," she scoffed at him in disgust. Then Annali, whose nature was so genteel and sweet, spit in Braen's face with all the enthusiasm she could muster.

Hunter had already begun to fortify her attack with others of his own. The ground beneath Braen turned to quicksand and the vines growing out of it began to draw him inexorably down into another suffocating fate. Insects appeared en masse, driving themselves between the small spaces of the ivy tethers to sting repetitively.

It was enough. More than enough. Hunter turned away from his besieged enemy, leaving him to Annali's dubious mercy. He flew over the frozen ground to Tatyana, scooping her limp body up into his arms, bearing her frightening deadweight with ease. He cradled her head gently on his shoulder, tucking her forehead beneath his chin as he searched for a pulse in her slender throat. The telltale throb of life was completely absent, driven from her body along with every other natural electrical impulse.

Hunter's heart began to pound in double time, as if it wanted to take on the functions of Tatyana's for her. He didn't have the skill to heal her and bring her back to life. Their Healer was Kaia. But since that remarkable witch wasn't here, he would turn to the next best medic among them.

"Annali, help me! We have no time!" he shouted in warning. He heard the panic in his voice; felt the sympathetic ache of pain racing up his arm and bleeding into his body along the path her blood had taken as it had invaded him.

Hunter knew Annali would follow him with all speed. She'd heard the rare emotion of fear in his voice and knew Tatyana's situation was critical. They left Braen behind without a second thought. The only way he could possibly escape the spells would be to teleport away from the location powering them. He would have no choice but to leave in order to preserve himself, and the tree would remain safe as always. Braen would also have to wash off that potion of Annali's, too, if he ever planned to be ivy-free. So long as it covered his skin, the ivy would thrive and follow, bursting anew from any viable ground. It was more than enough to chase the warlock off and keep him well away for the time being.

Chapter Eight

The Willow Coven converged on Willow House as a unit. They all strode into the conservatory and out of the storm of sleet, hurrying in order to preserve the life of their guest. Nox closed the exterior doors as Annali waved Hunter forward to a reasonably bare tabletop. He gently laid his burden along the length of it; his hands were tender and grateful as they lowered her head, his fingers brushing back her wet hair. Then he took up a position above her head and planted his feet, clearly there for the duration to watch over her.

Ryce, on the other hand, was pacing with obvious fury.

"I'm going to check on Gracelynne and repair that glass," Ryce bit out. "When I come back and when you are through here, Annali, you are going to tell me that you had no idea this girl was a dormant witch or so help me . . ." He drew in a hard, infuriated breath, turned on his heel, and left in a storm of anger.

Annali cleared her throat and focused on the task at hand. "Nox, I need blankets and clothes for her. Go to my room. My size will be far closer than Gracelynne or Kaia's. Get something soft and comfortable. Warm, too."

Nox nodded, the tension in the coven affecting even his casual ways. He left to do as she asked.

"Anna, she isn't breathing," Hunter pressed urgently.

"I'm aware of that, Hunter," she retorted. She bent intently over her collection of potions on the far table, contemplating carefully before choosing one of her powder sachets at last. "Step away, Hunter."

Hunter took a single step back from Tatyana's inert form. He felt the constriction in his chest and the protest running rampant in his mind even as he did so. He took a breath, trying to remind himself that this was only a temporary condition, this sensation of neediness and desperate desire for connection. Oh, he was irrevocably linked with the beautiful redhead for the rest of their lives, the sharing of blood having assured that, but he didn't think it would be practical to be so weighed down by it like this. He'd heard that eventually it would ease.

Annali stepped back, too, and then threw the powder at Tatyana. It landed against her body with a puff of dust. The innocuous little cloud of residue spread over Tatyana so gently that Hunter wasn't expecting the whiplash of electricity that burst out of the cloud and caused their patient's body to seize in a tight, arcing fit. The shock dissipated and Tatyana slammed back down onto the table.

She gasped for breath.

Hunter was over her in a flash. He forced her to look into his eyes, his hands encompassing her head and his thumbs against both her cheeks acting as a firm frame until she latched on to the blue of his gaze.

"Easy," he soothed, his voice deep and steady, its cadence purposely helping her find the natural rhythm of life. "Just breathe, angel. In and out," he encouraged. He didn't glance away once, not even when he heard Annali busying herself with the creation of her next helpful concoction. He was interested in nothing but saving the life of this woman who had saved his and Annali's. If they'd been struck as Tatyana had, they would have either died or fallen helpless and incapacitated, left to Braen's lack of mercy and diabolical intent.

This woman, Hunter knew, was an unexpected fortune. He'd known it the moment he'd first touched her. Even though the attraction had been physical at first, it hadn't taken long for him to see the treasure of her personality and intellect. The discovery that there was power and potential within her, too, was more than he could ever have expected. He was so stunned by her he had no idea what to feel. She was a stranger, both to them and to magic, who had risked everything to protect him, he who was Sentinel and protector of this mighty coven. Protecting his life, even at the potential cost of hers.

Now he returned the favor, guided her into regulating each breath she took, guarding carefully the spark of her life while Annali worked. Tatyana followed his calming instructions automatically, instinctively trusting him, although he could tell she was unaware of everything else. She couldn't speak or even form complex thoughts. She couldn't comprehend but the simplest of instructions.

To breathe.

"Be calm," he urged when her eyes grew wide, the new power she'd used highlighting them with jade fire. She was afraid to be so helpless, and he could feel her fear like a dagger stabbing into his soul. Hunter forced himself to control the emotion. "You're safe now, Tatyana," he soothed her firmly. "Annali is here to make you well. I'm here to protect you. I won't let anything harm you."

She was shaking. So hard he thought she might vibrate off the table. He cursed Nox for taking so long with clean, dry clothes for her. This time Hunter had the option of openly using magic to help her. He fitted his hands even more snugly to the contours of her face and spoke a Ukrainian spell. Instantly, a wave of warmth radiated out of his hands and entered her deeply chilled body. Now, so long as he touched her skin, he could regulate her core temperature.

Her shivers and chattering teeth eased considerably, although not all of her tremors were from the cold. Her respirations calmed and steadied. Hunter began to feel that he, too, could breathe easier. It took power to maintain the temp regulation, but he didn't waver even as it drained him little by little.

In a few moments, Annali rounded the other side of the table and Hunter helped Tatyana sit up in the circle of his arms so Anna could press one of her rejuvenating teas to her patient's lips. Hunter stroked his fingers down the graceful length of her throat, coaxing her to swallow when she couldn't seem to coordinate the reflex for herself. Soon the entire brew was in her belly, working its particular brand of magic. Hunter laid her back down just as Nox returned with a heavy robe, blanket, and flannel shirt.

"Those aren't mine," Annali observed with an arched brow of inquisition.

"Right, they're Dimitre's," he explained. "I guess I thought it would make her feel better to wear her brother's things. On a subconscious level at the very least. They are warm and dry and I figure that's all that matters."

"It's an excellent idea," Hunter agreed.

"Anyway, I'm going to check the property."

Lennox left quickly and Annali went about preparing another cup of tea for her patient, carefully measuring out specific tea leaves and other herbal ingredients in a cup, her complete attention absorbed in the task. Hunter, meanwhile, set the dry clothing down on Annali's stool.

Trying to maintain the connecting touch that he was using to warm her, he began to remove Tatyana's wet clothing. He started with her soaked sneakers, easily slipping them off until they both thumped wetly to the floor. Her muddied and torn hose were next. He slid his hand up her thigh and over her hip until his fingers touched the elastic band at their top. Realizing how awkward it was to remove the wet, clingy fabric with one hand, Hunter cursed the fact that he didn't have a spell for shedding clothes. It made him smile briefly as he wondered to himself why the usefulness of such a spell had never occurred to him before. Now that it had, he'd have to rectify the omission.

Hunter brought his other hand beneath her skirt to join in the effort of stripping off the stubborn nylon. As his palms slid over her backside he became suddenly aware of the incredible intimacy of the act he was performing. Unable to help himself, he looked into her shimmering green eyes as he slipped hands and sheer fabric slowly down her flawlessly smooth skin, the dampness of her legs warmed quite thoroughly by his spell. Hunter gave his head a single hard shake, trying to shed the inappropriate sensations writhing within his body as her skin glided along his palms. He discarded the destroyed nylons on top of her sneakers.

Before continuing on, Hunter turned his head to inhale a steady, purposeful breath through his nose and out of his mouth. He couldn't understand this. Sexual deprivation and predilection for redheads aside, he did not spark this easily and quickly off of women. Especially not helpless ones doing nothing to merit it. Hunter was disgusted with himself, but the assertion of his rational mind had no influence over his corporeal cravings. The well-meaning self-lecture was completely ineffective.

The right thing to do would be to leave and let Annali finish this task.

The minute he thought of that option, his mind protested with a flood of excuses as to why he couldn't leave. His spell to warm her, for starters. Then there was Tatyana's connection with him, which made her feel safe and calm. And again, Annali needed her hands free to work her healing potions.

All very sound reasons to remain and do what he must to help Tatyana.

In the end, he had to acknowledge that it was none of those reasons that actually motivated him as he reached for the hem of her short silk dress. If he was going to be a lecher, he might as well be an honest one, he thought grimly.

What does it matter anyway? he mused. She was already as good as naked with the wet silk clinging to her skin. And he was certainly adult enough to control himself no matter what he was feeling. Nothing could ever provoke him to take advantage of an innocent person.

With that logic to gird him, he peeled off the silk that clung to her every possible curve. The devilish red material stripped away to reveal an equally brilliant red lace and silk chemise, beneath which was still more suggestive underwear in a shimmering satin ruby. Against the paleness of her natural coloring, it was a wickedly sinful color, and unbelievably stimulating to the male eye. Actually, *she* was stimulating to the male eye. Tall, fit, and damned curvaceous, she was killing him.

His honor finally got the better of him. He quickly removed the chemise, but left her other lingerie firmly where it was before he lost all respect for himself. Clearing his throat of the tightness within, he reached for the towel Nox had included in his gifts of clothing. With an efficiency and forced detachment, he buffed her skin dry until she gleamed rosy and healthy. She was shivering again, his toweling hands having broken the warmth spell he'd been using. He sat her up and swung the flannel shirt around her quickly. Tatyana wound her arms around his neck once they were through the sleeves, clinging to his body instinctively. He tried to hold himself away from her because he was still wet . . . and still far too easily stirred by her nearness. She pressed a cheek to his, warm now while he was chilled through, nuzzling into him for solace. He paused in buttoning up the oversized shirt, drawing in a deep, thoughtful breath as the scent of rainwater, earth, and warming female rose from her skin. The combination was unimaginably appealing and Hunter found himself squelching a groan in the bottom of his throat.

Damn, but she was far too tempting. Even when she clearly had no intention of being so. She was barely cognizant of her surroundings. And as for himself, this was *not* who he was. The more he told himself that, the more Hunter hoped it would somehow regulate his behavior. Even as he robed her and wrapped her in a blanket, she persisted in her clinging grasp, silently seeking the contact of his vitality and security. Finally, with a sigh, Hunter took a lesson from the most basic instruction in the magic of the earth.

It's harder to work against the movement of nature than it is to travel with it.

In a nutshell, it was always easier, and sometimes wiser, to go with the flow.

Hunter stripped off his sodden shirt so he wouldn't get his clingy patient wet once more. After a brief drying under the same towel he'd used for her, he tossed both on the heap of her clothing and then turned fully toward her. She instantly slipped her arms around his neck again and snuggled against his chest. Hunter's eyes slid closed as he allowed himself to feel the rush of pleasure her contact and need triggered in him. It was nice to be needed again, a feeling he'd been relearning and indulging in a great deal since he'd first entered the conservatory tonight.

He tamped all of his inappropriate reactions down and focused instead on task management. He slid his hands into her bound hair and began to sort out clips and pins from the sodden twists of what had once been an elegant style. The dark mass of her hair was marred with mud and debris, but here he could help her with a few spoken words of magic. By the time it was freed from its tight bindings, it was falling in clean, wet waves down her back. Hunter exhaled a silent sigh of pleasure as the rich thick strands bled through his fingers like a waterfall of dampened claret silk. It dropped well below her shoulders, longer than he'd suspected, though it was cut shorter as it came forward until the front strands just barely touched her collarbone.

As if in response to what he was doing, Tatyana lifted her hands and slid them into the dampness of his hair at the back of his neck. A shocking bolt of stimulation ricocheted down his spine and into southern territories in his body, forcing muscles and flesh to clench in awareness and arousal. He grew hard. Oh, so very hard. His cock lengthened and thickened and heated with the fury of an undeniable arousal. Gritting his teeth, Hunter released his hold on her hair and reached up for the busy fingers crawling over his scalp. The minute she felt his hands on hers, she resisted his attempt to remove her touch, making a sound of protest that contained enough fear to cut him to the quick.

Then she found her voice; a hoarse, weak conglomeration of sounds that barely qualified as speech. Her crossed wires apparently didn't allow for English, so she was wrenching out Russian that was more an attempt to get impressions across than it was to make conversation.

"Cold . . . warm from you . . . Hunter . . . need you . . ." she rasped, turning her face into his neck so the words floated up his throat like heated puffs of erotica. Her lips brushed his pulse as they moved, lighting fires in his bloodstream that radiated heat like a sun, going through his entire body until he felt as though he was burning everywhere with unfathomable need.

"Here's some more tea. This will help sedate her so she can sleep. Rest will clear her mind." Annali turned around to face Hunter as she spoke and it was all she could do not to react outwardly at the sight that greeted her.

Hunter stood before the table, between the knees of their patient, wrapped up tightly in her hold while she nuzzled and cuddled him as if he were a huge, warm-blooded teddy bear. Meanwhile, the male witch had his eyes closed tightly and a priceless expression on his strained features. It was a cross between perplexity and raw sexual tension. Taking pity on him, she pressed her lips together and wiped all traces of humor from her expression. Hunter tried to draw away from the feminine trap he was ensnared in as Annali approached. It was unfeasible for him to do so without distressing Tatyana, so he relented with a sigh and turned a speaking gaze on Annali.

"I don't know what you expect me to do," she said, a giggle escaping her. "She's probably working on nothing but instinct and rudimentary thoughts after having her brain fried like that. Obviously she equates you with security and, umm"—Annali edited herself innocently—"sanctuary."

It was hard for her to keep a straight face as she said that. Presently, Tatyana combed her hands through his hair, down his neck and around his shoulders before heading back again. Somehow Annali managed to contain herself enough to have mercy on him when she saw how badly flushed the back of his neck was, even his ears tipped pink. She knew Hunter wouldn't be so flustered if he weren't already deeply attracted to Tatyana. He was trying to be gallant under impossible temptation, poor baby.

"Here, Tatyana," Anna offered with brusque efficiency, pressing the cup on her patient as she wriggled between the two of them enough to give Hunter some desperately needed breathing space. Annali heard him swearing vehemently under his breath in Romany. When she glanced at him, he had his back to her and his hands locked into fists so tight his knuckles had gone white. She pressed the tea on Tatyana. "Good girl," she praised every few swallows, managing to keep the other woman's attention while Hunter regained some composure. When he finally turned to face them, his expression was like grim stone and a quick pulse flickered at the base of his clenched jaw.

"I'm going to see her settled for the night and find myself some dry clothes. Tell Ryce I'll be down to keep watch."

Annali hardly thought that was likely. Hunter was so obviously exhausted. He showed every sign of having pushed himself too far. But, as always when she dealt with the coven males, Annali kept her mothering to herself. They would only argue with her anyway. Nature would force his compliance, she thought as she smiled slyly and flicked a glance at the insensate Tatyana. And nature would no doubt use every trick in the book to get her way.

Annali gave Hunter a noncommittal nod and stepped away from his target, watching as he swung Tatyana into his arms and carried her from the room.

Hunter flew up the stairs as if demons from the depths of hell were nipping at his heels. All he wanted was to see his charge safely into bed and to get himself dry and warm. It wasn't until he reached the top of the stairs that he realized there wasn't a room readied for Tatyana. So Hunter simply brought her into his own suite. He would arrange for a separate room after he returned below stairs.

He turned down the bed and slid her between the chilled sheets. There was a steady fire in the hearth in the outer room, but the bedroom was nippy. He set the thermostat, but he was still fighting off chills as he sought dry clothes from the wardrobe across from the bed. He stripped and re-dressed in a pair of gray sweats. He was searching for a warm shirt when he glanced in the mirror. The door to the wardrobe had tilted to reflect the occupant of the bed back at him. She was sitting up, her eyes wide and fascinated as she watched him. Hunter went exceedingly still for a beat, then he quickly reminded himself that, as disoriented as she was, it couldn't matter that he'd unthinkingly stripped completely naked a moment ago.

No. It didn't make any difference, he assured himself. She wouldn't even remember tonight by the time morning came around.

He rounded the bed and reached to ease her back into the pillows.

"Angel, you really need to rest."

The concept was apparently acceptable to her. She slid over to the opposite pillow as she grabbed his hand with surprising strength, dragging him toward herself, obviously intending for him to lie next to her. Resigning himself to the idea that he was a louse *and* a pushover all in one, Hunter slid down into the bed beside her. He was barely in contact with the bedding before she'd wrapped herself fully around him, squeezing him like a sexy, wriggly python. It was relentlessly blissful. Tatyana had incredible curves and her enthusiasm was like a fantasy. Not just because of her sexuality, although he certainly acknowledged he was enjoying it a whole hell of a lot, but also because of the sheer affection she was giving him.

He'd always craved this kind of enthusiastic physical affection from a woman. He'd grown up with zero physical connection with his parents, dark warlocks who offered their offspring nothing outside of the material. Braen and his other brothers had taken pleasure in the family's wealth and power, but Hunter had suffered in that cold, controlled atmosphere.

Now he was with a stranger who was bathing him in eager warmth, and it was like knocking on the gates of nirvana. Selfishly, he soaked in it, his arms circling her luscious body tightly. Tatyana was coiled around him, muttering happy, contented Russian to him that took away a lot of the guilt he felt for taking advantage of the situation. It was clear from the disjointed mumblings that she needed this as badly as he did, that her preservation instincts demanded it from him. Hunter knew that a large part of her reaction was the blood exchange; but that logic couldn't remove the peace he felt tightly holding a living being who wanted no one else to hold her but him.

He would go down to Ryce just as soon as she fell asleep.

"Annali, I'm waiting."

Ryce hadn't even bothered getting out of his wet clothing. As soon as he had repaired the window to Gracelynne's suite and had seen her safely at rest, he had stormed off in search of Dimitre's lover. Now he stood on the threshold of her bedroom as she shivered her way out of her clothes and into a warm dry robe.

"What do you want me to say?" she asked quietly, not looking at him as she wrapped up her wet hair in a fresh towel.

"I want you to say Dimitre didn't tell you about Tatyana either, Annie. I can almost forgive him, based on his newness to all of this and the fact that we are still working on settling his questions, concerns, and fears, but by the Lady, Annali, *you* should know better!"

"Ryce . . ." Annali sighed and faced him, hands on her hips. "Are you angry for Tatyana's sake because I didn't tell you or are you angry because you think I betrayed your trust?"

"*Think*? There's no damn thinking about it, Annali! You didn't just betray me, you betrayed the tenets of the Craft! Ones you swore to uphold. Does that change now because you are in love with a man?"

"Hmm. Let me think about that," she shot back with sarcasm. "Meanwhile, why don't you tell me about *your* betrayal of *my* trust? You know, a trust you swore to uphold the day you rescued me and brought me into this house? Or does that change because I am in love with a man?"

The accusation brought the High Priest up short, taking a serious amount of wind out of his outrage. "What are you talking about?" he demanded, although without force or righteousness. He didn't realize that the lack of emphasis only reawakened Annali's suspicions.

"I am talking about you sending my lover off with Kaia on her 'lecture circuit.' Like you would really let her go away on something like that when we are under such heavy threat? And that you sent her with Dimitre 'for protection'? He is the least skilled of all of us, despite the impressiveness of his power. Power is nothing until you learn to wield it effectively. You have pounded that message into me for eleven years."

"Annie . . ."

"Don't you 'Annie' me! You sent him somewhere dangerous and you made him swear not to tell me, didn't you? You are always preaching about how you want us all to find love and have families and real lives outside of the Craft one day, and what do you do at the very first opportunity? You take a man who I need to trust more than anything and you ask him to *lie* to me! Well, he didn't lie to me, and he didn't break his word to you because that is how important both of those things are. Instead, he came to me and said, 'Honey, I've been sworn not to tell you the truth about what I am doing, so I won't. But I won't lie to you about it either.' " Annali took a very deep breath.

"So when I tell you that Dimitre has been thrashing out what to do about his beloved baby sister until he has been tied into knots over it, then you need to know I am not exaggerating. Did I know? Of course I did. He tells me everything because that is how important I am to him. But he wanted to never tell her, or you, that she was a dormant witch, and I talked him out of that. I made him realize how dangerous it was to leave her out there uninformed.

"He was going to tell both of you by winter's end. But you know how proud he is. He wanted to be strong and in control before he thought about bringing his baby sister over into danger. He wanted to know he had placed his trust in the right people before telling her to trust them as well. It's only been two months since he was forced to cross over! Since he became a witch with this incredible power over the workings of time, power that he barely controls. Can you blame him for using caution when it comes to the girl he has practically raised since she was born?

"I'm sorry I withheld information from you and this coven. The moment I saw her here I knew it had been a mistake and I was going to tell you as soon as the opportunity presented itself. I know that doesn't make it right, but I was going to make her safe. You know I would never risk letting what happened to me, happen to her."

"I know you wouldn't." Ryce exhaled with tense frustration as he sat down on Annali's bed. For the moment she and Dimitre were sharing Annali's suite. Soon the suite on the third floor would be finished for them, and their future family whenever they chose to start one. It was Ryce's dream for all of them to live up on that third floor one day, all with families and a second generation of Willow Coven witches running around.

Annali was right, it had been wrong for him to make Dimitre lie to her, and he was glad the Tempus witch had found a way around it that kept both of his promises. It was one of the reasons he liked the man so much. He was intelligent and damn clever. Two qualities Ryce could already see in Dimitre's young sibling.

"Are you going to tell me where Kaia and Dimitre are, or is it still necessary to lie to me?"

Ryce shook his head. "No, love. Of course. I sent them to spy on the Pennsylvania coven."

"Oh my sweet Goddess," Annali gasped, her horror making her go pale, pale white.

"I didn't know it was Hawthorn Coven . . . or rather, Belladonna Coven. I had no idea it was Braen and all of them behind this. I should have known. I should have suspected there would be a reason why a new coven would decide to take us on first thing."

"Ryce, you have to get them out of there! You have to call them back before they are discovered!"

"I know that. But it's night, and that's when Kaia and Dimitre are most active watching the warlocks. They won't be back to their rooms until dawn. They certainly wouldn't bring cells with them that could alert anyone to their presence."

"What about a telepathy spell? You are more than strong

enough to reach that far," Annali insisted, her hands gripping the tie to her robe in agitation.

"Annie, love, it's the same thing as using a cell. Sure, I'll reach them, but they are on enemy territory. A spell that powerful will alert anyone even remotely adept to their presence. Please, try and stay calm," he urged her, getting up and moving to hug her. "Dimitre will be fine. His power is undefeatable unless Belladonna has acquired a dark Tempus. Hunter was just telling me what the odds of even finding a sane or in control Tempus are."

"Sanity never stopped a dark coven before," she bit out. "Evan was as mad as they came and he was High Cleric when they were called Hawthorn Coven."

"Yes, and he is a corpse with its head severed from its shoulders thanks to Hunter's blade. Braen is headed for the same fate."

"Braen." Annali shuddered at the mention of Evan's former protégé's name. She buried her face against Ryce's damp shirt.

"Something you need to talk about, honey?" he asked tentatively.

This was always a minefield. Whenever dark memories of her past loomed up between them, Ryce had to be very careful. He'd been successful at it for eleven years, and just because Dimitre had appeared to take Annali the rest of the way it didn't mean he couldn't still be her best confidant when she needed him.

"Let's just say that along with raping and torturing me those two weeks, Evan got a big kick out of enlisting Braen's help so he could watch everything from an observer's perspective."

"Oh, Annie . . ." Ryce whispered, closing his eyes and kissing her temple gently. "You never said a word about this."

"You know why I couldn't. Hunter would have gone ballistic, and it would have forced him on a road he might not have come back from. If you think losing him for a decade was hard on us, Ryce, imagine what it would feel like to lose him forever. That's what would have happened," Annali insisted. "His psyche would have been completely destroyed in the process of hunting down and assassinating his very own blood. I could never tell him that his brother had a hand in my hell, not once I learned they were related."

"Hunter has no loyalty to Braen. He broke from the cold, contemptuous ways of his family completely when he joined with me all those years ago. To him, Braen is just another warlock. Now, he is also the leader of the coven threatening Willow Coven, and Hunter is our Sentinel again. After facing his brother tonight, don't you think Hunter already knows it will be his job to kill Braen?"

"But then it will be because of his duty to the coven . . . not because he is avenging me. It may seem trivial or splitting hairs to you," she said, lowering her lilac eyes to the floor, "but it is important to me. And he is older now. Wiser and more skilled. It is different to face something like this at the age of thirty-four instead of the age of twenty-three."

"These are not trivial points," Ryce assured her softly, his hug tightening around her. "Nothing about this ever was. And you are right. This will be no easy task for him, but I believe he has the strength to face it now. A strength that he did not have back then."

"He has found the strength to face a lot of things, if he has come back here," she pointed out. "It will be rough when Asher returns to find him here."

"I expect as much," Ryce said. "So does Hunter."

"But you didn't warn Asher he was coming, did you?" She pulled back to look at him. "Do you really think that springing Hunter on Asher is the best thing to do? Or were you just saving yourself a few days of grief in the interim?"

"The decision was mine to make. Asher might have been the only dissident, but if I had asked for coven opinion I would have had to respect his pain and arguments. I cannot afford the luxury of that kind of fairness and democracy. If I pander to everyone's emotions, I will be unable to lead this coven or ensure our survival." He closed his eyes and bowed his head. "And make no mistake, love, we are fighting for our survival here. It was only by the intervention of our blessed Goddess that we found Gracelynne before she was murdered. Providence and dumb luck saved us from being torn to shreds that day they attacked us on the trail."

"The Great Mother sent Dimitre to save us. To save me, especially. Perhaps this time she has sent us Tatyana for an even larger purpose."

"To save us?" Ryce asked with a smile for her romanticism.

"To save someone," she stipulated.

Annali had a pretty good guess who that someone might be.

Chapter Nine

Okay.

She had been a very, very, *very* bad girl.

Tatyana confessed to the sin with a mental plea for forgiveness, exhaling as silently as she could manage. She was staring at an incredibly gorgeous man who was sleeping like a boy prince beside her. His face was just this side of angelic, what with that freaking adorable smattering of freckles that made him just about as irresistible in sleep as he was conscious. Consciousness, however, added a virility factor that sent angelic and adorable on a hike and welcomed the substance of sex and magnetism instead.

And that was why she'd been bad.

Well, there *had* been other reasons, she reassured herself. While she couldn't say logical thinking had returned to her last night, awareness had definitely increased at a far more rapid rate than she'd let on to her rescuers. No joke intended, of course. It had all been oblivion until she'd become aware that she was being stripped butt-naked by Hunter. Well, almost butt-naked. He had chickened out somewhere around the bra and panties, much to her never-ending gratitude. Disappointment. Whatever.

She'd been mortified as she'd waited for him to finish,

paralyzed with indecision. When she realized he expected her to be brain-fried, she had taken it happily as the perfect out. She'd pretend to be oblivious, and he'd be too much a gentleman to ever bring it up. It would all end swimmingly.

A good plan. Saved face all around. Everyone was happy.

Until he'd held her close and slid that shirt on. Then she'd gotten a lungful of earthy male warmth so delicious she could taste it. She'd been unable to resist a nuzzle, feigning innocence and taking blatant advantage. It had snowballed from there. In a blink she was all over him, barely able to resist the urge to lick him to death. He'd felt so good, so strong; his warm skin so smooth over fabulous muscular contours.

He'd saved her life. Somehow, that was the ultimate turn-on. She'd been crazy with the urge to bury herself in his vitality and heat. She'd also felt his attempts to repress his own reactions toward her. It made her insides do little happy dances to the tune of feminine superiority. She felt twinges of guilt, of course. However, she also reminded herself that *he* was getting off on a supposedly senseless girl, so she shouldn't feel all that bad.

Tatyana also had to claim a measure of honest insanity. She'd done some outrageous things in her lifetime, not the least of which had been in the past twelve hours, but where Hunter Finn was concerned she'd apparently lost all impulse control. Dragging him into bed with her? Suffocating him with a full-on body hug hadn't even been a coherent plan in her head. One minute she was getting the shocking thrill of a lifetime when she'd caught him stripping to full masculine glory, and boy did she mean *full*, and then before she knew what was happening she was wrapped completely around him and falling into a contented sleep.

My, oh my, but he was magnificent when naked, she recalled with a sly smile curling her lips at one corner. She'd gotten plenty of visual cues through his clothes as to his physical fitness, not to mention feeling it up close during the night's ordeal, but she'd had no idea a man could look finer without his designer clothing than he did with it. He was awesomely healthy, his muscles sculpted and lean without being obnoxious. The sinewy lines of his body flowed so perfectly. From broad shoulders to a sturdy spine, to a trim waist and hips and a muscular backside with a perfect flow into his rock-steady thighs. A flat belly with washboard definition, and the ultimate prize below it. She shivered happily with the memory. Mainly because, in spite of the freezing wet of his recently shed clothing, he'd been partially aroused. That had tickled her female ego silly. Not to mention some frank appreciation for the gifts bestowed on Hunter by his maker.

Who says craftsmanship is a lost art?

Too bad she hadn't had the guts to out-and-out kiss him.

Oh, she was probably suffering from post-traumatic something-or-other just because she was thinking such an insane thing, but she'd really wanted to know what his mouth felt like. Frankly, it was her opinion that he would suck in the kissing department. He had to. The law of averages demanded it. So far he scored off the charts on looks, charm, personality, natural tenderness, intelligence and . . . and special interests.

Tatyana went dreamy all over as she remembered once again the size of his 'special interests.' No one could have all of that going for him and be a great kisser besides. If he *was* a great kisser, then that could only mean he sucked at one other thing . . . and after seeing him naked and only *partly* aroused, Tatyana thought he'd have to work really, really hard in order to suck at sex. Not everything about Hunter Finn could be . . .

Magic.

Abruptly, she tried the word out in her mind, wincing slightly.

She couldn't have been dreaming. Flying. Fireballs. Lightning. The Big Bad Wolf. Or whatever that guy Braen was.

She shuddered at the memory of his malevolence and how palpable it had been. Worse, she remembered what it felt like. Putting aside the sheer pain of when she had been struck by that black lightning, she'd also felt a revolting contamination. It had felt physically filthier than when she'd been encompassed in mud and under fireball siege. Spiritually, it had been much worse. Most of the feeling had been purged by Annali's brews, but part of it still remained. It wasn't much, but it was enough to make her shiver violently.

And with that, brilliant cobalt eyes flicked open and looked into hers.

Tatyana's breath jammed up in her throat as she stared at Hunter. What was it about those riveting eyes that tossed her off balance? It was like being buffeted by a staggering storm, its highly charged ionic atmosphere piercing her from all sides.

Apparently her impulse control was still a little iffy, because she couldn't resist reaching out to touch his face. She drew unsteady fingers over the dark arch of an eyebrow, sliding down to his temple and continuing on until she was traveling over his roughly shadowed jaw. He had such a remarkable face, such truly handsome features; they held her in thrall and disallowed the release of her captivated fingertips.

She felt his hand come up to close around her wrist, holding her snug in his palm for a long series of heartbeats. Then, in an elegant fashion, he turned her wrist up to the brush of his lips, pressing a lingering kiss to the inside pulse. It made her exhale with a wild reaction of pleasure, heat sparkling up her arm in small sunbursts of energy that skipped from nerve to nerve.

He turned his hand in such a way that she observed the angry slashes across the inside of his palm where he'd forced the bite of the dual-edged blade. A wave of sympathy compelled her to shift the position of their fingers, her hand now cradling his and drawing it up to her lips. Gently, with the weight of his fingers curling against her cheek, she touched her lips to the wound in the seat of his hand. She felt a fizzy sensation against her mouth when she contacted his skin, as though she had sipped extra bubbly champagne. She smiled, enjoying the pleasant, titillating sensation. She looked at him through her heavy lashes.

"I think this is the part when one of us says 'We need to talk.' Only, I'm not sure which of us should do it," she remarked.

Hunter sat up suddenly, the expression of surprise on his face priceless. His hands came out of opposing directions and sank into her hair on either side of her head, holding her in a steady grip as he narrowed the distance between their faces to a six-inch space.

"That was one hell of a coherent sentence," he noted frankly.

"Thank you," she said with a bemused laugh, "I'm feeling extremely coherent." Although, having Hunter in her personal space like this was playing havoc with her senses. She could smell that earthy warm scent of him again. His hands were hot in her hair, against her ears and cheeks.

"I'm so very glad to hear that," he said huskily, his voice notching downward another octave. "That means you can understand me."

"Well, yes—"

And just like that, a very fine pair of male lips swept down onto her own.

Tatyana could have made an effort at shocked sensibilities, but that would have been a huge hypocrisy considering she'd just been longing to kiss him. His mouth fell tenderly against hers, and Hunter spent several seconds adjusting her to the fit of his lips, taking that crucial step that made all the difference in the world between mere competency and superior finesse when it came to a kiss.

His lips were so warm and she felt as if she were melting against them. She sighed softly into his mouth with irre-

pressible satisfaction. She felt a smile against her lips, heard
a low chuckle in his throat. Both quickly faded and were replaced by an exponentially increasing zeal that took her
breath away as he worked hungrily against her. Hunter's bold
mouth was everything amazing and sensual she'd hoped it
would be. Intrepid and confident, his kiss was as adventur-
ous as he was. Thrills of delight skittered up her cheeks,
shivering into her mind and making sure all of her senses
were paying full attention. Hunter's fingers tightened in her
hair, his hands rubbing through the silky strands with possessive captivation. Then, once he was certain he had her full
interest, he swept his tongue past her parted lips.

The man tasted like clean rain and a delicious masculin-
ity that made Tatyana voracious. Hunter fulfilled his every
promise, his kiss quickening through her with a whiplash of
igniting need. She couldn't breathe as heat inundated her
senses. Her hands had somehow found a home in his hair
and she was blindly holding him to the kiss just as much as
he was holding her.

Hunter had known it would be this fabulous to kiss her.

He was tromping all over his own good sense by doing
this. On some level, he actually knew that. But this was a
craving that had been clutching at him almost nonstop since
she'd first wrapped herself around him in the conservatory
last night. Now that she was coherent again, he had no shield
of honor left to ward off the impulse. She was aware and
willing and, blessed Lady, so enthusiastic.

Tatyana's lips were so sweet and succulent, and she had a
wicked sense of sensuality in her way of moving them. Her
instinctively reaching and shifting body made both his mind
and his body ache. His entire existence was strung taut with
the fantasies a mouth like hers inspired. Hunter wanted the
very essence of her flavor flowing over his tongue. *Yes*, he
thought with an inner groan as Tatyana made an eager, ap-
preciative sound that vibrated into his mouth, encouraging
him deeper. It was as though she could read his mind, her

sense of his intentions was so keen. An amazing turn-on; it sent desire ebbing and flowing through his spinning wits and pulsing blood, making his body respond with a singing arousal.

Tatyana felt him swiftly hauling her against himself, rolling her beneath the solid length of his body as his intensified kiss pressed her head down into the pillow. Dynamite explosions went off all over her body where her softness was suddenly melded to the astounding rock hardness of magnificent muscle. Her head spun as internal heat assaulted her from dozens of places at once, all of it reaching out eagerly to mingle with the extraordinary fire that was Hunter's body heat. She swept her tongue against his, tangling with him until she heard him groan from the intensity of her need and curiosity. He tasted so good it was definitely going to be addicting. Dangerously addicting.

There was no doubt about it; Hunter Finn was a very hazardous man. Even if she hadn't been witness to the events of the night before, she would have known it from his kiss. Hunter played for keeps, aggressive and blatant, letting it be known that he was not into games, not to be gainsaid, and definitely not wasting energy worrying about repercussions. The message was clear when she felt him move against her, shifting against her thighs and letting her feel how incredibly hard she had made him. *This*, he was saying, *is how much I want you. This is all that matters between us right now.*

"Mother Goddess," he groaned as he slid deeper and deeper into her mouth, "how you kiss!"

There was something about her, but he couldn't think to describe it while she was filling his senses like this. He could feel every curve of her body and each shift she made to settle them closer together. Hunter knew he was taking no prisoners, thinking of no limitations whatsoever when he probably should be, but he didn't give a damn. And clearly, neither did she. Her hands were running down his back, their touch like a message from heaven as they slid over his shoul-

ders and around his ribs with thorough curiosity. Her clinging fingers dipped into his sensitive sides, fingertips teasing
his hip bones at their crests. His blood boiled in response,
rushing loudly in his ears and weighting him with an erection that was excruciating as it throbbed against her. He felt
dizzy, like everything was so magnified that his senses were
on overload. Tatyana was just as affected, her wriggling body
misted with perspiration and clinging harder and harder for
contact.

"Touch me," she begged, her voice a wild, panting string
of words. "Hunter, please, please . . ."

The chemistry between them was unbelievable. From the
very beginning she had beckoned to him; aroused him even
from a distance. Having Tatyana under him changed the entire landscape of their attraction. Everything that had been
merely speculation the night before now appeared in the
realm of the achievable.

"Tatyana . . ." he rasped against her ear as his mouth found
the pulse beneath it. "This is crazy," he warned her raggedly,
even as his hand slipped from her hair and swiftly roamed
down the side of her throat. He felt the flannel collar of the
shirt she wore and touched superheated skin when he hit the
gaping neckline settled crookedly over the swell of her
breast. It only took a quick turn of his wrist before his hand
was cupping skin as smooth as cream, and a nipple was between his fingers. "Like this, Tatyana?" he demanded roughly
as his fingers pinched and rolled the sensitive tip of her
breast. She bucked, cried out. His mouth was back on hers;
sucking her lips at the same time he was toying with her
hardening nipple. "Tell me, angel."

"Yes . . . and more . . ." she moaned, moving so restlessly
against him that he threw back his head and let a coarse
sound of need claw its way out from deep in his soul. The
sound sang to her, so beautiful it was like a spell all on its
own. Yes, that was it. He was magic. "God, Hunter," she
gasped, "put your mouth on me."

They both reacted and reached to strip away the restriction of her shirt and bra until her generous breasts spilled free of satin and flannel. Hunter felt hunger for the taste of her spurring him hard. He didn't even bother to introduce himself with any gentility. The possession of his mouth was rough and aggressive. He caught up one dusky nipple with his teeth, and then he sucked her deep. She threw back her head, arched up wildly, and cried out. The force of the movement of her body was erotic, shifting him even though he was much heavier than she was. Tatyana was settling down and drawing up her knees on either side of his hips, her thighs now bracketing him in a very tender trap.

Hunter went mad for all of ten seconds. It was the only way he could describe the blinding insanity of feeling that seared through him as his cock cuddled up nice and tight to her extremely hot core. His mind de-evolved a million years and became a screaming impulse factory. If he listened to it, he was going to be very, very deep inside this woman in a few heartbeats. Hadn't this started out with just the intention of a kiss? Weren't there extenuating issues that made this unwise? Hunter could hardly remember or even care. Tatyana was wrapping her legs around him invitingly, shifting her hips as she ran seeking hands over his buttocks. Drawing him closer. Rubbing their pelvises enticingly together.

"I've never felt anything like this before," she uttered against his ear, her voice rough and sexy with arousal. "You feel glorious, Hunter . . ." Tatyana moaned as he shifted his hips in a deep stroke against her, rubbing her right through damp satin to stimulate her wildly. Her world was whirling as he repeated the movement, knowing exactly how to apply the right pressure over the right place. "Hunter!"

"Angel," he gritted out between tight teeth. "I can't . . . this is . . ." He couldn't get the words out, not when she lay like a four-star banquet beneath him. He looked down into sultry, wicked eyes that made his head spin. Her hands were all over his body. "You're . . . we're under an influence," he

told her hoarsely as her eager hands slid beneath the waistband of his sweatpants and sought the feel of his hard shaft.
"Tatyana . . ." he groaned as her fingers encircled him eagerly.

Before he knew it she had rolled him off of her body and
was swinging herself over him, mounting him like an expert
equestrienne, her hand stroking his length and closing around
his impressive thickness.

"My, my, my," she murmured as she gazed at him with
appetite in her eyes, her tongue touching her upper lip in a
blatantly sexy contemplation that tore him apart. "You're so
big," she marveled, "and so gorgeous."

She followed up the compliment with a tribute of hands
and fingers that made his hips buck up off the bed as he
groaned with mindless pleasure. His entire being throbbed
for release and she was dragging him closer and closer with
every artful stroke. She had a skillful, exquisite touch that
was so perfect in pressure and friction. Too perfect. Far too
perfect.

"Tatyana! You have to stop!" he commanded her, reaching to grasp her industrious hands. Hunter was gasping for
every breath, but she was pouting at him for spoiling her fun
and he swore she had no idea as to the agony this was causing him. Hunter dragged her up his length by her captured
wrists, wincing with every contact she made against his hypersensitive body. "Listen to me," he rasped, trying to stay
focused on why something that felt so good and so right was
actually, somehow, a problem that needed to be sorted out.
"We're under an influence you don't understand," he explained
hoarsely. "Please, believe me. I didn't mean for this to happen . . ."

Tatyana looked down at him with openly curious eyes of
the finest jade. She cocked her head to the side, licking her
lush lips slowly as she contemplated him as she might contemplate a very rich dessert.

"Influence?" she asked, making him grateful that she was actually hearing him on some level.

"Last night, when we traded blood. I meant to explain. But you were ill and I fell asleep. Then this morning . . . you looked so damned beautiful . . ." He trailed off, knowing in his soul it was a poor excuse. "I wanted to kiss you. I didn't mean to take it so far."

Tatyana smiled at him, obliterating right and wrong with a sexy, throaty laugh. "I wanted to kiss you, too," she told him with amusement. "Ever since last night."

"Yeah. I know the feeling," he sighed.

Tatyana freed her hands from his and pressed them on the mattress on either side of his shoulders, holding herself up over him as she smiled. "You're a good man, Hunter Finn. And you're right. We should talk about a few things. But that doesn't mean I will stop feeling the way I do. Wanting you this way."

"Come on," he said softly, reaching to close the buttons on her shirt and watching her swiftly flush. Just like that, from bold to blushing, even while she still lay suggestively over him with her desire stark in her gaze. "We'll talk. Then I want to make certain you're healed thoroughly."

"I feel fine." Tatyana cocked a sly brow, pairing it with a sneaky grin. "Don't I feel fine?"

She squirmed, and then laughed when he groaned and grabbed her by the hips to encourage her sexy ride for a minute before cursing and rolling her off him abruptly.

"Wretch," he ground out at her as he flung himself off the bed and straightened his clothing. He even fetched a shirt, letting it give him a sense of being armored against her when, in fact, there was only one part of him that was presently bulletproof. With a sigh he moved out to the sitting room and sat before the low fire. The clock told him they hadn't actually slept very long. No more than four or five hours.

Soon Tatyana bounced cheerily out of the room, dressed

in her borrowed robe now as she flounced into the chair opposite him with a grin and the primmest posture she could
humanly manage.

"Okay. 'Lucy, you got some 'splainin to do!' " she quipped,
snickering at her own joke when he couldn't help but smile.
She was taking this incredibly lightly. When he began to explain things, she would probably be royally pissed off.
Mainly at him.

"Let's start with the important basics," he began.

"You're all witches."

"Uh . . . yeah . . ." Hunter hesitated a long minute. She
said it as though she were talking about the weather, as if she
met witches every day. "How did you know?"

"Well, I realized you were casting spells, I heard the word
coven a couple of times, and," she added deprecatingly, "seeing as how I graduated kindergarten, I'm kinda smart like
that."

"Yeah," he laughed sheepishly, "that you are. Yes, we're
witches. White witches. Good witches. The ones who attacked last night are dark witches. Warlocks. Dark and white
witches . . . it's a good versus evil thing that sounds like a
bad gothic novel." He rubbed his hands together, feeling a
chill when he felt the mocking sting of the cut on his palm.
"I'm making light, but it's very serious actually. Witches die
in these battles all of the time. We were lucky last night.
Lucky not to lose you.

"I'm sorry you got caught up in this danger, Tatyana. I
want you to know you're under the protection of the entire
coven. I won't let anyone hurt you if it's in my power to prevent it." Hunter sat forward and clasped her hands, needing
to keep connected to her.

"Relax, Hunter," she soothed with a mellow tone as she
squeezed his hands. "I'm not going to have fits of fainting or
screaming. I'm a specially gifted person from an Old World
family. Witches, gypsies, and 'the sight' are all part of the
stories I heard growing up. I admit, I never believed . . . not

to the extent . . . well, what I saw last night . . ." She laughed and shook her head. "But that's the point of a secret, isn't it? I'm not supposed to know. No one is. You'd have kept me ignorant if I hadn't run out in the middle of it all. Correct?"

"Yes," he agreed grimly.

"Okay. So, I understand that you're witches. I can even grasp that I actually saw magic last night. Some pretty freaking awesome magic. I'm going to pass on the whole good witch/bad witch thing just now. So, here's the part I don't understand . . ."

Tatyana released his hand, peeling open the other while nudging her opposite palm alongside it. Last night, Hunter had asked her to trust his choice. Even though the choice was usually inevitable, he still wished he'd had the time to help her understand that.

Hunter didn't shy from his duty of explanation. What was done was done, and it had already been proven to have been for the better. "Tatyana, there are many complexities to witches and witchcraft. As we advance in skill, we each make choices along the way which often completely alter our lives and who we become."

"Sounds no different from the usual growing up and maturing," she observed.

"No difference at all," he agreed. "Witches are born. They cannot be made. Each of us is born with a specific connection to the magics of the world. We call them schools. But let's start with basics. There are two types of witches."

"Good and bad?"

"Actually, no. Witches, like people, aren't born good or bad. They choose their Path to become one or the other." Hunter brought them back to his original point. "Two witches are born; one is 'active' and one is 'dormant.' The active witch develops power quickly and will usually come to the notice of a mature witch who will mentor the child until he or she is old enough to choose a Path." He paused. "Now, the dormant witch has power, but it's latent. It often stays that way until puberty. These witches don't attract the attention of mentors because by the time they start manifesting ability, they're old enough to know it makes them different. They hide what they can do, afraid they will be labeled freaks or worse." Hunter watched her face, and he could tell it was the anger of recognition that tipped her cheeks and nose pink. He wasn't surprised. "These dormant witches are often mistaken for psychics, by themselves and by others. They can read minds, see the future, move objects with telekinesis, and so on. Some hide it, some cash in on it, and some . . . some can't handle it at all.

"The trouble is, these dormant witches are very vulnerable to warlocks and rogues." He held up a hand when he saw the coming query. "When active witches reach maturity, they choose a Path. They either choose to enter a coven or they go rogue. A rogue witch is sort of neutral. A free agent. They can be good, bad, or even indifferent. Rogues don't often grow to their full potential, so most witches choose to go 'in coven.' A dark coven or a white coven. Though we're not flawlessly good, a white coven strives for good intentions. Dark covens strive only to gain for themselves, using magic for power and prestige.

"Now, if a dormant witch is discovered by a rogue or warlock, they can do what I did to you last night, Tatyana. They can force a blood exchange. This will activate the dormant witch's power. The blood of the principal witch jumpstarts it."

"You . . . you made me a witch? I mean," she corrected herself quickly, "you activated me? I'm a full-blown witch now?"

"That is . . . it's not quite accurate, Tatyana," he stammered slightly. "Listen to me very carefully and don't interrupt me if possible. This will start off sounding unpleasant, but it will get better, I promise. Okay?"

"I . . ." Her eyes narrowed, but she nodded. "Okay."

"When I realized you were having visions of me, I knew

instantly that you were a dormant witch. Under ideal circumstances, I would've better prepared you, but with dark witches all around us, I couldn't risk you running around unclaimed."

"Unclaimed?" she said on the barest of whispers.

"If an active witch encounters a dormant witch, the principal witch can claim the quiescent witch. It's called making a familiar. The claim is made by blood exchange. This activates the familiar's powers, but . . . but the familiar will now be under the command of the principal witch. The principal witch can then utilize the familiar like a battery. A power source. The connection works both ways, but the stronger witch can block the less experienced one easily. These familiars . . ." Hunter hesitated for the first time, and then decided it was best just to push through, ". . . they lose all individual identity. They are slaves whose only purpose is to provide energy for the witch mastering them."

"Oh my God," Tatyana exhaled the words in horror, her complexion so pale that her freckles stood out starkly. She jerked her hands out of his, folding one arm around her middle as she leaned forward, clasping her free hand to her mouth and looking very much like she was going to be sick.

Hunter slid his chair as close to her as possible, ignoring her sharp flinch when he touched her cheek. "Easy, angel. Remember, it gets better."

"What can be better about having your entire life and identity stripped away?" she demanded, her throat working in a convulsive swallow.

"Nothing," he agreed firmly. "It's a horrible existence and I won't pretty it up. The fate of a dark familiar is one I consider worse than death. Dark familiars are often used as sexual slaves. Since their free will no longer exists, the principal witch extorts everything they can with the advantage." Hunter grabbed her before she could fly out of her chair from the revulsion that leapt into her wide, terrified eyes. "I know what you're thinking," he said fiercely, drawing hard on her hands as they curled into fists, "but I'm telling you the worst of it first so you can understand how narrow an escape you made last night; so you will understand why I had to force a blood exchange.

"Listen to me now." He made sure to enunciate every single word of his next sentence. "White witches don't keep familiars, Tatyana. We can make them and we can do all the same things rogues and warlocks would do to them, but we consider it an abomination. It's expressly forbidden for a white witch to exploit a familiar. The enslavement of another being for selfish purposes goes against everything white magic has ever stood for.

"When a white witch brings over a dormant witch, angel, it is only so that the neophyte can be released to the world of magic in safety. With free will. If I don't press my will on you from one witch's moon to the next"—Hunter shook his head in frustration, then clarified—"one full moon to the next, my ability to hold you enthralled in any way will be terminated for all time. It's my intention, as an honorable white witch, to be your mentor in the world of witchcraft. I will take nothing from you that you don't freely give, and you may freely take everything I offer that will be helpful to you. That is the white magic way.

"Now, you need to understand that the blood connection itself lasts forever," he told her plainly. "By that I mean it's like having a guardian angel watching over you. I will always carry a sense of you with me, wherever I go. You will always carry a sense of me as well. Unobtrusively."

"A . . . sense?"

"In a good way," he reassured her softly. "Trust me. If you are in danger, I will know it in an instant. If you are hurt, frightened, or . . . if you need my help in any way. The reverse is also true, from me to you."

"Okay, let me see if I have this straight," Tatyana said, exhaling long and slow between pursed lips before continuing. "You bring a familiar over and set them free to become a witch. And that's all? You won't . . ." Tatyana flushed rosily and Hunter could easily guess the thoughts plaguing her. "You only want to be a teacher for me? Show me how to be a witch?"

"Exactly," he said with intensity. "Tatyana, if I'd let you leave here unclaimed and unprotected, you'd have been in danger all the rest of your life. Now, you have every right to live that way if you choose to. I wish it was a choice you could have made for yourself. Sometimes dormant witches can live quietly, never exercising their psychic powers so they don't attract undue attention. It's risky, but possible. However," he sighed, "the coven we were fighting is formidable and astute. There are spells that uncover suppressed power. Just your being here would make them suspicious enough to cast one. Making you my familiar kept you safe from them."

"So, now nobody else can make me a familiar?"

"No one else. I've claimed you and my blood protects you. I'm sorry to make you a witch in such a way, without permission or explanation, but I hope you see . . ."

"No, I do see," she breathed, turning her hands over and grasping his tightly. "You were protecting me from a fate that . . ." Tatyana shuddered. "My God. I just never knew."

"Most don't. Your life will be very different now, Tatyana. You'll need to keep secrets, even from loved ones. You'll need to learn how to tame new surges of power. I could go on, but I don't want to overwhelm you." Hunter smiled, gently rubbing his thumb over her knuckles. "Understand, angel, I'm only sorry about not giving you an initial warning. Otherwise, I'm selfishly delighted to have you in my world. Magic is a phenomenal thing. I'm bursting with everything I want to share.

"There's also no reason for you to lose the things you love because witchcraft has entered your life. We all have our passions separate from magic. In fact, hobbies and magic tend to blend very well. But"—he waved his own excitement off—"there will be time to explain all of that. I don't want to overload you. I know you're trying to wrap your mind around the basics. Not to mention the amount of trust you've unwittingly extended to me."

She looked at him, tilting her head and studying him. "You asked me to trust you, and I will. I'd know if you meant me harm, Hunter. And you're right; I need time to assimilate all of this." She hesitated and he saw little stars of pink dotting her cheeks. "I do have one question though."

"Anything. My knowledge is yours, angel."

"You . . . you said we were being influenced . . . uh . . . earlier. What did you mean?"

Hunter released a breathy chuckle and smiled at her, though he had a hard time meeting her eyes now. "There are a few side effects with the blood exchange. A familiar is flooded with the veteran power of the proficient witch, and the virgin power of the familiar inundates the proficient. The consequence is a permanent vitalization of the sexual natures of both witch and familiar. They develop a heightened sensuality, a striking increase in pheromone levels, and become arresting to the opposite sex. There's a dynamic new sexual confidence, lowered inhibitions, and a . . . uh . . . rapacious carnal appetite."

"Oh God!" she gasped. "You mean I'm going to become a slut?"

"No, no," Hunter laughed, shaking his head when he got a cutting look. "Your selectivity will be the same as before." He hedged a moment, but he couldn't bail on her now. "Well . . . maybe for the very first week it will be a wild ride as we adjust, and you may not always make the wisest choices in some respects. I suppose our earlier conduct attests to that. I don't think either of us is the type to fall into bed after only a few hours' acquaintance. Although," he said pointedly, "I feel I have to add that the temptation was already there before we ever exchanged blood, Tatyana."

This time she was the one who laughed. She shot him a

look out of the corner of her eyes that positively sizzled. "I'd have to say that was very mutual."

"Okay, now, giving me looks like that will get you into a world of trouble. Damn!" Hunter stood up and paced away from her. Just one suggestive sentence and he was instantly twisting into hard knots. It was incredible.

"Sorry," she said, not looking at all repentant as she smiled with sly speculation. Hunter was filled with disquiet as he watched her wicked mind work behind her vivid eyes. Tatyana was already irresistible. Having her around the house while they were both on a sexual bender was going to thrash him. "So any other side effects?" she asked, settling back in her chair with a sensual wriggle and a smirk.

Did she mean *besides* his having a coronary at the tender age of thirty-four? Hunter laughed a little nervously to himself. He suddenly had insight into how Dr. Frankenstein must have felt.

"One other," he said. "You and I will find it very difficult to be apart until the second witch's moon has passed. This first week will be the most intense. I know you can feel it like I do already. But I promise it will ease."

"I don't understand. You said the principal witch controls the familiar."

"I won't try to control you."

"If a familiar has so much sexual sway, isn't the witch's position weakened? Your reactions to me, for example. You act as if I'm dominant in this situation."

"You're right," he said uneasily. "Normally the controlling witch isn't affected by the familiar unless they choose to be. They never lose control."

"Well," she said gently, pushing up out of her chair and crossing to him until she stood close enough to warm him with her body heat. "Not to be rude reminding you of it, but earlier, I didn't see you exhibiting any control. Or did you?"

"Honestly?" he said, his voice hoarse as her fantastic scent swept over him. "I have no idea how I managed to stop." Against all good sense, he reached to draw her up tight against himself. "I've never in my life felt anything like how I feel with you. No, Tatyana," he breathed, the truth stark in his tone, "I wouldn't lay strong bets on my ability to maintain control. I'd be very careful if I were you. I won't have you plagued with regrets a week from now."

"I'm sorry," she said softly, her eyes sweet and slumberous. Her warm breath skimmed his cheek as she wriggled a single, silky finger between their lower bodies. Tatyana slowly ran her fingertip up the hard ridge of erect flesh lying prominently beneath the fabric of his sweatpants. "I feel bad that you hurt like this," she murmured, waiting just long enough to feel a telltale twitch jolt through him before dropping her touch away. "I know how close you were, Hunter," she whispered. "I could feel it. Yet you held back to keep me from feeling cheapened or used, and I appreciate that."

"I was selfish, believe me," he argued, her boldness demanding truth whether she wanted it or not. It was important she not form inaccurate romantic images. "I'm not so gallant. To be honest, I was thinking that if I used you then, I would never be able to have you again." Hunter lowered his head so his mouth was near her ear, the touch of his breath making her shiver even as his words sank in. "When I have you, Tatyana, it won't be only once, and it won't be with regrets. I knew the minute I saw you that I wanted you. I knew after ten minutes of conversation with you that I was going to have you. After you ran out into the night to try and protect me, I knew I was going to have a damn hard time letting you go afterward. Am I clear here, angel?"

"Yes," she managed to whisper through her abruptly dry throat, her heated body rapidly parching her. *God, he's the sexiest man alive*, Tatyana thought keenly. She licked her lips as he pulled back to look into her eyes. He lifted his thumb to her wet lips and traced the moisture.

"Tatyana, you're going to need to stay here at Willow

House for the next few weeks at the very least. I'm sorry. I know this will disrupt your life—"

"Nope. No disruption at all. Here's just fine," she said quickly. "Right here, close by. Where I can learn things." *Lots of things*, she thought eagerly. *Boxers or briefs? Right side of the bed or left?* She smiled, taking a deep, excited breath.

Oh, she had a job (if not an assistant), an apartment she shared (with only *two* roommates) and a big brother who could pose problems, but all of that would wait for a while. To be fair, she couldn't say all of her excitement was centered around her handsome host, although there was a huge incentive there. There was also the idea of being a witch. Who wouldn't want to learn how to do magic? Granted, nasty warlocks on the rampage made for a major black mark, she thought with a little inner quiver, but she felt safe with Hunter and his coven.

With Dimitre's coven.

"Holy shit," she gasped.

My brother is a witch!

Chapter Ten

And just like that everything fell into place. This was why Dimitre had suddenly moved up here, quit his job, and refused her access to him. He was learning how to be a witch!

Witch.

"Witch. Witch. Witch, witch, witch." She said the word quickly, puzzling over the sound of it, watching as Hunter's eyebrow swept up with curiosity, a smile twitching over his lips. "Sorry. I'm used to that being a bad thing, that word."

"A bad thing?" he asked. He was used to those who looked on witches as evil. Knowing where he stood within the Craft, he didn't let blanket assumptions bother him.

"Shades of junior high school. When I was younger, I didn't realize that other kids couldn't see the future, or sense good or bad things before they happened. My family, being very Old World, simply said I had 'the sight.' It was a frequent enough trait in our family history that they accepted it just like one would accept a child with an extra toe. Their acceptance was normal to me. It was the fear and prejudice of the children and teachers that was a shock." Tatyana lowered her head and tried to hide a frown of consternation as the memories swam forward. "They called me a freak and a witch. I learned to dislike the terms." She laughed with the irony. "I guess they were right then, hmm?"

"No, actually. No one who uses the word 'witch' as a malevolent epithet is right. That, angel, is the most important lesson you will ever learn about being a witch. Only you can truly know what being a 'witch' will mean to you. Good, bad, or indifferent, it's your choice. I will tell you that coming into the Craft as a familiar will tend to send you in the same direction as the principal witch who brought you over. You are far more likely to become a white witch. Of course, in the event of my death, all influences will be severed completely . . ."

"Okay, this is a conversation we can have, like, *never*," she injected hastily, reaching up to cover his mouth as the words *my death* sent her heart sinking to her toes where it flopped like a fish out of water.

"All right, shh . . ." He soothed her by reaching out to rub strong hands up and down her arms. "You're very sensitive. Not," he said firmly at her sharp look, "that it's a bad thing. It's an observation. I've also seen that you have an instinct for witchcraft. You cast a spell last night purely on intuition. Would you care to share where it came from?"

"Oh." Tatyana bit her lip to keep from laughing as she flushed and waved the matter off. "It isn't important. Just beginner's luck."

"Actually, it's important to me, Tatyana," Hunter insisted, reaching to hook her chin with his finger, tilting her head up so he could look in her eyes. "Spells come from curious places and each one is unique. What you did wasn't just remarkable because of your inexperience. It's also something Spellcasters like Ryce and myself would very much want to learn."

"Well . . . it's silly really." She sighed and started again, rushing quickly through her explanation. "I used to get into trouble a lot for forgetting appointments, chores, homework.

I never watched where I was going. People would talk to me and I wouldn't hear a word they said. My mother used to scold me with a Russian phrase." She repeated it for him, and then translated. "It means: 'If your head is in the clouds too long, your feet will float off the ground.' It was the first thing I thought of when I wanted to get your feet off the ground, out of the conductive water. It's not much of a spell."

"It was a spell that saved my life and Annali's. For which, by the way, I hope I've thanked you profusely," Hunter pressed a kiss to her forehead as he drew her into a tight hug. A hug that felt like heaven.

"Actually, I think that's the first time. Nothing really profuse about that. But, luckily,"—she sighed with happy contentment—"I don't need profuse when I can get hugs." Tatyana hugged him back and laughed in a stream of uncontainable giggles.

"What?"

"Hmm? Oh, just marveling."

"Over?"

"How you've already managed to make hugging you feel like something I've been doing for a lifetime rather than half a day."

"I noticed that, too, actually," he murmured softly into her hair. "But I refuse to put it down to the blood exchange. I like to think I'm just a world-class hugger."

"Prepare for competition. With thirteen siblings, hugging is an Olympic event in my family and we're all gold medal contenders."

She heard him inhale the fragrance of her hair, his face rubbing slowly against it. "That isn't a family," he noted absently. "That's a small country."

She snickered and nodded in agreement. "Want the roll call?"

"Am I expected to remember it on demand? Will there be a quiz?"

"I might let you off if you're very nice to me. Ready?"

"Wait, I need pen and paper . . ." He pushed away from her and flopped down into a chair.

"Stop stalling," she laughed, turning to seat herself regally across from him.

"Okay. I'm ready. Let me have it."

"Okay. Descending order, name and age. The eldest is Rurik, age forty. Then Anya, age thirty-eight. Sashenka, a.k.a. Sasha, is thirty-seven. Larissa and Calina, twins, at thirty-five."

"Ah! I didn't consider twins. Bless your mother's heart," he chuckled.

"Believe me, she deserves it. Lidija, whom you heard me talking to last night, is thirty-three. Dimitre, whom you know about already, is thirty-two. Grigori is thirty. Konstantine, a.k.a. Konnie, is twenty-nine. Andrey and Sergei, twins, are twenty-seven. Katarina, or Kat, is twenty-six. And I, the youngest Petrova, am twenty-four. Voilà. My beloved parents are Jelena and Pyotr. That can be a bonus question for you."

"Good, because I can remember the names of anybody who spends twenty years changing diapers. That's a big family. How in hell did your father support you? And don't tell me your mother worked with a baker's dozen in kids running around."

"Actually, Mama did work. Pregnancy was very easy for her, I'm told. After they came to America, Poppa joined a prestigious architectural firm in Manhattan. Mama worked in medical offices or transcribed for doctors at home. It was enough to raise us well, keep us in clothes, and even left time for much love. I actually work with Konnie, Sasha, and Poppa. I'm an architect at Hayward, Smithfield and Rusakova."

"Wait a minute. HSR? One of the top three design firms in the city?" He looked staggered. "You work for HSR at only twenty-four years of age?"

"Well . . . yes." She frowned at him darkly. "And there

isn't any nepotism involved," she said sharply. "I earned my position on my own merit. I'm only a junior architect, of course, but I'm kicking ass already, I promise you."

"I don't doubt it," he said, his tone firm and quiet. "I never said you didn't earn your position. I was just impressed. That's all."

"Oh. Sorry." She made a long, sibilant sound through her teeth. "I'm sorry. I've gotten used to defending myself on a few issues. Being the baby of the family, I have to fight twelve siblings for every ounce of my independence. They're very overprotective sometimes. Sergei is a private detective, Grigori's an N.Y.P.D. detective, and Lidija's an advice columnist. With the three of them I can hardly make a move in peace. I think I'm beginning to get through to Lidija and Grigori. Sergei . . ." She shook her head with sisterly disgust. "He's hopeless."

Hunter sat back with a deep, thoughtful expression on his face. She watched him, trying to decipher his expression. He chuckled when she gave him an inquisitive look. "I was just doing some mathematics. You're the thirteenth child?"

"Yes."

"Am I getting this right? Is Dimitre the seventh child?"

"Yes, he is."

"In a family where witchcraft runs strong, the seventh and thirteenth children will almost always be witches. You said 'the sight' has run in your family for generations. That means there have been witches in your family for a very long time, whether they realized their potential or not."

Tatyana felt a sickening sensation rushing in her belly as something finally occurred to her.

Dimitre.

Of all her beloved family, she was closest to Dimitre. Dimitre and she shared the closest confidences, talking about everything, constantly checking up on each other, and always sharing their visions and instincts with each other almost as if they had a secret club between them.

But he had become a witch two months ago and, not only had he not breathed a single word about it to her, but he hadn't even told her that *she* was a witch! He had to have known it . . .

"That was why he didn't want me coming up here. Dimitre wasn't afraid I would find out that he was a witch."

"He was afraid you'd find out that *you* were a witch," Hunter realized as he followed her thought processes.

Dimitre had always protected her, mentored her, and loved her. Maybe in some twisted way he had thought he was protecting her, but when she thought about all the times she had carelessly indulged in her abilities, never realizing that a warlock could be near at any moment . . .

"Oh God," she choked out, horror rushing through her until she was shaking with it. "Oh God, Hunter!"

"Easy, angel, it's okay," he said, sliding off his chair to kneel between her feet, holding her hands as he tried to convey reassurance.

"It is not okay! My brother has known for two months the type of danger I've been in and he didn't even breathe a word! I could have been . . . I might have gotten . . ." And here she was now, safe and sound. But was it because of her trusted and beloved brother? No! It was a total stranger who had been forced to make a sacrifice for her, to keep her safe. In the middle of all of that danger last night he had made the right choice in an instant, never once looking like he had doubted himself. Even now, he knelt before her in support and comfort, in the place where her most beloved brother ought to have been.

Tatyana surged to her feet and Hunter quickly followed and caught her arm, turning her back to face him.

"Tatyana, you can't . . ." he began.

"Let go!" she interrupted, trying to yank herself free. "You have no idea how betrayed I feel! How angry I am! The one person in this world who I would trust with my life . . . isn't even who I thought it would be. It isn't who it *should* be!"

"Okay!" Hunter gave her a little shake. "What are you going to do, angel? Yell at him? Disown him? He's your brother and without knowing all of the facts, I am going to guess that he did what he did with the intent to protect you. Even if it was clearly misguided and wrong, he probably meant well. Think about it," he urged her. "Maybe he wanted time to get stronger or better acquainted with the members of this coven before asking one of them to make the kind of sacrifice—"

"Sacrifice!" she exclaimed, reaching up and clutching at his shirt tensely. "Someone sacrificed for him, didn't they? I already know any one of them would make that kind of sacrifice for me, and I haven't known them for two months! You don't even know my brother, but you did it, didn't you?"

"Yes I did, Tatyana," he said, fiercely squeezing her arms. "And look at what happened this morning! Look at us now. It's impossible for us to stop touching. We constantly focus on how we move around one another." Hunter closed his eyes, swallowing with tension. "Maybe, just maybe, your brother wasn't ready to watch something like this happen to you. You're the baby, remember? And that doesn't make him right," he added hastily, "it just makes him human. I am guessing it was Annali who brought your brother over into witchcraft. I am also betting that things are really intense between them. No big brother wants to think about exposing a little sister to all that sex and lust.

"Master witches and their nascent apprentices don't usually become involved sexually, although there is no rule against it and, as you can see," he reminded her on a whisper, his lips brushing her forehead, "it is very, very tempting. Your brother's only experience with it ended up putting Annali in his bed."

"And in his heart," she added softly.

"True. Thank the Great Lady, because Annie truly deserves to be loved by a good man. She has known true hell in her life. She has known what it means to be forced into becoming the familiar of a psychopathic warlock."

Tatyana lifted her head, covering her mouth as it opened in shock, and dismay blasted through the jade of her eyes.

"Oh no!"

"I think your brother has had a lot to deal with recently. Let's wait to give him a fair hearing before we judge him too harshly. The witch/familiar relationship can be an unnerving, exposing experience. Doubly so in Annali's case."

And yet, Tatyana realized, Hunter had undertaken it without even hesitating. "Why?" she asked softly. "Why did you do it?"

"I needed to," he said simply.

"As simple as that? It's so unnerving and complicated, but for you it's simple?" she huffed.

"Simple?" Hunter laughed out a hoarse bark of humor. "You disturb my concentration, you torture the hell out of me just because you *smell* good, and you . . ." He gave her a frustrated shake that was more a matter of drawing her closer to his body. His mouth lowered to a scant inch away from hers. "Feel my body against you, Tatyana," he ground out. "Do you feel how hard you make me without even trying?" He made sure that she did by placing a swift hand on her bottom, pulling her hips painfully tight against his. He groaned deeply, losing himself for a moment in the pleasurable press of her soft body. "My mind and my soul are burning," he whispered to her fiercely. "I know it's the same for you."

It was. She lit up like a flare with needs she could barely control. She felt wild and knew he felt it, too. His breaths came quicker and quicker, spilling hotly over her mouth like the endless tides of the ocean. The overpowering nature of the attraction between them would truly sink home later, when Tatyana realized that all of her irritation with Dimitre had been banished as if she'd flicked away some inconsequential piece of lint.

But for the moment, there was only Hunter.

Hunter was no longer trying to make a point. He was too busy looking at the hunger flaring in her eyes, feeling the sensual rise and fall of her chest, and the instant slink in her spine. Tatyana had a way of settling against him that made all clothing negligible. She eased in with a silky movement over his entire body until they were touching everywhere and he was burning up with the contact. Hunter watched as she licked her lips and lowered her eyes to his mouth, staring at him expectantly until he groaned.

"Tatyana," he said, obvious agony strangling his words, "if I kiss you, I may not be able to stop this time. It's that potent for me. I don't want to hurt you."

"Mmm," she purred softly, her lips brushing up against his in a slow, sexy rub. "How could you possibly hurt me?" she asked with careless curiosity.

"I wanted to wait a week . . . so you would know . . . so *I* would know . . ." Hunter was stumbling over his words, trying to hold on to his point and failing miserably as her lips teased featherlight against his and her hands stroked over his chest.

"Know what?"

Damned if he remembered.

He caught her taunting mouth with a sharp downward assault, forcing her to absorb his fervor. Her mouth scorched against his lips as he devoured her. She tasted as sweet as ever, filling his senses with honeyed flavor. The confection of her scent rose from her in appetizing clouds. Her fingers curled around his flexed biceps, the fullness of her breasts against his chest as she snuggled up against him. Tatyana made a low, frustrated sound that communicated her displeasure with the clothing between them. The sound of petulance vibrated into his mouth.

"It doesn't matter," he insisted as he swept her tongue into a deeply erotic dance. Hunter proved his point by reaching past the hem of her robe. He was quickly beneath it and the flannel shirt, touching her incredibly hot skin in wide strokes of hungry fingers along the length of her thigh and over the tempting arch of her hip. "By the Lady, you feel so good," he groaned.

"Do you want me?" she asked breathlessly, her hands sliding up under his shirt and splaying over muscles that jerked and danced beneath her touch.

"I—"

His response was cut off by a knocking on the door. Like the hard dose of reality that it was, it hit them bracingly, causing them to freeze in place. After a moment they both became aware of where their hands had been traveling to, and they jumped apart just as another knock sounded. Hunter swore eloquently and turned toward the door, but Tatyana stopped him, using firm hands on his shoulders to push him into the chair he'd abandoned earlier.

"It's not for you," she assured him. "Sit and . . . umm . . . calm down," she suggested while giving him a naughty lift of her eyebrows that somehow managed to make him laugh in spite of a turbulent storm of emotions and needs.

Tatyana checked to see if her clothes were straight as she walked to the door, the covert sweep of her hands making him chuckle again. She shot him a look just before opening the door to Ryce.

"Tatyana." There was no mistaking the surprise in Ryce's voice. Clearly he hadn't expected to find her in Hunter's suite. "I'm sorry to wake you but . . . there's someone on the phone for you. I was going to ask Hunter where he had . . . umm . . . put you to bed. The house is rather big, you see."

Tatyana stepped aside and welcomed him into the sitting room with a sweep of a hand. Ryce got his second surprise of the morning when he saw Hunter looking at him with amusement. He gave his High Priest a cheeky little wave. Ryce just closed his eyes briefly and drew a breath. Then he handed the remote phone to Tatyana.

"Yes, Dimitre?" she greeted without asking who it was.

Ryce crossed over to Hunter and opened his mouth to say something, but Hunter cut him off with a gesture to be silent. He was focusing on Tatyana's conversation.

"Tat, honey, are you okay?"

Tatyana wanted to be swayed by the massive wave of concern coming at her over the phone, but her temper got in the way.

"Don't you dare 'honey' me, Dimitre Vladimir Pyotr Petrova!"

Ryce and Hunter both winced when they heard the slap-down in her tone.

"Wow. All four names," Hunter mused.

"Quite," Ryce agreed grimly.

"Tatyana," Dimitre said quickly, "I'm on my way home. I'll be there tonight. When I get there I will explain everything—"

"Oh, well, don't hurry home on my account," she bit out. "There's nothing really left for you to explain. See, this houseful of total strangers already did the job on behalf of my forthcoming and trustworthy brother."

"They wouldn't have had to if my obedient and trustworthy sister hadn't broken her word and gone running up there without so much as a phone call!" Dimitre snapped back, his temper spiking as well.

"I wouldn't have if you'd called me and told me you were going to be out of town! You always tell me everything, Dimi. Or at least you did. Now I come up here to find that within the span of two months, the twenty-four years we have spent as inseparable siblings were just thrown aside! I can accept you falling in love and moving away and all that stuff, Dimitre, but I cannot accept that you would go through such a massive life change and never even consider telling me. And I'm not even talking about your not telling me I am a damn witch! I'm not even talking about the danger you put me in! *Knowingly* put me in! I am so mad at you I can hardly speak!"

Tatyana broke off on a sob, which she muffled behind her hand, pulling the mouthpiece of the phone away a little.

"Aw, honey, don't cry. Please," Dimitre said, his anger evaporating. He knew she was right and her anger and hurt were very justified. He'd screwed up. Annali had warned him, but he had let pride and big brother role-playing get in his way. "Just remember this, I have never set out to intentionally hurt you. Everything I did, whether it was right or wrong, I did to protect you. You know I love you."

"I know that, but you have to stop treating me like a baby, Dimi. I'm going to be fine and I'm going to make decisions for myself about this like any adult would. Like you did. Don't think you're going to come here now and take charge of me. Hunter is my master witch, and I'm his apprentice. He's going to teach me about witchy stuff. You're going to explain yourself and then go off and be with that sweet Annali. By the way, I could eat her up with a spoon, she's just so adorable. I approve so very much. I think she has way too much class for you, but . . . the heart wants what the heart wants," she said with a breezy attitude and wave of her hand.

Hunter was completely bemused. She'd gone from fury, to hurt, to exerting independence, and now she was actually busting her brother's chops. All in the span of a minute.

"Look," she said with a sigh, "we'll talk when you get here. Just drive safely please?"

"I will. Hey Tat?"

"Yeah?"

"What's he like? Hunter, I mean."

Well, there's a trick question, Tatyana thought.

"I can't get into details about it right now."

"Meaning he's sitting right on top of you," Dimitre guessed.

Well, not anymore, she thought with a stifled laugh.

"See you later, Dimi." Tatyana hung up the phone and exhaled in a rush as she looked at Hunter and Ryce. She smiled wanly and said, "Well, I think that went well. What do you say we try world peace next?"

"How about we stick to getting some breakfast?" Ryce countered. "We'll sit and talk some. You have to have a thousand questions."

"Aww . . . are you really going to limit me to a thousand?"

She gave the men a wink and a flirtatious wrinkling of her nose before tossing Ryce the phone and heading out of Hunter's suite.

"Braen," cooed a soft, feminine voice from the stairwell.

Braen looked up from his task of spreading ointment over the nasty bites and stings he had suffered during last night's battle. He could have had a familiar tending him, or even Odessa, who was just now coming down the stairs, but he had been in a very bad mood when he had begun the task and he hadn't wanted to be abusive to his lover. And familiars just annoyed the hell out of him sometimes.

"What do you want, Dess?"

He watched her legs come into view as she descended the stairs, black fishnet stockings leading up curvy legs to a black miniskirt and bustier made of soft leather. The cuteness of her black Betty Boop curls was belied by her dark, gothic makeup, not to mention the multiple black-inked tattoos on her pale shoulders. She had a black widow spider, with the bright crimson hourglass on its belly, tattooed on the rise of her left breast, too. Her breasts were small, but the bustier did a fantastic job enhancing them.

Odessa knew her lover was in a foul mood. He had achieved none of the victories he had set out to accomplish this week and it infuriated him. Still, sometimes an evil mood could be a good thing . . . for her, at least. Braen tended to get very extreme in bed when he was pissed off, and she rather liked extreme.

She tsked her tongue when she saw what he was trying to do. She felt bad for his discomfort. After all, despite their tremendous power, their bodies were terribly human. They healed and hurt just like normal humans did unless magic was used.

"Lover, why don't you get a Healer to help you with these?" she asked as she moved quickly to take the salve from him. She reached first for his back, an area they both knew he couldn't reach by himself. "We have at least four of them, don't we? Why should you suffer?"

"I want to suffer," he bit out. "I want to remember every minute of this indignity. And I'm going to remember exactly who did it, too. Of all the witches in this world!" Braen slammed his hand down on the table before him. "That up-start Barbie doll of a familiar!"

"Annali," Odessa said grimly. "You ought to let me go take care of that one."

"How? With the exception of the three witches they are missing, Ryce won't let any of them out of that house now. She barely leaves as it is. And it was bad enough that blond bitch ties me up like a Christmas goose, but then Hunter shows up! Of all the fucking people!"

Braen grabbed a glass from the desk and pitched it against a wall in fury. Odessa let the burst of temper ride over him, waiting until he settled down, muttering epithets under his breath in a variety of languages as he resumed his seat.

"Well, at least we know now what we will be up against," she said with soothing logic. Odessa got a kick out of play-ing the voice of reason, just as much as she got a kick out of using taunts and goading. She could work Braen up either way if she wanted. Right now, Odessa wanted him calmed down so he could think clearly. She wanted her High Cleric to destroy Willow Coven just as much as he did.

"The problem is opportunity," Braen said. "We were supposed to bring down Witchcraft Barbie last night, making Ryce more vulnerable. Not only did we fail at that, but now Hunter is there to protect him. You and I could have taken on Ryce and slaughtered the cocksure bastard, but we can't take on him and his Sentinel."

"No one is infallible. Think of the little Elemental," she whispered seductively in his ear. "What a powerful fighter they said she was. No one could ever defeat her one-to-one, they said. But you destroyed her. In another few minutes, she would have been dead." She laughed low in her throat. "Ryce thinks he rescued her, but a woman like that, with that much power, can't recover so quickly from such a sound defeat. Soon your memory-obscuring spell will start to wear away, and slowly she will remember . . . everything."

Odessa followed up the observation by running a hand down over his muscle-hardened belly until she was rubbing her palm along the fly of his jeans. She knew full well how Braen loved to relive his conquests in his mind over and over. She also knew that they could often spur him on to his next action.

Despite his discomfort from his wounds, he grew very hard under her taut caress. Braen had really enjoyed himself that day, tearing up Ryce's property as he beat his little Elemental witch to hell and back. Odessa was right. He was glad he had missed the opportunity to kill her. Not because she had given him the fight of his year, but because it was so much more enjoyable to think of what her returning memory would start to do to her. She would be useless to Ryce for a very long time. She would also be a burden and a drain on his valuable resources.

"Gracelynne," he groaned with obvious pleasure, stimulated by memories, thoughts, and Odessa's touch.

"And your little Barbie doll, too, remember?" Odessa's nimble fingers unzipped his fly so she could contact him better. "You had her long before she ever even knew what a po-

tion bottle was for. You could see it in the way she shook and
trembled with fury. She remembers. She knows what your
cock felt like deep inside her."

"She will never forget," he agreed.

"And that isn't the end. You have other surprises in store
for them. Things they could never expect. You already know
how to use their white, happy little ways against them. All it
will take is a little time and your magnificent power." Odessa
moved in front of him, pushing back the table to make room
for herself. "And I had an idea you might like."

Odessa dropped down to her knees and Braen grinned.

"I love it already," he said.

She laughed. "Oh, well, this, too. But, I think you'll like
my other one even better. All we'll need is some help from
my mother."

"Adaliah? How is a Weather witch going to do me any
good?"

"I'll tell you in a minute," she promised, lowering her
dark lips to her task.

Chapter Eleven

Hunter looked out at the snow with his usual appreciation for the beauty of such things, but he was also very aware that Tatyana's brother and Kaia were driving home in the middle of this blizzard. She and Ryce were both worried about the missing witches. The storm's precipitous appearance was reflective of the abrupt changes going on inside of Willow House. Because their coven was so closely in tune with the forces of nature, there was a good chance that the turbulence within the house had changed the ice and rain into this unexpected snowstorm. When emotions ran high in a witch, it provided a source of power. When that power wasn't used, the excess energy bled out into nature and manifested itself in things like rainstorms, a twilight bark among dogs or wolves, or a simple unexpected fog. When an entire coven ran high with adrenaline and unresolved tensions, storms and other wilder manifestations were very possible.

They could countermand the storm, of course, if they had a Weather witch, but they didn't. Anyway, it was sometimes best just to let the energy play itself out.

"Hunter, come away from the windows and sit by me," Annali encouraged from behind him, her cajoling tone too loving and sympathetic for him to ignore.

He drew up one of the stools near her workbench. Hunter didn't bother examining the components she was working on; the extent of her knowledge in potions was completely beyond him. His mind boggled at the amount of botanical and chemical information she could hold in her head at once. At present she was cooking a small beaker over a Bunsen flame, watching with fascination and taking continuous notes.

"You're worried. There's no reason to be," she chided without looking up.

"You're kidding, right?" She was referring to the fact that he was worried Kaia wasn't available yet to check over Tatyana. "That black-hearted bastard poisoned that lightning strike, Annie. The lightning alone was enough to scramble her brain. The poison could be a time bomb waiting to detonate."

"I sensed nothing last night. Only the stain of darkness itself, which I did a fair job of removing if I do say so myself. Tatyana woke this morning coherent and looking the picture of health." Annali looked as self-satisfied as a cat presenting a dead mouse to its owner. "You doubt my capabilities?"

"Hardly, sweetheart. But it's a fact that Kaia is the Healer among us and she'll know best. I have to tell you, though: you've come a long way since I've been gone and I'm very proud of you."

Annali turned back to her mixture, but he saw the pleased color rushing over her cheeks at the compliment. "As have you. You're very confident. You weren't so content with yourself when you left."

"Let's not talk of the past," he dismissed easily and without emotion.

"Braen didn't disturb you?" she asked, arching a brow as she focused steady, seeking eyes on him.

"No more or less than usual," he responded vaguely. "My focus was on Tatyana. And on you."

"Tatyana," she mused, engaging in avoidance of her own

when he tried to direct the discussion to her precipitous behavior in the battle. "I'm amazed you so easily made her your familiar, Hunter. You never wanted to take on apprentices. You used to say the idea horrified you."

"Not horrified," he corrected. "It was off-putting, maybe. The idea of giving a part of myself away . . . well, I don't suppose you need an explanation," he finished pointedly.

"No, I don't," she admitted quietly.

"But you're right," he said. "I've never taken on an apprentice before. I didn't see how I had any other choice last night, though. I couldn't in good conscience leave her exposed. That," he stressed, "would've been horrifying."

"And how do you feel now?" she asked.

Hunter hesitated. Annali was uniquely qualified to discuss the situation with him. It was incredibly disconcerting; to be so drawn to another that common sense and reason became completely submerged in the heat of a moment. Anna would understand that.

Without meaning to, Hunter took too long to respond to Annali.

"I see. You don't feel you can discuss this with me," she said, hurt obvious in her tone and shimmering in her wounded eyes.

"Annie . . ." He couldn't lie to her when that was exactly what he was thinking, but he suspected she thought it was for a different reason. "Never think I don't trust you, Annali. You are now, and always will be, a sister of my heart as well as my coven. My faith in you is absolute." He reached out to pick up one of the small hands she'd fisted tightly. Gently, he massaged away the tension within it. "I'm just a little overwhelmed by everything that's happening. By the way it's making me feel. Part of my brain keeps telling me that I'm allowing my inexperience with the blood bond to control my behavior, and because of that I'm taking advantage of an innocent young woman."

"You feel what you feel and you are human as well as witch, Hunter."

"Yes, well, there's the other part of my brain that . . ." He looked up away from her and laughed wryly. "This is the part I have trouble discussing with you. It's very disturbing. And it's taking me a little while to remember you aren't seventeen anymore. You will forgive me for that, won't you?"

When Hunter had left the coven, Annali had still been unsure of herself and trying too hard to make up for beginnings that hadn't been her responsibility. She'd also had a case of hero-worship, dogging his steps and hanging on his every word. However, just before his departure, she'd shown him another side of herself, one he would never forget. She had shown him a serious glimpse of the woman she would become as she stepped out of the shadows that her capture and torture had cast over her. She had shown him the woman of ten years later.

"But you're right," he said fondly, "it's wrong of me to forget you're no longer that frightened, angry girl." He squeezed her fingers once, then brought them to his lips. "You've become a beautiful, compelling woman of impressive intelligence and strength of character. I can see that as clear as day, even if I'm occasionally blinded by memories of your younger self."

"It's understandable," she agreed, standing up and moving close to him, reaching to add her free hand to their mixture of palms and fingers. She bent her forehead to his shoulder. "You knew me best back then."

"You wouldn't allow anyone else near you," he reminded her.

"I know." She was quiet for a long time, and then she spoke softly, "Sometimes it seems like it happened to someone else. Other times, it's all around me. We've both come to terms with our past, Hunter, but I will always be the girl you rescued, and you will always be my hero, whether you want to be or not," she said, tears filling her voice. Hunter let go of her hands so he could wrap her up tightly in a hug of love and protection.

"Aww, honey, I love being your hero," he laughed softly. He reached to frame her face with his hands and brought her teary eyes up to meet his. "Don't condemn me if I am uncomfortable discussing my sexual predilections with you, or asking you to discuss yours."

"But if it will help you in any way, Hunter, I would gladly do it. Maybe this time," she teased gently, "I will be *your* hero."

"Anything is possible," he agreed. "Will you let me think on it? Give me some time to gather my thoughts and questions?"

"A wise idea," she agreed with a nod before she leaned in to kiss his lips warmly. "You've become more careful and thoughtful, I think."

"You've become incredibly gorgeous. Have I told you that?" he complimented her, just to see her blush and preen. He laughed at her, kissing her warmed cheek before turning her away and sending her back to her stool.

As soon as Annali stepped out of his line of sight, Tatyana suddenly appeared within it. Apparently, she'd been standing there for some time, if the expression on her face was anything to judge by. Hunter surged to his feet, holding out a placating hand as he stepped between her and Annali.

"Tatyana," he warned as her eyes narrowed meanly on Annali. "Take a breath, Tatyana, and *think* about what you're doing," he demanded.

"It's no use," Annali said from behind him, tension in her voice. "She can't overcome a familiar's jealousy. Not this soon. Trust me on that."

"Yes, she can. If I can regain control, so can she," he argued.

"You? What do you mean? You are the master and she is the familiar. You are in complete control," Annali insisted, looking confused.

"No. Not between us. Now isn't the time to discuss this," he said sharply, just as Tatyana growled nastily in her throat and lunged for Annali. He snagged the furiously jealous hellcat by both arms, jerking her back just in time to spare Annie from a set of clawing nails. Annali gasped when the other woman hissed violently, lunging against Hunter's hold.

"My Lady Goddess, Hunter, I've never seen anything like this!"

That got Hunter's full attention and his eyes widened as he jerked Tatyana back against his body and forced her to be still.

"I thought jealousy was part and parcel of our enhanced connection and hypersexuality," he demanded.

"Jealousy, yes. This is . . . I have no idea what this is," she exclaimed, gesturing to the other woman. "She's like an animal, Hunter." She gasped. "Wait. Did you just say *our*? Hunter, are you behaving like this, too?" she asked, gesturing to Tatyana. "Uncontrollably emotional? Possessive? Jealous?"

"No . . . I don't know," he snapped as he struggled to keep Tatyana under his control. She was nearly as tall as he was and her strength was fueled by intense emotion. "I have to get her away from you. We'll talk about this later."

With a jerk that whipped Tatyana up off her feet, he hauled her out of the conservatory.

Heat seethed through her mind, painting her vision with the scarlet of congealing blood. Fury rooted around in her gut and rage screamed for release as she bucked in frustration against the hands gripping her arms. She spewed out Russian curses; the very best ones that Rurik had taught her at age twelve, much to their mother's dismay. Tatyana threw her weight around by kicking her feet up off the floor and wrenching her body. She was being dragged away from where she wanted to be, away from the target of her wrath.

How dare she touch him! How dare that blond witch invite his kisses and laughter and smother him with her own! After what she and Hunter had nearly meant to each other that morning? Was the bitch blind? First she stole Tatyana's brother's affections, and now this? She wanted to take Hunter, too? No one could be ignorant of the chemistry between her and Hunter! She'd done it on purpose, *the conniving little whore!*

"Enough!"

The roar of Hunter's command penetrated the haze of her mind a moment before his weight crashed hers to the ground, forcing her facedown into a bank of freezing snow. The cold and wet slapped reality at her like a backhanded strike across her face. She was wearing nothing but a thin cotton dress Annali had loaned her. Finding herself suddenly knee-deep in a blizzard had her gasping in shock and horror as every inch of her skin rippled tight in goose bumps and shivers.

The redirection worked. She was jolted completely out of the furious grip of uncontrolled jealousy so foreign to her natural personality. As soon as the snow and ice enveloped her, she completely forgot that jealousy had even existed. All she was aware of was slush and snow soaking into her front, and the heat and weight of Hunter leaning over her back and holding her down into it. The contrasts were just about killing her as she quaked and trembled, trying to speak without screeching.

Then, for good measure, Hunter backed off of her just enough to flip her over onto her back, saturating the rear of her body with ice as well. Tatyana sucked in a staggering breath of absolute shock, her entire body clattering with rough, spastic movements that were more like seizures than shivers.

She was getting really sick of being cold.

Her eyes whipped open and stared up into the new familiarity of Hunter's snapping blue gaze. "Are you insane?" she gasped up at him, twisting her body to try and buck him off of her. "It's freezing out here! Get off of me!"

"Not until you cool down," he contradicted her sharply.

"Cool down? I'm a freaking popsicle! What in hell possessed you to throw me into a snowbank? Are you some kind of kink freak or something? This is demented!"

Hunter's mouth opened to say something, a look of sheer shock writhing across his expression, before he snapped it shut wordlessly. He reached out to wipe snow from her ruddy cheeks, pushing back the wild streaks of her cinnamon red hair. He looked seriously into her eyes, a frown toying with his lips.

"Are you calmed down now?" he asked.

"I'm always calm! Well,"—she relented quickly when he cocked a brow at her—"discounting fireball attacks, but I think that was understandable under the circumstances!"

He seemed to digest her reply for a moment, watching her warily as if for some kind of trick. Finally, he removed his weight from her body and kneeled over her. He reached out a hand, which she took, and hauled them both to their feet. Tatyana immediately set about brushing off slush and ice as her teeth chattered hard enough to give her a headache.

"Freakin' snowstorm and a maniac throws me out into it!" she mumbled with vehement outrage.

"Better that than you taking off my friend's skin five nails at a time," he retorted.

"What friend? What nails? What in hell are you talking about?"

Hunter drew up short when he felt the realness of her confusion and indignation. She was dead serious. She had no idea why he'd dragged her out there.

"You mean to tell me you don't remember flying at Annali like you wanted her pretty head on a silver platter?"

His words stopped all of her motion and for a moment her

eyes narrowed with that gleam he'd just seen a few minutes ago. "You think she's pretty?" she demanded.

Uh oh.

Was this blood bond between them really capable of heightening emotion to such an insane degree? Well, if their sexual attraction was anything to judge by . . .

"Crap," he muttered in frustration, running a wet hand through his hair.

Willow Coven could not afford this kind of volatility within its ranks just now. They were already weakened without Gracie, and Asher was still missing in action. Next time, as Braen had warned, Belladonna Coven would be prepared for the fact that Hunter had returned home.

"Tatyana, try and focus, please," he begged her softly. "Don't you remember that not five minutes ago you were furiously jealous of Annali?"

She snorted and looked at him like he'd lost his mind.

"I'm not the sort to become jealous," she declared. "I'm the youngest of thirteen kids. Jealousy was a waste of time, so I never bothered."

He could believe that. However, he knew what he had seen. She had the capacity for jealousy, just like everyone else on the planet. She just kept it well hidden. After what he'd just seen in magnification? He'd bet she was more than capable of feeling possessive anger.

"Well, take my word for it. Before you hit that snowbank you were hissing and clawing like a crazed cat." Hunter wisely avoided reminding her why. She'd walked in on him being affectionate with Annali and it had snowballed into hell having no fury. "Something bizarre is going on with this bond between us, Tatyana. Our emotions and needs are magnified, sometimes beyond our control."

"Why?" she asked, looking very uncomfortable all of a sudden. This time when she shivered, he knew it wasn't entirely because of the cold.

"Come here. Let's go inside before you freeze to death."

He gestured her forward, but she hesitated. Hunter understood. He'd felt the same way that morning. She didn't trust herself.

"It's okay. I'll be with you and I won't let you do anything you'll regret," he assured her.

Too cold to worry too much about it, she hurried beneath the fall of his arm and let him bring her inside. It wasn't until then that she realized he'd initially brought her out into a central courtyard, rather than beyond the actual perimeter of the house. It had an exit that led off of one side of the conservatory, but there were also three other entrances so that all four points of the compass were represented, all edged by gardens with a fountain in the center.

Tatyana didn't bother with any further observations. She was so wet and cold that ice was forming on her hair. Hunter brought her in the door opposite that of the conservatory, the one fully across the courtyard. She comprehended that it was so she and Annali wouldn't meet, and Tatyana wished she could remember what it was she was supposed to have done and why she'd done it. Try as she might, the memory wouldn't come back. It made her feel out of her own control, a feeling she didn't care for. If it was this bad being the familiar of a white witch, how horrid it must be for . . .

She could barely finish the thought.

Hunter swept her indoors. She was surprised to find herself in an enormous room, the vast windows on all sides steamed with condensation, an indoor pool sprawling out before her in artful curves. A stone garden at one end framed a centerpiece waterfall tumbling from a height of about fifteen feet. Palms and ferns grew along rock steps at the sides of each level the waterfall struck before it eventually splashed down into the pool. At the opposite end was a large sunken hot tub with stairs leading both to the walkway and into the pool.

The water was bubbling and steaming and that was all

Tatyana wanted to know. She broke away from Hunter and ran to the hot tub. She nearly threw herself into the steaming water, screeching when it felt hot enough to burn in contrast to her frozen body.

"Oh yes, yes, yes," she groaned. "Ouch, ouch . . . mmm . . ."

She looked up when Hunter's deep chuckle floated down over her.

"Which is it," he asked. "Yes, ouch or mmm?"

"(D) All of the above," she told him. "Oh, this is heaven. And hot! I'm half frozen thanks to you!"

"I was just keeping you from doing something you might regret. I'm positive Annali would have regretted it."

"I don't suppose you'll tell me what she did that freaked me out, will you?" she fished hopefully as she floated in a lazy circle around the circumference of the tub.

"No, I don't suppose I will," Hunter agreed grimly. "I'm not reminding you just in case you go all Freddy Krueger on her again."

"Oh, come on! You must be exaggerating," Tatyana scoffed.

"I never exaggerate."

He didn't have to exaggerate. Life, he thought, was intense enough. He watched her bob and dip in the steamy water, her thin dress as ineffective at hiding her figure as the wet silk had been the night before. Annali had loaned her something in simple white cotton and Tatyana wasn't wearing a chemise or bra at present. Hunter knew this because he was fixating on the dark thrust of her nipples through the now sheer fabric. The temperature contrasts had worked wonders on the rigid tips of her breasts and they were so visible she was as good as naked. Better actually. There was something damned alluring about being able to see her, yet knowing she was still fully clothed.

Hunter was freezing, in spite of the heat climbing up his body and the steam of the room, but he wasn't as bohemian as Tatyana was. He wasn't about to plunge in with her sense of instant gratification. She thought nothing of jumping in with both feet. He'd learned at a young age to monitor his every action, reaction, and movement. That was the reason why this screwed-up bonding was especially disturbing to him. Without judgment and reserve to properly manage his impulses, he was afraid of what might happen. Everyone always credited him with remarkable wisdom and control in the face of chaos, but no one knew what that took. No one knew what impulses he had to repress in order to maintain that even keel.

He envied her abandon. He was getting a clearer picture of who this woman was, despite the distortion created by the blood bond. She was courageous and bold, that much was certain. Under those shy blushes lay a vixen who only exposed herself to one she could trust with that side of her nature. The heightened sensuality of the blood bond was bringing it out in spades, stronger as she came to be familiar with him. Much as his urge to seduce her with all the force of his own passion came out when he got close to her. His normal approach would never be so brutish . . . so barbaric. He couldn't seem to help himself, however, and he couldn't make himself feel regret for his coarse, domineering behavior.

It felt too good.

That was it, Hunter realized. The thoughts and feelings were genuine. It was the impulse control that was damaged, that part of a person that years of experience normally tempered. It was as if it were wiped completely away. They were being taken over by their impulses.

He instantly related the theory to Tatyana.

She was silent and thoughtful for a long minute as she digested the information. She found one of the seats in the tub and settled down, the curtain of her hair skimming on top of the water and fanning out around her. Soon she looked as though she were surrounded by a wine-colored sea anemone. It was the most beautiful sight Hunter had ever seen in his life. She looked like a sea sprite . . . or Aphrodite about to be born from the ocean. His entire body clenched with desire, need rooting profound and low and turning him steel hard with want.

God, he thought, *I'm never going to survive this.*

Not if he had to withstand these kinds of onslaughts every five minutes.

If he didn't figure out how to ease these assaults on his senses and emotions, he would be throwing her into his bed and using her to exhaustion by the end of the day.

"So you're saying what we feel is being greatly magnified," she said.

"Yes," he agreed, clearing the hoarse catch from his throat. "It is."

"But the original feelings are real."

"Yes."

Tatyana tilted her head slightly, her pretty pale eyes speculative as she ran them with slow, blatant appraisal over his body. She stopped when she spied the rampant evidence of his present feelings and thoughts.

"I see," she said, a silky, sensual note creeping into her voice. "So if I didn't like you to start, I'd probably hate you by now and wouldn't be able to bear the"—she smiled slyly—"the sight of you."

Hunter had to agree with the hypothesis, because, at the moment, he wanted to reach out and strangle the little tease to death. Or pull her head into his lap. Only the knowledge that she was working under the influence of an enhanced sensual nature saved her from either fate. His hands did curl into fists, however, as he went about forcing himself to resist many more wild impulses.

"That appears to be the case," he said stiffly.

"I was attracted to you from the start," she mused, standing up in the water and leaning her elbows on the ledge behind her so she could lounge back casually. The material of her wet dress pulled taut across the resulting forward push of her breasts. "So now I find I'm extremely attracted to you. Beyond reason, perhaps. That would explain why I have such incredible urges to strip you naked and . . . mmm . . ." she paused to contemplate all the possibilities.

Good. Hunter was damn well contemplating them, too, and in about five seconds he was going to do more than just contemplate. The sexy little witch was purposely pushing him. How was he supposed to fight that? Why would he want to?

"I've a question, then," she said unexpectedly, altering his one-track thoughts abruptly. "How can we keep ourselves from hurting others? You said I almost took Annali's head off. This morning when Ryce told me a joke at breakfast you just about took off his."

"I did not," he denied sharply. "I would never be disrespectful to Ryce."

"Really?" She laughed with an irreverent snort. "Hunter, you told him if he touched me one more time you were going to stab your fork through his hand."

All flirtation instantly banished, Hunter looked at her completely aghast. Seeing his horror, she clucked her tongue sympathetically. He knew she was telling the truth, even though he had no memory of it. He no more remembered his jealousy than she had, the incidents being repressed for some reason.

"Well, at least I didn't threaten him with magic," Hunter said weakly, finding a seat at the edge of the tub. He kicked away his shoes, cuffed his pants up to his knees, and sank his cold feet into the hot water, suddenly needing the small comfort. "That would have been unforgivable."

"Ah, but you would never think of using magic against Ryce, so you wouldn't do that. I, however, am admittedly capable of entertaining the thought of scratching someone's eyes out, though I'd normally resist that impulse."

"But I'd entertain stabbing a fork through my best friend's

hand?" Hunter shuddered. "Resisted impulses or not, it makes you reevaluate the kind of person you think you are."

"Stop that," she scolded, wading through the water and standing between his dangling feet so she could fold her arms over his thighs and look up into his eyes. "It's only human to think vicious thoughts now and then. Especially when sparked by . . . well, I'm guessing it was jealousy. You know, that really keen kind you feel at the beginning of a relationship when things are so new, intense, and hungry, but you don't know each other well enough yet to trust? There's no faith in fidelity because you have no real understanding of the other person's code of honor or morals. I mean, for all you know I'm nothing but a tramp, tramping my way up the Hudson River."

"For all you know, the women in this house are all my exlovers who I'm seeing again for the first time in ten years and I'm feeling some nostalgia."

"Exactly!"

She smiled.

The smile faded.

She frowned.

"You aren't, are you?"

Hunter chuckled, leaning forward to nudge her forehead with his. "No, silly. Annali was barely eighteen when I left, Kaia needs a man who will drop a small planet on her head in order to gain her full attention, and Gracelynne . . . Gracie is . . . hard to explain. Not without betraying certain confidences. Suffice it to say, she's had a hard life and she's going to need someone quite different from me as her mate." He laughed softly, a fond smile on his lips. "We're so compatible, all of us in this house, but not to the point of physical intimacy. It would be like bedding your sibling." He shuddered at the taboo. "What about you?" He gave her a teasing grin. "Are you whoring your way up the Hudson River?"

"Eww. I said tramping. Whoring sounds so much nastier." Then she laughed at herself. "I say that like I'm taking it personally. No. I'm decidedly non-whorish. Non-trampy. Oh, you know what I mean!" She pinched him on his thigh when he snickered at her. "I was dating someone last month, but Sergei scared him off before I could consider anything serious. Lucky for me. Turned out he was married. God, I hate liars." She shook her shoulders as if she was shedding a slimy creature from her back. "Before that, I'd been having a serious dry spell. Which actually could explain why I'm incredibly horny right now," she added matter-of-factly.

"Could it?" Hunter asked, his voice dropping low enough to hit his toes.

Tatyana looked up with a half-smile on her lips. They were smoldering again. Those sapphire blue eyes that burned like a butane flame. When she looked into those eyes, sometimes Tatyana wanted to wriggle inside and see what it would be like to be burned by those flames.

"Yes," she said. "It's been a while since I've been to bed with anyone. About two years, I think. I've been working to make a name for myself. No time for extracurricular activities. What about you?"

"You mean am I horny . . . or how long since I've had sex?"

"Well, both, I guess," she chuckled, giving him a suggestive eyebrow wiggle that could prove to be his downfall.

"Yes, and I'd have to say about four years."

"Four years? Sexy, gorgeous, *yummy* guy like you with the sensuality and appetite you have? You have to be pulling my leg."

"I was"—he cleared his throat—"living with Romany clans. There's . . . it wouldn't be wise," he finished lamely, unable to form coherent sentences under the onslaught of her very personal compliments. The feel of her nails absently traveling up and down the fabric of his slacks over his thigh wasn't helping matters. Having this discussion while her head, for all intents and purposes, was in his lap . . . well, that was just plain torture.

"I see," she said, an 'aha' tone to her voice.

Those mischievous eyes were back and they were doing a number on him all over again. Every time she moved it was like silk underwater, slow and sensual with undeniable beauty. She moved to seduce, whether she was meaning to or not. At the moment, she was meaning to. Her hands both came to rest on his thighs, stroking them softly in a steady rhythm, up and down. It was incredibly suggestive. So was the slow way she licked the water from her lips.

"Why don't you come in here with me," she invited silkily. "We can be cozy hot while the snow falls all around us." Her hands slid up to his damp shirt, her fingers tugging the fabric. He reached out and covered her hands, staying her.

"Tatyana, no . . ." he protested very softly. "It's safer the way we are, angel."

She laughed uproariously at that, perplexing him for a minute. Then she slid her hand right between his legs, cupping the full length of his erection firmly. Her eyes fixed on his just before she leaned forward, deliberately stuck out her tongue, and touched it to the back of the hand pressed vertically along his rigid shaft. She licked leisurely up from the wrist, over the back of it on up the longest finger, right to the very tip, before finally flicking her tongue off.

Enough said.

After that morning, four years of celibacy, and the raw suggestiveness of what she'd just done, Hunter was shocked that he hadn't come right then and there, just by watching that naughty pink tongue. Even so, he was throbbing with urgent need and it was taking every ounce of his willpower to keep himself sitting still at the edge of the tub. She was still touching him, so he suspected she could feel the pulsing twitches running through his cock in time to his racing heart. Did she know he'd never been as hard as he was now? Did the devilish little vixen know . . . ?

"Hunter," she gasped, "you're hurting me!"

Hunter blinked. To his shock, his hands were wrapped in a vise-like grip around her upper arms, so tight that the skin bordering his fingers was turning purple. He instantly eased the touch, unwilling to let go completely for fear the bruises that were sure to appear would be visible already. She was looking up at him expectantly, her eyes so beautifully voluble.

"Tatyana . . ." he struggled to say, barely able to manage her name or an apology for hurting her.

Her hands slid away at last, but there was no relief. Instead his nerves screamed with the loss. She moved to the steps that would lead her to him, Aphrodite ready to make her entrance into the world. He was shaking as he watched her mount those steps. He could do nothing to control it, his every nerve on overload. A sleek, wet cape of beautiful red hair, pale, freckle-dusted skin, and the body of a goddess. He was doomed. He knew it the minute she stepped with bare feet onto the stone and turned to extend a hand down to him, bending forward slightly, her breasts jiggling in a fetching manner beneath the wet transparency of her dress as she did so.

"There's no need for this, Hunter," she said softly. "Why should we torture ourselves with resistance? Why waste what could be such a stunningly sensual experience? Hmm? It's the perfect solution, you know. Lock me away with you, Hunter, and make love with me. We'll protect the others with our absence, yet we'll still be close to the coven in case you're needed. We can exhaust each other into good behavior."

"That isn't reason enough," he argued hoarsely, even though every cell in his body was screaming an affirmative. "I don't want to do anything you'll come to regret. What happens a week from now, Tatyana, when discrimination returns? I need your trust and friendship in order to guide you. I'll lose that if I allow this. No matter how badly I want to, angel, I can't." He tried to draw away from her. "Ask me again in a week. Then I'll know it's me you really want.

"Two years of celibacy, Tatyana, tells me you're as discriminating as I am when choosing partners. I've told you how dark witches use their familiars for sex. Even though they are compliant and even begging for it, it's still rape because their natural will is subverted. If I do what you ask, I'll be no better than Braen or any warlock. Please. Don't do this. Don't tempt me when it's so painful to resist you."

"Well," she said softly, a sharp contrast to the uneasy swallow and hollow laugh she released. It sounded flat and insincere; her eyes were filling with pride and pain. "I guess the master witch does have all of the control after all."

She stepped backward away from him, her arms coming up to cross over her breasts. She looked as if he'd just punched her in the stomach and then kicked her besides. Hunter surged to his feet, reaching out for her. Tatyana turned and ran, wet hair flying and bare, damp feet slapping on the floor at as fast a speed as she could manage while slipping on smooth surfaces.

Hunter barked out a curse, the word echoing in the vast room over the sound of the waterfall and the bubbling hot tub. *Hurt her now or hurt her later*, Hunter thought, *I'm damned either way*. And either way it sucked. But this hurt, he tried to console himself, was temporary. A few days from now she would feel far better about it than she did now.

He hoped.

Like all their emotions, the pain of rejection must be highly intensified. How must that be feeling to her right now? Hunter's heart tripped a strange beat at the idea. Worse yet was the knowledge that he was the cause of it. He'd give her some time, but he had to eventually go and ease her way somehow. He couldn't just leave it like this.

In the meantime, he had to speak with Annali.

Chapter Twelve

Tatyana ran through the house and, in the span of a few minutes, managed to get completely turned around and lost. She lost track of floors, stairs, and even how many turns she'd made. She began to find strange rooms she'd never seen before, for the first time coming to understand how enormous the house was. Becoming cold again and feeling like a foolish drowned rat that couldn't even find a decent place to privately sulk, she felt tears begin to run down her cheeks. Her heart had become so chill with pain, but ironically, her tears were hot. Swiping at her face and fearing she would run into Hunter, Tatyana ducked into the next room she found, slamming the door shut behind her, venting a little of her furious hurt.

Jerk. Rat. Bastard. Rat bastard, she added, trying combinations now as she looked around herself wildly. She was in some kind of strange room without a central floor. She was standing on an oval balcony that ran the circumference of an oval room. Above her a fresco in bright pastel wound around an enormous oval skylight that was trimmed in gold and pretty plaster fairies. The rest of the ceiling was a white plaster trimmed in gold, but it looked as though it had been woven like one of those child's potholder kits she'd had as a young girl, only the ceiling was far neater than any weave she'd ever managed.

The balcony was a sturdy wooden balustrade at waist height with spindle posts set so close together they could barely be seen through. The curving walls all around were painted in a mural that had no start and no end that she could see, only a perfect continuity of figures in more pastels and brilliant primary colors that turned out to be a depiction of . . .

Alice in Wonderland.

Of all the things in the world, why would someone paint a balcony with scenes from Alice in Wonderland? How odd she should end up here. It was almost as if someone were sending her a message, or having a very good joke at her expense. Brushing that self-pitying idea aside, Tatyana approached the banister so she could look over it and down into the room that was below her.

She certainly hadn't expected to see beautiful cribs of sparkling white, carefully arranged dressers and changing tables. Little beds just the right size for a child just out of its crib tucked up with plain white sheets for now, but which would no doubt bear bedding that was the child's preference when the time came. There were toys still in their packages to keep the dust off of them; others were laid out at the ready. Play blankets, swings, bundles of fresh clothing zipped and tucked in clear plastic. Cedar toy chests, little blackboards, easels and paint simply waiting.

Everything a child could want. Everything a baby could need.

Waiting.

And this balcony so parents could come and sneak peeks all day long with the children none the wiser, making it easier for their nanny if it was a bad time to disrupt routine or disturb a nap.

Tatyana felt her heart leap out of her chest. It lodged tightly in her throat and new tears filled her eyes. Suddenly everything she'd seen, done, and felt shifted, spun, and changed.

All because of what she saw when she looked down into that empty, echoing room.

Hope.

And for the first time since she had learned their secret, she suddenly saw the witches once again as merely people. People who one day hoped to fill all those cribs and beds. Who planned to live their entire lives together, sharing their magic, but even more, sharing their families and the futures of their children. Loyalty, dedication, and total commitment. So much commitment that the room stood empty still. What must it take, she realized, for a witch to find love. Find love and reveal what they were and what it meant to be a witch. To share that meaning and then hope that the other person would come to care for the coven. Care enough for the coven to want to live among them, inseparably, for always. To live among them with their dangers and their blessings and consider giving birth to a family.

Oh, the odds of all the things that would have to come to pass perfectly in order for those hopes to be achieved. Tatyana felt her heart pounding madly, still stuck in her throat no matter how she tried to swallow past her tears of lonely empathy. What manner of man or woman could ever be selfless enough to accept so many conditions? What manner of being did one have to be to ever be brave enough to risk asking?

Dimitre. Her very own brother was that brave. He dared to love in this difficult setting, to take risks no future husband or father would want to take for his family, just so he could be there for Annali . . . and for his new coven.

She had an overwhelming urge to find Hunter, her entire body pounding with the pulse of her need. She forgot her stung pride in an instant, this need was so strong. Then it wasn't just Hunter. It was Annali, Ryce, Lennox, and Gracelynne. Who were all these people? What was the witch like in each of them? Hunter had said they all specialized in something that called to them. Outside of the witch, what lay

within the person? Was there any separation between the
witch and the human? Had there ever been?

So many questions that her head was spinning.

Suddenly she knew how she would be spending the next
week after all.

"We need to talk."

"We need to do much more than that," Hunter said grimly.
He sat back in his seat, a glass of neat vodka dangling between his fingers. Ryce entered the firelit parlor and both
men glanced anxiously at the darkening windows. "Have
you heard from them?"

"No. Dimitre and Kaia's cells are both going straight to
voicemail. We're just going to have to wait this out."

"I hope that's what they did. I hope they pulled over and
just decided to wait the storm out." Hunter took a swallow of
his drink. "But I guess that's wishful thinking. They would
have grabbed a land line and called us, right?"

"What we need is a good Weather witch," Ryce said as he
crossed to pour himself some whiskey. "We also need to figure out what we're going to do about Braen and the Belladonna coven. I don't like the idea of sitting here waiting
for them to make their next move."

"How long have you had Dimitre and Kaia spying on
them?"

Ryce laughed, moving to sit next to Hunter. "You're the
second person to figure that out. How did you know?"

"Because you'd never let our Healer go off just to give
lectures when you felt the coven was in such dire threat. Especially not a threat that causes you to call me home after ten
years. You kept the big guns close to the house and snuck the
two weaker witches out under the radar. I figured after you
told me about Dimitre's power, you were counting on him
using it to get them out of harm's way if things turned sour."

"Right. He has the defense, and Kaia has the knowledge. She knows what she is looking at when she spies on a coven. It's a bit of a learning experience for him as well. Made him feel like he was contributing essentially to the coven."

Hunter nodded, understanding how it must be difficult to be the awkward novice while also being a man in his thirties who was used to having a measure of control over his life.

"So how long?" he repeated.

"A week. Enough to get some fair intel, from what Kaia said to me."

"I should wait for that information before I think about what manner of message to send to my brother," Hunter said, his animosity apparent. "What were you thinking of? Fire and brimstone? Or would you prefer just pissing him off and making him act before he is ready?"

"Oh, no," Ryce said, his tone low and cold. "I no longer have a message to send. I'm going to throw the whole damn dissertation at him. That warlock bastard stepped foot onto *my* lands. Twice! He attacked me on my home soil. He put my house and my loved ones under threat."

Hunter didn't need for Ryce to finish the picture he was painting. He understood the man's fury perfectly, just as he understood that the retaliation for this offense would be total and obliterating.

"Then we wait for the others to return. We gather our information and we make a plan." Hunter grinned a little wickedly. "Something different. Something they won't be expecting. Braen knows you well, Ryce. He'll know you're pissed off and will expect you to take swift action in response."

"Yeah, well, he knows you, too. But we're not going to act right away, and that's what is going to keep him guessing. While we're figuring all of this out, I want to concentrate our magical energy into strengthening the house defenses. No one should leave the grounds, especially not alone. We have to be wary of lures and traps. He's going to try to draw us out."

"One at a time. He's trying to pick us off like ducks in a gallery." Hunter lifted a quizzical brow when he spied Ryce's expression of dark contemplation. "Something else on your mind, Ryce?"

"Actually, you are," Ryce returned. "This is a hell of a time for you to have an apprentice splitting your resources and attention. I don't know what the hell is going on with this blood bond you've made. Annie told me what happened. She's really worried and so am I."

"I can control it," Hunter said quietly.

"Can you? Does that mean my hands will remain fork-free?"

Hunter winced. "It's some kind of impulse control problem. I'm hoping, now that we are aware of the trouble, we can avoid most confrontations that might develop."

"Hmm. An assassin who cannot control his impulses. I'm still not comforted here."

"Damn it, Ryce! What do you want me to do?" he demanded. "I can't change what has happened. Did you want me to leave her out there where someone could snatch her up and spend two weeks fucking up her mind and body? Don't you think what we did to Annali was enough? I took one look at Tatyana and I knew I couldn't hesitate. Hesitating and carelessness is how Evan found our Annie in the first place, remember? None of what happened to her would have happened if it weren't for us leading him right to her. That was not going to happen again!"

"Of course I didn't mean you should have left her unprotected," Ryce snapped, the reminder of his part in Annali's past not sitting well at all. He didn't need his old friend's memories of it to feel guilty as hell. He had his own. "I'm just trying to encourage you to find a solution!"

"Well, I've been thinking about that," Hunter returned with hard sarcasm, "and so far my only solutions are to lock her up for more than a month, although there's that whole pesky brother thing to deal with. Or, I can tie her to my bed stark naked and exhaust myself on her. Unfortunately, there's still that pesky brother issue about to come up and, also, last I checked white witches didn't do things like that."

"Well, they do," Ryce stipulated with an unexpected grin, "but it's got to be consensual."

The observation took the steam out of Hunter's anger and frustration, making him chuckle softly. Nodding, he toasted his friend with a brief raise of his glass. "Blessed be, my brother."

Ryce sighed, rubbing the tension in the back of his neck. "You know, it can't be coincidence that two blood bonds in this family have gone wonky."

Hunter looked at him with surprise. "This is the first I am hearing of it."

"At first, Dimitre's bond with Annali was normal. She was immune to his power, etcetera. Then suddenly the immunity failed for no explainable reason. Now you are connected to his sister and experiencing this hyperactive impulse effect? Not to mention the physical attraction, too, by the sound of it. I have had five blood bonds. I felt increased sexuality and even some strong attraction to my students, but I could easily ignore it. Not saying that makes me better than you, mate."

"I wouldn't think so," Hunter said with a shrug.

"Just that even with ten years in the wind I know this isn't normal for you."

"Yeah," Hunter agreed darkly. "Just what we need, right? Me, involved with another witch's sister. Again. We both know how that turned out the first time."

"That's not fair. Not to you or anyone else. You always took too much responsibility for Amber."

"I didn't have any other choice. There was no one else to blame. Now it's ten years later and I come back just to make the same mistake all over again? Gracious Lady, I thought I'd become better than this."

"You cannot liken this to what happened ten years ago.

You're a different person and these are extreme circumstances."

"Maybe you could have convinced me of that if it was just the blood bond attracting me to her, Ryce, but I promise you, I was hot for our new little witch the instant I touched her, and finding out she was Dimitre's sister didn't faze me in the least."

"Annali and Dimitre went through this intense attraction, too. It was wild for them as well. There is no rule saying that you cannot touch your apprentice if the familiar consents, and if you never touched anyone's sister . . . your dating options would truly suck. If you recall, Tatyana is very vehement about living her own life with her own choices. You don't even know Dimitre. He shouldn't be a factor in your decisions just because you think history is repeating itself. That's an insult to Tatyana."

"An insult? Where do you get that?"

"Because she isn't Amber. Amber was so vastly different from the woman I met last night, it's like tomatoes and strawberries—only the color is the same." Ryce shot him a sly smile. "But you always had a thing for redheads."

"Yes, I know," Hunter replied with a groan. "I cannot afford this distraction right now. You are so right."

"Then change it from a distraction into a strength. Maybe instead of fighting with yourself and with Tatyana, you should seriously consider that . . . maybe it's not wrong for you to be attracted to this woman. Maybe she is something . . . someone you need. You and I both believe that things happen for a reason. The Mother Goddess sent Dimitre to heal Annali for us. Maybe, just maybe, Tatyana is Her gift to you for the same reasons."

"You think I need healing?"

"There isn't a person on this planet who couldn't stand for some healing. But witches, those of us who have to see hard things and make hard sacrifices in the name of the Mother and all things good, I think She rewards us for the

things we do for Her. I think it keeps us honest and faithful.
And sane."

"I don't feel very sane at the moment," Hunter remarked,
dropping his empty glass on the table.

"Right. I hear that's normal when there's a woman involved," Ryce chuckled.

Tatyana didn't sleep.

She couldn't. Not while knowing her brother and Kaia
were traveling in this horrible storm completely unaccounted for. Not while knowing there were evil witches out
there who would do anything to get hold of a Willow Coven
member. It was bad enough this witch Asher was completely
unaccounted for. Now Dimitre, too?

Strangely, of great comfort was the fact that no one else
seemed able to sleep either. She'd been given her own rooms,
but she was too restless to stay in them. So, she wandered all
over the house. One after another she encountered Dimitre's
new friends, in various places doing the various things they
did for comfort. Annali was in the conservatory bent over
her beakers. She invited Tatyana in for an impromptu lesson
on potion making and how magic was used in the process.

Nox was playing billiards. This time she invited herself.
Konnie had taught her to play since she'd been tall enough to
reach the table and she really enjoyed giving Nox a run for
his money. She also enjoyed his irreverent personality and
the British native's love for storytelling. He told tales about
every one of his friends, and she knew them better for it already.

She purposely sought out Gracelynne when Nox said she
was awake in her rooms and that she wouldn't mind a visit at
all since she couldn't come down yet. So she paid that visit
and got to see the tragic courage of a woman lost. But instead of giving Gracelynne the sympathy of a stranger, she
treated the visit just like the others, as an opportunity to

learn from an incredibly gifted witch. Whether it was learning about magic or those within the house, no opportunity was to be wasted, she felt. Tatyana knew that there was a very real possibility any one of them could fall victim to the threat of war that hung silently over the house.

Hunter didn't see her again until the next morning. He had been aware of her the entire night, hearing her and glimpsing her through doorways and around corners. It was amazing, he thought with consternation, how two people stuck within the boundaries of the same house could actually manage to not meet. Wasn't she at all interested in making some form of contact with him? Some kind of recompense or apology or . . . *contact*?

There was no logic to it. No matter how big the house was, it seemed unlikely that they wouldn't trip over each other at some point. Especially when one of them was purposely looking for an opportunity to run into the other.

Tatyana always seemed to be with someone else. However, since he wanted her to get to know his family, he didn't disturb her when she was engrossed in conversation or activity with one of them.

Or all of them.

There wasn't a single member of the household, except the still absent Asher, whom she hadn't talked to during the course of those hours. Now it was just before noon and Hunter could hear her laughing in the library, and it was Ryce's deep voice egging her on into further gales of the luscious sound. Every time she laughed, it cut through him like a siren's song, calling to his every last nerve and vital function. His heartbeats and breaths quickened, his skin shimmered with anticipation. He imagined outrageous and decadent things about her laugh and how he'd coax it out of her while she rolled across his bed in her delight. Just the thought of it shortened his patience to a near zero.

Unable to tolerate not seeing her any longer, he impatiently pushed into the back entrance of the library, edging

around the far stacks until he could see her at last. She was
on her back on a brown leather couch, her long, beautiful
hair hanging over its edge, gleaming with the burnished gold
hue of the lights. Ryce sat on the end of the couch where her
feet lay. Her feet were crossed at the ankles, bare, and resting
by the heel of her bottom foot on Ryce's thigh. Ryce had a
casual hand around the top ankle, which was twitching
rhythmically back and forth.

Tatyana was, of all the worst possible things she could be
doing, casually sucking on a round lollipop. The confection
was the size of a golf ball. She gestured with the candied
stick as she spoke, sucking it between points she was making in the conversation.

"A lift," she was correcting her British compatriot, "is
what you get when you're a movie star past your prime.
When your face or boobs sag." She ticked the pop back and
forth between her breasts for emphasis, although there was
positively nothing sagging about the fully taut globes that
were, even without benefit of a bra, exactly where they ought
to be. "It's called an *elevator*."

"And a flat is what you get when the lift on a movie star
goes awry?" Ryce queried devilishly.

Tatyana immediately tore into peals of laughter, her
pretty toes lifting up to nudge Ryce in a pectoral muscle as
punishment when she couldn't speak to him for lack of breath.
Ryce was chuckling and fending off her pedicure. The
laughter calmed and the lollipop began to slide in and out of
her mouth again as Ryce extolled the virtues of the Queen's
English. Then Tatyana pooh-poohed the Queen and war was
declared. Before Hunter knew it, she was calling Ryce a
limey bastard and telling him to go back to his bloody Queen
if she meant so bloody much to him. Ryce told her bloody
Americans have no right to use words like *bloody* and *limey*
and he dumped her off the couch and over onto the floor so
her belly was down and her backside was up and she was
cussing and giggling and trying to talk around the candy in

her mouth just as Ryce leaned over her, drew back his hand, and whacked her on her bottom quick and sharp.

Tatyana squealed, laughed, spat garbled invectives, and struggled to right herself as Ryce threw a leg over her knees and pressed a hand onto her back to hold her in place while he whacked her again. Tatyana was red-faced and screaming with laughter and curses, the lollipop removed as she hurled all over her shoulder and tensed in preparation for his next assault.

There was a resounding smack, but Tatyana was surprised when she felt nothing and suddenly Ryce let her go. She wriggled around until she was face up and saw Hunter and Ryce looming over her, Hunter's hand gripping Ryce's in what looked like a very painful grasp as the two men stared hard at each other. Hunter looked furious, his cobalt gaze spitting raging fire at his friend. Ryce was struggling to maintain his composure, but Tatyana could see he was disturbed to be nose to nose like that with Hunter. Tatyana realized that Hunter had stopped Ryce from striking her and was now letting the other man know how much he resented him putting his hands on her body.

He was jealous.

That meant trouble. After getting a blow by blow from Annali about her own behavior in the conservatory the day before, Tatyana knew it as sure as she knew her name. Hunter looked as if he had been pushed to the edge of a mighty cliff, and someone had just snuck up behind him and screamed. Tatyana flew to her feet, flinging her body between the two men with a laugh and a hasty, "Hey, hey, Hunter, how's it going? I was just coming to look for you. I was wondering if, while we're waiting for Dimitre, you could show me a spell or"—she grunted as she pushed against his powerful frame with all of her weight and leverage—"two. Don't want,"—she managed a half-inch of movement before she gave up being subtle and bored her shoulder into his solar plexus and put everything she had into shoving him away from Ryce like a linebacker pushing back a training dummy—"to waste the opportunity." She panted when he finally lost balance and stepped back two steps. "Whew!" She grabbed his arm, linked hers through and began to tug him toward the main doors, waving Ryce off surreptitiously; glaring at the witch when he had the balls to smother a chuckle while Hunter was still within punching distance.

Tatyana was all but exhausted by the time she forced Hunter out of the main doors with a shove. She slammed the doors closed and pulled her treat from her mouth with a pop as she glared at Hunter.

"Are you out of your mind? What were you going to do, punch your best friend in the nose?"

"That," he hissed, "would have been the least of his injuries. And while you are questioning my actions, Lolita, you might want to look at your own behavior!"

"Lolita!" Her hand fisted around her lollipop with annoyance right before it landed on a thrust-out hip.

Hunter groaned inwardly. She had no idea how fetching she looked standing there like that in her bare feet, with her red toenails peeping out beneath the swing of the skirt of yet another dress she had borrowed from someone. Not to mention she was still rosily flushed all over from her earlier play and laughter.

"Do I look like some overscxed teenager to you?" she demanded.

Yup. She surely did. Especially with that damned lollipop in her hand. She was at least a decade his junior, probably barely in junior high school when he had left the coven. She was tall and beautiful, undeniably a full-grown woman, but there was an unquestionable innocence to her personality and her youth. She was able to laugh with that lack of restraint that told him she hadn't yet known any of the real heartaches of the colder adult world. The ones that made even your laughing moments come up a little short and speculative.

As for oversexed . . .

She looked like a siren. A beauty only myth could capture and no man could bear to look away from. Certainly not this man, Hunter thought with agony as his body instantly rippled with awareness and very blatant need. Her eyes skimmed over him with that hooded, sultry contemplation that she didn't even know she was employing. She held every inch of her body in constant sensual motion, small shifts so subtle that they could be seen only in the overall effect, but the impact was felt like an earthquake shaking his libido. Her hair flowed around her in wild streaks of color ranging from blatant cherry to mahogany. She reeked of sex. The potential of it; the nature of it. She smelled of it, he noted as he inhaled deeply of her. Musk, promise, and femininity. The sweet scent of the sugar melted on her tongue, the flowery aroma of shampoo in her hair, all a lure that taunted.

Tatyana's indignation evaporated as Hunter leaned nearer and nearer with every increasingly labored breath he took. The intensity in his indigo eyes kicked up her pulse and made her breath stop in her throat. She bumped back into the wall behind her and his hands lifted to box her in by pressing to it on either side of her shoulders. She saw him inhale, long and deep, his eyelids lowering slightly with a flicker of blatant pleasure as he came always closer to her. Her mouth was gaping slightly in shock, though she didn't realize it until he let his electric blue eyes rest on her lips. Before she could close them, his mouth lowered to hers, his tongue darting out in a slow, sensual sweep across her bottom lip. He moved back, tasting what his tongue had found, his sexy mouth gleaming wetly at her as he did so.

"Sweet," he murmured, reminding her that her mouth was covered in sugar.

"It's the . . ." She gestured with the lollipop vaguely, holding it between them.

"Taste it," he bade her, the rough vibration in his voice making it sound like a growl.

Suddenly, finally, she understood. Fiery intent lit the jade gems of her eyes, a sultry smile curved her lips. As erotic as her unconscious sensuality was, when she put effort behind seduction it blew Hunter completely away. She took the time to twirl the pop deftly between her fingers, and then slowly rested it against her lower lip. She rubbed it there, to and fro, for a smallest moment of motion, and then her tongue came out to flick against it suggestively. Hunter's hands fisted against the wall, knuckles and tendons creaking with the violence of his grip on himself as his eyes followed every motion of her wicked mouth. She kept her eyes on his even though his focus shifted back and forth between them and her mouth. Finally, she fully sealed her lips around the round candy and sucked the globular sweet deeply into her pink mouth. When it popped back out at last, sugar and wetness coated her lips and her tongue came out to lick it away.

Hunter didn't give her the opportunity to steal the treat from him. He swooped in to claim her, wrenching her mouth under his savagely as his hands sank into her hair and his body slammed hers up against the wall. The lollipop hit the floor with a clunk as her hands came up to clutch at his back and shoulders.

Tatyana felt the barbaric claim of his tongue plundering her mouth and she welcomed him with equal wildness. Sugarcoated and heated, she took him prisoner in her mouth, sucking on his tongue and dancing a needy tango with him until she made him groan. Her mouth was full of the rough, masculine sound. His hips met hers, grinding forward with a deft shift that made his hunger so clear. She felt him throbbing with it right through both of their clothing, so full and so much like smelted steel as he rubbed, hotly aroused and in need, against her. Then his hand skimmed fast and blistering down her body, making her twitch and strain for him as he swept over her breast, her belly and then insinuated his hand between their melded hips. His palm cupped her, seeking heat and finding it, his fingers spreading over her through her dress, making her gasp and surge up on her toes excitedly. A tornado of fire swirled up through her, starting at the center point of his touch and whirling wildly across branches of nerves she'd never known she had. Her belly clenched and liquid slid from her body in hot invitation, drawn to his seeking fingers.

Then he pulled that glorious contact away, grabbing her thigh instead and dragging it up along the outside of his own, settling himself against her completely in an invasion of rock-hard flesh and scorching heat. His kiss plundered her mouth, his erection ravaged her through their clothing with an all-too-keen stroke and thrust that had her gasping into his mouth when the eroticism of it began to overwhelm her. He was exhaling hard and harder into her mouth as he rocked forward and she reached to meet him with a wild undulation of female sensuality. Her hands joined the effort, gliding down to grasp the tight, straining muscles of his ass, pulling him forward and urging him on.

Suddenly Hunter's hands dove beneath her skirt, shoving it up her thighs to her hips so he could stroke his hot palms over her bottom, his fingers curling around the fabric of her panties. He was going to pull them away. He was going to free himself as well. He was going to put himself inside of her and thrust so deeply he would send shockwaves through her entire body. He was going to make her scream his name until the whole damn house came running.

Hunter ripped himself away from her when the sheer violence of that need left him shaken and shocked. He was leaving them both blind and breathless as he staggered back until he hit the opposite wall of the corridor, but she had reached much too deep inside of him. Somehow, she had tapped into the part of himself that he reserved for his duties as Sentinel, the brute . . . the primal warrior.

"I must be mad!" he rasped hoarsely, bending weakly at

the waist as he struggled for breath. "The more I keep apart from you the more I want you, Tatyana." Hunter resisted the urge to roar like a savagely wounded beast even though that was exactly how he felt. "I can't . . . I can't do the right thing! I don't know what it is!"

His honest and devastating pain hurt her, like blunt, stinging slaps of reality. She didn't mean to upset him and torture him. In fact, she'd set out to avoid doing exactly that. She had avoided him to ease his need for her, to learn about the people he loved . . . and to learn about him from them. She didn't want to be just a bed partner to him. He had been right about that. She suspected that he had something so special within him, waiting for her to uncover, and she wanted so badly to find it. She wanted to know who he truly was. What his dreams and wishes and hopes were. No one here could tell her those answers because he had been gone so long they hardly knew him anymore. At least, not outside of the essentials of his personality that would never change. He was the only one who could tell her all she wanted to know, but every time they came close, their physical bodies overruled their minds. Purpose blurred. As did boundaries. His honor pained him greatly, and she adored him for how hard he fought to treat her well, but they couldn't get anywhere if this hunger was always going to overwhelm them.

The intensity of the attraction was supposed to have eased, he said, the first day promising to be the worst, but it had done just the opposite. She could see it in every part of him. Hunter was straining for control with a fury that had not been there yesterday. She longed to go to him, to comfort him, but she would be no comfort to him if she closed the distance between them.

Tatyana wanted to close that distance more than anything. Her heart throbbed with the need to do it, as did her body, and she didn't hesitate to admit it. She needed to be with him. In all ways possible.

Suddenly Tatyana knew a moment of pure stillness. Even

her heart seemed to go quiet, although she knew very well that it still raced to the tempo of their passion. Then, in that self-silent instant, clarity rang a gentle bell through her mind. As it grew in resonance, she felt the bracing hit of it like she had felt the shock of the snow Hunter had thrown her into the day before.

He is a white witch, her mind whispered logically, *and white witches do not control their familiars.* Apprentices. Using the word *familiar* was something of a misnomer. Familiars were slaves, controlled completely by another for their own selfish ends. Hunter would not . . . *could* not be party to anything remotely like what dark warlocks put their emerging witches through! So why . . . ?

Why on earth would he treat the volatile chemistry between them as anything other than it was? It was powerful, perhaps even a bit wild as it was enhanced by their raw sensuality, but she could feel the conduit between her nascent power and his masterful resources, and she had to believe . . . no, she was positive she would know if she were being manipulated in any way.

She wasn't being played by mystical forces. These forces were purely natural. The only manipulation going on here was in Hunter's own mind as he tied himself into knots with laces of nobility and integrity that she suspected might just be more about protecting himself, rather than about protecting her.

Tatyana smiled widely, straightening from the wall and smoothing her clothes into place. She knelt quickly to retrieve her candy from the floor, wiping a hand over the wood to remove any stickiness. She headed for the nearest bathroom without looking back and washed her hands after throwing out the lollipop. She didn't need to turn or look in the mirror to know he was looming in the doorway, staring at her with covetous, famished eyes, his hands gripped closed in restraint.

Her fresh understanding of the connection between them

allowed her a new freedom, but it was freedom he didn't yet share. He was still bound by the idea that her reactions, as well as his own, were influenced.

Hunter's eyes, already riveting, swept around like those of a lazy predator sizing up an approaching mate. Then there was the moment when he shifted to the stalker, the moment she knew damn well that he had marked her for his own. Even now, in the doorway, as he leaned his forearms up against the frame, his eyes were fixated on her like those of his namesake. A hunter. Born and bred and determined to take down his target.

Her.

All she needed now was to coax him into catching her. Since he was the only one who knew the truth of who he was now, in the present and not ten years ago, he was the man she must spend time with in order to get to know him better. But besides that, she was eager to begin learning what direction she would be going in as a witch. From all she had seen, there were almost no two witches alike in the entire house, except maybe Ryce and Hunter. They were both Spell-casters. Annali was an Alchemist. Kaia a Healer. Gracelynne was an Elemental witch, able to call elements by will without spells. Lennox called himself a Symbolic witch, able to cast magic by drawing symbols in the air or on surfaces. Dimitre, amazingly, was known as a Tempus witch. A witch who could control time, or jump his consciousness into the past memories of another person. A way to observe history without influencing it. She knew now there was a seventh member of the house, a witch called Asher, who was off somewhere unknown to the rest of the coven at present. Ryce said Asher was a Spiritus witch, a witch who could call spirits and things beyond 'the Veil' to do his bidding.

Where would her power lie? What would her abilities be? There was truly only one individual who could show her. Yet, how could she learn when he was avoiding her? There was only one solution, and that was to stay as close to

Hunter Finn as was humanly . . . and even supernaturally . . . possible.

The thought pleased her and she smiled a wicked, tempting smile as she angled her face away from the mirror so he couldn't see it and try to decipher her thoughts. Her heart was racing in her breast. Hunter might be infused with animalistic passion, but at his core he was a principled man who couldn't live with himself if he thought he'd done something to harm another. That was why he kept doing what seemed to be the impossible, pulling away from her when he so clearly didn't want to. How to surmount that logic? she wondered.

"Hunter," she said softly, keeping her face averted, her back to him, "what is the difference between what's happening between us and when a witch controls his familiar?"

Tatyana might as well have slapped him across the face, that was how much the query startled and stung. His head even jerked back as if she'd actually struck a blow. Apparently she *did* feel she was being controlled after all, he thought bitterly. Frankly, he couldn't blame her. It was why he couldn't even resolve the conflict within himself. He could see no lines between what was genuine desire and what was the influence of their magical bond.

But there *was* a difference, he amended with a frown, between the passion passing between them and the depravity of what he had known dark witches to visit on their familiars. He refused to have her equating the two and making this into something black and evil. It was a little out of control, yes, but its origins were genuine and not dissolute.

"What passes between us is a mutual attraction, Tatyana. When a warlock forces his will on his familiar, she's like a puppet to him. A doll whose life and spirit are repressed. She is forced to merely watch from behind distant eyes while her body is violated. Or, worse, the warlock can temporarily convince the familiar she lusts after him. He can make her crawl and beg and . . ." He stopped, swallowing hard and looking down at the tiles of the floor angrily. "He can turn an innocent into a whore, make a slut of a virgin, and make her think she loves every minute of it until the crushing moment he releases awareness back to her."

"I see. So I'm lucky then that my rather whorish behavior of late can only be blamed on myself."

Hunter sucked in a shocked breath and burst into the bathroom, finally crossing the threshold he'd been using as an invisible barrier. He came up behind her and grabbed her shoulders roughly. He spun her around and forced her to look up at him with a palm clasping her chin, fingers and thumb pressed into her face tensely.

"You are *not* a whore! You wouldn't have the first clue how to be one! Is that how I've made you feel? Do I make you feel used and . . . and devalued? Just a body with no personality, unique existence, or special soul? Because I will damn myself straight to hell if I have! I never meant—!"

"Shh . . . no . . ." she soothed him quickly, her hand coming up to cover his mouth, cutting off the stream of self-loathing before it could get any worse. "No, honey, no. You haven't got it in your soul to treat a woman in such a terrible way. Why in the world would you ever think that? Why would you think any intention you've had toward me would be a bad thing? Because our sexuality is being magnified? Because who we are is being magnified? Don't you see, Hunter? If a scientist scraped you up and put you under a microscope, he could magnify you a thousand times, a hundred thousand times, and all he would ever see is Hunter. He would only see you. The good in you. If there is no evil in you, how can it possibly be made larger?

"If you want me, Hunter," she whispered, her fingers releasing his mouth in order to trace its fullness and beautifully sculpted lines, "and it's magnified a thousand times, it's still only you wanting me. Me wanting you. No wickedness, no badness, no deceptions or mistakes that will ever need apology. Do you understand me? You're not a warlock, and

I'm no slave. You sacrificed yourself to make very sure of that. I'm free to decide, just as you are. So *decide*, Hunter, once and for all. Not in the heat of the moment when you might feel guilty later, when your thoughts are hazed over, but now, when your feelings are all focused on protecting me. I trust you to listen to the honesty inside yourself."

Hunter looked down into her eyes. Strange, how right before a moment of truth there was first a mad rush of chaos. As he focused on the pretty jade gaze waiting patiently for him to wade through his confusion, she seemed, suddenly, so wise and at peace, as if she knew a secret he didn't understand. But he wanted to understand. He needed to. He felt that truth beating in his brain like a drum.

He had continually devalued this connection between them, treating it as something base and unnatural that must be stopped, but the bitter taste of that truth didn't set well with him. It never really had. Because the reality of the matter was this connection was as legitimate a fruit of nature as his magic was. If the enhanced nature of it came through his magic, it was still coming through a source of *white* magic, and Hunter didn't want to doubt the purity of his power.

So . . . perhaps it was the past looming over him, influencing his choices with her? Was he afraid of repeating the same mistakes he had made so many years ago when last he was in this house? Hunter wanted to believe he had learned from that long-ago tragedy and wouldn't repeat it.

Chaos calmed to the sudden stillness of understanding as he realized it was all about fear. He had never claimed to be a fearless man, but was he letting it control him? Through their magical link, she had a direct line into the heart of everything that he was. He felt her pushing into places no one else had ever had access to within him. If she continued getting so close, so deep inside of him, what would she see? What would she feel? What would she think of the savage within him that wanted her with such blind craving and intensity? What would she think of the witch who was, for all intents and purposes, an assassin for his coven? What of the man and his past saturated with mistakes?

Despite these fears, a part of him realized he needed desperately to finally pull someone in that close. He was so tired of his solitary ways, and weary of fearing no one would ever truly know and accept him, mistakes and all. And it scared the holy hell out of him to think he could possibly want or need another human being so very much. He had essentially been wandering the world without any deep attachments for a decade. Now he'd stumbled back into the nest that had birthed him *and* his worst mistakes. So far, his family here had given him blind love and acceptance, just as family should. But what Tatyana offered was neither safe nor comfortable. It was well beyond that blindness of a family who no longer truly knew him.

Yet, he found he craved his connection to her just as deeply as he had longed to return home. He craved *her*. He needed her, and wanted to be needed by her. No, not just physically. How it had gotten beyond that so quickly he didn't know, but so it was. Where it would end was also a mystery, but these were natural human mysteries, not magically induced ones. Magically enhanced perhaps . . . but not magically generated.

Wise little witch, he thought as he looked at her. Age and wisdom, it seemed, didn't necessarily go hand in hand. Too young for him? Hardly that. Too smart for him was more likely, he thought with a chuckle. She smiled at him when she heard the soft laugh, her eyes sparkling knowingly. Goddess, she was breathtaking.

"I'm a damn lucky man," he murmured to her.

"And don't you ever forget it," she rejoined.

He laughed at her, catching up her hand so he could bring her palm to his lips. "There is so much more to you than meets the eye. You've charmed me, and my coven, all in a day or two."

"Well, I'm a stray. Good-hearted people can't resist a stray," she said with an easy shrug.

"A very good point." Hunter began to kiss the tips of her fingers slowly, one at a time. "So, angel, you've duly conquered my reservations." He smiled a wicked little smile that darkened his gorgeous eyes to a sinful shade of sapphire. "What would you care to do with me now?"

"I'm so very glad you asked."

Chapter Thirteen

The door to the bathroom slammed shut as Hunter stumbled back into it, all of his grace abandoned for the sake of trying to maintain balance. Tatyana had turned into a snake, a serpent with a sinuous body, taut muscles, and a voraciously curious mouth. She had stripped his chest of his shirt, the article of clothing hanging useless off his arms while her hands slid eagerly over his skin, molding willingly to every contour and muscle she could find. Her mouth, meanwhile, was drifting teasingly over his left nipple, her tongue and breath just barely ghosting over the sensitive spot until he was hissing a soft, sibilant sound between his clenched teeth.

His hands tangled blindly in her glorious auburn hair and he coaxed her head back until he had her mouth under his. The eager sweep and flick of her tongue filled his brain with explosions of pleasure. The kiss became so rough that their lips bruised against each other, though without any complaint from either of them. Hunter finally released her captive head and sought the curves of her writhing body as they slithered against him in a sensual crush that overloaded his senses.

Tatyana felt his palms rushing down the curve of her

spine, cupping and gripping her ass and drawing her in tight to his solid body. He burned with heat from head to toe, making her skin mist damply and her breath pant in short spurts into his mouth. He had eased his possessive kiss into long, lapping strokes of his tongue, making it clear how much he savored the taste and feel of her mouth. She was dizzy with the sheer sensuality of his kisses, but more than that, she was provoked.

The deep 'v' of her neckline and the soft material of her dress allowed her to pull it off her shoulders, wriggling it down until her breasts were plumped out above the neckline just to the line above her tightened nipples. She drew one of his hands from her backside and placed it on her left breast, letting him feel the warmth and luscious fullness of it, the tease of the nipple hidden just beneath. He tried to pull back and see her, but she renewed the fervor of their kiss instead and the persistent massage of her body against him until she was fairly sure he didn't know which end was up and couldn't figure out which curiosity or fantasy concerning her wild body to fulfill first.

Once she had Hunter's every sense occupied in a whirl of sexually charged input, Tatyana slid her hands down over his ribs and traveled the fine contours of his hard belly. She felt the muscles beneath her fingertips contracting tighter and tighter the lower she went. By the time she passed his navel, he was completely tensed and breathing as though he'd run a marathon. Her fingers slipped past his belt, beneath his waistband, then curled around the slim leather from both the back and the front, gripping it tightly on either side of the shiny buckle.

Hunter could feel her knuckles rubbing teasingly against the skin and fine hairs of his lower belly, her fingertips just a breath away from touching him with real intimacy. He was hard as hell and confined only by the fabric she held. He should say barely confined. He could feel the warmth of her fingers—that was how very close she was.

"You're teasing me," he accused hoarsely.

She had been industriously kissing his throat while he had pulled back to fight for breath. Now she lifted her busy mouth in order to smile up at him provocatively. "Am I?"

He felt her fingernails tap against his skin in a brief, taunting flick of her fingers. "Yes!" he said tightly, closing his eyes because he couldn't bear looking at that catlike sexual confidence she radiated for a minute longer without doing something extremely barbaric like screwing her brains out on the cold tile floor of a bathroom. "We should go upstairs . . ." he tried to suggest reasonably.

Hunter suddenly felt his belt sliding free of the loops of his slacks, the quick slide and crack of the leather forcing his eyes open just as the metal clink of the belt hitting the tile mingled with the echoing of their quick breaths. Her wide, compelling eyes somehow showed both innocence and decadence all at once, captivating him completely as her lashes lowered to hide all clues to impending mischief.

"Upstairs," Tatyana murmured silkily, "is so far away."

He could hardly argue with that.

Especially when he felt the distinct motions of her deft fingers sliding down his zipper and then gliding against his hips as she gave release to his swollen erection by pushing away all the material confining him. His gratitude came out as a ferocious invective, but by the delight in her laugh it was clear she understood him perfectly. She rested her forehead just at the top of his breastbone, her face tilted downward so she could look at him. Hunter could barely hold a breath and he was shaking with the intense stabs of hot arousal she was instigating so cleverly.

"Hmm," she hummed with blatant appreciation in her tone. "My, my, I *am* a lucky girl," she mused breathlessly.

Hunter groaned at the implication of her candid observation and a streak of heat surged through his body, pulsing through his shaft in a visible throb of reaction. Tatyana made a tiny little gasping sound of delight and laughed breathily with pleasure. Then, finally, she touched him. Warm, silky fingertips against hot skin wrapped over steel. She wasn't tentative so much as she was fascinated and savoring every delicate sensation. She started at the flushed tip, tracing the cap with a maddening thoroughness. Hunter's nerves sang a chorus of insanity, his entire soul throbbing with want. Wanting *her*.

She lost patience with tiny details and he was suddenly helpless as his aggressive little minx took the hot length of him into both of her hands, exploring him with sure, curious strokes that stole his breath and his reason far, far away.

To Tatyana, he was beautiful. It was such a delicious sensation, holding him in her hands and at her mercy. The rush of it, the feel of him, sent heat washing wetly through her whole body. There was a telling throb of demand between her legs, her clit fairly twitching with interest and her hollow body whispering fiercely of cravings too long suppressed. His legs were braced apart enough to allow her to move over him, straddling his thigh just enough to coax friction against her heated sex. She wriggled against him impatiently, but she took her sweet time stroking her way to fabulous familiarity with him. He was lengthy and beautifully shaped, but also so deliciously thick. Within her hands he was burning and rigid, every firm pulse of desire in his body reflected in a surge of vigorous blood to the already heavily engorged length of cock.

And suddenly she wanted to lay claim. Her entire body demanded it along with her mind and soul. *Take him. Devastate him with pleasure. Make him yours*. As she contemplated the impulse, her fingernails raked through the thatch of black curls from which he sprang, stimulating a shiver through him that made her smile with feminine dominance. Her hands closed around him and a sound of response struggled out of him roughly. *Yes*.

Yes.

Hunter's head dropped back against the door with a soft

thump as he was besieged with swirls of heat and stabs of
pleasure that exceeded anything in his former knowledge.
She shaped him and caressed him, her face tilted down still
so she could watch herself touching him, and that alone was
an incredible turn-on. He swelled to outrageous proportions
under the silky stroke of her eager fingers, until his pulse
roared in his ears, tension clutching him in violent anticipation. He groaned savagely as she flicked her thumb over the
moistened tip of his prick. His head rolled to the left and he
caught their reflection in the large mirrors along the wall just
as she dropped down before him.

"Tatyana!"

He meant it as a warning, for all the good he thought it
would do. He wasn't afraid to admit that he didn't know how
much more of this he could bear. He had been pushing the
envelope of control for two days now, and he was quite close
to losing hold of what little restraint he had remaining. But
one look at her sly features in that mirror and he knew she
was determined.

Tatyana was too excited and too delighted to pay him any
heed. She liked the idea of giving him so much pleasure he
wouldn't be able to see straight. She loved how he felt, heavy
and bold in her hands, the slightest stroke of her fingertips
causing him to shudder. She slid one hand over his hip as she
took a moment to nuzzle his belly. He smelled so good, so
manly and sexy, the tang of musk and aroused male tickling
her senses delightfully. She felt his hands clutching her hair
and scalp spasmodically, more clues to his excitement and
loss of all senses other than those she was manipulating.

Tatyana knew what *he* had wanted. Lovemaking and romance and sweetness. She wanted that, too. Later. She was enjoying herself far too much now. She released a laugh against
the sensitive skin of his lower abdomen that made him dance
with stimulation beneath her lips. She slid her hand up the

beautiful length of him, tracing a nail along bulging veins as she purposefully exhaled a hot breath across the head of his erection. It was a sexy little warning; a preview of what was next on her to-do list.

"Angel . . ." Hunter gasped just a second before a non-angelic tongue flicked across sensitive nerve endings, setting them afire with violent throbbing pleasure that was incredibly close to agony.

Hunter swore, then groaned, then growled out her name as her lips closed around him and her industrious tongue began swirling eagerly around and around the head of his cock. With so much of her hair bunched up in his hands, he found himself forced to look into the mirror if he wanted to see her as she tortured his body. He sucked in a staggering breath as he caught sight of her blissful expression an instant before she made a perfect seal with her mouth around him and drew him deep within.

Heaven. Right there on earth in the incongruous setting of a slightly chilly bathroom. It was quite the concept and Hunter appreciated it with the numbness of thought that came when one's brain was completely focused on sensory input. Tatyana pulled back playfully, right on the very brink of releasing him, and then her snug hand was sliding over his moistened shaft until it met up with her teasing lips and tongue.

And that was just about the last detail he was going to remember with any clarity. That and the understanding that she was really, really enjoying herself. Enjoying her supremacy over him and his raging body. *Well, more power to her*, Hunter thought numbly. At that point, he could only kick back and enjoy the journey. She was clearly determined, and she definitely had the skill to override his opinion on the matter. Tatyana proved her talent by working up a perfect rhythm between the draw of her devilish mouth and the stroke of her hand until Hunter was blinded with bliss and drenched in sweat.

"Oh, baby," he groaned helplessly, stringing together curses and exclamations of his building pleasure as his hips moved blindly into her intensifying tempo. "Tat . . . by the Lady, *Tatyana!*"

It was meant as the ultimate warning, his grip in her hair tensing, and he thanked all the power of the universe that she heard and understood him. She freed him from the torture of her perfect lips and together they dragged her up his body. Before she drew her next breath, Tatyana was the one with her back to the bathroom door. Hunter had swiftly reversed their positions and was simultaneously flinging away his clothing even as he was reclaiming her wicked mouth. His hard urgency was quite contagious, and she was a very eager helper as he grabbed hold of her by both thighs and drew her hard up his body until her knees hooked up past his hips and she crossed her ankles behind his back to make certain she stayed there.

Hunter was well into savagery by the time his hands plunged under her skirt and snapped the fragile material of her thong undies, stripping them away between heartbeats.

"You maddening, beautiful little . . ." he rasped against their conjoined lips.

"Yes, yes," she agreed almost dumbly. It was hard to make sense of anything when she craved him so badly. But even as she sought and wriggled invitingly against him, she was deprived of the satisfaction she required. For the moment.

Hunter eased back from her just far enough to slide his hand between their bodies and snugly into the juncture of her thighs. His smooth fingertips slipped against skin and moisture, following the contour of her lower belly and pubic bone, past the soft feminine mound completely denuded of hair. This only made his progress increasingly slicker as he went and he broke from kissing her to bury his face against her throat while he groaned soulfully.

"So damn wet and hot. Always so hot," he accused her. "In action or in actuality." He punctuated the observation by running his center finger right to the spot just above her sensitive and yearning clit. Hunter took a moment to ignore her straining and reaching body's demand for stimulation, drawing away and then close again, gauging her reactions with careful attention as she squirmed and begged him in wordless little moans of frustration.

Hunter was more than ready to take her. His engorged prick was dripping with the need of it, but now that he had taken charge, there were one or two curiosities he needed to satisfy first.

"In just under five minutes"—he breathed hotly into her ear—"I am going to be fucking you until we are both blind from the pleasure of it." Hunter shuddered when she whimpered out spastic little moans of need in acknowledgment. "But I think I want to drive you just a little insane first."

Hunter gently bit her earlobe as he skimmed over and past her flushed clitoris and sought for where he really wanted to be. She squealed as the pass ratcheted up her nerves with blunt stimulation, her knees tightening against his waist. His erection lay rigidly along the bare softness of her bottom, a teasing reminder of just how close he was to heaven, even as he circled the entrance of her vagina. Full wet lips bordered his path, but her position around him left her easy and wide open to him. It wasn't but an instant before he had a finger three knuckles deep inside of her.

"Hunter!" Tatyana gasped roughly, her hips shifting forward and her walls sucking tight against his finger as though she wanted to draw him deeper still. Hunter drew his head up so he could focus on her expression. Her heavy lids lifted to reveal darkened jade pupils full of the smoke of lust and pleasure. Her entire face was flushed pink and her mouth was swollen from their kisses as it opened in incoherent sounds of response and need. He watched her pretty features

tense with indefinable ecstasy as he began to draw his thumb
over and around the sensitive little nub of nerves so close to
where his finger slowly was joined by another.

Now he stroked her. From the inside, from the outside,
from every point he could reach that he knew gave her pleasure. Anything to see that wild abandon written over her
again and again. To feel it in her uninhibited body movements in his arms and against his body. When she arched her
back hard, it thrust her breasts up under his nose. It took only
an instant for him to tear back that final inch of fabric and finally suck a pebbled nipple deep into his voracious mouth.

The combination of stimulations made her cry out wildly,
made her tense like a taut bowstring. Close. She was on the
very edge. Hunter could feel it. "I need you to come, Tatyana," he groaned. "Come hard for me, angel."

"No!" she cried, clumsy hands fumbling at his thick shoulders, her nails scraping his skin even as she shook her head
in a wild cloud of red. She meant that she didn't want to
come without him, but all she could voice was the one word.
His fingers glided in and out of her body rhythmically now,
his thumb claiming permanent residence against her tender
clit. She could hear her own pulse roaring in her head and
the cadence was crying out for him.

"Yes," he hissed in dominant countermand. "Come now.
And then again when I plunge myself inside of you. Do it.
Let go. I need to see you . . . later I know I'll be too . . ."
Hunter growled roughly in frustration, pushing her entire
body hard against the door in emphasis. "*Come for me!*"

He was a man used to wielding power, and that moment
was no different. Tatyana gave in to his demand to leave him
behind, unable to hold on any longer in any event. She
gasped in a deep breath, tensed like she'd been instantly pet-
rified, her entire body reaching . . . reaching . . . and Hunter
knew one last stroke would shatter her. It was a slick, circu-
lar stroke of his thumb that detonated her. He watched her
mouth open and knew she was prepared to scream, and to

his surprise he was already muttering a wildly quick spell to soundproof the room. When she let go, it was his name that screeched out of her, or at least a reasonably close version of it, and he forced her to ride her crest as long as he could before she gasped and pushed a hand against him to signal overstimulation. He quickly withdrew his hand from her, but it wasn't in him to wait long enough for her to recover a single breath, never mind a few of her wits. Hunter took himself in hand and muttered an unintelligible apology just before he guided himself into her with a deep, crushing thrust.

She was still so tensed from her orgasm that he felt snug resistance the whole way. The surprise of his entrance also caused her to tighten around him reflexively. Hunter's mind rushed with colors and sensations and he almost missed her remark after her initial gasp of surprise.

"Oh God yes! It's about freaking time!" It made him laugh, a low chuckle against her cheek, which drew back into a grin beneath his lips. She giggled breathlessly even as she tugged him deeper forward with a squeeze of her subjugating legs. "Well," she said breathlessly, "it's true! I feel like I have needed you inside me forever!"

"And yet we've known each other barely forty-eight hours." Hunter punctuated the remark by slipping half free of the wonderful clasp of her body. "And now I'm going to blow your mind right here against the not-so-romantic bathroom door until you scream my name again. I think I liked that."

"Oh!" She gasped when he drove back into her. "Did I do that?"

"Yes. And Goddess knows you look gorgeous when you come all over me like that. This time, though, it's my cock you'll be baptizing instead of my fingers." Hunter punctuated the observation with a well-timed dive into her hot, tight channel, nearly driving himself incoherent in the process. Speech flew away as he braced his feet and pitched his weight forward into her again and again, his forehead resting against hers as she mauled his back and shoulders trying to catch a better grip that would not be achieved. In an instant all measure and cautions were obliterated, and he reached to grab hard hold of her soft, lush hips.

Tatyana felt like she was the center point of a firestorm. He was so hard as he drove himself inside of her, so incredibly overwhelming and hot. She'd never known she could feel so raw . . . so much like she was rushing toward the edge of the galaxy and wanting to leap off. He plunged deeper and harder, like a man obsessed, until her hands slipped off of him from the sweat of his body and her mind reeled back to that precipice she'd fallen from instants before he'd claimed her. He was holding her so tight she knew she'd have bruises to show for it come morning, and she didn't even care. He was building up in low, rough sounds of pleasure, one groan on top of another, rushing to release just as she was. She wanted it so badly. His release. She needed to feel him explode apart, completely under the sway of the magic their bodies produced together.

Suddenly he let go of her, shifting swiftly to catch her under her legs, hooking her knees into the crooks of his elbows and spreading her further open as he pushed her knees toward her shoulders. He and the door were the only forces holding her up now, but she couldn't even think about that. All she knew was that the shift had sent him singing squarely over her G-spot, and with more freedom of movement available to him, he double-timed his thrusts.

"Time!" He growled it like a command. "Time to come again, sweetheart. I feel it. In you. In me! Goddess!" He spilled out a harsh phrase in Romany and Tatyana felt suddenly as though she'd been struck again by lightning, only this time it was blue and pure, hot and beautiful. The strike of it locked her up in spasms so glorious she couldn't even draw the smallest of breaths. White light streaked across her vision and her sensitive hearing captured Hunter's massive roar of release even as his hips and body surged into her hard enough to potentially split the wood of the door that braced them. He was gasping and spewing Romany phrases or invectives . . . she couldn't decide which . . . even after he collapsed against her, his head on her collarbone and his lips on her skin. She was partially blinded by her hair and sweat, she couldn't seem to grab a breath for her life, but none of it mattered because she was swimming in obliterating bliss right along with him.

"I'm not leaving you," was the first thing he said that made sense to her.

"Well, good," she chuckled. "That's nice to know."

Hunter laughed softly at himself as well as her. "I meant for the moment. From . . . this connection." He slowly released the hold he had on her legs, stroking her thighs sensuously as he coaxed her legs around his waist again. He reached between them to caress the point where they were joined, making her gasp and tighten up again. Hunter hummed speculatively at her sensitive, anxious little body, running eyes already rediscovering hunger up to hers.

"Have you ever . . . ?"

"Felt so connected to another person?" she finished for him curiously. She reached for his face, taking it between both hands. "Never. Not even Dimitre. And I am sure I never will."

"How?" he asked hoarsely. "How are you so sure?"

"Are you saying that you aren't?" she countered, a sliver of apprehension entering the moment for the first time since the door had slammed shut.

"Oh no," he swore with low vehemence. "But I'm used to sensing things like acts of fate. I'm so aware of all that had to happen to put you here, in my sphere and in my arms, and I know I have some damn serious tributes to make to the Lady Goddess and our ancient Blessing Tree."

Tatyana didn't have a chance to question or reply to that. Hunter's head snapped up so suddenly that she could swear

she heard a ligament pop. She watched with morbid fascination and dread as his fine blue eyes narrowed and his thoughts
and attention turned obviously inward. He was sensing something and, by the accompanying frown, it wasn't something
pleasant or welcome.

"What is it?" she asked, her hands gripping his shoulders
nervously.

He looked at her, almost as if he had forgotten she was
there with him, a fact that normally would have filled her
with consternation, but she was too alarmed to be bothered
with her ego when she saw that look come over him.

"Asher has come home."

Chapter Fourteen

Tatyana was a little baffled as to why the arrival of a member of Hunter's coven would distress him so. He had hold of her hand as he drew her through the house and she smoothed self-conscious fingers through her hair and over her clothes, trying not to look as though she'd been engaging in illicit behaviors. He, she thought with consternation, looked as though he'd been doing nothing more important than reading a boring book.

She pushed her shallower concerns aside, however, as her apprehension at Hunter's mood and reactions began to take over. She could feel the tension radiating off him in powerful waves. She could almost feel the harsh cadence of dread in his pulse, even though his expression never reflected it. As Hunter pulled her into the main front hall, she was riddled with curiosity over what could cause that kind of a reaction in this kind of a powerful man.

As if a silent call had gone out, all the members of the coven began to enter the room from different points at the same time. Annali from the hall near the conservatory; Lennox from the rear hall; Hunter, Tatyana, and Ryce from the area of the library; and even Gracelynne from the stairs to the east. As Hunter drew her to a halt in the center of the hall, positioning her between himself and Ryce, Tatyana got her first good look at the coven member who had been MIA.

The Spiritus witch known as Asher wasn't as tall as the other males of the coven, but he was still a unique looking man and very attractive in his own way. Asher had an intensity about him, aquiline features set beneath a slightly wild cap of strawberry blond hair and only slightly darker brows. His eyes were a soft, doe-like brown, but the gentle color was belied by the dark expression brewing deep within them as he watched each member of his coven approach. His gaze settled at last on Hunter. A frown to match Hunter's tugged at an otherwise fine mouth, erasing the dimples that'd ghosted near his lips only a moment before as he'd watched the approach of the entire coven with bemusement. The witch gave his keys an absent jingle as he allowed a certain grimness to overtake his expression.

"My, my," he mused in a rich baritone, "what an interesting greeting this is. And so very . . . complete." He glanced at Hunter, appraising him for a long moment. "Welcome home, Sentinel," he greeted him, not sounding very welcoming. It was the first time Tatyana had witnessed anyone be anything other than warm and hospitable to Hunter, or anyone else within the coven for that matter. Yet, she wasn't all that surprised. On some level she had sensed this would happen. She had become aware that the coven wasn't entirely pleased with Asher, and that Asher wasn't going to be pleased to see Hunter.

"You don't look surprised," Hunter countered with directness.

"Don't I?" One of Asher's dark, red-gold brows cocked up an inch as a sarcastic curl rippled over his mouth. "Forgive me. Was I supposed to dance?"

"Hardly," Hunter said flatly.

Asher let his shadowy, assessing eyes fall on Tatyana and the fact that Hunter's fingers were laced tightly within hers. "Well now, isn't this cozy. You've come complete with your own entertainment and everything. Aren't you going to introduce me to your little"—he paused quite purposely to make sure his derision sank in—"friend?"

Hunter took an aggressive step forward, but his progress toward Asher was interrupted when Ryce and Lennox stepped between the two increasingly hostile men. Though he was physically stopped, Tatyana could feel the violent energy Hunter flung toward the other man. It was clear Hunter wanted to do serious damage to Asher for his barely veiled insult.

Tatyana was shocked. She didn't know what to make of what she was witnessing. There must be some connection between this awful meeting and the reason why Hunter had left all those years ago. It was the only thing she could figure.

"Asher"—Ryce spoke up sharply—"I wouldn't be testing anyone's patience right now if I were you. This woman is a guest of honor in this house and she will be treated as such, or you will answer to me. Provided I get to you before Hunter does," he added darkly.

"Hmm," the newly arrived witch said with lazy speculation. "I'm feeling a little hostility in the ranks."

"Where the hell have you been for the past five days, Ash?" It was Gracelynne who demanded the answer as she continued to limp down the remainder of the steps and struggled to get up in Asher's face. "Leaving the coven with no forewarning and no notice of where you would be? For five days? When you knew full well we were investigating a powerful dark coven? When you knew we were already short Dimitre and Kaia?"

For the first time something other than malice and sarcasm filtered across Asher's features. He looked over Gracelynne with slow, considering eyes for a moment, going very still as he took in all of her injuries and bruises.

"Gracie . . . what happened to you?"

"What happened? *What happened*?" she railed, her voice rising sharply. "I called and called for you, Asher McBride, that's what bloody happened!" The accusation struck like a whip, all the harder because the tough little woman's expression shattered with her emotions. "I screamed. I cried. I *prayed* for you to come! How dare you barrel in here spewing anger and righteousness at Hunter when you've done no better yourself, and *you* don't have the errors of youth and inexperience to blame it on!"

Tatyana watched as the brightest, tiniest little sparks began to snap through the tight curls of Gracelynne's ginger-colored hair. Hunter suddenly let go of her hand, reaching to gently take Gracelynne's shoulder under his comforting fingers.

"Gracie," he soothed, "don't upset yourself like this."

"I'm not upset, I'm bloody furious! He has no right. No right at all! You bastard. You selfish son of a bitch!" Gracie was leaning against Hunter's hold as she flung the abuse at Asher with all the fury a woman in pain could muster. The small sparks expanded to miniature snaps of lightning that jumped through her curls, forcing Hunter to lean out of the perimeter of the halo of electricity around her head.

"Gracie, you'll make yourself sick like this," he said more firmly, giving her a gentle little shake before braving her anger and conductive static to lay an arm of comfort around the small creature's shoulders. He embraced her snugly to his chest and immediately Gracie grasped at him and broke into a sound of complete pain and sadness too strongly weighted with misery to be called a simple sob.

Hunter was casting a look at Tatyana that begged for her understanding as he held the tiny witch in his embrace. But she wasn't truly paying attention to him. Instead, she was distracted by the brief, sardonic smile that twitched over Asher's lips. There was something strangely blasé about his expression and reaction. It wasn't what she would have expected from anyone in this coven. No more than she would expect it of one of her brothers.

Asher turned to look her dead in the eye for a long second, the contact giving her a momentary chill. Then he turned back to Hunter.

"So," he said coldly, "you waltz in here after a decade of abandonment, after leaving here in disgrace, and suddenly they're all ready to forgive and forget? Is that the deal, Ryce? I've been here for the past ten years, but he hasn't. Now he's just going to step right back into the shoes of Sentinel, and death and dishonor are to be swept under the rug?" He shook his head and laughed as if they were all out of their minds, and he was disgusted with the lot of them. "Look. It's simple. Either I start packing, or he stops unpacking. I'll give you a day or two to decide. Meanwhile, I need a drink. I'll be in my room."

With that and a neat dodge around any explanations of his whereabouts, Tatyana noticed, Asher pushed past the gathering and stormed up the steps leading to the east wing of the house. As soon as he had disappeared, Annali and Ryce both surrounded Gracelynne with gentle touches and sounds of soft comfort. Gracie remained most receptive to Hunter, however, and Tatyana thought she was beginning to understand why. When she'd been under attack, Gracie would have screamed, cried, and prayed, just as she had said, for every member of her coven. Not just Asher. Something had kept them all from hearing her, from rescuing her from the brutalization she had suffered. In her battered psyche, they had all failed her.

All except Hunter, whom she wouldn't have thought to call for because he had been gone for so long. He, by a chance of timing and fate, was the only one whom she felt had not let her down in her most dire moment of need. It was a convoluted logic at best, and a sure sign of the damage she'd suffered. Tatyana felt a pang of sharp sympathy for the other young woman. Especially since she had spent some time with her earlier and had begun to get a feel for her personality. She'd been subdued, but it was obvious that she normally had a sassy streak a mile wide along with a heavy dose of grit and courage. Gracie had flashed strong glimpses of these traits at Tatyana when she'd realized there was someone 'weaker' than herself in the household now. It had bolstered her flagging spirits to feel useful and protective of Tatyana in her neophyte state.

So now, the new witch made herself extremely small and faded back away as if she weren't even there. If she were to comfort Gracie, it would undermine the other woman's growing sense of strength. Tatyana wished to preserve that feeling between them, believing that it might be an avenue of healing for Gracelynne in the future. She was no psychologist, but she'd learned a lot growing up with twelve brothers and sisters, especially the art of navigating a fragile ego.

Soon Ryce fell away from comforting Gracie as well, leaving her to Hunter and Annie. They each wrapped themselves around a side of her petite body, and as a trio they slowly climbed the stairs back toward her suite in the east wing. They talked softly, their low tones echoing off the high ceilings as they went, and the remaining members of the coven watched until they disappeared.

Then Tatyana rounded on Nox and Ryce, her mouth pressed into a determined line and her hands fitted onto her hips. "Would anyone care to explain what the hell all that was about? Because I have to tell you, I'm mighty confused."

"Unfortunately," Ryce said carefully, "it's not our place to tell you about this. Hunter will have to tell you himself if he wishes to. You're our guest and a welcome apprentice, but there are some histories among the coven that . . . that . . ." He shrugged a shoulder a little helplessly.

"Are none of my damned business?" she supplied helpfully.

"Something like that," the Brit agreed.

"No. It's okay. I get it," Tatyana said with a shrug. "I'll just wait and see what Hunter says. Meanwhile," she sighed,

looking up the stairs after her absent information resource,
"I'm going to go relax somewhere alone."

"Just don't—"

"Go outside. Yes, I know," she said with an impatient wave
at Ryce that matched her tone as she climbed the stairs.

Tatyana walked slowly around the balcony, alternately
throwing pensive stares down at the empty room below and
stopping to study the excellent artistry of the 'Wonderland'
mural. It was extremely quiet, except for the sound of her
bare feet on the floorboards. She tried to imagine what it
would sound like, a room full of children created by these
magical people.

What terrible thing had occurred to drive so enormous a
wedge through this close-knit household? Until Asher's
wrench in the cogs, Hunter had seemed to be settling in.
Everyone had seemed to welcome him home. What had gone
so wrong so suddenly?

She needed to know. Not because of curiosity, but because it had so dramatically affected the life of the man who
had just become her lover. Why had he left ten years ago,
and what did that have to do with Asher? What wouldn't a
man let go of after a whole decade?

Tatyana left behind the sadly silent nursery and began to
walk the dark hallway. She'd had her share of feuds with her
siblings, most especially with Calina, whom she had never
understood completely, but never anything of so powerful a
nature that it would drive them, and subsequently their family, apart.

"You know, it just figures you'd be a redhead," Asher remarked from the shadows of a doorway several steps away.
Tatyana drew to a halt, his attempt at a lazy drawl putting her
on edge. There was something rigid and dangerous beneath
all that obvious casualness as he stepped away from the door

to lean one of his arms against the near wall. She could feel his eyes roaming very slowly over her, picking her apart and appraising her with blatant rudeness.

"Excuse me," she said, moving to push past him. His hand snapped out quick as a whip and grabbed her upper arm, stopping her cold. Then she saw the white flash of teeth as he smiled.

"My, oh my. You are much better built than I first thought. Tall and pretty. Great tits. I can see why Hunter likes you."

The way he said 'likes you' would have made a lesser girl feel dirty. Luckily, she was not that girl.

"Yeah, well, I'm told I have a mighty fine ass as well," she retorted tartly. "Both of which are two assets more than you can ever lay claim to."

Asher chuckled at that, a genuinely amused sound as he moved close enough for his body heat to radiate into her.

"Let me tell you a little secret, Red," he said softly, straightening up so he could reach out and stroke her cheek with two slow, gentle fingers. "Hunter isn't the saint he appears to be. He never was. Oh, I know you see how the others adore him and they probably visibly relish his return, but trust me, there's a reason why he was shunned by this coven for ten years." He reached out and flicked back her hair with his hand, but she refused to flinch away from the deceptive warmth in his deep brown eyes. "And boy is it a winner."

He made another sweep at her hair, and once he'd exposed her neck he leaned in and sniffed gently, his lips curling in a mocking smile. "You smell like him, you know. It's all over you. But I suppose it's nothing a shower couldn't cure, eh?"

Tatyana jerked back on her arm with all of her weight as suddenly as she could, but his grip tightened to a bruising degree, and with an awesome display of physical strength, Asher dragged her forward and shoved her through a nearby door, following after her and slamming and locking the portal as she stumbled for balance.

Feeling genuine panic now, she began to back away from him, a scream of terror building in her throat.

"Oh, don't do that," he chided, wagging a finger at her. "I just wanted to have a little uninterrupted discussion with you. No running away, no screaming or whatever feminine histrionics you can think of. After all, I'm a white witch. What do you think I'm going to do to you?"

Tatyana wanted to believe him. She wanted to believe an entire coven couldn't be fooled for all those years. This was just . . . some kind of repressed anger toward Hunter, and Asher was taking it out on her. He hadn't hurt her really, just intimidated her.

"I have nothing to do with any of this," she reminded him, backing up into the far wall of the room. It was someone's bedroom, she realized. Or potential bedroom. A nanny perhaps, considering the proximity to the nursery. The furniture was covered in sheets, showing it to be as yet unused as the nursery itself. "If you have an argument with Hunter, I know he would prefer you be straightforward with him about it."

"Oh, so you know him in ways other than the biblical sense?" Asher asked as he let his eyes roam the room briefly. Maybe she was crazy, but he seemed to look at the bed too long for her comfort. "And here I thought he was just fucking you."

"Hey!" she snapped. "Watch your mouth, you pig!"

It was a big mistake to yell at him. Tatyana's temper had popped off out of nowhere, and Asher clearly didn't care for it. He stormed across the room in three broad steps and she thought he was going to grab for her.

He did. Around her throat. Asher sealed one large hand around her windpipe and major neck arteries, his nails burrowing into her skin, and he yanked her off her feet as he slammed her back into the wall. Tatyana tried to breathe, but it was impossible. Her head struck the wall and she saw stars.

"Oh, wait," he said in her reddening face as his body

crowded against her, "you can't scream this way. I think I'd like to hear you scream."

She watched in terror as he murmured a quick spell, sending a flash of cobalt blue color around the room.

"There. Not only soundproof, but no pesky sensing of your emotions by the others or any other such nonsense. Now, let's work on that scream, eh?"

Asher released her and she fell to the floor, sucking in breath on a long, gagging gasp. She coughed until she thought she was going to throw up. Apparently, Asher had no patience for this.

"Come, come. Up you go."

Tatyana didn't know how she found the strength or breath, but when he leaned down to grab her, she whipped against him like a Fury, finding the flesh of his arm and biting down for all she was worth. He was the one to scream. At first. Then he used his free hand to grab her by her hair and yank her head back as if he would rip it from her neck. The instant she let go and cried out, he swung out a powerful foot and kicked her square in the center of her back. Pain exploded down her spine and across her chest. He flung her forward into the wood floor, and her face hit with a brutal smash. He kicked her again in the stomach, and again in the face. Tatyana had no clue how to cope with this brutal attack. All she could do was cry out under each blow. Soon, she was blank with agonizing pain and dizziness, just like a limp doll, too stunned to move.

Asher grabbed hold of her and flung her up onto the bed.

"No reason why we can't get comfortable," he said, chuckling to himself as if he'd made a fabulous joke. He arranged her limp limbs to his liking and hovered over her. "Now, I like a feisty girl as much as the next guy," he said, showing her the blood running down his bitten arm, "but if they see this, then they will know it was me in here. The whole point is to keep them guessing, now isn't it?"

Tatyana watched through swelling eyes as he fished into

his back pocket and stuck a square packet between his teeth. She realized it was a condom just as he grabbed for the skirt of her dress.

Tatyana screamed.

"Oh yeah, baby. Music to my ears! Never was into sloppy seconds, but this time, I gotta make the exception."

She tried to hit him, sobbing hysterically as she flailed and kicked out, but he just seemed to enjoy it as he wedged himself between her legs and unbuckled his belt.

"Aww, don't be like that. Look, honey." He held up the foil packet. "I'm practicing safe sex, which, I gotta say, some people around here obviously haven't been doing. But hey, maybe he doesn't mind getting his bastard on you, right? Unless you're on the pill? Are you on the pill? Cause I would just love to ride bareback. Been a long time. Yes? No? Not going to tell? Okay, how about we save the bareback until I flip you over? Hmm?" Asher laughed when her eyes went wide with increased horror and she tried to fight him off again, screaming as hard and as loud as she could, deafening her assailant. "Uh oh, I think someone's a virgin! Oh God, you just made me hard as a rock, honey. Wanna see?"

"Show *me*, you miserable little fuck!"

Hunter reached for Asher and, grabbing him by his clothing, tore him off the bed and flung him with all of his might into the wall across the room. Asher hit the wall and slid down hard to the floor. Giving him no time to recover, Hunter grabbed him again and punched him over and over across the face, pausing only to shake out his hand when he struck it wrong. To his shock, Asher used that instant to cast a powerful single-word spell, sending Hunter exploding back across the room, slamming the back of his body into a dresser near the foot of the bed.

The rage in the room was overwhelming. Tatyana's battered body reacted violently and she rolled to vomit over the side of the bed. Her head screeched with agony as more people ran into the room, adding to the cacophony of shock and horror. She saw Asher standing up in front of the window, throwing out his arms in a theatrical shrug.

"I guess this means I'm caught. Oh, damn."

Then he turned and flung himself straight through the glass of the window. Tatyana heard a woman scream, and a man shouted. Shadows rushed toward the window.

She lost consciousness.

Ryce, Nox, and Annali looked out of the window in horror at Asher's body lying in the snow at broken angles, blood coloring the white of it red.

"Sweet Mother, Ryce! Do something!" Annali screamed.

"Leave him," Hunter rasped as he picked himself up from the floor. "Let the bastard rot!"

"Hunter!" Annali gasped, aghast as she spun around.

That was when she saw Tatyana in the bed for the first time. Her hand flew to her mouth in dismay as the world of her nightmares seemed to come to life right before her eyes. Hunter staggered over to the bed to Tatyana, covering her beaten body with his own, gathering her to himself as unmitigated fury burned tears into his eyes. He cradled her gently, trying to comfort and inspect all at once, his throat clogging with emotion as he encountered her blood everywhere he turned. It was an image he had prayed never to come across again in his lifetime. He had seen it once, eleven years ago, when he and Ryce had rescued Annali from Evan's pit of hell. Now, to see it here, in Willow House . . . the idea was inconceivable.

"Annie," he croaked out as he rocked his burden in his embrace. "Annie, help me."

"Nox, see to Asher," Ryce instructed quietly. "If he survived, put him in stasis. I want answers for this. I don't know who did this, but you can damn well be sure it wasn't Asher McBride. Annali, help Hunter."

"What are you . . . ?"

"I'm going to find Kaia and Dimitre."

Annali nodded and hurried to the bedside where she was needed.

"Ryce, be careful. This could be exactly what they want," she warned him, panic causing her heart to race madly.

"If someone got to Asher, then they could have gotten Kaia and Dimitre. This girl is not going to wake up"—Ryce pointed to Tatyana and his voice broke—"to hear me say her brother is dead."

"No!" Annali gasped. "No! I would know! *She* would have known!"

"Annie!" Ryce barked. "You keep on task! You help her! I won't bring Dimitre home to a dead sister either!"

Annali swallowed back her sobs and nodded, tears spilling down her face. Ryce turned and leapt out of the same window Asher had, except he cast a flight spell that sent him soaring across the property. Nox followed suit, lowering himself gently to the ground in Asher's wake.

Annali turned to the stark tableau waiting for her. It wasn't until she really saw Hunter's eyes that she realized he had come to care for the little redhead far more deeply and swiftly than anyone had expected. She touched his shoulder gently, drawing his attention to her.

"Let's take her out of this room. It's freezing in here. She will need you, so let's bring her to your suite."

"Okay, what the hell? I finally get service and no one at the house is answering?" Kaia shook her head, the straight fall of her black hair rustling against the collar of her coat. "Something isn't right."

"I've been saying that since this whole damn trip started," Dimitre hissed. "No cells. No landlines. Being forced to stop overnight. I don't like it. It's too damn coincidental."

"Or . . . you're just the most paranoid person there is and now you've got me thinking the same way." Kaia sighed and rubbed at her forehead.

"What kind of Healer gets a headache, anyway?" he teased her, prompting her to backhand him in the chest just like his sisters always did. He laughed and kept his eyes on the road ahead.

"Any Healer who spends a week with you," she retorted. "I swear I can't wait to meet your sister. I have to meet any woman who put up with you for years and survived."

"Annali puts up with me just fine."

"Well, that's because she is blinded by love. When the sex and lust wear off, you'd better start to behave, buddy."

"The sex and lust are never wearing off," he chuckled. "Annali and I—oh shit!"

Dimitre slammed on the brakes when he saw something land in the middle of the road in front of the car. It was a huge mistake on such icy roads. The car started to skid and then, just as suddenly, it stopped. Kaia and Dimitre jerked in their seats from whiplash and they both grunted as their seatbelts tightened with bruising force. Dimitre was the first to recover, quickly checking on his passenger before looking out of the window.

"Ryce!"

"By the Lady!" Kaia hissed. "Let me out of here 'cause now I'm going to hit *him*!" She yanked her seatbelt free and scrambled out of the car as Ryce lowered his hands from the seize spell he had used to stop their skid. Dimitre was right behind her.

"Are you out of your mind?"

"You just took an eon off my life, Ryce Champion!" Kaia shouted.

"Kaia, Dimitre, something has happened and you are needed at the house immediately."

Kaia knew Ryce best, so she knew that when he spoke in that tone it meant something very, very bad had gone down.

Dimitre was instantly subdued as well, not as familiar with the tone, but taking it just as seriously because both the woman he loved and his baby sister were in that house.

"It's twenty minutes by car," Dimitre said, looking back at his vehicle.

"We may not have twenty minutes. I need you both. Now."

Dimitre whipped back around to face the High Priest, his heart beginning to thunder with dread. He could understand him needing Kaia, because she could heal, but there was only one of two reasons why Ryce would need him right away.

Annali or Tatyana.

"Take us. Now," he demanded.

"Hold on. This could feel a little strange," Ryce warned.

Then he cast a teleportation spell, sending the three of them on their way.

Braen was furious.

"Odessa!" he bellowed savagely as he stormed through Belladonna House. "Odessa, get your Goth ass down here right now, damn you!"

"I'm right here," she said dryly from a nearby alcove. She was leaning against the wall with her arms folded beneath her small breasts, dressed in a sheer black negligee that was split up the entire length of the gown to just below her crotch. She wore black patent leather knee boots with it, and a matching black garter and stocking set. Her hair was slicked back, possibly because she was fresh out of the shower. "Someone is in a foul temper," she observed. "Something wrong, lover?"

"Wrong? No, actually, everything is just fine now."

Braen grabbed her by the arm, marched her into the nearest room with furniture in it, and threw her ahead of himself. She laughed as she caught her balance and turned to face him, hands on her slim hips and darkly painted lips pouting.

"Aww, honey, what happened?"

They were in the dining room, which was fine with Braen. It provided a nice table. He grabbed Odessa by the arm again and flung her into the table. She sprawled against it and he caught her and turned her, forcing her to bend at the waist until she was facedown against the polished surface and he was kicking her feet apart. He grabbed the sheer silk thing she wore and tore it furiously from her pale body. Odessa snickered, until he struck her hard across her bared backside.Then she gasped.

She wasn't wearing panties, which he found frustrating because he would have liked to have torn those away, too. He jerked at his own clothing, freeing the raging erection he'd had been suffering with for the past half hour. He reached for a condom and tore it open, prepping himself in record time. Without preparing Odessa anymore than he already had with his rough handling, he jammed himself up inside of her. She squealed, partly from the pain of his raw entry and partly from excitement.

Braen reached out and grabbed her by the back of her neck and started to pump into her with brutal force.

"Now, you scream for me! You hear me? Scream!"

Realizing what he wanted, Odessa instantly began to struggle against him. Fighting him hard and screeching for him to stop. The play made her wet, quickly, easing his thrusts into her enough to provide him with an opportunity for more speed. Braen took advantage savagely, gritting his teeth together as he kept repeating himself.

"Scream. No one can hear you. No one will rescue you! Oh, Christ . . . !"

It didn't bother Odessa when he came almost instantly. She knew he'd make it up to her later.

Chapter Fifteen

Tatyana awoke with a savage indrawn gasp, jerking into an upright position. She regretted it instantly as fire exploded across her ribs and face. Large, warm hands reached out to take hold of her and she screamed. Jerking around, she looked up into cerulean blue eyes. Recognizing Hunter, she immediately threw her arms around his neck, suffering from the contact with her bruised and battered body, but unable to do anything else but hug him to her.

"Shh, baby, shh. You're safe. I've got you."

"Oh God!" she sobbed. "I thought . . . he said you couldn't hear me!"

"I will always hear you!" he promised her fiercely. "No magic can interfere with a blood bond, angel. He didn't know you were mine. Thank the blessed Maiden."

"He was so evil! How did he get in this house? I thought we were safe in the house from him!"

"Oh, honey . . ."

"I know you fear you're just like him, but you aren't! You could never be!" She sobbed harder, barely able to catch her breath as her ribs kicked back horrid pain with every indrawn breath.

Hunter looked over the bed to Annali, fear in his eyes at Tatyana's incoherence.

"She might have a concussion," Annali said quietly as she reached to extend one of her fragrant cups of tea to him.

"I need a bath," Tatyana whispered. "Please. Please."

Annali bit her lip, remembering the sentiment all too well.

"Take her in. It can't hurt her and it will calm her down."

"He's all over me," Tatyana sobbed. "He wanted to soil me to get revenge on you. And I didn't see him . . . I didn't know until he was on me!"

"Shh." Hunter tried to soothe her as he swallowed back impotent rage. He no longer had a target to direct it toward, and for her sake he needed to keep calm. "Let's go get you your bath, angel."

"So much fury," she murmured as he picked her up from the bed and carried her inside the bathroom. "Don't let go!" She cried out the protest when he went to set her down in order to fill the tub. Annali stayed him with a touch on his back, reaching to do it for him, filling the tub with the hottest water she could bear, knowing only that would satisfy.

As if timed perfectly, Tatyana and Annali both gasped and raised their heads.

"Dimitre," they both exclaimed.

Annali all but burst into tears to know he was safe and to feel him in the house, coming closer to her.

"No, no, no. No, Hunter. No." Tatyana shook her head and buried her face against his chest. "No. He can't. I can't."

"I'll tell him, Tatyana," Annali said softly. "Don't worry, sugar. I'll keep him away until you're ready."

"He's stubborn."

"Darlin', I've lived with the man for two months. You think I don't know this?"

Hunter almost dropped to his knees when he saw Tatyana smile. Annali hurried out of the room, trying to figure out how she could stop Dimitre from doing an end run around her even though he would sense Tatyana's pain.

"Let's get you in the water. Kaia's here now and she can heal you up."

"Don't leave me."

"I'm not leaving you," he promised.

"Come with me," she clarified.

Hunter hesitated as he understood her request. He didn't think it was a wise idea at all, considering factors like the trauma she had suffered and a big brother in the house. He was amazed she was letting a man anywhere near her.

"You aren't Braen," she whispered against his ear.

Now where had that come from? he wondered.

"If Dimitre comes up here, he isn't going to like it very much if he finds you in a bath with me."

"I need you," she said softly, her jade eyes fluttering open. "In the tub or out, you still have to help me bathe. Annali will keep him away. She has magic."

Hunter turned a smile against her hair. She said that as if Annali were the only one with magic. Perhaps as far as Dimitre was concerned, she was right.

"Okay, honey. If you really want me to." Her affirmative was to pluck open the top two buttons of his shirt. He gently caught her hand in his, stilling it. "Your job is to relax and wait for me to do this myself. Got it?"

"Yes."

Since the tub was sunk into the floor, it made sense to go in together. He set her down and held her steady with one hand while he stripped himself with the other. He watched her warily, especially when he went for his belt, looking for any adverse reactions from her. In truth, she just seemed impatient. She was in pain, feeling who knew what kinds of emotions, and waiting for him to obey her demands. He kicked away his clothes, bent to lift her up again, and carried her into the hot water.

"Holy hell! She made this hot!" he complained.

"Mmm. Feels good."

Once he had them in the water, the jets tumbling lightly in a way he hoped soothed her without hurting her, he expected she would want some distance. Instead, she settled in his lap and kept her arms around his neck. She laid her head on his shoulder and closed her eyes. Hunter knew she had likely busted some ribs. It couldn't be a comfortable position for her, yet she acted like it was heaven on earth.

"Thank you," she murmured.

"Anything you need, angel. Just ask me."

"I mean thank you for saving me from Braen."

Hunter's brow furrowed as he tried to figure out why she was choosing now to thank him for that. It was too odd.

"You're welcome," he said with a mental shrug. Asher had severely scrambled her head, he figured.

She relaxed against him fully, calming down enough that he couldn't feel the thundering fear rushing through her blood any longer. She sighed and started to pet him along his throat, shoulder, and chest.

"You're so pretty," she said with a little smile.

Hunter had to smile back at that, kissing her temple gently.

"So are you," he said. "Are you okay? Want to turn?"

"Okay," she agreed, letting him turn her gingerly until she was sitting in the water between his legs, her back to his chest as she reclined along the length of his body. "Kaia's coming," she sighed.

Sure enough, she was right. He didn't know how she knew, but he could sense his coven mate entering his outer rooms. Tatyana hadn't even met Kaia yet, so how could she sense the other witch's arrival? He figured it must be because of Tatyana's bond to him.

"Soap. Bubbles. You're naked." Tatyana reached for a canister on the edge of the tub and knocked it over, spilling bath gel into the water in a huge glob before Hunter could snatch it up and right it. As if she had timed it perfectly, the water jetting out of the sides of the tub began to froth up a fat blanket of bubbles. The bathroom door opened moments later to admit a short, pretty Native American woman. She was dark-eyed and buxom, an exaggerated hourglass figure making her look cuddly and sexy all at once. When Kaia saw Hunter holding Tatyana in a growing pile of bubbles, she smiled and flashed deep, charming dimples at him.

"Hunter! Blessed be!"

"Blessed be, Kaia."

Kaia hurried across the room and knelt beside the tub, smiling at the couple. "And blessed be to you too, little sister. Your brother worries for you."

"It's his job."

Hunter snickered at the blasé remark and the weary, dismissive wave-off that accompanied it.

"She's not all . . . here," he warned Kaia.

Kaia narrowed her eyes on her patient. "She is more there than you think. I see she talked you into joining her?"

Hunter looked sheepish. "Was that bad? She wouldn't let go and I figured it was best not to fight her . . ."

"No. This is very healthy. She wasn't raped, and this behavior indicates she doesn't feel violated in her own mind either. She feels like she was merely beaten. It is as though . . . she never doubted your arrival."

"I barely made it in time to keep him from . . ." Hunter closed his eyes and kissed Tatyana's temple fiercely. "I never expected Asher hated me so much that he would do something like this."

"Braen," Tatyana murmured.

"Is there ever an explanation that can justify why any man does this?" Kaia asked.

"To split up the coven." Tatyana blew at the froth of bubbles building up in front of her, wincing when her chest

protested the deep breath. She lowered her voice in affecta-
tion of a male. " 'The whole point is to keep them guessing,
now isn't it?' " she said mockingly.

Puzzled, Hunter tried to get a look at her face.

"Dimitre's pissed," Tatyana remarked. "Really pissed. Annali knows how to make him calm. Ryce is all kinds of upset.
Oh, but Asher is finally back, which is good. He doesn't hate
you, you know."

"Kaia, she's rambling," Hunter said worriedly. "She keeps
doing that."

"Yes, I see that. But that doesn't mean she isn't saying
something important. Here. Let me heal her a bit, check out
the damage." Kaia reached out as Hunter shifted Tatyana closer
to her. Gentle hands with long, elegant fingers touched Tatyana's face, seeking the damage done by the trauma she had
been through. "Poor thing. Asher really did a number on her.
I just don't understand what could possibly have—"

"No. Aren't you looking?" Tatyana complained.

"Yes, sweetheart, we are," Kaia assured her. "Hold her
head, Hunter."

Hunter did as instructed just as Tatyana's eyes slid closed
and her body went lax in his hold.

"Is she okay? She seemed really altered," he asked.

"She was seriously concussed. Bruising and a little bleeding can do that. He destroyed her ribs on that one side. She's
lucky she didn't puncture a lung. Hunter, I cannot believe
Asher McBride would attempt to rape an innocent girl. And
even if he were going to, why would he do it under his own
roof? Knowing witches were all around him?"

"Kaia, I can't talk about this," he told her stiffly. "If I
do . . . I feel like my head will explode. All I want right
now is to take care of Tatyana. I don't want to try to understand the way hatred can warp someone's mind."

"Asher doesn't hate you!" Kaia protested. "He's come to
terms with Amber's death! He no longer blames you for it.

The only thing he still feels hurt over is that you . . . well, you know."

"Then why did he target Tatyana? He knew she was my lover, that's why. You don't think he wanted to do this to get back at me for sleeping with Amber? How am I supposed to understand any of this?"

"Slowly," she advised. "Listen to your instincts. The bond saved her, and it will save you, too."

"By the Lady, Kaia, I don't think I have it in me to wade through mystic bullshit right now."

"All right, honey," she mollified him. "Let's bring her back to bed. I'll heal her some more. I can't do it all the way because . . . I need to use a lot of magic if I'm going to save Asher's life."

"He's still alive?" Hunter demanded. "And you're going to let his victim suffer so you can spare him?"

"Hunter," she chided softly, "we have no idea what is really going on here. We can't ignore the fact that he went missing for five days and within minutes of entering this house behaved in a way that was completely out of character. Then to jump out of a window? Something is very wrong with all of this."

"What's wrong is you all trying to make excuses for him! I don't believe this!"

Hunter angrily reached for a bath sponge and used it to quickly bathe away all removable traces of Tatyana's ordeal. The rest would be up to Kaia. Together they got her out of the tub, dried her off gently, and carried her back to his bed. Hunter dressed in a pair of pajama bottoms before going to the bedside to help Kaia. Together, they used all the magic they knew to help Tatyana heal.

Dimitre ran both hands back through his golden hair in frustration.

"Annali, I don't even know this man! How can you tell me to leave her up there with him?"

"Doesn't my judgment help you with that in any way? You have lived Ryce's past memories of Hunter on one occasion. In a way you do know him."

"Yeah, and I watched him decapitate a man with his bare hands. Not a very comforting image, babe."

"Kaia's up there, too. This isn't my idea. Tatyana begged me to keep you away until she was ready for you." Annali moved closer to him, adding her body warmth to her argument.

Dimitre cupped her shoulders with impatient hands, rubbing at her arms. "I'm not used to letting others take care of her. I've done it since the day she was born."

"I know, darlin'," Annie soothed him softly. "But *this* is your family now, and you need to trust us."

"Like I trusted Asher?" he bit out.

"I don't know who that was, darlin'," she said, "but I guarantee it was not the Asher you and I know."

"That's like the neighbors of a serial killer who always say 'he was such a nice boy' in interviews," he grumbled.

"Yes, but there's magic involved in our world and that makes all the difference."

Dimitre relented finally. He could feel Tatyana through the special bond they had always shared, and her pain had faded already. She was calm and resting. Calming himself, he wrapped his arms around Annali and pulled her tight and close, kissing her warmly. He hadn't seen her in a week and relief was finally catching up to him as his worry for his sister was cautiously relegated to a secondary place in his mind.

"Are you okay?" he asked her softly. "Ryce told me things over the phone . . . and I've been worried about you."

"What things?" she asked, her supple body going suddenly stiff, sending him on alert.

"That you were attacked by Belladonna Coven. That you threw yourself in front of the Blessing Tree. That you faced down their High Cleric. Was there more than that I should know about?"

Annali sighed deeply and Dimitre knew that there was.

"It's just that Braen, Belladonna's High Cleric, used to be Evan's protégé back when they were Hawthorn Coven. It's not the first time he and I have met," she added quietly. "A fact he took great delight in reminding me of."

"Ah babe, I'm sorry," he said roughly, hugging her close as he struggled with the spike in his temper. All of this time he had thought Annali's offender had paid for his sins against her. Now, to find out there was another who had yet to pay, it was difficult to see past the haze of red fury.

"Don't," she whispered against his ear, when she felt the tension that whipped through his strong body. "One day he will face his crimes. Don't poison yourself with hate from now until then. He has no power over us unless you do."

"That isn't the only reason," he said fiercely. "Braen wasn't at his coven the day you say Gracelynne was attacked. If he has a history of violence toward women, how can I not suspect him of it?"

"It was very likely him. He is powerful. I can't imagine who else could pull it off."

"Then that means she was probably raped, Annie," he said.

"Yes. Probably," she agreed with a catch to her voice.

She went still in his arms all of a sudden and Dimitre knew she had just come to the same conclusion he was reaching.

"Once a rapist, always a rapist," he spat. "And who else would have the power to overtake Asher like that? If that is really what happened."

"Oh, Sweet Lady," she breathed. "We let him in. He used Asher's body to cross the protection wards and we just let him in. Your sister said . . . ! But, how did she know?"

"Know what?" he demanded.

"She knew! She somehow knew it was Braen. She said to

Hunter 'I know you're afraid you're like him. You're nothing like him.' Dimitre, Hunter is Braen's biological brother. He's always struggled with proving himself better than his darkly magicked family. Somehow she knew Braen had got past the wards and possessed Asher to do it."

"Do we know what kind of witch she is yet?"

"No. But with this kind of stress, I have a feeling we are going to find out."

Tatyana awoke again the next morning. She knew it was morning because the sun shone brightly enough through the window to give her a ringing headache. She groaned and rolled over, surprised and delighted when she found herself landing against a large, hard male body. She was full of aches, pains, and bruises, not to mention the memory of a harrowing encounter the day before, but it all faded away the moment she realized Hunter had stretched out beside her in bed and kept her company all night long. He was wearing loose black pants, like cotton pajamas, and was bare-chested. She was extremely naked. She was beneath the covers, he was above.

Tatyana smothered a giggle. It was such a puritanical thing for him to do, considering they had made love and bathed together the day before. It simply told her more about how caring he was and the lengths he would go to see to her comfort while keeping most of his chivalry in play. She stipulated 'most' because she supposed he might have slept in a chair or elsewhere entirely if he were really going to try to be a gentleman. Then again, she liked that he was *just* honorable enough . . .

The rest was very much male instinct and proprietary behavior. Something else she seemed to like . . . on Hunter at least. It was like the first time she had awoken beside him. He had been untamed that morning, overcome with his passionate self. Honor had kicked in just in the nick of time.

Just enough, but not too much. Although, she was very interested in seeking out that untamed side without honor making an appearance.

"I feel you thinking at me," he murmured before he opened his eyes.

"Yeah?" she countered. "What am I thinking?"

"I am never sure if I want to know," he said with a wry chuckle. He turned his head, looking her over carefully before drawing an arm around her and hugging her close. "Are you okay? Do you mind me holding you today?"

"It doesn't hurt," she assured him.

"No, I meant . . . because . . ."

"It still doesn't hurt," she said as she reached to hold him. "You stopped it before it reached that point for me."

Tatyana reached over to kiss him gently on the mouth. He tucked a hand into her hair at the back of her head and held her as he let her touch him at her own pace. He had to admit, it felt really good to feel her kiss again. Yesterday had seemed to turn on a dime from fantasy to nightmare, and he barely knew how to react this morning to all of it. Yet, she seemed relaxed and comfortable with what she was doing.

"How do you do that?" he asked softly, stroking back her hair as it fell over him. "How do you adapt from one crazy moment to the next and make it look so . . . easy?"

She smiled a little, drawing her lip between her teeth a moment. "I think it all goes back to that big family thing. It's controlled chaos. Things are happening nonstop. If you fall apart over one thing, you can't manage the next one. The only thing that truly affects most of us is if one of us is seriously hurt. Believe me, all of this was harder on Dimitre than it was on me. It was harder on you, too."

"Are you kidding? When I saw you on that bed, heard what he was saying to you, I just . . ." Tatyana felt his hands close spasmodically around her head, her shoulders, and then her arms. "I wanted to kill him. For the first time, I felt this uncontrollable desire to kill someone who wasn't a warlock, and to take inconceivable joy in it." Hunter saw her eyes go wide. "It sounds monstrous, I know. I'm sorry."

"No, no, I'm just trying to figure out . . . who wasn't a warlock?"

"Asher."

"Well, of course not. He's one of your coven mates," she snorted. "What does he have to do with yesterday?"

"Right, angel," Hunter said slowly, giving her an odd look. "You met him right after we had . . . umm . . . after the bathroom."

"Uh, no, I didn't. I've never met Asher."

Hunter sat up, slid back against the headboard and drew her close.

"Tatyana, take a look at yourself. You're covered in bruises. You met Asher in a really bad way yesterday," he reminded her, his brow furrowed with worry. Kaia said she had healed the concussion as well as Tatyana's broken bones. What was wrong with her memory?

"Hunter," she mimicked his tone, "I never met Asher. I encountered Braen. Remember? He cornered me in that room, beat the shit out of me, and tried to rape me. You're the one who stopped him, for God's sake. You watched him leap out of the window and get away. Why would you think Asher did this? Asher doesn't hate you. Think about it. Braen is the only one who would benefit from hurting me to get to you. He was trying to split the coven. I guess he figured if he . . . if he attacked me and left no clues as to who did it, you all would tear each other apart looking for a culprit among yourselves." She shuddered and snuggled closer to him. "I'm so glad he didn't succeed. This is a very special place."

"Honey?"

"Mmm?"

"What does Braen look like?"

"Black hair, like you. Black eyes. Nasty scar on his face. He had a tattoo I didn't notice the first night, right here." She indicated a point low on her chest. "Some kind of knife with symbols on it."

"An athamé. It's a power symbol." Hunter touched her face gently. "Angel, we have to get up. Think you can come with me to see Ryce?"

"And Dimitre. He's waited long enough. First, I need to make sure I look only half like hell, instead of completely. Dimitre having a freak-out is never a pretty sight."

"I can imagine," he chuckled.

Dimitre hadn't slept well. Granted, the reason was two-fold, he thought with a small smile as he reached to stroke the back of Annali's neck before bending to kiss it. The kiss made her scrunch up her shoulder and laugh, reaching back to push him away.

"I'm trying to concentrate," she scolded him.

"I'm trying to kiss you. Why do we always do what you want to do?"

She scoffed out a laugh. "I'm not even going to dignify that with an argument."

"Because you know it's true. For example, I wanted to see my sister. You said no, so we didn't see her. Then, I wanted to go to sleep, and you jumped me like I was some kind of Thoroughbred."

"Dimitre!"

"Eww. TMI, brother dear. Too much information."

Dimitre whipped around, an actual flush burning across his face as he met his baby sister's eyes. They were sparkling with her usual impish mirth, making him feel the sudden suffocating realization that he hadn't seen her in far too long.

"Tat!"

She ran up to meet his step forward, flinging herself into his arms and hugging the hell out of him. She felt his fear and his worry in every nuance of his embrace, his breath drawing in raggedly as he kissed her bruised cheek. Dimitre could smell makeup on her, heavy foundation, and knew she was hiding more than she was showing. Tatyana only wore eye makeup as a general rule. She had hated the feel of foundation on her face since she'd been very young. He was surprised she even owned any.

He set her back down on her feet and put her at arm's length. Her pretty jewel jade eyes were gleaming with tears and she even sniffled. She wasn't much of a crier, but she was sensitive as hell whether she liked to show it or not. Looking at her bruised face just about wrecked him, but if she had worked so hard to minimize the effect, then she was also working to minimize his reaction to it.

"You look like you went ten rounds with Tanya Silvada, that bully who lived down State Street when you were twelve, remember?" He cocked a grin at Annali, taking brief note of the tall, dark-haired male standing beside her whom he knew was Hunter Finn. "When Tatyana was twelve, this new girl on the block thought to make a name for herself by picking on my little sis. She must have thought beating up one of the popular girls would earn her some points in whatever crowd it was that she was looking to get in with.

"She didn't do her homework, though," Dimitre noted with a chuckle as he looked back to his sister. "Tanya didn't bother to find out Tat was the baby in a family of big brothers who had been wrestling with her since she could first grab on to them. Tat came home looking like shit after that fight. She walked in the door and my mother damn near had a heart attack. So Tat says . . . 'Oh, relax, Mom. It's not like she broke my nose or anything. Oh, by the way, I got suspended. And, umm, you might be getting a call from Tanya's mother, because *I* broke *her* nose.' "

Dimitre mimicked his sister so perfectly that Tatyana reached out and swatted him on the shoulder. She glared at Hunter and Annali, who were laughing.

"Well, I did. I just wish I'd done more than bite Braen yesterday. He caught me off guard," she said with a frown.

The room instantly sobered at the reference.

"Did she say Braen?" Annali gasped.

"You'd better come with us. We're going to talk to Ryce."

"It's called an Interior Doppelgänger spell. It's extremely complex. The casting takes well over a day to get it right and it requires a lot of energy to pull it off. Between Braen and his familiars, he would have been able to do it." Ryce paced in front of the fireplace in irritation. "I should have known Asher would never leave us voluntarily. I kept making up excuses about why he would leave without telling anyone where he was going. I guess I figured if he'd been taken by the Belladonna coven, you and Kaia would have seen them bring him in as a captive."

"Explain this spell," Dimitre urged him.

"The caster basically wears another person like a skin. It doesn't displace the other person's spirit, it just paralyzes it. Asher probably saw everything that was happening, but couldn't do anything to stop it. It was a clever way for Braen to get into the house and to start trouble."

"He always was a shortsighted prick," Hunter said bitterly. "He couldn't even wait five minutes before he was trying to gratify himself on an innocent woman. If he'd held off, he really could have done some damage."

"He could have tried. This family is tighter knit than Braen is capable of imagining," Ryce countered. "I should have seen so many things and I feel like a complete ass. Asher wouldn't have redelivered that ultimatum from ten years ago, I don't care how surprised he was at seeing you."

"But he wasn't surprised," Annali recalled. "Not even when he acted it toward Gracelynne."

"You think that was Braen? The one who attacked Gracelynne?" Tatyana asked, wrapping her arms around herself in a hug as she shivered.

"I think it was," Hunter said. "And I think he got off on watching Gracie get upset like that. Probably part of why he went after you so quickly, angel."

Dimitre looked up abruptly when he heard the endearment, watching as Hunter slid a hand gently around the back of his sister's neck. Exactly as Dimitre had done to Annali earlier. Up until that moment, he hadn't taken notice of any chemistry between the master witch and his novice. Now, he couldn't help but see it. If it hadn't so clearly been a gesture of comfort, and an obviously effective one as his sister relaxed her hug on herself, he might have gotten pretty upset about it. He might have seen Hunter as taking advantage of the bond they'd developed. But the blood bond enhancement was purely about sex. He could honestly say that, in the beginning, his motives toward Annali had been more obsessively about sex than anything else. What he was seeing from Hunter was tenderness, plain and simple. He recognized it because he'd done the very same things to ease Annali as they'd worked through her traumatic memories.

He sighed when Annali reached to take his hand, giving it a squeeze. He supposed she'd seen where his attention was directed and this was her way of reminding him that his sister was an adult with her own life to lead. He had already reminded himself, so he guessed he was a step ahead of her for a change. He had always prided himself on being the one family member who didn't treat her like a baby, who had tried to cultivate her independence. The way he had been behaving these past couple of months wouldn't have proven that theory.

But who could blame a brother for worrying? He'd witnessed, through Ryce's memories, Hunter committing an act of brutal assassination. True, that act had saved the woman Dimitre loved from a life of hell, but there was something a bit nerve-wracking about placing a beloved sister in hands that wielded life and death with such accuracy and force.

Then again, who better? Hunter had just saved his sister from being raped and, by the sound of it, killed.

"He meant to kill her," Dimitre said aloud. He watched his sister startle and the immediate way Hunter stepped up closer behind her chair. "It's something you said, Tat. He was planning on healing the wounds you gave him, and . . . and even though it physically wasn't his own body . . . well, why bother with a condom?" He shifted uncomfortably; the whole concept left a bad taste in his mouth.

"No witnesses," Ryce agreed grimly. "No blood, marks, DNA . . . It was what Gracelynne's attacker was aiming for as well. Same M.O."

"Great," Hunter said sarcastically. "It's not bad enough I have a warlock for a brother, but he just has to push the envelope and be a serial rapist, too."

"He thinks it's his due," Annali said quietly. "He has spent years and years taking everything he wants the instant he wants it, and sex is no different. To him, it's all consensual. Or it should be. We're all just waiting around for him to prove his prowess to us. To show us his power."

"No. He knows full well his behavior is designed to destroy a woman's psyche. He is counting on it. He's using it to weaken this coven," Hunter said darkly. "That's why he did Gracie for himself and was taken by surprise by you, Annie. To him, you were already weakened by him and Evan. Tarnished goods, so to speak. Remember how shocked he was when you fought him off at the Blessing Tree? It never occurred to him that you had not just recovered, but flourished in this place."

"And might I just add a hearty *neenerneenerneener* on your behalf," Tatyana said. The tension in the room broke with that, making the coven chuckle as one.

"How is Asher?" Hunter thought to ask now that he realized the truth of what had happened.

"Not great. Kaia is exhausting herself trying to save him. Only Nox's stasis spell is keeping him alive at the moment. But I have faith that between her magic and her medical skill, our Kaia will prevail."

"Why throw him out a window? I mean, besides trying to kill him. Or is that all it was? Hunter would have done the honors himself in another minute or two," Annali noted. "I would think that would have made more impact on the coven. Wasn't that his goal? To damage our morale?"

"Except he couldn't escape the wards around the house if his host died within its boundaries," Ryce informed them. "He needed Asher's body to get out of the house just like he needed it to get in. It's a limitation of the spell Braen was using."

"Another is that he couldn't use Asher's magic, he had to use his own. That's why he was spellcasting," Hunter said.

"Okay, so here's a question . . . how are we going to kill the bastard?"

They all looked at Tatyana when she asked the question with her arms crossed and her foot bouncing impatiently.

"Right. Good question," Ryce agreed. "Easy to ask, but not so easy to execute. He knows this coven too well. He's been gathering warlocks for years just to contend with us. There are only two advantages we have that he didn't plan for." He first pointed to Dimitre and then to his sister. "He wasn't prepared for Hunter before, but he is now. He knows nothing about you, Dimitre, or your power. That doesn't mean he doesn't have a Tempus of his own, though, so you can't be cocky about it. Unfortunately, we have no idea what advantage number two is yet." Ryce cocked a brow at Tatyana. "Whatever it is, Tatyana's magic is untried and bound to be erratic at first. And until we do figure out her magic and how to use it, we need to lie low and heal our people. We need Gracie. She's big guns.

"Now, that's exactly what he isn't going to want, so we need to keep alert. We can't take any more injuries. Kaia simply isn't strong enough to cope with so much all at once, and Annali can only do so much picking up the slack. Hunter, Nox, and I can do rudimentary healing, but we need to store magic in other ways if possible. First off, we need to change some of the wards on this house. That's the first thing he's going to attack and you can bet he got a good look at them both times he passed through. It's only a matter of time before he figures out how to unravel each one.

"Nox and I will work on those," Ryce said. "Hunter, you have one job. Find out what your apprentice can do. Dimitre, all I can say is practice. Really stretch yourself. Not drain yourself, stretch yourself. Annali will show you what I mean. Annie, I want you making potions that pack a serious punch. If you need supplies, let me know, I will teleport a basket and list to Raven's occult supply shop. No one, and I mean no one, is to leave this house without my express permission and one or more witches accompanying them. Even so, it had best be a damn emergency. Someone do me a favor and nail that directive to Kaia's thick skull for me?"

"Consider it done," Hunter chuckled.

Chapter Sixteen

Braen was, once again, in a bad mood.

After carefully orchestrating so many opportunities to get the best of his enemy, one by one they had slipped through his fingers. First, Adaliah's storm. Adaliah, Odessa's mother, was a powerful Weather witch. She had socked in almost all of New York with that awesome blizzard once Odessa had pointed out it was a surefire way of keeping the missing witches away until he had a chance to utilize the captive Asher to his best advantage. Braen had hoped to keep them all separated, providing an opportunity to pick them off. The problem was the two that had been missing had gone out from under his radar, slipping right past his spies. Now, the storm was ended and, sure enough, just as his spies had caught sight of the Healer bitch and her unknown witch escort, within minutes their car had been left abandoned on the side of the road and they were nowhere to be seen.

Second, the fiasco with his Interior Doppelgänger spell. He had burned out every familiar he had and a great deal of his own personal magic as well to cast that spell, and he had done it perfectly. But to have it so easily ruined! And when he'd been so close to that little redhead he could practically smell her sweet little pussy just begging for a good ride. Because God knows Hunter wouldn't know what to do with a hot little bitch like that, whether he'd marked her already or not. His baby brother was far too noble and honorable and all that bullshit to really use a woman to her full capacity.

Now all the witches were safely home and his Doppelgänger spell had ended most unsatisfactorily. The only plus was knowing he'd made certain Asher had landed badly enough to guarantee a broken neck. They would be short one witch next time they clashed. Not a very strong witch, but admittedly he'd been a useful one.

At least for *his* purposes.

Still, he was furious as he tried to figure out how his traitor of a brother had managed to penetrate his muting spell so he could come storming in like some pathetic white knight to save the girl, cheating Braen of his prize.

"Of all the times for him to come back, he had to pick now," he complained bitterly to his companion.

Odessa laughed, her darkly painted lips parting to flash white teeth and a red tongue. Even without her clothes on, her dramatic makeup, black hair, and starkly pale skin made her look Gothic.

Braen reached up to grab her by her throat, cutting off her laugh and giving her a mean shake. "What's so funny?" he demanded.

"Braen, you're cock-deep inside of me and your mind is an entire state away. You're lucky I'm not pissed off." She smacked his hand away and leaned forward so she was nose to nose with him, her small breasts brushing against him. "If you are bored with me, lover, let me know. I've got a half dozen familiars with nice healthy pricks at my beck and call."

Braen obviously didn't like the sound of that. He wrenched her over until she was beneath him on the bed. His focus returned to the task at hand and he began to pound himself into her.

He did his best thinking while he was fucking around

with Odessa. Whether it was alone or toying with their familiars together, he always obtained a certain clarity as he relaxed into the pleasure of pumping himself to orgasm. Odessa was a bit of a nymphomaniac, so she got off without much effort on his part. When he did put effort into it, she was like an animal.

They were perfect for each other, really. She had made a better leader out of him. They lived together, something he had never done with any other woman. She was fast rising in power and was just about ready to be proclaimed Dark Knight of Belladonna Coven; the equivalent of a white coven's Sentinel. He had dreamed of finding a perfect match for himself, thinking he could finally out-power Ryce Champion because he refused to train and elect a new Sentinel for Willow Coven.

And then he went and brought Hunter back.

Braen had been livid to find out Odessa had gotten her little ass kicked by Hunter so easily in that initial battle. She had underestimated him, not believing his claim of being Sentinel. It had given Hunter all the advantage his brother had needed.

Stupid bitch, he thought angrily, his fury projecting into the crashing connection of their bodies. Odessa . . . well, of course she got off on his violence. She came hard, then successively, but he wasn't ready to finish, so he kept up his abuse, and his thinking.

He needed a way to get at that cursed coven. Until he got rid of them, they would keep picking off pieces of *his* coven and he wouldn't be able to achieve any of the goals he had wanted to achieve. He was fairly certain he could take on Champion with Odessa by his side, but he needed to get rid of his brother and that potion-making whore first. Yeah, she'd been sweet in her time, his mentor Evan letting him play with her, but now she was powerful and clever. Tricky as hell. Total waste of a perfectly good familiar. Maybe she wouldn't have been as much fun after her mid-twenties, after the horror of her situation had burned her mind and soul out, but the body would have lasted.

Instead, she had led Ryce and Hunter to Evan and had gotten the greatest warlock of all time slaughtered over her. Annali. Hunter gave a damn about her. So did Champion. If he struck at Annali, then maybe . . . But how? He had already tried to lure her out using the Blessing Tree. His brother had thwarted that ploy.

What he would really like was to get his hands on all of the women of Willow Coven.

"I've been inside two of them already," he muttered, closing his eyes and replaying those pleasures in his mind. Annali as a young girl of sixteen, screaming and weeping, and then that amazon packed into a little body who'd given him a hot fight before he'd finally nailed her. He'd been so worked up after that clash it had been all he could do to get the clothes off her before he'd been ready to come inside her. He'd almost forgotten to wear a condom. Except there was no way he was letting any of those white magic bitches get pregnant with his child. So they could make an abomination of righteousness out of it? No thanks.

Now he'd missed his chance with Hunter's little red-headed lover. She hadn't used magic on him, so he doubted she was a witch. It had been difficult to sense her, muffled as he was with another man's skin and soul all around him. Still, he'd fucked her up sufficiently to mess with Hunter's head. He had to accept that as enough of a victory.

That left the Healer.

Oh, yes, the little Indian squaw. All round in the right places, big breasts, fuckable ass. She was the one who defied Champion most often, always leaving the grounds to go to the hospital or clinic. It was only a matter of time before she would leave again to tend to her patients on the outside.

"Oh, yes," he groaned as he contemplated the possibility of catching her. "Except, this time, she dies. No getting away at the last minute like the other two. Yeah. With no Healer, it will be only a matter of time. They can't stay in that house forever."

"Kaia," Odessa moaned between cries of pleasure.

"Yes. Kaia."

"You want to fuck her? Before we kill her?"

"Yes," he gasped, feeling his orgasm approaching faster with every word. "You can hold her down for me, Dess, right?"

"I'll bind her with a spell. I'll make her beg for you. Would you like to hear her scream, or beg for you? You can tell Champion she begged for it like a two-dollar whore. Tell him she sucked your cock dry and let you fuck her besides."

"Oh God!" Braen jammed himself into Odessa and came furiously inside of her, spewing and spewing until he cried out again from the pleasurable pain of the dry contractions of his drained cock.

He collapsed over her, not even noticing her own screams of release or that she could barely breathe from it. He sighed and grinned. He'd known he'd get his mind cleared if he just got Odessa into bed. Now, he had a plan.

"You're going back to New York," he chuckled. "I need a doctor."

"Just . . . tell me what happened. Whether it was really Asher or not, it doesn't change the fact that something happened. Something that drove you away from people you call family for an entire decade."

Hunter paced restlessly from the conversation area before the fire in his sitting room, to the doorway leading into his bedroom. It was obvious the topic made him uncomfortable. His agitation was rubbing Tatyana's nerves a little raw.

"We're supposed to be figuring out what kind of magic you can do," he hedged awkwardly.

"Oh, we will. After you tell me. Until then, you are S.O.L., my friend."

"You know, it's your maturity that really fascinates me," he mocked.

"And you won't get me off the topic by insulting me about my age. Although I will want to know how you picked up on how to push that button so quickly," she said with consternation.

Hunter had to grin at that. Actually, she had given it away in her phone conversation with her brother that first morning they'd spent together.

"Look, it . . . I just prefer to leave the past in the past," he said with a sigh.

"And we will, after you tell me. I don't want to walk around with my imagination to depend on. I have a very evil imagination. It's one of my wicked womanly powers. Much worse than magic."

"Is that right?" he asked with a laugh as he turned and crossed over to her.

"Oh yes. Lots of exercise involved. I can jump to conclusions in a single bound. I'm more powerful than a murder motive. I'm faster than the town gossip. I am deadly and I must be stopped."

"I couldn't agree more," he chuckled as he leaned over her and reached for her mouth. She pulled back, a hand holding him at bay.

"What are you doing?" she demanded. "You are not going to change this subject."

"I haven't kissed you properly since yesterday," he argued.

"Then you better talk fast," she said a bit breathlessly as his eyes burned down at her with that butane intensity that made her heart race.

"Let's work out a barter system," he counter-offered. "I tell you something, you give me my kiss. We can work exponentially from there."

"But I thought we were supposed to be doing magic,"

Tatyana said lamely as the warmth of his breath skimmed silkily over her cheek. She suppressed a shiver.

"If you can cheat, so can I," he said, a very wicked gleam in his hot eyes. He reached up and touched a foundation-covered cheek, frowning instantly. "Unless I'm asking too much. Damn, it's like . . . you make me forget in an instant everything you've been through, just with that saucy little attitude of yours and all that pluck you toss out so easily."

"That's okay," she assured softly. "I want you to forget. I don't do victim very well. It's like with that bully Tanya . . . I wear my bruises proudly because . . . well, I won. Doesn't matter how I won, just that I did. It's over now. He failed and you made that happen for me." She reached up with graceful fingers and plowed them through his hair, making him turn toward the caress with a pleasurable sigh. "I only need one thing from you to feel truly better about all of this."

"What? Anything you need, angel, just tell me."

"What happened ten years ago?"

Hunter sighed and resisted the urge he had to turn the minx over his knee. Some other day, he thought, allowing the wicked desire to enter his eyes and expression, leaving her guessing as to its origin.

"About a year after Ryce and I rescued Annali, I got involved with one of the other witches in the coven. Amber. She was Asher's twin sister. I was twenty-four and she was eighteen. She and Asher had lived here since they were sixteen. She'd had a crush on me since day one, and I was too young and too egotistical to see beyond being flattered."

Hunter turned and sat down on the couch beside her with a deep sigh, rubbing at his eyes. "She turned eighteen and it was like a gun going off at a starting gate to her. She thought that was what I'd been waiting for those two years. For her to be a grown-up." He laughed dryly at the idea of anyone being a grown-up at eighteen. "She sure came on like a grown-up," he recalled without accusation. "I barely knew what hit me. At twenty-four I was still thinking more with my hormones than anything. I was too dense to realize that she was in love with me, and I was in love with the sex." Hunter looked at her. "I hate telling you this. I'm not proud of it. It nearly destroyed this house."

Tatyana got up from her seat and, facing Hunter, she threw a leg over his thighs. She settled her bottom on his lap and leaned forward to give him a slow, deep kiss. It was amazing, really, the instant sensation she had that she was truly starved for him and his affection. All of her focus zeroed in on the feel of his lips; her palms cupped his face, which was dark and roughly unshaven still. She ignored the potential for whisker burn and slid deep inside of him in search of his tongue.

Hunter groaned under her slowly seductive reward. He reached for her head and enveloped it in his big hands as she made slow, sensuous work of his mouth. When she pulled back for a breath, he could hardly hear over the rushing sound of his blood.

"How?" she asked as though there had been no break in the conversation. "How did you almost destroy this house?"

"Asher found out about me and Amber and went napalm. His sister swore that I loved her and . . . that's when I realized she was on this whole fairy-tale trip and I'd really screwed up. I tried to break it off gently, but there's no such thing as a gently broken heart. Especially not when you live in the same house with the one who hurt you, and you have to see him constantly all day long. I tried to make it easier on her by leaving for long stretches of time. One day, while I was away, she and Asher and Annali were out to a movie and they got ambushed by a trio of warlocks. Annie was still doing only rudimentary potions then, and Asher's magic doesn't lend itself to offensive attack. Amber was the only one who could really fight the enemy. She was a Conjurer witch. Basically, she could create something out of nothing with the power of her mind. But it's a highly focused power. You need a great deal of concentration and experience to be any good in a firefight."

The telling was becoming more difficult for him, and he couldn't seem to stay connected to her eyes. Tatyana knew that was because he was afraid of what she would think of him afterward. She reminded him she was very much still with him by kissing him again, stroking her thumbs soothingly over his cheeks.

"She tried her best to fend the warlocks off while the entire coven was racing to help them," he continued after a moment, this time seizing on her jade gaze as though it were a life raft. "Turned out I was closest because I was already out of the house. They'd taken the fight off into this glade right outside of town. Annie was cut down, nearly losing an arm in the process. Asher was always good with weapons, but he could only do so much against magic. He fell. Amber was facing three-to-one odds, *and* the thought that her brother had been killed. I was just running up to where Annali was when Amber conjured the only thing she could think of that would take out the trio closing in on her.

"She made a bomb. I never even saw it, never had a chance to cast a single spell. I was too far away, maybe too inexperienced. I never expected her to self-sacrifice like that. When the explosion hit I was . . ." Hunter shook his head. "I was too far away to do anything, not that there was much I could have done. And . . . you never expect someone to survive something like that blast. Not when it takes out trees and . . . everything. Asher found her maybe seconds before she actually died. I wasn't there but apparently my name was the last thing she said to him. I don't need to guess how much that hurt him. He let me know every minute of every day afterward. I put up with it for a month after Amber's funeral, and then he delivered an ultimatum to Ryce. Him or me. Willow Coven couldn't have us both. And I knew . . ."

"You knew Ryce was going to pick you," she filled in for him.

"If he did that, we'd lose Asher to going rogue or dark witchery. I had no doubt in my mind about that. The betrayal would have been the final straw for him. So, since I was already hating myself for all the stupid mistakes I had made, including getting there too late to do anything to help her like a Sentinel was supposed to do, I left. I didn't let anyone argue, and Asher never knew it was my choice and not Ryce's." Hunter laid his head back and stared up at the ceiling a long moment. "It took a decade, but I realized what was and was not my fault about that day. I accepted my mistakes, and stopped taking on extra ones that were only in my mind. I'm hoping the same is true for Asher."

"Was it hard to come back here as Sentinel? To re-accept that level of responsibility?" she asked.

"Actually, it was easier than I had expected. I was born to be Ryce's Sentinel. He and I . . . we met when we were just boys, fully empowered, the both of us. I was from a witching family, he was not. Except, my family . . . my family produces witches like Braen. He's one of three of my warlock brothers, you know."

She gasped. "I had no idea!"

"Not something I like to publicize," he said grimly. "Only one thing kept me from that path, I believe, and that was Ryce's influence. He was a natural-born leader. Me, with my roots in dark magic, I had just enough power in me to be a killer and just enough conscience to be doing it for good reasons. At first Ryce had his work cut out for him teaching me white ways. After a while, it came naturally to me. Soon I was the family disgrace. I was also twice as powerful as any of my brothers.

"Ryce's wealth allowed him independence at an early age. We built this house and started our coven. First Kaia. Then Lennox. The twins and then Gracie. You know about

Annali. Ryce has done well here. This coven has a reputation
even in Europe. I got to hear bits and pieces of stories over
the years. It was like writing home."

"But now you are home. And I see why everyone feels as
though you never left. Ryce may lead and finance, but you
are as much a part of this coven's foundations as he is. You're
part of the reason it's even here. Technically, you and Ryce
were Willow Coven long before this house was built. How
old were you when you met Ryce?"

"Ten. He was thirteen. I was a spoiled little shit," he
chuckled. "I had used magic to get everything I wanted from
the day I first cast a spell. He was from a family of privilege
and never saw his parents, so he was autonomous by then,
but not spoiled. He was devoted to white craft, following in
the footsteps of his mentor who had died a year before I met
him. Can you imagine him taking on a ten-year-old snot
with dark magic in his blood at the mere age of thirteen and
actually mentoring him?"

"Ryce? Yes." She laughed and cuddled up to Hunter. "I
can only imagine him being born a powerful adult. Ryce and
potty training just don't compute."

"Oh, man," Hunter chuckled. "But can I tell you a secret?
I think it would compute . . . if he was a father. He's a natural. And if you listen to him long enough, you will hear him
talk about families and love and witchcraft like it's a triad of
power like the Maiden, Mother, and Crone. The three as-
pects of our goddess," he clarified. "I think he craves a family of his own blood in this house, as well as wanting us to
have ours."

"It shows," she said. "I saw the nursery. It's just . . .
waiting."

"Yeah, he likes to go through it and update everything
whenever something is really bothering him. Or at least he
used to."

"It looked pretty up to date," she assured him. It made
him grin like a fool.

"The more things change . . ."

". . . the more they stay the same. I just hope Asher survives. And I am glad that, in my mind, I can only see Braen with me in that hallway and in the room. Asher doesn't deserve to be part of that memory. But it's so strange because I know that at the time, I couldn't see through the spell, however, right afterward I think I could. Now I see nothing of Asher. I don't even know what he looks like."

"Good. No matter what troubles he and I have had in the past, Asher is a good man who has suffered a lot for his craft. Including the pain he is in now. It would be unfair if his image was blackened in your memories before he even has a chance to know you and you to know him."

"I agree." She exhaled slowly. "There now, see? That wasn't so bad, was it?"

"No," he agreed with a grin. "But I think we're going to have to go well beyond a couple of kisses to make this barter fair." Hunter's hands slid down over her back and Tatyana smiled slyly at him.

"I gather you have something specific in mind?" She snuggled forward, her full breasts settled up against his chest. "Or can I choose?"

Just the question sent a spool of heat tumbling and unraveling down the length of his entire body. Hunter tried to catch a breath as her smile turned cunning and knowing. She knew she had excited him, just as she knew it would never take much effort on her part to do so. Something about her just tripped every single wire he had.

"I can go either way," he joked hoarsely, harkening back to the night they had met and making her explode in a grin.

"Mmm, that sounds like fun," she practically purred against the corner of his mouth. Her spine made that slinky movement that always captivated him and Hunter was suddenly very aware of the heat of her body penetrating through his clothes.

"It's . . . I'm . . ." he stammered, trying to draw coherent thoughts together as her tongue began to dart out in little licks against his lips. "By the Lady, you are so damn beautiful," he declared hotly as his hands ran down her body.

She laughed at that, pulling back to give him a look. "You can't possibly mean that in the aesthetic sense," she challenged him.

"Oh, but I do. I mean it in every sense. And you'd know if I was lying. A few bruises and some mushy makeup doesn't keep me from seeing what I want to see. It certainly doesn't make you any less sexy or make you burn any less hot," he whispered as he caught her bottom in his hands and used the cupping hold to tilt her into his waiting mouth.

Tatyana felt his hands squeezing her gently, but there was a vibration inside of him that told her how much he was holding back. As usual, she mused. Still, she knew she wasn't likely to unleash so much as a mouse from inside of this man while looking like she'd just done ten rounds in a boxing ring. That big beast inside of him just scratching and growling beneath the surface and waiting for her to release him, it would have to wait.

But for now . . . for now she was burning. Hunter shifted restlessly beneath her and she felt that impatience radiating through her body. She was wearing some kind of buttoned-down dress of Annali's, something handy as she'd gotten dressed quickly that morning at Hunter's impatient request that they go see Ryce. Now the convenience of it made her grin with lascivious intent. She slid forward and snuggled deep into his lap, her bare sex pressed to his fly where he'd be better able to get drenched in her heat. In reaction to the contact, Hunter sucked in a breath and his hands shot up along her bare thighs under her skirt. He grabbed hold of her by her hips and pressed her down against himself as she rocked against him.

All the while, she began to unbutton her dress from the top button on down. When she had gone far enough to put her cleavage on display but still shy of her navel by a couple of buttons, she lightly danced her fingertips down her breast-bone and over the inside swells of her breasts.

"I think I would choose to have you put your tongue on me, right here," she remarked invitingly as she slowly drew apart the two sides of the dress. "All the other parts of your mouth would also be welcome." She drew aside fabric to expose a pretty pink nipple, the fair color still outstanding against her even fairer skin. She scraped a fingernail across herself as she pulled her dress aside, causing her nipple to tighten up into a tempting point.

Tatyana saw his attention was completely riveted to her exposed breast, his chest rising and falling hard with his aroused state. She thrilled in the power she had to affect him, the knowledge of it sliding in wet, heated ribbons down her body. She used a pair of fingers under his chin to tilt his attention up to her eyes.

"What would you have chosen?" she asked, a soft smile on her lips as they brushed in gentle kisses over his brows.

"Probably something like this," he rumbled roughly against her cheek just before he slid a hand from her hip and sought between her spread-out thighs. It meant feeling the back of his own hand pressing against his fly, but just then he really needed a little counter-pressure. He felt her tense up in preparation long before he made it past her labia and into the drenched valley they protected. He found her clit almost immediately, causing her to gasp and jolt forward against him. The movement brought that delightfully bare breast against his mouth and he took advantage instantly, catching her rigid nipple between his teeth briefly before flicking his tongue in play against her.

Her hands split directions, one diving into his hair at the back of his head, the other hurrying to finish her task of un-buttoning her dress. She moved in counter-motion to the stroke of his fingertips, her hips undulating in soft, subtle circles that radiated up her entire spine. It was so incredibly sexy, such an amazing turn-on. She was so naturally full of sexual appetite and so able to express it, she made Hunter lose his mind to her desires.

Tatyana shucked her dress back off her body, making herself a naked, open treat for her as-yet fully clothed lover. Hunter could barely decide how best to use his body to please her. He loved what her pleasure did to her. The little ways she moved, the unchecked sounds she made. She was panting hotly already, her eyes closed as her lithe body rode the stroke of his hand with growing ecstasy. He ached with hardness just watching her, the pulse hammering through his cock an unreal force. It begged him to be inside of her, and then the begging quickly turned into demands.

Hunter barely felt her hands pulling his shirt apart, never even realizing she'd unbuttoned it as well. He lurched forward off the couch, spilling them both onto the floor in front of the radiant heat of the fire. She was beneath him now, and she complained in a sultry mewl when he removed his hand from her to strip his shirt off. He reared up onto his knees as he did so, looking down at her gorgeous body lying before him, her knees parted around the intrusion of his hips.

Bruises colored her all down one side.

The shot of rage came out of nowhere, even as he struggled to fight it back. This, he realized, would allow Braen victory over them both. If he let his anger control him and ruin their intimacies, his brother would have driven a wedge between them just as definitive as if he'd succeeded in his intended acts.

Tatyana wasn't fooled for an instant. She saw and felt every emotion that rocketed through his warrior's soul, including the fight to keep it all at bay for her benefit. She reached up for him, catching him by the face and drawing him down to her kiss.

"It's okay," she hushed and soothed him, ignoring the answering anger she felt toward the man who had done this to them. She refused to allow him the opportunity to defeat them. What they had, she knew, was so much stronger. "Look

4

at me and see only who you need," she coaxed him softly. "See only what you want, honey," she whispered against his ear. "See the woman who wants you to make love to her."

Hunter drew back to look down at her and blinked dark lashes over brilliant blue eyes. He smiled as he let his gaze roam over the length of her perfect body once more, reaching a hand to stroke down over her curved breast, in-swept waist, and the lush swell of her hip. Her smooth, pale skin was dusted with the lightest smattering of freckles, a tempting pattern that beckoned for him to touch and taste.

"I have never had a woman dazzle me the way that you do," he confessed to her heatedly as he stroked her warming skin. Firelight touched her, making pinks pinker and peaches golden, her hair turning into a nimbus of coppers and reds.

Tatyana smiled up at him, reaching to touch his bare skin and following his beautiful eyes as they tracked over her body again and again. It left her dizzy and breathless the way he seemed to worship every inch of her, ignoring everything except her textures and responses. He lowered his head to her soft belly, nuzzling her with hot breath and coarse whiskers. The combination stimulated and tickled, making her gasp out loud, her braced feet raising her up off the floor. The movement drew all of his attention downward, his mouth tracking below her navel.

He drew up just far enough to watch himself touch her, his fingertips coasting over bare, smooth skin where hair ought to have been.

"You shave," he observed, glancing up at her to watch her face as he so gently navigated the edges of her sex.

"Wax, actually," she said breathlessly.

"Okay," he said.

"Why? Is something wrong with that?"

"No, sweetheart. You're perfect. Either way, you'd be just perfect. I was just observing things about you. For instance, you're the prettiest shade of pink right along . . . here."

His finger slid between the slick lips of her pussy, enjoying the feel of his effect on her body. Her position with her knees apart allowed him an excellent view of that soft shell pink that darkened in intense degrees the closer inside of her he traveled. His touch slid all around her. The simple sound of the wet movement and the sensuous aroma of her that rose up to him made him crave her on his tongue. He lowered his mouth to her, kissing her over her denuded skin, his tongue dipping for a preliminary taste of her.

Hunter stopped and swallowed back a groan as a fierce tremor of need shuddered through him. He swept his fingers over her, separating her so she showed herself to him in perfect pink depth. Her clitoris glistened wetly, like a small jewel. Craving overcame him and his tongue darted out to stroke over her. Her reaction was dynamic, a gasp that rang off the ceiling and a seeking lift of her hips when he drew away without satisfying the clamoring need of her hungry little body.

After that, there was no way to keep him from her. She was too sweet and salty on his tongue to let her escape without a thorough tasting. And the more his lips and his tongue stroked against her, the more she writhed and moaned with ecstatic feeling. Her fingers were latched into his hair, the act of holding him to her both amusing and erotic. He didn't want to be anywhere else, and she didn't want him anywhere else. It was a perfect partnership.

What he really wanted he was rapidly working her toward, if her concurrent cries of pleasure were anything to gauge by. The sound of her was delighting him and killing him all at once. Without altering his successful technique at all, he reached to free his throbbing cock from his pants, desperately in need of relief. He then focused on her sensitive little clit, wriggling a finger inside of her as he tortured her to her last nerve. She was tensing tightly around him, gearing up for the release he wanted. He forced a second finger into her and worked them into her as he savored the last moments of her climb.

Tatyana threw back her head, her entire back bowing up off the floor as the feel of his mouth drove her over the edge. She was full of his fingers, longing for it to be so much more than that, as the dance of his tongue caused her to explode with spasms of pleasure. She screamed out, tears and stars dancing in her eyes as her blood roared through her body. She felt him remove himself from inside of her, his mouth fastening on her to catch the creamy heat of passion oozing from her body.

When he was satisfied she was done, he moved away from her limp, panting body and shed the remainder of his clothes. Hunter slid back up her form quickly, the slide of her damp skin like heaven against his own. She clutched for him eagerly, parting her legs wide for his approach. He spent a long moment at each breast, laving and sucking, pulling roughly at her with eager teeth as if his body wasn't demanding release with everything he had. He wouldn't rush. He had rushed the first time. He needed so badly to enjoy every nuance of her this time.

He reached for her mouth, listening to her moan softly as she experienced the taste of herself on her tongue. He shared the essence gladly, her reaction burning through him. She was so sexual a creature that he couldn't imagine anything they might do turning her off. That was a theory he was willing to spend a great deal of time testing.

At last Hunter settled against her, letting himself rest in contact with the outrageously receptive heat of her. Knowing she waited just for him was like winning an incredible sweepstakes. His reactions were the same. Unbelievable excitement, disbelieving pleasure, and heart-pounding anticipation for what would come next. How to spend this gift? What way to make it go furthest? To make it last?

"I have to take you, Tatyana," he groaned as his cock slid against her wet folds again and again in restless need.

"Yes, please. I'm waiting," she begged, lifting seeking hips for him.

"But I'm going to warn you now, angel," he breathed against her ear. "I am not going to come until you do so at least twice more. So don't you even try to make me. There's only one thing that is going to set me off, and that thing is listening to you and feeling you orgasm all around me. Got it, honey?"

"But . . ." She panted a moment, having a hard time reconciling herself to taking more pleasure without him. Hunter had learned quickly that she got off on making him feel good. This time, he wanted all her attention turned strictly inward to herself. At least until the end. "Okay," she relented with frustration when the closeness of their bodies begged her to do anything to have him inside of her. "Anything, Hunter. Anything you want. Please!"

The last *please* came out as a loud cry of relief as he found his place at the entrance of her vaginal tunnel. He didn't waste a single moment longer before pushing into her in shallow, increasing thrusts. Her head whipped side to side, her hair a wild cloud of wisps and tendrils.

"What feels good, hmm?" he taunted her softly after finding her ear. His body was coated in the sweat of restraint, his penis aching for full penetration into her tight little body. It knew how eager she was, felt the way her walls grasped and sucked at him as they tried to pull him in deeper. "Tell me, angel. What feels good? How am I going to make you come unless you tell?"

"Oh God! Please, I need you inside me!"

"I am inside you," he teased her.

"Deeper! All of you. Fill me until I burst," she begged him, her nails scoring his back in desperation. She needn't have worried. Her way with words guaranteed his response in a powerful, hard-driven thrust of solid flesh through yielding muscle. It was all to rev up her responsive mind, and it worked. The instant he was fully inside of her, she ripped into orgasm.

Hunter cried out with her as she clutched around him and

tried so hard to milk him of his seed. She gasped and panted, clutching him with hands and body, writhing under him with the most incredible passion he'd ever seen in another person. To find someone like this, with her heart, courage, and intelligence besides . . . and someone with magic! She was a rare and precious treasure and he realized it with the chilling certainty one gets when one is touched by the hand of fate.

He closed his eyes and nodded acceptance to himself, then looked down at her. "That's one," he rasped. "Now this one, I'm going to fuck it out of you like crazy."

Chapter Seventeen

Tatyana was being rolled onto her side, Hunter straddling her bottom leg on his knees while he drew the other over his hip. Once he had her in place, including the momentary adjustment of a pillow under her hip to elevate her just right, he quickly entered her again, thrusting himself heavily into her.

He had done it on purpose. Turned aside, she couldn't really touch him. All she could do was focus on the feel of his cock rubbing over all the nerves inside of her body. She could see him braced in a powerful kneel, his magnificent body on full display in the firelight, his strong hand wrapped around her thigh while the other stroked her skin. Tatyana could see him moving into her over and over, his focus completely on his rhythm and his fascination with the curves of her body. His choice of position had seemed unusual at first, but she quickly came to understand why he had wanted it. He was thrusting right across that singular spot inside of her that made her mind fall apart and turned her nervous system to spaghetti.

Tatyana was frustrated that she couldn't touch him, her hand reaching for his and covering it just so she could feel him.

"You just can't help yourself, can you?" he laughed breathlessly.

"I need to touch you," she gasped as he turned her completely away, facedown now, his hands running up the back
of her body until she heard him make an almost savage
sound of appreciation.

"No matter which way I turn you, angel, you just get
more delightful with every inch." He took hold of her hips
and pulled her back onto her knees. She automatically put
her hands under herself so she was on all fours and she
moaned deeply when he squared himself into position for
entering her again. His fingers traced her with teasing ca-
resses against her aching clit. His cock dipped into her
lightly, refusing her the satisfaction of depth and power . . .
of the fullness she craved with all of her being.

"Hunter," she complained. "We had an agreement, I
thought. You know very well that every time you touch me, or
even so much as look at me, it drives me crazy. I know you
know it because I see you do it on purpose to get your way.
Not this time. This time you just feel how hard and hot you
make my cock, you feel how hungry I am for the textures of
this delicious body of yours. Feel it until you can't feel anything else. Until you don't want to feel anything else."

Hunter ran his hands up over the pale, naked curves of
her backside. His fingers slid up her sensitive spine as he
slowly and fully sank into the tightness of her. The moan she
released actually shuddered through her entire body, and he
felt an answering response strangling him. It was unbelievably erotic to tease her like this, but he may have been asking
a bit much of himself. She was still too new to him. Too un-
explored and unexpected. He couldn't get over her sheer
sensory appetite and it aroused him insanely. He tried to
clear his mind and think, tried to construct a plan for pleas-
ing her, but all he could focus on was the erotic sounds she
made when she felt him plunge deep inside of her. He began
to seek them out with relish, but it was unraveling his con-

trol thrust by thrust. Her sleek body slid in his hands as perspiration coated her skin, that slink in her spine amazing to
watch as she rode back against him in a frantically quickening rhythm.

She dropped down to her elbows, bracing herself harder
in counterforce and allowing him a new depth and pitch.
Her head dropped down, her hair sprawling over the floor.
Tatyana looked down the front of her body and could see his
cock sliding in and out of her. She saw how wet she had
made him by the gleam of the firelight and it was incredibly
exciting.

She also saw a sudden advantage that made her smile
with wicked mischief. She could feel him reaching a fever-
ish pitch, knew he was struggling for control so he could
focus on making her feel pleasure, but the truth would always be that it was his pleasure that really triggered hers.
Even the thought of her little trick made her incredibly hot,
her body burning up in preparation of release. A release she
needed so very badly.

She waited until she saw him close his eyes, his head
dropping back slightly as he lost himself in what he was
feeling. Then she shifted all of her weight onto a single arm,
reached down her body and between her legs for him. His
stroke into her brought him over her fingers and palm, ending with her cupping and massaging the heavy sac between
his legs.

"Holy . . . you . . . oh, no . . . no, no . . ."

She smiled when she felt him go rigidly still inside of her,
his hands clamping down on her hips. She felt him struggling fiercely for recovery as his body burst with the need to
come inside of her. She didn't relent, her fingers, nails, and
palm stroking his hypersensitive skin, feeling the tightening
tension pulsing through the heated flesh she toyed with. To
make it just a little more difficult for him, she tightened
every muscle that surrounded him.

"Oh, you sly little . . . by the Lady, you . . ." he gasped,

unable to complete his sentences until he realized he was
fighting a losing battle. "Son of a bitch!" he exclaimed at
last, grabbing onto her tightly as he started to plunge into her
like a madman.

That mad desperation, that inability to resist her, that was
what got Tatyana off. She braced both hands once more,
feeling him battering himself against and into her until her
head reeled with the pleasure of it.

"Oh God! Oh yes! Hunter, I'm . . . I . . ."

"You damn well better!" he growled ferociously just as he
jerked into her in clumsy, off-rhythm thrusts and shouted out
the coming of his release.

Tatyana felt it all. His release, hers. All of it flooding into
her from every direction until she was seizing with it in
every molecule of her body. It was as though she could feel
the rush of semen jolting from his body from his perspective, the almost painful pleasure of it that made every nerve
go completely haywire. She could feel him pulsating deeply
inside of her even as she did the same all around him. She
couldn't stop her outcries, which seemed to go on endlessly.
She was on overload, tears falling hotly from her lashes as
she felt Hunter holding on to her, vibrating with tremors as
he sucked for breath as deeply as he could.

Tatyana was barely even aware of him moving and lifting
her up into his arms. He carried her straight into his bedroom, laying her in his bed and sliding in beside her. He
gathered her close, kissing her in whatever spots he could
reach without releasing her from his hug. At last he settled
near her ear, his breath warming it and her neck.

Hunter didn't say anything, his mind still reeling in the
aftermath of how she affected him. He had never been so out
of control as he was when he was with her. Others had
sought to tap into the wilder side of him, but none had succeeded in the slightest. He had always held himself steady;
he was, in a sense, untouchable.

She touched him. In so many ways. With so much depth.

He had spent enough years making certain his sexual encounters were emotionally detached to know when he was in serious threat of being very, very much attached. His lifestyle had left no room for things like commitment or love or any other romantic notion, and now was no different. His was deadly work; even now his family was under a dire threat they might not manage to survive intact. As it was, they could lose Asher.

But he felt a responsibility to Tatyana as well. Her own life hung in the balance every moment she stayed there. The idea sent Hunter's heart racing in a spiral of very real fear. It forced him to relive that moment again, when he had seen Asher's possessed body looming over her, ready to violate her even as he taunted her with disgusting imagery. What if he hadn't gotten to her in time? Goddess, he *hadn't* gotten to her in time. Not in time to spare her pain. That was his job. Just as it had been with Amber; it was his responsibility.

"I feel you thinking at me," she whispered.

Hunter couldn't help smiling at that. "You are assuming way too much if you think I can put together coherent thought after what you just did to me."

"Don't try to dodge me, buddy. I grew up with the master of that trick and . . ."

Tatyana sat up with a gasp.

"Oh crap! Dimitre!" She turned to shove Hunter in the shoulder. "Get some clothes on!"

Bemused, he watched her fly out of bed and run naked back into the sitting room. It wasn't until he heard the knock on the outside door that he realized why she'd freaked out all of a sudden.

"Ah, hell," he groaned as he hurried to get out of bed.

Dimitre gave up on knocking and walked into Hunter's suite. It was purely an act of habit. He'd gotten very used to the coven's liberal approach to privacy. Sitting rooms were fair game in the private suites; bedrooms and bathrooms, obviously, demanded respect. It never once occurred to him that there would be a reason to alter that assumption, forgetting that until then, he and Annali had been the only couple in the house and the only ones having sex within its walls. None of the other single witches brought outsiders to the coven in order to protect their secret selves.

He was expecting Hunter and his sister to be working on her magic, just as their High Priest had demanded they do. He completely forgot all the times he and Annali had worked all kinds of magic, neglecting his powers completely, every time they had been alone in the beginning of their relationship. Sex magic, she had liked to call it.

Even so, as shocking as it was to walk in and find Hunter Finn belting on a robe rather hurriedly as he came from his bedroom, it didn't compare to seeing the beautiful woman by the fireplace struggling to button up her dress while kneeling amid discarded clothing and the obvious signs of illicit behavior.

He took one look at her, her golden blond curls dancing with firelight and her lavender eyes looking up at him with extraordinary guilt, and he felt the entire world careen off its center.

He stood frozen, as if he were stuck in his own ability to freeze time, watching her fly to her feet and run to him. If she touched him smelling of another man, he was certain he was going to explode.

"Stop!"

He made the command, throwing out his hand, and flinging power from his core. Up until that moment, whenever he did this, the entire room or house would freeze in time. He hadn't learned how to control it yet, and when emotion like total devastation was involved, anything could happen.

It did. This time she was the only thing to freeze. Flames continued to flicker in the fireplace, and Hunter was still moving toward him.

"What are you doing?" Hunter demanded. "For the Mother's sake, Dimitre, she's a grown woman! She can make her own choices!"

Dimitre finally did explode. He swung at Hunter, shouting in fury. Hunter dodged him easily, catching the roundhouse punch by the back of Dimitre's wrist. As gently as he could, he forced the witch to follow the momentum of his own strike right off of his feet. Dimitre hit the floor with a grunt.

Physically, the blond witch was no threat to Hunter. Magically was another story, he knew, as he glanced over to Tatyana's frozen form. Leaving Dimitre facing the floor, he cast a binding spell that kept his hands and body locked down where they were. He was hoping that without hand gestures and without being in his line of sight, Dimitre couldn't target him.

"You son of a bitch!" Dimitre shouted, making Hunter consider a muting spell as well. However, they needed to talk.

"No more or less than usual," he retorted dryly. "What is your problem, Petrova?"

"Are you fucking kidding me? You're sleeping with her!"

Hunter sighed. "Yes. I'm aware of that. Why is this such an issue for you?"

"Because I love her, you miserable bastard!"

"And now you can't love her because she slept with me? Or is it because you don't think I'm good enough for her? Frankly, my friend, you aren't going to think anyone is good enough for her. And you have to get over that."

"I swear to God I'm going to kill you for this," Dimitre hissed. "I thought you were after my damn sister, and that was hard enough, but Annali is mine! You hear me? She's mine! I'll kill you for touching her!"

"Anna—?" Hunter swiveled his head between Dimitre and his sister, completely puzzled. "What in the name of the

Lady are you talking about? I wouldn't ever touch Annali! No more than you would touch Tatyana!"

Dimitre laughed, but it was a mirthless, pained sound. The sound of a man with a heart that was breaking. A man shattering into pieces.

"I find you in here alone, the two of you dressing, and you just admitted to me you were screwing around! She's standing right there, frozen in time like an evidence exhibit!"

"Wait . . . Annali? Annali is frozen in time? Right here?"

"Oh my God, I can't do this," Dimitre rasped.

"Dimitre!" Annali exclaimed as she came running into the room. "Hunter, what are you doing?"

Annali scrambled onto the floor beside the man she loved and Hunter released the binding so she could touch him. Dimitre shoved himself away from her, staring at her with real tears in his wounded eyes. He flung his attention between the blonde reaching toward him in moving supplication, and the one he had frozen.

"Don't! Don't touch me!" he demanded of the moving Annali, keeping his hands down so he didn't freeze her as well. "Is this a trick, Finn?"

"If it is, it's of your own making. I see two different women here. Your sister, Tatyana, whom you've got frozen like a popsicle, and Annali, your lover. Not mine. Yours. This one is mine." He moved to Tatyana, his mind moving through his vast inventory of spells as he tried to come up with something he could use to countermand the magic her brother was using.

Annali gasped and turned on Dimitre with every ounce of indignant Southern fury she could muster. "Dimitre Petrova, you think I slept with Hunter?" She reached out and slapped him so hard across the face that Hunter winced.

"Ow! Son of a . . . ! Okay!" Dimitre grabbed her recoiling hand and looked into her furious lavender eyes. "I would never think anything of the kind unless I saw it for myself!

Never! So, when I came in here and found you half naked, and him just as good as, and a room that, forgive the indelicacy, reeks of sex, what was I supposed to think? If it's not you, Annie, then it's someone who looks a hell of a lot like you! That," he pointed to the replica of Annali, "is not my sister! That woman is your spitting image!"

"That is Tatyana!" Hunter and Annali argued in tandem. "Don't you know your own sister? I thought you two could sense each other," Annali said hotly. "We don't know who you are seeing, but that's your sister." Annali looked back at the redhead stopped in mid-motion. "But nice job isolating your magic, baby," she praised him in earnest.

As confused as he was, Dimitre knew without a doubt that the blonde in motion next to him was his Annali. She was forever finding the good side of even the worst situations.

"You know, I never thought I'd be trying to convince someone's brother that I am sleeping with his baby sister," Hunter grumbled. "Would you mind freeing her? I'd like to figure out what's going on here."

Dimitre moved to do so, reaching for the other Annali and feeling a surreal shiver down the back of his neck as he touched her and slowly freed her from his time trap.

Tatyana found herself stumbling into her brother and abruptly realizing that Annali had appeared out of nowhere. Hunter had completely shifted positions. It was as if she had blinked and stepped into an entirely different moment in time.

Understanding struck and she put her hands on her hips and glared at her sibling. "You used magic on me!" she accused him. "What'd you do that for, you big jerk?!" She looked from him to Hunter. "Did he do something stupid? Are you okay?"

Hunter found her concern amusing, rather than insulting as he might have. More than that, he was getting a kick out of watching her brother's expressions.

"Holy shit, that sure sounds like my sister," Dimitre acknowledged. "And I can feel her psychically. But I swear to God, she looks like Annali!" He reached up and poked a finger against his sister's cheek, getting his hand slapped for his trouble.

Hunter quickly explained the trouble to Tatyana.

"It's some kind of spell."

"Yes, but who cast it?" Annali asked.

"Let's go find Ryce. Maybe he can figure it out. Give me a second to umm . . ." Hunter let the sentence hang and moved to retrieve his clothes from the floor. He got dressed while Annali glared at Dimitre alongside his sister.

"Okay, stop that. It's just too freaky getting stared at by two of you. I mean, two of *you*," he clarified pointing to the real Annali.

A few minutes later the quartet was interrupting Nox and Ryce's reconstruction of the house wards. Ryce turned sharply, annoyed at their entrance into the room he used for complex spellcasting.

"Sorry, Ryce," Hunter said, "but we have a problem."

Ryce watched Hunter reach back and pull forward Yelena Suarez, a sultry little black-haired beauty Ryce had been having an ongoing affair with whenever he was able to find time away from the coven. Circumstances had been keeping him out of her bed for the past few weeks, and he had missed her lusty little appetites. However, he had never told her where he lived, and she absolutely was not invited into the sanctity of the coven.

"What in hell is she doing in this house?" he demanded of his witches, a sharp cancellation gesture ending his current magic. "And why would you ever bring her in this room? Are you out of your minds?"

Hunter looked from Ryce to Yelena with a strange expression on his face and then asked, "Ryce, who do you see here?"

"Who do I . . . ? You're the one that brought her here, Sentinel. Why are you—"

"Just humor me," he encouraged dryly.

"Yelena. Suarez. She's a . . . she's my . . ." He ran a hand back through his hair a little sheepishly. "Right, well, she's my current mistress then, if you must know. But she doesn't know what I am or where I live, so this cannot be her."

"It isn't," Hunter agreed. "It's Tatyana."

"Like bloody hell it is," Nox argued over them all. "There's Giselle, that tiny little redhead from Raven's shop."

"Whoa, now even I'm confused," Tatyana complained.

The other two men gasped when Tatyana's voice came out of the image of the woman each thought she was.

"It's a glamour," Ryce marveled, coming up to Tatyana and reaching to touch her face. Hunter frowned, but he allowed it reluctantly.

"A very specific glamour. She's different to everyone," Nox noted.

"Not to me," Annali snorted.

"Or me," Hunter added.

"Me three," Tatyana said, raising her hand before she brushed Ryce's touch away.

Hunter was trying to think. Could a glamour be cast through the wards while they were being repaired, from an outside source? Had Braen cast a delayed effect on her, hoping to cause even more chaos among them? Or . . . had she cast the spell herself?

Hunter sucked in a hard breath and suddenly turned to look at her. Holding her between his hands, he studied her long and hard. Sure enough, even though he was looking at Tatyana, he was looking at a very perfect Tatyana. A flawless one.

"No bruises. You have no bruises," he said quickly. "We all know for a fact that you do, and when it was bothering me earlier . . . you said . . ."

Tatyana recalled what she had said and hurriedly slapped

a hand over Hunter's mouth, blushing thoroughly as she looked at her brother and the others.

"Hunter!" she warned through gritted teeth. "Shut up!"

Ryce chuckled at her reaction. "Tatyana, we need to know what you said so we can figure out what's going on."

"Let Hunter figure it out," she ordered.

"Two minds are better than one, angel," Hunter reminded her. "And the more the merrier. Besides, they're going to find out eventually."

"Oh, crap," she groaned, burying her face against his chest as it burned with embarrassment.

"Yeah, let's hurry this up. It's freaking me out watching you get hugged on by my woman," Dimitre complained.

"You mean you see Annali?" Nox asked, chuckling. "Now there's just something wrong with that, mate."

"Tell me about it," he grumbled.

"The boy genius walked in on them . . . and thought Tatyana was me," Annali sniffed. "As if I would cheat on you!"

"Well, you used to be in love with him!"

"I was not!"

"I'd say it was a crush, really," Ryce mused, "wouldn't you, Nox?"

"Infatuation, actually," Nox suggested.

"Hero-worship," Hunter injected.

"Men!" Annali growled with a stamp of her foot. "You are all irredeemable! I swear!"

"So tell us what you said to Hunter, Tatyana," Ryce said with a grin, returning to the matter at hand.

Tatyana just kept her face right where it was and shook her head vehemently.

"Dimitre, darlin', give your sister some dignity. Ryce will explain later when she doesn't have to face you," Annali coaxed him. Dimitre frowned, the whole situation displeasing him and disturbing him.

"I'd feel better if I could see this spell reversed."

"Dimitre Petrova, you move that fine ass of yours out of this room this instant or I swear to the Goddess I will tell every soul in this room what *you* said to *me* last night when we made love."

"Whoa!" Dimitre reached out and this time he was the one slapping a hand over his lover's mouth, knowing full well she made no empty threats. "Umm, okay. Tat, I'll see you after you fix this. We're going. Bye."

Dimitre dragged Annali from the room as she snorted giggles from behind his hand. Once they were out the door, Hunter turned to Ryce with a sigh. "That is one scary power that boy has. I'm lucky he didn't stop time in the entire room. He just singled out Tatyana, although I doubt it was his intention. Otherwise I would be dead before I knew what even happened."

"Yeah, that's the unfunny part of this," Ryce agreed. "So, what'd she say?"

"I'll try to quote it perfectly. 'Look at me and see only who you need. See only what you want . . . see the woman who wants you to make love to her,' or something very close to that."

"Far out," Nox murmured. "Right, then, I get it. Everyone who looks at her sees the woman they want. Dimitre saw Annali. Ryce sees his mistress. You want Tatyana, so you just see her. Annali doesn't want a woman, so it doesn't work on her. Nice little spell, that."

"Except I don't think it's a spell," Ryce mused. "It was about bruises, you said?"

"Yes. I just wanted him to see past them. To not let them bother him," she sniffed.

"To look beyond the surface. You wanted to bring his mind beyond its limitations. Emotional limitations. As a result, you're walking around in an unlimited glamour that is making men see you as the woman they desire without limitation." Ryce cocked a brow and grinned at Nox. "Giselle, eh? Never knew you had a thing for her."

"I bloody don't!" Nox protested. "The spell's gone wrong or something. I wouldn't go for a non-magic girl. Too complicated even with a magic one."

"It wouldn't kill you to take her as a lover so long as she knew the limits," Ryce argued.

"But I don't want to. She's all cute and that, but not my type."

"Well, I did make the wording reciprocal. Maybe she wants to make love with you, rather than the other way around," Tatyana suggested.

"There you go. That's it exactly. Hey, that's cool. It's like scrying for a girl who's hot for you," Nox chuckled. "That'd take the guessing out of it."

"Where's the fun in that?" Ryce laughed.

"So how to reverse this?" Hunter prompted.

"I think it's up to Tatyana. Seems like she's using the power of suggestion here, not a spell."

"Well, whatever it is, it's giving me a headache. This is all giving me a headache," she complained.

"What it is really is a sign of magic," Ryce pointed out. "The first since that spell out by the Blessing Tree."

"It's vague. It could be any number of schools," Hunter said, shaking his head. "Spellcaster, Ritualist . . . Presage . . ."

"It could be anything," Nox interrupted. "We all can do glamours. It's just that this one is rather strong."

"The desire behind the suggestion was strong," Ryce remarked. "It's a good sign," he assured Tatyana. "It says something about your power level."

"Terrific. But can you help me fix it before I completely weird out my brother?"

Chapter Eighteen

"Hey, brat."

"Hey, jerk," Tatyana greeted in return when her brother tugged on her hair before kissing her on the cheek she turned up to him.

"How are you doing?"

"Well, I have a headache, possibly from the idea of my boyfriend and my brother having a fight, possibly not. I haven't decided."

"It was a perfectly understandable mix-up."

"Yeah, well, I'm sure Annali is very pleased to know you have such faith in her," she said dryly.

"I'll let you know as soon as she starts talking to me again," he sighed.

"Ooo, a bit miffed is she?"

"Pissed. With a capital P. Worst thing is, she's talking but not talking. Hard to explain. I'll work it out."

"No doubt. You have that talent," Tatyana laughed.

"So it's 'boyfriend' is it? What's it been? Two days? Three?"

"Hmm, I don't recall. What was it for you and Annali? Maybe that will jog my memory."

"Touché," he chuckled. "But are you expecting you and Hunter to go the way Annali and I are going?"

"I'm not expecting anything," she said quietly, rubbing at the ache in her forehead. She knew what her brother was getting at. He didn't want her to risk getting attached so quickly to a man she knew so little about. He was worried she might get her heart broken. "I never expect anything."

"It's just, you're young yet, Tat. Nothing says you have to—"

"Yes, Dimitre, I get it," she snapped, turning sharply to look at him. "I'm not some idiotic schoolgirl with a crush on a movie star. I know he's a witch. I know he's a killer. I know he is ten years older than I am and twice as powerful as I ever hope to be. I know I would be insane to think someone like that will ever want to settle down, never mind settling down with a 'child.' Okay? I get it."

Dimitre was speechless. She had hit every point he might have made right on the head, except hearing her say it all like she had made it sound damn cold and unflattering to her.

"Listen, honey, I'm just—"

"Well stop, okay? Stop worrying about me so much! You didn't worry about me one damn bit these past two months, and frankly, I seriously underestimated the freedom of it." She stood up, grabbing the book she'd been reading on the different schools of magic and hugging it tightly to her body. "And for God's sake, call Mama. You've been a real bastard to her. You hurt her when you didn't come for Christmas. We always come for Christmas. All of us."

"I was in Pennsylvania!"

"Yeah. Okay. You tell her that. I'm sure that'll make her feel so much better."

Tatyana left after that sarcastic parting shot.

"How is he?"

"Better," Kaia said wearily. "He's out of stasis and holding his own. I've repaired everything life-threatening either by magic or conventional medicine. He's lost a lot of blood. I could use a trip to the clinic."

"You'd have to account for that blood."

"There are ways," she said with a shrug. "Fact is, he needs it and I am too weak to help anymore."

"What about Dimitre or Tatyana?" Hunter asked. "I know none of us can donate, but surely you can see if they can."

"No. They are both A positive. I already checked. The only universal donor in this house is Annali, and I can't use her."

"Well, why in hell not?" Hunter made a frustrated noise when Kaia gave him a look. "Don't give me that doctor-patient privilege crap," he snapped. "Is she sick? Was this something Evan caused?" Kaia hadn't been a full-fledged doctor and had still been just learning to be a Healer when they had first brought Annali home. It was possible she had missed something in that first year that he didn't know about.

Kaia sighed. "You know, the problem with you and Ryce is you both think you have a right to know everything that goes on in this house. I can't use Annali because she's anemic. She has a long history of it, in fact. That's why I never use her. Now that you know, maybe you can do me a favor in return. Help me convince Ryce to let me go get some blood for Asher."

"I'll talk to him. Maybe if I convince him to send me with you it will make him feel okay about it."

"Great. I appreciate it."

"Meanwhile, can you get some sleep, Kaia? Maybe Annali can watch over him for you?"

"Would you ask her?"

"Sure. Hang in there."

Hunter left the private clinic at the back of the house. The medical setup had come in handy quite often over the years, he was certain. It serviced only the coven's needs, and now that Kaia was licensed it was probably much easier to supply the mini clinic. The shortage of blood was merely a reflection of how critical Asher's injuries had been. He didn't envy Kaia working alone in there. She'd performed surgeries on Asher he was positive weren't meant to be done singlehandedly. What surgery was? Nox's stasis spell was the real advantage. It stopped all vital functions, suspending them until the spell ceased. It was what had made those impossible surgeries possible.

Hunter walked into the rear section of the conservatory, making his way through the series of hothouses until he reached Annali's office. He pushed open the door and spied her across the room. She was bent over her lab sink, washing her face and hands. He could see the remnants of a spilled potion on her lab table and dripping onto the floor.

"Anything I'm going to have to duck and cover for?" he teased her, knowing how volatile her mixtures could be.

"Hmm? Oh," she smiled wanly, "no. Actually, I was just recorking some of my extracts and . . . I dropped one."

"Butterfingers."

"Exactly." She straightened up and grabbed a towel to dry her face and hands. Hunter could see the spattered mess across her pretty pink outfit and knew she was going to be peeved about that. "Did you need me?"

"Actually, Kaia does. She needs relief in a bad way. Can you send her to bed and watch Ash?"

"Of course. I'll go as soon as I clean this up. The mess just reeks."

"I kinda thought it smelled like roses. Strong."

"Reeks," she asserted. "And you're right. It is a highly concentrated roses extract."

"You know, this reminds me . . . I was going to ask if you wouldn't consider helping me put together a small gift for Tatyana. A reward for when she really comes into her magic."

"Oh. I see." Annali waved her hand at the strong odor of roses. "A personalized perfume?"

"A little less complex. Maybe . . . a little more umm . . . provocative."

"Ohh, okay. Let me think about it. I'll come up with something soon. Okay?"

"Great. I—" Hunter cut himself off and looked up suddenly. Annali tensed. "Something is . . . Tatyana is upset, I think. I'm going to go check on her. You'll go send Kaia to bed?"

"Sure thing, sugar."

Hunter barely heard the acknowledgment. He was already on his way out of Annali's lab. He hurried up the stairs, following his sense of his apprentice witch. He found her in his suite, sitting curled up before the fire in a chair with a book open in her lap. Her eyes were closed, though, her head tilted back and lines of obvious pain etched over her face. He could see she had also been crying, her tears leaving marks in the foundation she was using.

"Hey, honey," he said with soft concern as he knelt before the chair she was in. "What's going on?"

"Nothing. Just my brother being a jerk and giving me a big headache, that's all."

She sounded angry, but she welcomed his hug just the same and let him pull her close in a comforting hold.

"Did you take something for this?" he asked, gently touching her temple near her closed eye.

"A half a billion Advil. I'm waiting for them to kick in."

Hunter closed the book in her lap and set it aside, drawing her down completely into the cradle of his lap as he sat down cross-legged under her. "Are you going to tell me what Dimitre said to piss you off?"

"I don't think so," she sighed. "It's not worth repeating." Especially not when Hunter's present tenderness made her want to forget her brother's dire warnings about her lover's unlikely need for a long-term woman in his life. Besides, neither one of the Petrova siblings could claim to know this man well enough to guess what he really wanted. Unfortunately, for her, it was becoming a problem, all of this not knowing. "Can I ask you something?"

"Sure, angel. Ask me anything."

"Are you really staying here?" She looked up at him, wincing at the firelight until he brought a hand up to guard her eyes. The gesture was so thoughtful, so sweet, she felt her throat closing up with confused emotion.

"Yes. I am. This is where I need to be now. Probably for the rest of my life, Goddess willing. Hopefully, being older and wiser will make me appreciate the coven more. I think it makes me appreciate a great many things more," he said softly, his thumb stroking over the bruises she was hiding.

"Do you mean me?" she asked with a little sob. "Because I'd like it if you did mean me."

"Oh, honey," he said, gathering her up tight to his chest, his lips brushing over her face, "of course I mean you. I'd be an idiot not to realize what a treasure you are. Do I look like an idiot to you?"

"No." She sniffled. "I don't understand why I feel this way. I'm not an insecure person."

"Wanting to know how someone feels about you doesn't make you insecure." He sighed. "And honestly, I'm glad you asked. Because now I can ask you right back."

"You want to know how I feel about you?" Tatyana plucked nervously at the material of his shirt. "I feel confused."

"Why?"

"Because I know I hardly know you, but"—she looked up into his eyes—"for some reason it doesn't matter. I feel like I know everything that's important. Which is childish, right? After only a few days?"

"No, sweetheart, it isn't childish," he said firmly, staring hard into her eyes. "It's called a blood bond, and it's magic. It connects us, allowing us incredible shortcuts to familiarity. I imagine it's why your brother and Annali became so close so quickly as well. And while the pull between us is supposed to fade over time, I am feeling just the opposite. I realized that it isn't because the bond's gone wrong . . . it's because it's going right. Really right." Hunter was unable to resist bending toward her mouth, kissing her gently. "I was afraid to say anything because you are so young . . . and I mean that in the sense that I can't imagine why you would want to saddle yourself with a man like me when you have a whole new future ahead of you. Even so, I couldn't bring myself to do anything that might scare you away or encourage you to come to your senses."

Hunter laughed awkwardly when she simply stared at him. "I need to know you more," he said roughly. "I've barely tasted the surface of you. I certainly haven't reached a satisfactory depth." He had to smile when she snorted out a giggle. "I like that your mind is even dirtier than mine. It's very comforting."

"I'm glad to help. I'm thinking of moving in with you. I think you'd like that. I have a list of reasons this could bene-fit both of us, if you need them."

"Not at all," he murmured. "For how long?"

"Umm, until you kick me out?"

"Sheesh, that long, huh?" He bit his lip and affected thinking about it, making her heart pound at the crazily of-fered compliments and sentiments. "Well, just so you know what you are getting yourself into. I'm going to be a huge pain in the butt when it comes to teaching you magic."

"Okay. But that means I get to be really demanding in bed," she stipulated.

"Fair enough," he growled softly. "So, I guess I should say something to Ryce, then?"

"No need to rub it in that he isn't getting any," she said flippantly.

"I meant that you are going to live with me. With us, I mean."

"With you."

"With me, in the coven. A definite us."

"I like being an us," she breathed lustily.

"Yeah, me, too." He grinned down at her, his fingers unable to keep from stroking through her hair and across her skin. She seemed soothed by his touch, something that pleased him immensely. "How's your headache?"

"Mmm, this makes it better. It's just been so noisy lately. Everyone is so jacked up with tension. Dimitre is in a bad mood because Annie is mad at him. Which, I partly don't blame her for and partly feel bad about."

"The point she is missing is that the suggestion of your spell demanded he have no choice but to see the woman he wanted most. It was out of his control, on the one hand, and a compliment to his devotion to her on the other. He could have seen Angelina Jolie."

"Ooo, good point. I have to tell her that. And, ooo! You could have, too! But you saw me. How cool is that?"

"Extremely cool," he chuckled. "But you did make it reciprocating, and frankly, I don't think I'm Angelina's type. Don't believe Nox's claims to not want the girl at Raven's shop. He's determined to find a magic girl, but honestly, you can't pick and choose who you fall for sometimes."

"Another lesson you are learning?" she asked softly.

"More so every minute."

She sighed and smiled.

"Honey?" he asked, his brows drawing down in a frown. "Are you thinking something specific right now?"

Tatyana laughed. "That is such a girl question."

"I'm serious."

"Not really. I'm just basking in the whole 'us' thing at the moment."

"Okay."

Hunter cradled her tight and pushed up from the floor and onto his feet. He carried her into the bathroom.

"What are we doing?"

"Taking a bath."

"Oh. That sounds nice." She relaxed a moment as he

walked past the mirrors and she abruptly jolted in his hold. "Wait!"

"I knew it," he sighed, stopping and putting her feet down on the ground. "I thought maybe I was imagining it."

They both leaned toward the mirror to check out her eyes. They weren't bright, but they definitely had a soft glow to them that indicated she'd cast a spell.

"What did I do this time? And why didn't you say something?"

"I was going to, but I figured you would notice for yourself if your eyes were different. You see, sometimes when I look at you, your eyes seem to glow from just your personality. Your wit and humor. Obviously, I'm completely biased."

"Oh. That's very sweet, Hunter, but this glow means I'm using magic. Except, we don't know what I'm doing. That has to be bad, right?"

"No. The magic must be latent. Or rather, passive. Sometimes we have power that only we can see and interpret within ourselves. Your eyes would be a full-on neon green if you had cast magic again deliberately. I think the only reason the glow in your eyes wasn't noticeable during the glamour was because the suggestion hid it. This is a minor alteration, something only those closest to you might notice. Even I wasn't sure. So, let's take a nice long bath and see if we can't get rid of your headache and figure out what is going on all at the same time?"

"Hey! Multitasking! That is very 'now' for a guy like you."

"And what does that mean?"

"It means you spend an awful lot of time lusting after old and decrepit magic."

"Hey. Watch it, you." Hunter spun her around, bouncing her back into the mirror harmlessly as he crowded her against the reflective surface. "Headache or no headache, you'll get taught a lesson about respecting your—"

"Elders?"

"Betters, you brat." Hunter grinned when she snickered, his fingers moving to make rapid work of her button-down dress.

"Aren't we going to need water?" she giggled, squirming between his body and the cold glass as he unbuttoned her to her navel and then reached inside to cup her breast in a warm, rough hand.

"Eventually."

"I thought sex and headaches didn't go together," she whispered against his cheek, and his head bent to look at her as he pushed fabric aside.

"I heard that was a myth. Sex can cure a headache."

"Mmm, I bet some male doctor thought that one up," she laughed. Tatyana shrugged back with a wriggle that made her breast dance in his hold, and her dress slid down off her body. "I am always naked first," she complained to him.

"Isn't it great?" he chuckled.

"For you. Okay," she amended when he bent to catch her nipple between his lips, "for me, too." She released a little sound of pleasure, rising up on her tiptoes.

. . . *isn't anything you can say right now that will* . . .

"Whoa."

Hunter felt her stiffen and murmur a halting command and he straightened to look at her. "Did I do something wrong? Are you okay?" he asked quickly.

"No. Yes. I mean . . . no, you were fabulous," she assured with a sigh. "I think I need that bath, though. I need to relax. I'm thinking too much."

"At your service." Hunter left her to turn on the taps and began to strip off his clothes. Tatyana watched him with blatant appreciation when muscles flexed as he bared his skin for her. The instant he was fully naked she reached to touch his aroused penis, stroking her fingers over him from base to tip. He was only half as hard as he could be, but she knew that would change quickly under her touch. So did he. He caught her hand up, kissing her palm. "Bath first. Once you feel better, then you can torture me all you like."

. . . in the name of the light, the dark, the holy void . . .

Hunter stepped into the bath and drew her in after himself. Just like the day before, he settled her between his thighs with her back to his chest. He drew her soft hair over his shoulder, guiding her into laying her head back as well. She sighed as he petted her from the forehead down over her hair.

"That feels good," she purred softly, reaching up to touch his face with gentle fingers. She came across his lips and felt him kiss her fingertips. "Why didn't you tell Ryce that Kaia needed blood?"

"Hmm? Oh damn!" he swore, sitting up sharply. "I completely for—hey, how did you know . . . ?"

Hunter didn't finish the question. Not that she knew the answer, but he suddenly thought that he did.

"Tatyana! Tatyana?"

"Stop telling me you're sorry. It won't change the fact that you didn't trust me," she murmured.

"Tatyana, stop it," he said sharply, giving her an attention getting shake. He watched her head wobble limply, her unfocused eyes glowing bright as blood ran down over her lips and chin from her nose.

"I know what happened to me. I remember. I don't want them to know I was raped. They'll never look at me the same way again," she muttered.

"Damn it!"

Hunter didn't know what was upsetting him more. Seeing her dripping blood from her nose into the bathwater or listening to the altered accents of her voice as she poured out the thoughts of his disturbed coven mates. First Annali's Southern cadence, and then Gracie's cockney lilt. Hunter decided to go with his gut and he suddenly plunged her underwater, jerking her back up again immediately. She gasped and coughed, flailing for a moment before realizing he was holding her tight and forcing her to keep still.

"Stop," she coughed. "I don't . . ."

"Then listen to me very carefully," he said into her ear, his voice resonant and loud because it was so close. "Imagine you are in a prison cell. Cinderblock walls all around you, but no bars anywhere. No way in and no way out. Thick walls. Impenetrable. Okay? Are you with me?"

"Yes," she said, aware of him grabbing a washcloth and wiping up her face.

"Tell me what you hear in this place. This tight cell with nothing coming in or out."

"Quiet. Silence. Just your voice when you speak and my own."

"That's good enough for now. You have to maintain that silence, okay? While you do that, I'm going to tell you about your magic."

"I have a headache," she groaned, touching her pained head.

"Yeah, and I realize why now. Did you read about the Mentalist school at all, angel?"

"No."

"Mentalist witches . . . well, it's all about the power of the mind. Empathy, telepathy, telekinesis, pyrokinesis. The power of suggestion. Holokinesis. Hallucinations."

"I'm having hallucinations?"

"No, honey, but you can do it to another person. Holokinesis is projecting a lifelike 3-D image of something that everyone can see but it isn't real. Sweetheart, this is one of the most powerful schools there is. But very few witches have the discipline to keep from frying their own brains. It's like your brother. He has a massive potential for power, but also a huge risk factor for losing touch with reality. The nosebleed you have, the headache, are both very dangerous warning signs. You need to keep that wall around you or you will give yourself a stroke." He swore at himself. "It came on so gradually. You probably didn't even realize all the things you were sensing. You might have put half of it down to your usual psychic noise and the other half to intuition. I should have realized this was why you saw through Braen's spell over Asher."

"I only saw it with hindsight. When it was happening to me, I didn't even notice."

"You're a novice. How are you supposed to know? I'm the one who is supposed to take care of you."

"You do take care of me. The instant you see I need it. Don't be so hard on yourself." She turned her head and looked up at him, reaching to rub away his frown. "Now that you know, you can teach me everything to help me. Like, if I have to keep this prison around my mind, how do I learn to use any of this power? What if I get tired? What about when I am asleep? Can I fry my brain in my sleep?" she asked, nibbling her lip worriedly.

"Unfortunately, anything is possible. Fortunately, I have spells that can help us with that until you learn better control. I can seal the room at night. You won't be able to hear anyone's thoughts or feelings except maybe mine."

"But then, how will you know if the coven needs you?"

"Ryce will break through the spell. Or Nox. Or hey, cell phones work."

"Cell phones?" Tatyana giggled.

"A good old-fashioned knock on the door?"

"Oh yeah, I'm sure. 'Excuse me, could you stop throwing fireballs at me so I can politely awaken my Sentinel?' That'll happen."

"Smart ass." He smiled when she laughed. "It's only a temporary measure to help you, and it's my job to see to it. Everyone here knows that. They understand there's going to be hard situations while you and your brother are training. The idea is to make the investment and take the risks for the benefit of developing a powerful witch in the long run."

"Am I still bleeding?"

"No."

"Good, because I feel like Carrie after the prom sitting in this water."

Hunter chuckled at her flair for imagery. "How about a nice shower in our little cinderblock cell? See, each thing you do has to be brought into that enclosed space. It helps keep you aware of protecting yourself."

"Got it. One co-ed prison shower. Mmm, sounds sexy." She reached to open the drain in the tub and stood up. Her pale body gleamed wetly as she stepped out and crossed to the glass shower and its multiple sprays, which she had working perfectly within minutes. She stepped under the water just as Hunter joined her.

Showering with her was somehow suddenly a far more erotic idea to him than bathing with her had been. Maybe it was because he had been seeking to soothe her in the bath. Now he was just . . . watching her bathe. She let the water rinse over her, running it through her hair and rushing it over her body with the use of her hands. After a few minutes of watching her hands flow over her own skin, Hunter was humming with attentive desire for her. She grabbed up shampoo for her hair and tossed it to him. He caught the bottle and she turned her back to him with a grin thrown over her shoulder.

"You've been fantasizing about washing my hair since you first thought of us coming in here."

"I love your hair," he said after clearing a catch in his throat. "The color, the length, and the way it feels in my hands and on my skin . . ." Hunter sank his hands into her deep, dark hair and worked up the shampoo lather as well as his own delight. She stepped back closer to him.

"My headache is going away. It seems so much quieter now that I realize it's just you and me I'm listening to."

"I'm glad." He turned her and tilted back her head to rinse the soap away. "Once we're done here, I have to take care of Kaia's request. Nox and Ryce are still holed up anyway and I can't really interrupt them twice. It wastes magic. After that is resolved, I'd like to take you to bed for a while. If that's okay with you."

"Oh, I'd really like that, actually," she said agreeably, stepping up to rub her body against his, her fingertips trailing down his back. "But, do we have time before Ryce is finished?"

"Yes," he said roughly, watching her sly smile as she reached for some soap.

"Good. Because I still need to wash, and so do you."

She laid soapy hands against his chest and began to slide slickly over him.

Chapter Nineteen

"I'm not arguing about this anymore."

"Good, because I didn't want to argue about it in the first place," Dimitre snapped. "All I want is for this to be okay between us. I want to know what I have to do to get you to forgive me."

"I'm not . . . I don't know!"

Annali paced the length of the infirmary, just as she had been doing since Dimitre had hunted her down there. She was incredibly confused, hurt and aching with the need to be held, but the man she loved was the cause of all of those feelings and she didn't know how to handle that contradiction.

"Babe," he pleaded softly, coming up behind her and stopping her circuit with a touch on her waist. "My sister cast a spell that demanded I see the woman I want, the woman who wants me, when I looked at her. Despite my idiocy with Hunter, doesn't it mean anything that it was you I saw and no other? I mean . . . I love you babe, so much, that I see you everywhere I turn anyway. I can smell where you've been. I feel comfort in the wake of your presence. Whenever I do see you, all I can think of is how I need to have you very, very soon or I will go insane. When I saw that whole scene upstairs, I was in complete shock. My mind couldn't even accept it. I fell apart and all I could think was, 'I can't do this.' My heart was breaking so hard that it still hurts. I can't lose you. I can't exist without you. I can barely breathe knowing you're angry with me, Annali."

Annali turned around to face him, tears running down her face.

"How can you love me and not know I would never do something like that to you?"

"I do know it. Even in the moment I was making up excuses in my mind, blaming Hunter for things . . . things worthy of his brother."

"I love you, Dimitre. I gave everything, risked all of my trust, and fell in love with you. I couldn't give that to anyone else. I don't think I even know how."

"Anna," he said softly, reaching to cup his hands around her pretty face. "Annali, please don't expect me to be perfect. No one can live up to that. I told you, I might screw up, but it won't mean I'm not crazy about you."

She sighed, relenting at last and sliding her arms around him. He seized her offered hug with full enthusiasm, making her squeak with the pressure he exerted around her.

"I won't doubt you again," he promised her. "Do you believe that?"

"Well, you better not. Next time I will beat it into your head with potions."

"Annie? Where's Kaia?"

Dimitre and Annali turned to face Ryce, both slightly startled by his appearance. The High Priest looked a little tired; his day of casting had clearly taken its toll.

"In bed, I hope. She was exhausted and needed rest. I know she was anxious about Asher, though. He needs blood and she wants to get it for him ASAP."

"He'll have to wait. I don't want anyone to go out. I did some scrying and I can sense warlocks all around us. Make certain someone keeps Kaia in the house for me, will you?

You know how determined she can get when a patient's life is at stake."

"I would think she'd know better," Dimitre scoffed.

"We'll revisit that assessment after you've lived with her for more than a decade," Ryce said dryly. "Just watch her. I need to rest. Nox is already sleeping. I'll check on Gracelynne before I go down for the night. Your sister is with Hunter. Seems like we're safe and snug, right?"

"We're fine, Ryce. Please go. You look exhausted," Annali encouraged him.

With a nod, he headed back out of the infirmary, off to find Gracelynne.

Hunter woke with a start when he heard his name.

The room was pitch black, not even moonlight intruding on the darkness because the shades had been drawn for privacy. The wards might keep warlocks from touching the house, but they didn't necessarily keep them from spying in windows. Hunter wouldn't chance any of his private time with Tatyana being observed from the outside. He turned toward her as his eyes adjusted a little better. Her bare, pale skin stood out starkly. She had shed the covers and lay sprawled on her belly over much of the mattress. She appeared to be sound asleep, but he could swear he had heard her calling for him.

Given her new powers, she might very well have. She could be dreaming and calling out to him telepathically. Interesting thought, that. Was she dreaming about him? If so, he wondered if it was something nice and erotic. Considering the exponential growth of his appetite for her, and the heated sex they'd had earlier, he would love to know.

"She's pregnant, you know."

Hunter felt his heart freeze in time, as sure as if Dimitre had commanded it. He flicked his attention up to Tatyana's face. She was still asleep, but . . .

"Who is?" he asked in a whisper.

"Our Annali."

Hunter turned sharply, looking for the source of the information. Now his heart was racing. It had been ten years, but he recognized that voice.

"Amber?"

"Yes, Hunter. Don't look for me. Can't see me. You can only hear me."

"By the Lady," he breathed, "how are you doing this? I'm not a Spiritus witch."

"No. But Asher is helping me. He doesn't need his physical health to use his magic. His coma is allowing him to act as a conduit. It will tire him, though, so I have to be brief."

"Amber, you didn't come here to tell me about Annali."

"Yes and no. I came to warn you. If Annali goes with you tomorrow, she will lose her child . . . possibly her life. You have to convince her to remain behind."

Hunter didn't bother questioning her. Asher and other witches like him had taught him that the world beyond death moved independently of time. Amber might already have witnessed dozens of possible futures. She was merely trying to prevent one of them.

"When you said 'If Annali goes with you,' what did you mean?"

She laughed, her voice just as soft and girlish as he remembered. "You always did know how to work the world of magic to its optimum. I can't tell you that. It will come to you soon enough. Even I must obey certain rules."

Hunter heard movements, just a brush of a breeze, then a touch that was cold and eerie across his skin. He watched as Tatyana's hair blew against her face and she shivered. He quickly drew up the comforter over her.

"She is very pretty," Amber noted, a wistful tone obvious in her voice.

Hunter didn't know how to respond to that. He had never in his wildest dreams imagined meeting with Amber again.

His entire chest ached with tension and he worried about her.

"Don't worry so much, Hunter," she scolded softly near his ear, as if she sat between him and Tatyana. "I am really beyond all of the things that kept my mind so narrow when I was alive. You learn a lot once you come here. I've seen your future, and hers as well. All the things that have happened happened so you could be here with her. She was meant for you. But, this you have already figured out."

"Yes. I have. I'm not sure she has, though."

"If she is meant to, then she will. In her own time."

"Amber? Are you . . . happy?"

"Oh yes. Very. I miss Asher terribly. And sometimes it is sad to just watch you all and not be able to speak with you . . . to join you. I miss you very much."

"I'm so sorry I wasn't there for you, Amber," Hunter said, his voice roughening with emotion.

"I know you are. I'm sorry these years have been so hard on you. I didn't want that. After a while, neither did Asher. Did you know he has been looking for you?"

Hunter caught his breath in surprise. "No. I didn't."

"For three years now. I tried to help him, but our contact has to be limited. He would never have moved on otherwise. I never came across any spirits who had been in contact with you, though. I suppose you moved too much to form any attachments."

"Something like that," he agreed.

"All I could assure him of was that you weren't dead. So, he kept looking by conventional means. It is hard to search for someone who not only doesn't want to be found, but lives a secret life to begin with. He wouldn't have wanted to draw attention to you."

"Honey, you're fading," he said worriedly.

"Asher is tired. I'm going to leave. Please, keep Annali safe. This baby will mean great things for Willow Coven. Your lover and her brother come from an ancient line of witch-

craft. Their children will save many innocent lives one day. I
need to go. Take care."

"Good-bye Amber."

Hunter felt the coldness fall away from him, and Tatyana's body heat radiated to him once more. He reached for
her, drawing her up against him. She complained in her
sleep, but soon turned toward him and snuggled up against
him for warmth. Her bare skin felt cool along her back and
warm along her front, a result of being exposed to the chill-
ier room air as she slept on her tummy. She was warming up
quickly, though.

He had a lot to think about because of everything Amber
had said, but all he could focus on at first was Tatyana.
Amber was right, of course. He had already come to realize
she was very special to him.

Well, okay . . . special was a mild term for what she made
him feel. It had been less than a week, but already he couldn't
imagine letting her go. When she had told him flat out she
was staying with him, literally moving herself in, he had
nearly expired from joy. He had to admit, he had played it
pretty cool. However, now that he knew she was a Mentalist,
he could kiss any emotional secrets he had good-bye. He'd
like to come clean himself before she snatched it out of him
on her own. He was just afraid she might think it was too
soon. Insincere. Cavalier.

And if he was going to be honest with himself, he was
just afraid, period. He'd never felt this way before. He had
learned how to love and be loved in this very household—
Ryce had taught him—but he'd never fallen in love before.
Was it possible he was mistaken? How could someone like
him even know if he was right about something like this?
Also, how much could he really offer Tatyana? Clearly, she
deserved everything.

But did everything include his dark magic genetics? Six
known generations of warlocks, and he'd been the first, and
only, to walk away. Even now his brother threatened all of

their lives with his poisoned desires and magic. Braen had raped women Hunter loved like sisters, and had almost done so to Tatyana as well. If she were destined to have powerful children who would contribute to the cause of good, would that future be endangered by his familial influence in the mix? Ryce had preached that no witch was born predisposed to good or evil, and he often used Hunter himself as an example, but was it really true? Would he and Tatyana be able to raise his offspring completely away from the influences of darkness?

The selfish rush of pleasure that hurried over him at the thought of giving her his children nearly floored him. Hunter buried his face in her sweet-scented hair and tried to breathe through his dizzying desire. A wife. A child. Home. It had all seemed inconceivable only three weeks earlier. Ryce's scry had brought home within reach again. If that could be regained, couldn't the rest be gained as well? He couldn't broach all of this with Tatyana now, not until after she had become the strong witch she was meant to be. Not until she had learned to live with him. Not until he could coax her into maybe loving him.

For the first time in years he had an incredible urge to run to Ryce for advice. Even the impulse made him smile. Ryce was sure to be asleep though, resting from a long day of spellcasting with Nox. He could figure his way through this on his own. If she read his thoughts and emotions, well then he'd have to deal with the consequences. Until then, he would just have to take it a day at a time. A step at a time. Familiarity and trust. Love. And the rest . . . ?

What right did he have to pursue all of that when he might be unable to offer her everything?

Knowing he wouldn't be able to sleep, he slid away from her, apologizing softly when she complained again. He dressed in pajama pants and belted on his robe, then walked out of the living quarters. He hit the main part of the house and instantly thought of Asher and Annali. He walked back to the infirmary, the floors chilly under his bare feet as he went. He entered the clinic and found Annali asleep in a bed not too far from Asher's. Dimitre was sitting up, reading something thick and old that was probably from Ryce's vast library.

"Hey," Dimitre greeted, surprised to see him.

"Hey. How is he?"

"Same. He was running a slight fever before so I figured I'd keep a close watch. I don't want to have to wake Kaia unless it's imperative."

"How's Annie feeling?"

"Tired. She puts a lot into her work."

Hunter wondered if Dimitre even knew about Annali's pregnancy. Did Annali? He quickly thought back to Kaia's smooth dodge about why she couldn't use Annie's blood. Also, when he had walked in on Annali earlier, she had been washing her face as well as her hands, hovering over her sink. Had she been ill? Morning sickness?

None of that meant either one of them knew, and it didn't seem to be his place to tell either of them if that were the case. Not unless he had to in order to keep her safe from whatever was coming their way.

"Listen, I'm sorry about what happened earlier," Dimitre said awkwardly as Hunter pulled up a chair and straddled it backward.

Hunter chuckled. "Don't worry about it. I doubt I would have done any different if our roles had been reversed. Although I wouldn't have just been managing the instinct to kill, but the skill as well."

"Yeah, something I'd actually appreciate lessons in one day."

"Anytime. I'll teach you to kick my ass good and proper next time."

"I appreciate that," Dimitre chuckled.

"Seriously? That stopping time trick is great, but you

need a follow-through. Some blade work. Maybe a tanto or long pike. I have some ideas. Less mess, just as sharp ideas."

"Speaking of ideas, something has been on my mind," Dimitre confided.

"Oh?"

"Yeah. Something Ryce said earlier. First, I need you to explain just how well your brother knows the habits of this coven."

"As well as if he lived here, except for the capacity to understand the tenets we work toward and the things we value. Actually that's wrong, he understands; they just have no worth to him."

"Okay. About my sister . . ."

Hunter stiffened, his posture straightening. "Yes?"

"Relax." Dimitre chuckled. "I was just wondering how the magic thing is going for her."

"A few problems, nothing too major. I figured out her school."

"Hey! That's great!" He paused when he saw Hunter's expression. "It is great, isn't it?"

"Eventually. At first . . . not so much. She's a Mentalist. It's as difficult to manage as your school is. More so because the number of talents involved is triple or more. You have sheer power and eventually will control a frightening ability; she has abilities that will require years of practice and a lot of focus to control. Just keeping herself sane is going to take hard work."

"They say the same about my power, but I haven't experienced that so much."

"You've also been isolated. Wait until the first time you are in a real crowd. You'll be jumping into past memories you would never want to see or experience. Everything from the horrendously boring to . . . well, I was told you went through some of Annali's past."

"Some of yours, too. Via Ryce. The night you rescued

her." He glanced at the 'her' in question. "I watched how Evan died."

Hunter didn't so much as blink. Dimitre was part of Willow Coven now. He knew what was expected of all its members, especially its Sentinel. Hunter wouldn't apologize for his tactics, or for any warlock deaths, however brutal they had been. Most especially not Evan's. He had carried out that assassination with joy, and he would do it again.

"I admit, I was a hypocrite about it. I didn't like the idea of my little sister hanging around with a man who cut the heads off of other men like it was nothing. But then you came to her rescue when she needed it most, and all I could think was, thank God a man like you was there to save her. I realized I wouldn't want it any other way. I will kill one day. And so will she. I understand that. I wish it weren't that way, but . . ." He shrugged.

"So then, tell me why you want to know about her power."

"I was just wondering . . ." He leaned in close and whispered. "Do you think she could do that trick again? The power of suggestion thing, making everyone think she is someone else? If so, how long can she hold it? See, I figure if it could fool someone as powerful as Ryce . . ."

"Then it could fool someone as powerful as Braen," Hunter finished for him. "Someone has a sense of irony. You want to do a version of his trick with Asher right back at him?"

"I guess so. I have a plan. It's dangerous, though. I'm terrified to even suggest it."

"Run it by me, and then we'll go from there."

Kaia fiddled with her defrost. She could still see her breath in the car even though it was starting to warm up at last. It was a bitter cold day, despite the glaring bright sunshine.

Or not.

Kaia instinctively touched the brake pedal when a heavy darkness crossed over the sun, thick clouds gathering out of nowhere. As she approached a corner and was about to turn, something massive and dark suddenly fell onto the center of the hood of her car. Out of reflex, she screamed and slammed on the brakes. The car began to skid and the anti-lock brakes began to jerk in short spurts of release as they, and Kaia, tried to correct her panicked mistake.

Her heart racing, she finally came to a halt and looked onto the hood to see what she had hit. In the back of her mind was the understanding that the laws of physics, as she understood them, dictated that the process of deceleration ought to have thrown the object from the hood. The object in question should not be crouched in wait, staring with glittering dark eyes into the windshield and directly at her.

The object in question being a darkly beautiful girl.

Odessa rose smoothly from her crouch and stood up in the center of the hood, her black and red painted lips curving in a smile.

Kaia watched her leap off the hood of the car as nimbly as a gold-medal gymnast. She landed firmly in the snow and ice, her black clothing making her stand out sharply against the white landscape behind her. She was dressed in the gothic manner that was so popular with the rebellious younger generation. She had opted for a thick, Spanish-lace skirt with skintight black Capri pants beneath it, no doubt for warmth. A goal that seemed defeated by the short black shirt that stopped just below her small breasts, baring her entire midriff of supremely pale skin, including the tops of her hips and the malachite and silver chain ringing the circumference of her waist through a ring in her navel. Her hair was dyed a flat, pure black; her nose, eyebrow, and ears were all pierced a varying number of times. With it all she wore an incongruous long black trench coat and thick combat boots.

Kaia knew in an instant she was in trouble. She scrambled out of the car, knowing it was useless to try to flee, and fought back panic as other dark shapes began to land in the road around her.

"Kaia," Odessa greeted her as though they were long-lost friends, even holding her arms out. "So good to see you. Braen sent me to tell you he is very much in need of your . . . services. And he would be so grateful if you would . . . come for him."

"Hmm. Let me see. Umm, that'd be a big fat '*no freaking way.*' But really, thanks for thinking of me." Kaia's bravado barely held when she felt a warlock pass close behind her. The bane of a Healer's magic was that Healers needed to touch their target, whether to heal or harm. Without contact, Kaia was useless. She knew very well that these warlocks had no such limitations. And they knew better than to come in contact with her while she was still conscious.

"Oh, really? You have something better to do? Coven mates to heal, perhaps?" Odessa mused, looking all around the area. "Not very nice of them to leave you out here all alone."

"Why don't *you* leave me alone? Then, for once, you will be equal to Willow Coven," she mocked the other woman. The warlocks were going to do their worst no matter what she said or did, so she might as well get her licks in.

Odessa's dark eyes flashed with wickedness.

"You know what, I'm going to have a lot of fun with you," she pronounced. Then she nodded to the other warlocks and Kaia braced herself for the inevitable.

She wasn't expecting the bolt of chain lightning that crashed into the quartet of warlocks, jumping from one to the other in violent blue arcs and blowing every one of them back off their feet. She screamed a little in shock and surprise, her heart racing as she jerked her attention to the sky and saw Hunter descending toward her.

Hey, angel. You okay? Hunter greeted her in her mind as his booted feet hit the icy ground. The man was dressed to kill, literally. All in black, his clothing close fitting but flexible. He wore athamés on his left hip and biceps, probably one in his boot as well. His casual manner hid a barely repressed fury that she could feel in every fiber of her being. The Sentinel of Willow Coven took it very personally when one of his witches was attacked.

Odessa was the first to regain herself. She cast a flame devil between Hunter and his sister witch, forcing them apart. Kaia stumbled back into the grasp of a warlock who grabbed her around the throat and started to throttle her. But it was the red haze of rage he was using to power his effort that was damaging to her. He shoved her back against her car and her feet slid out from underneath her. Her head rang with the purity of evil intent that ran through these warlocks and she suddenly knew exactly what they had plotted. She knew why Odessa wanted to provoke this fight, and what she planned to do with her spoils.

Her breath was clogged beneath the restrictive hand, and her nose began to bleed. Instantly she thought of her brothers and used what little breath she had to suck blood into the back of her throat and spit full bore into the warlock's face, spraying him with brilliant red. He let out a rather high-pitched squeal for a man, letting go of her and swiping madly at his face. He growled with fury and lunged for her.

"Tatyana! Duck!"

She obeyed, diving for the cold ground near the car. Ryce blasted in out of nowhere it seemed, blowing the warlock right off his feet with some kind of percussive force. Once the warlock was lying in a heap on the side of the road, Ryce leaned down and offered the disguised Tatyana a hand up. Even under the stress of attack, Tatyana had maintained the strength of her magic suggestion. She looked and felt exactly like Kaia. Even the height difference was maintained in his mind. He could even sense her just as though she were his sister witch. That was unexpected. But it was also obvious that she was paying for being in among all of this wrath. She was bleeding heavily from her nose and he could even see a burst blood vessel in her right eye. Her eyes were glowing a bright amber.

Ryce turned to see Hunter. He was taking on three to one odds and Ryce needed to help him, but Tatyana looked like she was in bad shape.

"I'm fine," she said, reading his mind. "Go. Please. There could be others. I'll sit in the car."

"Right. You watch your back, understand?" he warned.

"I'll yell if I need help."

Ryce nodded and whipped his attention back to the fight going on across the road.

Hunter knew who the immediate threat was. The other two warlocks were incidental. He bee-lined for Odessa, casting as he went. Snow from the sides of the road suddenly exploded in her direction, pelting her with solid ice pellets, road salt, and road debris. She screamed out in fury and Hunter saw he had drawn first blood. He cast behind himself, a blowback spell to deter the other warlocks at his back, flinging them several yards away from himself and Ryce and Tatyana as he quickly turned back to Odessa.

The Goth warlock screamed out her next spell, and the ground shook in warning beneath his feet. Hunter instinctively reengaged his flight spell right before the ground ripped open beneath him, swallowing up roadway and Kaia's car. Ryce was suddenly occupied with snatching Tatyana up out of the car and trying to scramble back out of the path of the ever-widening hole in the earth. The body of the warlock they had killed fell into the chasm. Tatyana's feet slipped down into the widening hole just as Ryce cast flight on them and took them away to safety.

Odessa remained a step ahead as Hunter was distracted with watching Tatyana get pulled to safety. She cast a hail of fire over them, the large stones pelting and burning the vulnerable witches. Hunter ignored the pain and danger with ease, years of calm in a fight keeping him centered. He trusted

Ryce to care for his woman, so he turned to the imperative target.

Odessa.

Odessa was scrambling. She was young yet, and he could soon see that she was struggling to keep up with him spell for spell while managing her fear as well. She had not felt fear the last time they had met. This was because she had not believed his claim of who he was. She believed him this time and she knew he was definitely a man to be feared. Anyone who had grown up more powerful than her High Cleric had to be a man she should fear.

"Come, come, Odessa," he mocked her as he set down on solid ground. "Surely you can do better than this biblical bullshit. Next you know, it'll be locusts and a rain of toads."

He advanced, a new spell in Romany thundering out of him in a voice meant to intimidate, as well as to pour magic into the casting. Odessa barely knew what hit her. The geasa knocked her off her feet and pinned her to the remaining roadway. She was bound to the earth now, unable to move or gesture, the paralysis cutting down her repertoire by more than half because so many spells were best focused with accompanying gestures. She could still speak, though, so she was still dangerous. Hunter flew across the distance just as she countermanded his spell with a powerful magic rhyme. She was sitting up just as he reached her. His athamé sang out of its sheath and with a savage cry he stabbed it through her shoulder, forcing her down again until the blade had pinned her to the blacktop. Then without so much as thinking, he grabbed for the dark witch's head and wrenched it hard off of her spine. The snapping of her neck was accompanied by a gurgled cry, and then she fell silent as she dropped from his hands.

The Sentinel wasted no time before turning to face the other two warlocks who were trying to rush him.

"Back off!"

Hunter flung out both hands in warning, his palms flaring with electric blue power to match the blaze of his eyes. Lightning arced from the fingertips of one hand all the way to the other, like a juggling act of deadly force. He stood with his feet braced hard apart as he faced the two warlocks of Belladonna Coven. After what had happened to Asher, Hunter was spoiling for a fight. What was more, he was spoiling for blood. He would be fully within his rights to destroy them. They had threatened members of his coven.

The faces of these witches were fresh ones. He hadn't seen them the night of the original attack. The High Cleric in charge of Belladonna Coven would generate as many witches as he felt necessary to defeat Willow Coven. Even if it cost him some precious measure of power in the process.

"I've a message for your Cleric," Hunter announced, his voice booming out across the frozen road. "Tell him . . ." He smiled, his teeth gleaming like the fangs of a predator. "Never mind, I'll tell him myself."

Lightning leapt from his hands even as his feet lifted from the ground in flight. Two bolts, one to the left and one to the right, found their targets, arrowing through the miniscule shields each of the warlocks tried to throw up to defend themselves. The scent of burning hair and charring flesh, both so sickeningly unmistakable, began to cloud the air. Hunter continued to feed power into the charges, refusing to release even when he was fairly certain the witches were both dead. This wasn't about simply killing the witches, however. This was, as he had said, a message. Braen would find the remains of his subpar forces and would know that Willow Coven was through playing nice. Braen would know exactly who had done this, and exactly what it meant. Hunter would be coming for the heart of Belladonna Coven, sooner rather than later if Braen dared to attack a Willow witch or cross into their territory again. Even lurking at the edges of their property would be considered an act of war, and the Sentinel of Willow Coven would answer in kind.

Whether he would heed the warning would be up to the Cleric.

Once he began, Hunter wouldn't quit until there was nothing more than ashes left of the two warlocks. As it was, he would have to dispose of Odessa's body and seal the hole in the road. They could leave nothing that would attract attention from outsiders.

Hunter cast a spell, kicking up two small dust devils out of the ashes of the dead warlocks. The ashes burst into beautiful red and gold flames, and then became feathers of two magical phoenixes. The birds flapped into flight with their long wingspans, their bright plumage gleaming like suns in the starlight. Their extra long tail feathers trailed elegantly behind them as they flew off slowly and majestically toward Pennsylvania and Belladonna House. Tomorrow, when the birds reached the house, they would seek out Braen as instructed and burst into flame before falling into piles of ash at his feet. Hunter rather liked the entire poetic bent of the idea. It would deliver his message quite nicely.

It would also piss Braen off in a major way.

Hunter's eyes found Tatyana and he sighed when he realized it was over, and she was safe.

He had done what he had been born to do.

And it felt wonderful.

Chapter Twenty

Ryce laid Odessa's body down on the floor of the basement. It was blasted out of the mountain rock and would provide an additional dense barrier besides the house and wards that would keep anyone from discovering her. This was crucial to the second part of Dimitre's plan. The part both he and Hunter were now balking about, despite having been the ones to suggest it in the first place.

"This is a bad idea. We should just send her body back to Braen along with the others. It'll be enough of a warning—"

"It will piss him off and you know it," Ryce cut Hunter off. "He will bring the war here and he won't care who sees it. Whether we win or lose we will be forced to leave this state and I will not lose my home because of that bastard."

"My sister is bleeding like a stuck pig, Ryce! She can't do any more of this!"

"She can, after she rests. Kaia will heal her of any damage caused by the magic paths."

"You know damn well that isn't the problem. She made it through this time, but she could have a stroke the next," Hunter railed as he paced sharply across the cement floor.

"Not to mention her blood loss."

"We just got a supply of blood from the clinic. If she

needs it, she can get it from Kaia. If we run out, Kaia can get more blood from you, Dimitre. Why are you two arguing with me? You know damn well we can't turn back now. Odessa reeks of your brother, Hunter. If she isn't his mistress, I will eat my spellbook. The Lady knows she's certainly twisted enough to suit him. You heard what Tatyana said. They weren't going to kill Kaia. They were going to kidnap her. They were going to serve her up to him like a concubine. Hasn't he hurt enough of our women to suit you? You know he won't be satisfied until he's raped every last one of them, and that includes Tatyana. She's the one that got away, and don't you think for a minute that isn't infuriating him. When he comes for her, and he will come for her"—Ryce bit out to the men who loved her—"he will see to it she pays for her escape. Most of all, Hunter, she will pay because she is yours. Why do you think he targeted her in the first place?"

"All the more reason to keep her away from him!" Hunter practically roared. "She has no defenses! If he catches her—"

"He won't kill her. Not until he's had his fun. That will give us the time we need. We're doing it. This argument is over."

Ryce moved to leave the basement.

"When did you become a goddamn dictator?" Hunter lunged for Ryce, but Dimitre plowed between the two men and shoved hard against his sister's lover. He saw the fear behind Hunter's rage, and he recognized it instantly. It was the fear of a man in love. One who was terrified of losing the object of that love.

"Willow Coven was never a democracy," Ryce shot back. "I ask for opinions and perspectives because I respect all of you. In the end you know this is my decision. Someone has to make hard choices, Hunter. Normally you would be right beside me as I did this. This time, your heart is on the line and you can't see clearly. Neither one of you can." Ryce took a breath. "Annali isn't staying behind either. Kaia will tend to Asher and Grace. I need Annali. We are shorthanded enough as it is."

"No!"

"Absolutely not!" Hunter spat over Dimitre's protest. "You can't bring her."

"Kaia has no offensive power unless she lays hands on an attacker. Annali is one of my most powerful offensive witches. I need her, and that is final. Not unless you can give me a damn good reason why you two keep trying to hold her back here."

"She's *pregnant*!"

Hunter's bellow echoed around the basement. Dimitre went lax, his mouth dropping open in shock. Ryce dropped back against the door he'd been about to open, his grip on the knob turning his knuckles white.

"She's what?" Dimitre asked. "No, she isn't! She would have told me!"

"She may not realize it yet," Hunter said with a frustrated sigh, running a hand through his hair. "Damn it, I'm sorry. I didn't want to be the one to tell you. I know she will want to when she figures it out."

"Which begs the question, how do you know about it?" Ryce asked.

"Because I had a visit from Amber and she told me. She also told me that Annali will lose her baby if she joins this fight and might lose her life as well. Asher wouldn't have risked what little strength he has to act as a conduit for Amber if he didn't believe it was imperative we know."

"Hunter, help him!"

Hunter reacted from instinct, grabbing Dimitre's arm as the other man's knees went out from under him. He fell weakly to a kneeling position and looked as pale as chalk dust. Ryce had the temerity to chuckle.

"Breathe, Dimitre," he instructed dryly. "Hunter, smack him. Make him breathe."

"Fuck you," Dimitre gasped.

"He's breathing," Hunter noted with a chuckle.

"Right. So Annali stays here then," Ryce acknowledged with a shrug. "You could have just said as much from the start, but I see why you didn't. Tell Annie we're sorry to ruin any surprises. You'll have to tell her, you know. She won't stay behind otherwise."

"Yeah, I know," Dimitre said with a nod as he sat back on his heels and braced his hands on his thighs. He gave his head a shake. "Oh man, this is so . . . messed up. Damn it, I haven't even asked her to marry me yet!"

"Well, you're in the position. Want me to go get her?" Hunter teased him.

"You be quiet," Dimitre barked. He took a breath and pushed up to his feet. "Ryce, I need to talk to you alone. You go check on my sister, would you?" he requested of Hunter.

"On my way." Hunter moved past Ryce, giving him a dark look as he passed him. "Can we at least agree that if Kaia says Tatyana's in too much danger we can try to come up with something else?"

"If that is how she feels, then have her come talk to me about it. I'll consider everything she says."

Hunter wasn't pleased with the concession, but at least it was a concession. He hurried from the room in search of his goal. Once he was gone, Dimitre turned to the High Priest with a noisy swallow that betrayed his tried nerves.

"What can I do for you, Dimitre?"

Ryce knew Dimitre would continue to argue about his sister, and of course Ryce didn't blame him. However, he hadn't made this choice lightly. He never did. What the Priest would prefer was the opportunity to celebrate this key step in achieving his lifelong dream of cultivating a coven where a new generation of witches could be born. He could only wish that Dimitre would realize just how much that meant to him.

"Ryce." Dimitre cleared his throat. "Annali considers you her closest family. You've raised her through the most harrowing times in her life and you helped to create the beautiful being that . . . that I love. I wanted to wait because I wanted to have more to offer her when I approached you. More control of myself. More power to protect her. And while I haven't completed those goals, I have every intention of doing so. I swear that to you. So . . . I would like your permission to marry her. She wouldn't consider saying yes unless she was assured of your approval."

It was rare for Ryce to be taken off guard completely, but it did happen on occasion. Here he had been hoping for just a thread of understanding from his new coven mate, only to have Dimitre astonish him by clearly comprehending how he saw himself as a father to the witches he loved and protected in this house. While he had no right to give or refuse permission for anything concerning Annali because she was a woman of full age and free will, a woman not even of his blood, he probably would have been insulted had she married without some consideration of his feelings for her.

Now, despite his surprise and the emotional impact of Dimitre's words, he managed to find his voice.

"I couldn't think of anyone better for our Annie."

Hunter brushed his hand over Tatyana's hair, waking her from her dozing. She smiled at him, but didn't sit up or move. She looked exhausted. Her eyes were still aglow from her use of intensive magic, but she looked like herself again, including the damage to her eye.

"Hey. How are you feeling, angel?"

"Tired. But I'm happy. I'm so glad this worked. Kaia says Asher is so much better already from the blood transfusion. And I never thought we'd get someone like Odessa today. She is really close to Braen."

"I know. Ryce told me," he said, leaning forward in the chair next to the bed she was using in the clinic while waiting for Kaia's assessment. The Healer was presently occupied with Asher. "Angel, are you sure you want to do this? Are you sure you want to get that close to Braen again?"

"Want? Not really. Need? Oh yeah. I'm looking forward to it."

Hunter grabbed up her hand and squeezed hard. "Honey, do you even see yourself? You are pale as hell. You're exhausted. Every time you come across strong emotion you start to bleed."

"I know. And I know you and Dimitre are worried. But it's a good idea, Hunter. Just . . . let's do this. Let's get it over with. I want it over with so Gracie can start to heal and this coven can relax. I want to go outside. There's no freedom here while we live in fear of attack. Hunter, this was your idea. Yours and Dimitre's. It's a good idea, and I can do it. I just need some rest and a little time cuddled up next to a certain Sentinel I know. Can we do that, please? I don't want to worry about all the things that can go wrong. I'm scared enough as it is."

"Okay," he said softly, moving to sit beside her and drawing her up into his arms. "Okay, angel. I'm sorry." Hunter closed his eyes as he hugged her tight, and with a deep breath he exhaled the tense fear pent up inside of him. He knew holding it inside would be just as bad for her as for him. She was too tired to struggle with keeping herself walled in properly, and it was obvious her mind was open and a little raw.

Kaia came into the room shortly after that to find him holding her and petting her along the length of her hair. The image made her smile, but she hid it under a professional façade very quickly.

"Okay, let's see what kind of damage you've done," she said briskly. She shooed Hunter back away from the bed, so he stood with his arms folded tensely over his chest and hovered worriedly at the foot of it. Kaia did a quick neuro exam conventionally, saving her already overtaxed magic. All of Tatyana's reflexes were acceptable, except Kaia didn't care for the sluggish response of the pupil in Tatyana's damaged eye. "Hunter?"

"Yes?"

"I am going to heal her. Tonight I'd like you to cast a dampening spell around her bedroom. This way she can sleep in perfect silence and get the rest she needs. Actually, the sooner the better, if she has nothing else to do." She turned to Tatyana. "Eat in bed. Relax. Read. Do whatever you like, but remain inside the room. It will seal you off from all the random emotion in this house. I believe if we do this, tomorrow will go much easier for you."

"But . . ."

"No. No 'but.' Just do it," Kaia said sternly.

"But, is Hunter allowed with me or no?"

Kaia seemed to think about that for a moment. "Yes. He can stay with you if he controls his emotions. I really want you to stop using magic for a while."

"If I make any mistakes I'll banish myself," Hunter promised seriously.

"All right then, just give me a few minutes and you can take her up."

Dimitre found Annali in the conservatory bent over her lab sink.

"Babe?"

She jolted upright with a loud sniff and quickly scrubbed tears from her cheek, as if that would keep him from realizing she'd been crying.

"Babe, what is it?" he asked with instant concern and sympathy, hurrying over to her. The moment he turned her into the warmth of his body, she burst into tears again.

"I don't understand! Every time I try to work, the smell of something just suddenly makes me so nauseated and I can't . . . I can't . . ." She exploded into sobs, frustration and, no doubt, hormones fueling her upset.

"Aww, babe," he soothed her softly. "It's okay."

"It's not! This coven is counting on me for tomorrow! I have to make these potions!"

"You have hundreds of potions already. It's enough. Just relax."

"Don't you tell me to relax!" She shoved away from him, and then shoved at him again for good measure. "You who gets completely freaked out if one tiny thing is out of your control? Please!" she scoffed.

Dimitre wasn't ready. In a moment of total panic he realized he wasn't ready for this. For any of it. He was completely ill-equipped to deal with a pregnant witch, a new wife, a nascent witch for a sister, worrying about tomorrow's offensive, and, oh yeah, still trying to figure out his own damn powers. Apparently, she was right. He did get freaked out when things were out of his control. But he must be getting better at it, because ever since he'd met Annali things had spiraled out of his control, and he had managed to find love and a whole hell of a lot of happiness in spite of it. Or because of it.

"Annali?"

"What?" she snapped.

"Babe, I love you more than I will ever be able to express, but if you are going to be like this for the rest of your pregnancy, I have to warn you there's a chance I'm going to lose my temper right along with you every once in a while. I just thought it'd be good to get that out in the open. You need to know that, just because we argue, it doesn't mean I'm not crazy in love with you. Okay?"

"Oh . . . okay," she said, blinking big lavender eyes at him. "Did you say . . . ?"

"Yes, I did."

"But I'm not . . ."

"Yes, you are," he countered.

"But you can't possibly know that . . ."

"Yes, babe, I can."

"Dimitre!"

"Yes?" he asked, trying not to smirk, but not succeeding.

She looked like she wanted to smack him. Or possibly hug him. Maybe both.

Annali decided to grab for her sink again and give in to a fierce tide of morning sickness. Dimitre reached out to pull stray coils of her hair back out of her way, rubbing her back and soothing her with soft, reassuring words. He explained how he knew what he knew, and then he explained that, in spite of the shock of it all, he was ridiculously happy. He hoped that she was, too.

After a few minutes of retching, a few more of sobbing intermixed with some rather hysterical laughter, Dimitre eventually figured out that she was, indeed, very happy. And of great comfort was the fact that she was equally scared out of her mind. It was comforting to know he wasn't alone in his bone-chilling terror over becoming a parent.

He would wait until after tomorrow before making plans to ask her to be his wife.

Braen paced the length of his house down its center hallway, then turned and came back again. Of all the things he hated about revenge, it was the waiting. He had been waiting for over a decade to get the better of Willow Coven, and he was on the very cusp of achieving his goal. Unlike Willow Coven, his house was not a commune of witches. His property housed his coven in various locations, but the house was his alone. Odessa lived there, of course. And her mother, Adaliah. He didn't mind Adaliah's presence. She was a quiet, reclusive woman who rarely left her rooms. It had made Odessa happy to bring her into his home and her gratitude had earned him much pleasure in her bed.

So, despite Adaliah upstairs, he was by himself. Something he rather enjoyed on most occasions. The only thing making it so unbearable was the anticipation of Odessa's success and the prize she would be bringing to him. But, of course, he had to wait. Wait until Kaia's need to tend her patients overrode her need to obey her Priest. Braen chuckled because he knew the Healer's habits all too well, and it was only a matter of time. All he needed was just a little patience.

Braen reached the front of the house when he heard a strange sort of cry, the high-pitched cawing of a bird. He opened the front door, remaining within the warded borders of the house while checking to see if there was any danger around. After a moment he stepped out onto the porch. As soon as he did, two brightly plumed birds, their feathers an amazing display of yellows, scarlet, and oranges, swooped into his presence. They hovered in flight for a moment before suddenly bursting into flames, the creatures screaming their cries as they changed from those of a bird to those of dying men.

They fell into two distinct piles of ash at his feet.

It was Braen who ignited next, his fury exploding in a primal shout of rage. He stomped his foot into the messy ashes and screamed out the curse of his existence.

"HUNTER! Goddamn you!"

He wasn't stupid. He knew a message when he saw one and he recognized the signature of his brother's magic anywhere. The phoenixes were a snide touch, a reminder that his brother's once-dead position in Willow Coven had been reborn.

"I thought they were rather poetic, actually."

Braen jolted and whipped around to face Odessa. He had been so incensed that he hadn't even felt his lover near him. The beautiful paleness of her skin was like backlighting for the darkly painted erotica of her lips. Her black cap of curls and the equally black head-to-toe latex rubber outfit she was wearing made her look like a predatory panther on the prowl. She stood with supreme confidence, her feet braced apart on high block heels, the shiny black boots zipped up tightly over her calves barely distinguishable from her latex catsuit.

"In a bad mood?" she asked. She waved a disgusted little hand at the ashes under his feet. "They served their purpose. Why get upset? I am safe and I was successful—isn't that all that is important?"

"Of course it is," Braen said, a whole new rush of excitement overriding his rage. "Where is she? Were you followed? They will come for her."

"No, they won't. They think she is dead. They think she's . . . ash." Odessa kicked a foot at the pile nearest her. "Oh, they'll want revenge, but they won't be in as much of a rush as they would have been if they thought we had her."

Odessa stepped back and revealed the small bound and gagged form of the tiny Native American doctor who had been her target. He should have known she wouldn't fail him, he thought as his heart pounded with glee. He grabbed Odessa by the wrist and jerked her against his body, his hand grabbing her ass with a smack and his mouth pushing over hers hotly.

Tatyana did everything in her power not to gag or react in any way that would give her away. Her heart was pounding with the realization that the trick had worked. Unfortunately, it was working far too well. She had tried to prepare herself for the possibility of Braen's hands being on her again, but nothing could prepare her for the reality of her repulsion and disgust as she recalled his evil intentions toward her. Unlike him, however, she refused to give herself away so quickly. She had tasks she needed to accomplish, and she was going to succeed.

Braen released her quickly enough and stepped hurriedly over to the bound Kaia. He crouched down to meet her wide, fearful eyes, careful not to touch her.

"Well, well. My little Indian squaw. You know, Dess, I've never eaten Indian before," he chuckled.

Tatyana laughed at the disgusting remark with as droll a wickedness as she could muster. She looked at Kaia and knew the little Healer was trying to tell herself she was in no real danger. But Kaia needed to believe that it was real. Braen had committed enough violence against women to know how they would react. If Kaia didn't act that way, she could blow everything. At any time, Braen could decide to cast any number of spells that would allow him to see the truth, not the least of which was a mind-reading spell. As it was, Tatyana had had only a few moments of familiarity with Odessa's mind in order to pull this charade off. She could make a crucial mistake at any time.

"I am curious as to how you're going to manage this," the fake Odessa mused. "You can't touch her without her trying to give you a heart attack or something."

"How did you get her here?" he countered.

"No skin-to-skin contact." She smiled. "Bit hard to enjoy her without skin-to-skin contact, Braen."

"Too true. But I have an excellent shield I can teach you. It's like putting a condom all over your body, except we won't even feel it."

"Ooo, clever," Tatyana cooed. She saw Braen reach out for Kaia and quickly moved forward to grab the Healer by her arm, jerking her up to her feet. "Let's bring our toy inside. I need a drink and a shower before we can start playing."

Braen stood up, a thunderous expression crowding his features. "I don't need you to start playing. You think I want to wait any longer than I already have?"

She pouted, throwing Kaia back against the porch rail roughly before moving close to him. The one thing she remembered, the one thing she had to remember, was that Odessa never showed fear to Braen. It was what infuriated him and attracted him to her. She sidled up warmly to his body, closing her eyes for a moment and envisioning Hunter to make her body behave realistically. She needed to calm him. There was too much emotion swirling around her. She couldn't raise walls and maintain an illusion at the same time, so she was left open to it. A nosebleed or anything like it would ruin everything.

"You promised," she purred against his ear. "You said I could hold her down for you. You said I could make her beg for you."

"True," he relented, his body posture still stiff. "But Dess, I've been waiting. My cock aches for it." He reached between their bodies to rub himself through his fly.

"It won't take long, lover. I promise."

"Then come inside," he invited, opening the door and grabbing for Kaia on one side as Tatyana took her on the other.

It was the only way to pass across the wards. To be invited or taken across by the caster or a dweller within the wards. She and Kaia walked into the house of their enemy. She found it to be cavernous and echoing, a crude expression of wealth, as though he had no time for details. His greed obviously ran toward other types of riches rather than those decorating his home.

This would be tricky. She wasn't sure of the floor plan, the others who might live there, and where things were located. She had been intensely focused on Odessa's personality and her relationship with Braen when she had invaded the other woman's mind in preparation for this moment. Luck was with her, though, and she spied a wet bar in the corner on one side of the huge room. She threw Kaia down onto a couch and strutted across the room. She felt the Healer's fear spike off the charts when Braen took the opportunity to toy with her hair.

"What would you like?" she asked, hoping he was specific.

"I think some whiskey. Would you like some too, witch?" he whispered loudly against Kaia's ear. "A little liquid courage for you before . . . well, *before*." He chuckled at his ominous vagueness. He reached down and stroked a hand over Kaia's denim-clad backside. "God, I love a big ass. Dess, you know I adore you but you have such a miniature behind. This is some serious ass on here. Good for the grabbing, better for the fucking."

"Now, now, you promised," Tatyana scolded as she hurried back with their drinks.

"I didn't say I wouldn't touch," he shot back. He took the glass she handed him and downed the double shot in a single swallow. He slammed the glass down on an end table and turned his avaricious attention back onto Kaia. "We should bathe it," he remarked. "I hate to wash away that lovely smell of fear, but I think of all this dark skin under soap and water and I just start to ache."

"What a fabulous idea," she agreed as he reached for her and drew her down into his lap. He shifted so he could take her hips in hand and rub his prominent erection against her bottom.

This was too much. For both of them. Tatyana had to draw the line and pray that she had done enough. She reached out when Braen buried his face against her neck. His hands were traveling up toward her breasts. Tatyana grabbed the gag from Kaia's mouth and the Healer witch sucked in a breath before burning precious magic to cast a powerful unlocking spell. The ropes binding her fell from her body and both she and Tatyana lurched to their feet and faced Braen.

In one hand, Tatyana held the glass with her drink in it; in the other she held one of Annali's potion bottles. She threw it down on the ground just as Braen was struggling to get up in a fit of outrage. She grabbed Kaia, who was stiff from her bonds, and they dove behind a couch.

Braen was already done casting before the potion exploded under his feet. Out of nowhere strands of webbing appeared, flinging themselves over the two women. At first it was a light annoyance, but quickly it began to cling and suffocate, restricting their movement. Just when they thought they were going to be cocooned to death, the effect of the spell vanished, the webbing dissolving all around them.

"He's out," Kaia breathed with relief. "That stuff you put in his drink did the trick . . . along with the blast. Thank the Goddess."

"Braen! What is going on down here!"

A beautiful older woman, the perfect picture of a tragic heroine with her black hair falling free down her back and a white gown that swept across the floor, rushed down the stairs. She was porcelain pale and had wide blue eyes. She might have seemed much younger if her face looked as if she had ever smiled.

"Odessa! What has happened here?" the warlock demanded. She reached the landing and turned to see Kaia. She pointed at her with regal disgust. "You! You are white!"

"Well, there's some irony for you," Kaia said dryly, making Tatyana snicker.

The woman heard her and narrowed her eyes on Tatyana. "You are not my daughter! Pretender! Where is my child?"

The rage that tore through her caused all the doors to explode open and violent winds to whip into the house. The woman raised her hands and seemed to force the winds to attack the two white witches invading her home.

"Weather witch!" Kaia cried.

"Go to the back door! I'll get the front!"

The women split apart, running against the violent hurricane force of the wind, dodging furniture and objects that flew at them. Tatyana felt as if she was at ground zero inside her head as well as outside her buffeting body. The pure wrath of Odessa's mother, combined with Kaia's fear and the uproar of a rousing clan of warlocks all around her made her feel as though her head were going to explode.

Tatyana had no choice but to fight through all of it. She reached the front door and forced herself against the wall so the sudden shift in the wind couldn't drive her out of the door, defeating everything she had worked for. She thrust her arm through the door, her head ringing with wind shear and an emotional tempest. When she felt a warm, masculine hand clasp her forearm, she nearly sobbed with relief. She pulled, trying to drag him in even as he fought to enter. He couldn't cast through the wards until she helped him across them. The minute Hunter forced himself over the threshold, he let go of Tatyana and gestured forward with his fist, his shouted Romany stolen away by the furious winds. Everything flying toward them changed direction like metal to an electromagnet, targeting the Weather witch. She screamed as she was bludgeoned.

A stone paperweight slammed into the warlock's forehead and in an instant everyone was falling to the floor as the windstorm died. They all lay there gasping for breath. Tatyana, Hunter, Kaia, and Nox, whom Kaia had admitted through the back door. Adaliah was out cold, and so was Braen.

Hunter recovered quickly, knowing they were still on a property with well over forty active warlocks on it of varying skill and power. Ryce and Dimitre wouldn't be able to hold them off forever and they needed help. But first . . .

The Sentinel gained his feet, seeking the one and only target that was his responsibility in this offensive. He was covered by debris, sprawled on the floor like a drunkard. Disgust tore through Hunter as he grabbed his foul excuse for a brother up by his clothes and threw him onto a sofa.

Tatyana watched Hunter close in again on Braen, his body gleaming with reflections as the decorative blades on his biceps and hips caught the sunlight pouring in through windows broken by the wind. In an instant a blade was out of its sheath and flashing with blinding light as Hunter grabbed his brother by the hair and poised to strike.

Suddenly Tatyana felt emotion exploding through her head, thoughts rapidly following. The conflict in Hunter was brutal and noisy, a screaming match of emotional frenzy. He despised Braen and all that he stood for. He hated his brother because he was a symbol of all that was tainted within himself. He was proof of the evil of the genetics of his family. He was horrified every time he realized that he, too, would have been on this path, were it not for Ryce. He was terrified when he thought about the potential evil Braen or he could pass on to another generation.

For these reasons and a thousand other egregious sins, he knew Braen must die. It was justice. Justice for Annali and Gracie and Tatyana . . . for every woman Braen had violated over all the many years of his sexual maturity, including the ones currently locked away somewhere as his familiars. They could be free only if he were dead. This was Hunter's duty. This was his birthright.

So why did his blade hesitate at his brother's throat? It was as though something black and restless was crouched eagerly inside of him, waiting for him to commit this act. Brother murdering brother, a sin as old as creation. It was as though he knew he was flirting with darkness, and the good inside of him screamed in warning.

Hunter pulled back, gasping for breath and grinding out a sound of frustration. He held Braen down by his throat, the scar he had given him glaring up at him and reminding him of how it had felt those weeks after he had done it. More conflict, half of himself glad he had done it, the other half distraught over that sense of pleasure he'd gotten from it. Then it had been saving an innocent young woman, this time . . . this time Braen was defenseless and not even conscious.

He knew Ryce needed him. His duty, everything he was, stood beside his Priest, acting as his magical second, stepping up should Ryce fall and need him.

Hunter was so blinded by his inner turmoil that it wasn't until he felt wet droplets on his hand and focused on the heavy crimson color that he realized Tatyana had come up behind him and was leaning over his shoulder. Her hand reached for the wrist pinning Braen down. It was the lightest touch, but immediately caused him to loosen his grip and sit back. He looked up at her, seeing her painted and dressed up like Odessa, but with her own face and hair now. With her own blood running rapidly out of her nose.

"Tat!" he ground out, his fingertips reaching to swipe away the rivulets of blood.

"It doesn't matter," she whispered as she leaned forward over Braen to kiss Hunter on the corner of his mouth. He was baffled by her actions right up until he felt her body jerk hard and heard a very familiar crunch of sound.

The sound of a blade pushing through flesh, cartilage, and bone.

"Tatyana!"

He grabbed her by both arms and jerked her away, revealing his brother beneath them on the couch with one of Hunter's own athamés plunged through his throat, and Tatyana's inexperienced hands clenched around the handle as her victim's blood welled up over her fingers. It was a killing blow, except it wasn't an immediate one. She could hear Braen struggling for breath, drowning in his own blood, and Hunter knew it. He saw her look down at what she had done, watching it resolutely. When Braen finally fell still and silent, she turned up glowing eyes of jade to him.

"It's over," she whispered.

Then jade disappeared as her eyes rolled back and her entire body collapsed in his hold. Hunter fell to the floor with her, trying to make himself react in those few heartbeats before she started to seize violently.

"KAIA!" He screamed the witch's name as though Armageddon had fallen upon the earth and the end of all things was imminent. Hunter realized that if anything happened to Tatyana, his world would come to a crashing end. Nothing else would matter to him.

He grabbed up her hand and held it tightly, ignoring his brother's blood smearing between their palms, as Kaia came scrambling over the floor to them. The witch laid her hands on Tatyana's thrashing head and closed her eyes, trying to focus in the madness of bodily circuitry gone wild.

They were both abruptly distracted when a series of explosions began to take place outside.

Kaia turned sharply to Hunter. "You leave her with me! Ryce needs you!"

Hunter couldn't even speak the denial, just shook his head as he looked down and saw blood leaking from Tatyana's ears.

"Hunter, listen to me. I can't heal her until you leave! Your emotions affect her too strongly. The emotions of the others in battle make it worse. The sooner you end all of this, the better her chance of surviving! You have to go!"

"Blessed Lady, Mother of all, please—" Hunter found the voice to pray at last. "Please keep her safe. Keep her with me."

Now that Kaia had put the need for him to take action into acceptable terms, Hunter all but tripped over his own feet to get away from Tatyana. He ran for the door with a war cry building in his throat and plunged himself into the pitched battle between Belladonna and Willow Covens.

Chapter Twenty-one

Tatyana opened her eyes with a light flutter of lashes, the darkness of the room startling her at first because for some reason she had expected it to be sunny. Sunny like it had been . . .

She gasped softly, recalling the offensive against Belladonna Coven. A moment of pure fear raced through her from not knowing who had prevailed; the darkness of the room was suddenly a prison. Or potentially a prison. Panicking, she jolted upright and flung out her hands. The bedding, the shadows around her, it was all just ghostly lumps that could be anything or anyone.

Until her hand touched warm, bare skin stretched over hard muscle. In an instant all of her other senses unlocked, allowing scent and sound and sensation to wash over her.

Hunter.

She knew the feel and smell of him better than she knew herself, it seemed. His mind was quiet, lost in the ether of his dreams. She ran her hands over him to assure herself that he was okay. She found small bandages over his right shoulder blade, his right forearm, and on the small of his back. The wounds indicated he'd been caught from behind at some point.

Distressed by this, but so glad he was alive and well, she leaned over and kissed his bare back.

"Thank God," she whispered, sighing with relief. So much relief that tears stung her eyes.

As if on cue, Hunter jerked awake. He turned beneath her, reaching to draw her down on to him, welcoming her hug with one of his own. He loved the way she hugged. She threw her whole body and soul into it, giving affection he had never realized he craved so much. Then again, he craved everything about her.

Tatyana was on the verge of tears as she all but throttled him with the squeeze of her arms. She wasn't a big crier, but something about him just made her speechless with the urge to do so. In this case she thought it was relief to see him safe, but she was also beginning to realize that in all cases there was something far deeper lying beneath the surface reasons. She buried her face against his strong neck, breathing him in and fighting with her emotions.

"Do you think"—she gasped softly—"would you think I am childish if I asked you if you believed in love at first sight?"

"A week ago, I would have," he confessed in a voice still roughened with sleep.

The distinction he made had her suddenly feeling like she was soaring inside. Now she was tearing up for whole new reasons.

"But not anymore?" she asked, drawing back so she could see his beautiful eyes. It was too dark to make out their brilliant color, but they were no less beautiful to her.

"No. Not now. Now I would have to say I am a powerful advocate for it." Hunter reached out and pushed a hand through her hair, inspecting her face very carefully. "How do you feel?"

"Light as a feather," she breathed, reaching for him with her mouth. She felt as though she hadn't kissed him for a lifetime. He must have felt the same because his arms drew her even tighter against his body as he made slow and heated work of their kiss. When he broke off, she thought to ask him, "Is everyone else safe? Dimitre?"

"Fine. Nothing Kaia can't heal over a few days' time. We're bursting at the seams with recovering familiars at the moment, but otherwise everything is as it was."

"Tell me what happened," she begged him. "The last thing I remember . . ."

They both realized the last thing she remembered and Hunter hushed her softly as he kissed her forehead.

"First, tell me why you did what you did," he demanded.

"Because you couldn't. To you he was always going to be a brother. I felt the war inside of you. I knew which side would win. You would have killed him because that is what you had to do in the name of good, but . . . you would have paid for it heavily in conscience. He couldn't be dismissed as just another warlock, just another source of evil. To you, it was murder. Fratricide. It was beyond good and evil. To me . . . to me it was just good and evil. Witch versus warlock. I had no such conflict. If Dimitre suddenly turned into this Darth Vader type witch, I could never kill him." She shuddered at the thought. "It was just better the way it happened."

"You've never killed anyone before. I'm just worried . . ."

"Oh, don't be," she said with a snort. "First of all, after what he did to me and so many others? It was a relief to do it. Second of all, the worrying thing is Dimitre's job. He'll get jealous, there'll be all this machismo again, next thing I know you'll be arm-wrestling and male-bonding . . ." She shuddered dramatically.

"Shut up," he chuckled, rolling over until she was lying beneath him. He dipped down to the irreverent grin on her lips, lightly kissing them closed until they both lost sight of everything except the feel of one another as lighthearted affection turned into deepening passion.

Hunter shifted his body over her, redistributing his

weight for her comfort and also to allow her the freedom to wrap her arms and legs around him, which she promptly took advantage of. He sighed against her mouth in pleasure at her grasping limbs and mobile hands as they slid over him. After a long chain of kisses that singed his skin, she cupped his face and drew him away from her so she could look at him.

Tatyana brushed her hand through those charming spikes of black hair hanging over his forehead. "Is it all over?" she asked him softly. "Really? Braen and that horrible place of evil?"

"It's all over. For now. There will always be others."

"Well, hopefully not until after I am an aunt again," she laughed softly.

"You know about that?" he asked with momentary surprise. But he was rolling his eyes even before she gave him a look. "Right. Telepath. Empath. A.k.a. big fat busybody."

"Hunter!" She pinched his side, making him jolt on top of her. She found she actually liked the feeling of his powerful body shifting hard over hers. She renewed her clinging grasp on him, ignoring his chuckling to nuzzle warm lips against his neck. She was really developing a penchant for that strong expanse of tendons, muscle, and the thriving pulse near his throat. Mainly because she always got a definitive response out of him. He hummed deeply in approval and his frame shifted with arousal as she licked his skin and skipping pulse.

"Oh man," he groaned as her legs rubbed restlessly over his, "I have never met anyone who can change gears as quickly as you do. And no, that isn't a complaint." He reached down to slip a hand under her tank, his fingers skimming her belly softly. He slowly enjoyed the warmth and texture of her skin, the smooth softness of it leading him right from one curve to the next until his nails were stroking along the underside of her breast.

Because he was lying flush along the center of her body,

Tatyana could feel the prodding growth of his erection against her. She had been dressed in loose pants and he wore his usual pajama bottoms, so it was easy to feel him through the thin materials. She slid her hands down the bare expanse of his back, minding his bandages, and eventually running slow fingers up over the flexed muscles of his backside.

"I feel like I haven't touched you in ages," she confided breathily. "I feel vacant without you inside of me."

"Ah, Tat," he sighed roughly as he rose up on the strength of a single arm so he could watch himself peel up her tank and expose her breast. Now that she was getting used to her abilities, she could easily understand the wash of emotional desire that was separate from the physical within him. She could feel his sense of worship as he caressed her and used his fingers to tug stimulation through her nipple.

She could even hear the chaotic rush of his thoughts.

So beautiful. So damn perfect. Need to taste her.

It was her only warning before his lips brushed over her areola and his tongue darted out to do just that. He tasted her in little flickers of contact at first, but it was only a minute before he was sucking her strongly into his mouth and making her squirm and moan in the process.

I'm going to taste you everywhere, his thoughts promised her. *From your pretty little nipples to that luscious pussy that tastes so sweet.*

"Oh God, yes," she groaned, "put your mouth on me."

Hunter drew back slightly to look at her passion-flushed face, realizing what she was doing and unable to help grinning. "I'll do that and more," he agreed, "but first I need you naked, angel."

She agreed and they both worked to strip her, and then him as well, before returning to their embrace. Hunter felt the gorgeous softness and warmth of her bare flesh the same way he would a miracle balm. She soothed, cured, and vitalized all at once. His heart thundered with excitement as she drew his head back down to her breasts, encouraging his appetite for her as he moved between pert, pink nipples and soft-skinned mounds. There was just something so amazing about the feel of her that he couldn't keep his hands still or his body at peace. In fact, he grew more chaotic by the minute, his thoughts following suit.

Tatyana marveled at the duality she found struggling within him. There was a tender lover, the side that needed so badly to treasure every essential he could find in her. He longed to make slow, heartbreaking love to her for hours on end, giving everything, taking only her pleasure for himself. The thought of this excited him beyond measure in so many ways.

But the second side . . . here was the wild beast. He was unwelcome in the bed of his lover, in Hunter's mind. He reserved this brute for the battlefield, relegating him to it and thinking quite firmly that this was the only place he would ever belong and be acceptable. However, the bestial side of Hunter lurked much closer than he was comfortable with whenever she stirred his passion so wildly. He mistook the beast for the viciousness inside of his brother that had caused him to do such abominable things to women.

This was when Tatyana realized Hunter feared he would always be tainted by the evil in his family. This was when she heard his awful worries that he couldn't possibly offer her any part of himself without extending the stain of evil along with it. The beast would always be a part of him, a crucial part that allowed him to be a merciless killer among his own kind. But in his mind, it would never really be acceptable for her. For their lovemaking. For the future that might one day mean bringing polluted children into her world.

Enough! she thought fiercely. She was going to nip this ridiculous predisposition theory right in the bud. Ryce had said it, and so had Hunter—no witch was born good or evil. It was a choice. Even being raised in the darkest of families, the influence of a single white witch had made the difference in Hunter's life. Wondrous good plucked out of a den of evil and set to flourish. She could easily imagine what being raised in a whole houseful of white witches would mean for Hunter's children.

Though that was all well and good, it wasn't the man of honor she needed to contend with at the moment. Right now, she needed to flirt with this so-called monster inside of him. Only by fully embracing it with her body and her soul could she prove to him that he was not his brother, and he never could be. Ironically, though, it would be Braen's actions that would show her the way. His behavior toward Odessa had been sexual, but not deviant . . . yet. He had never humiliated or devalued Odessa. Everything they had enjoyed together had been by mutual consent, although the enjoyments themselves had been perverse on many occasions. So here she would borrow from Braen to heal Hunter, something that would have infuriated the twisted warlock and satisfied Tatyana to think of it.

Tatyana pushed Hunter from her body, rolling them as one over the bed until she was poised above him. The aggressive maneuver and position stimulated that more savage side of his need, and she kissed him and licked him with aggressive sounds of pleased hunger down his breastbone and on to his belly. She had caught his hands by the wrists and held them down on the bed so he couldn't grasp her as she crawled down his body. She teased with her tongue below his navel, flicking it against the sensitive skin. She exhaled hotly against the wet saliva left behind, let her hair tickle over his tautly obvious erection before pursing her lips and blowing a stream of heated breath down the length of his thick shaft and the sac beneath. Her lips were just a half inch away from his flesh the entire time.

Then she kept sliding down away from him and climbed off the bed. She released him, turned her back on him, and left the bedroom. In the outer suite there was a fire burning and it lit the room in gold and orange. She strolled naked toward the fire, enjoying the heat on her bare skin as she ignored the furious cursing coming from the bedroom and her abandoned lover. She let her wicked smile show itself as he stormed out after her and found her bent slightly at the waist, warming her hands and displaying the charms of her backside as he approached.

"What the hell is going on?" he demanded, his attention torn between his anger and the sight of her body on full display in the firelight.

"I got cold," she said with a shrug.

"You got—? Tatyana, get your ass back in my bed right this damn second!"

Tatyana settled her hands on her waist and turned slowly to face him. She made certain he was distracted by the way she held her body before she sniffed indignantly.

"Who in hell made *you* the boss of *me*?" she demanded. "I said I am cold. I'm staying until I get warm."

She turned back and bent to warm her hands again, thrusting her backside at him again with an impertinent little waggle. That waggle sent firelight over her curves and her exposed sex, showing the gleam of liquid coating her nether lips and revealing her obvious arousal.

Hunter marched up behind her and grabbed hold of her by her hips, dragging her back against his own so his turgid flesh stroked through her saturated pussy. She gasped, grabbing for his hands as he growled, "I'll warm you up and then some."

"Hunter," she complained with a laugh even as she wiggled back over him. "Come on now, be nice."

Nice? How could he be nice when he was being drenched in her steamy juices, when he was so close to being inside of her all it would take was one quick adjustment? She wanted him to stop? To pull away?

Tatyana engineered her withdrawal herself, turning under his grasp until they were chest to chest, his cock thrust up hard between them. She reached down, encircling him with a snug fist, using the wetness coating him to stroke him with glorious smoothness. It was all he could do to keep his legs locked under him and his hands from clamping down too hard on her shoulders as he grabbed her by them.

She rubbed her face against his chest, cuddling her breasts against him again. "What is it, honey?" she asked with a sexy pout in her voice. "What can I do for you? Would you like me to get on my knees for you again? Only this time, I might not stop. I could make you come in my mouth or all over my breasts or—"

"Stop!" He bellowed the command, giving her a hard shake. Tatyana knew why. She was provoking that dark beast and Hunter heard it growling in his mind, saying *yes! yes! yes!* to all of her suggestions, wanting that pleasure so greedily and forcing Hunter into a haze of numbed reaction. His cock throbbed in her hand, oozing pre-cum over her stroking fist. Instead of obeying his command to cease, she raised the stakes.

She ran two fingers over the bulbous head of his flushed penis, wetting her fingertips thoroughly even as she stimulated the sensitive nerves there. Then she raised her fingers to her lips. She took one onto her tongue with a seductive little sucking as she gave him a look of pure jade fire from beneath her lashes. Then she switched fingers and licked the second one clean with flicking little strokes of her tongue.

"Sweet Mother," Hunter hissed as he drew her sharply against his body and crushed her mouth under his kiss. This was the first real sighting of that creature she was seeking. She felt the savagery, recognized it from those glimpses she'd had in the past, felt the fierce animalism that thundered through his mind and thoughts.

Hunter grabbed her wrist and drew her arm tightly behind her back, pulling her hand up her spine until she just started to feel pain. Just enough to thrust her breasts up high to him as he held her in his control. His free hand closed around one of them, holding it up for the bite of his teeth. The pain was negligible, the pleasure outrageous, and Tatyana's head fell back with an ecstatic moan. He kneaded her flesh, toying and sucking so hard she came up on her toes to help facilitate his actions. Her entire body squirmed against him, setting him on fire with want. Desperate, desperate hunger. All of a sudden he was starving for her. He couldn't be content until he was pumping himself inside of her. He couldn't rest until he was wearing her around his aching cock.

He suddenly grabbed her up and flung her over his shoulder. She squealed in surprise as his hand grasped her around her thigh to secure her, his fingers tickling very close to warmth and wetness. He stormed back into the bedroom and flung her down onto the bed with a hefty bounce.

"Hunter, what . . . ?"

He responded with only a burning glare from hot blue eyes before he grasped hold of her by both of her knees, pulling her legs up and apart so he could look right between them. Tatyana felt his thoughts like a raging fire. *There. Heat. Pleasure. Tightness and wetness waiting for me.* She heard him rumble out a growl of need in his mind. His large hands reached out to seize the tops of her inner thighs and he held her stretched apart, watching her body tremble in excited anticipation. He could smell her arousal. He could practically taste it. He bent to do just that, his tongue sliding right through the center of her parted labia, coating his tastebuds in her essence and feeling his entire being beginning to quake in response to it.

Just as he dipped for more, she pushed against his hands and gained freedom from his tongue. She rolled over and crawled on hands and knees away from him once again, her backside prominent and her flushed pussy pouting prettily at him.

"Where in hell are you going?" he demanded with a roar as his hand clamped down on her ankle.

She tossed back her hair, her spine curving as she looked back at him over her shoulder. "Wherever I damn well want to go," she countered. "I was thinking right here." She braced her hands and knees apart, opening herself to his view as she braced her weight on one hand and reached down the flat of her belly with the other until her fingers were sliding through her own wet flesh in full view of her overstimulated lover.

"Holy shit," Hunter rasped out in a choked prayer as he watched her long, graceful fingers seek out her clitoris with slow, teasing strokes, each one of which he felt as if she were running those fingers right up his cock. She sighed softly into the bedding right as she found her own entrance and slid a finger inside of herself, withdrawing it wetly and switching for another. Enthralled and acting on automatic, Hunter's hands reached to stroke over her backside and the backs of her thighs as his full attention was riveted on watching her take her own pleasure.

Oh, yes, baby, his thoughts ground out in rough rasps of encouragement. *Show me, angel . . . show me. Oh man, I could come just watching you do this!*

His internal litany excited the hell out of her and she found her full focus turning on to what she was doing. She moaned as her own touch sent jolts of stimulation through her nervous system. Knowing his full attention was on her was making her crazy. She almost forgot that what she was doing was supposed to be for him. In the long run, at least. Tatyana collapsed from under his hands, frustrating his need to touch her as she rolled over and slid extremely close to the edge of the bed. Close enough that her knees bracketed his hips and his cock dripped eagerly onto the pussy she was playing with.

"Enough!" he rasped aloud. "Enough teasing!"

Hunter reached out and grasped her by her arms, half lifting and half shoving her back into the center of the bed. He climbed after her, his big body caging hers as he pushed her legs apart roughly and approached her with wildness burning in his eyes. He braced a hand by her head, his breath coming in gasps now as he took hold of her leg. He was seconds shy of breaching her, of shoving himself so deep inside of her that they wouldn't be able to separate. Then he was going to fuck her out of her mind and his. Twice. No, three times. He didn't care what she said or how she might try to deny him this time; now it was his turn to take and tease and torture her until she screamed.

The sheer violence of his thoughts froze his breath and heartbeat in his chest. His entire body went stiff with shock and dismay even as the animal clawing its way free of him roared at him to continue. It demanded victory over her. She must be conquered with deep, vicious thrusts. She had begged for this, taunting him to insanity.

"No!" he gasped, suddenly trying to pull back from her, only to find himself trapped in the vise of her legs and arms. Her hips rose as her weight drew him back forward, causing his phallus to plow through the heavenly field of her waiting and wanting sex.

"Yes! Do it! Do it now! Fuck me, Hunter. Deep, and hard! Now! Please, now!"

Hunter felt himself go completely blind and deaf to everything but the savage inside of himself. Suddenly he was there, shoving himself into her with no warning and no gentleness. He stuffed himself deep, but it wasn't enough so he slammed harder and deeper into her, all the while sobbing out rasps of, "I'm sorry. I'm sorry! I'm so sorry!"

The apology stopped with a wild masculine sound of furious pleasure. He thrust himself into her as though he were drilling for deep oil. She was crying out, the sound skipping over his senses and slowly making him realize that it was bliss bursting from her lips. Now suddenly he had to come. Right that instant, no waiting. He couldn't bear not coming inside of her a second longer. The bed protested his violence with her body in loud creaks of wood and springs, but she begged for more in a lusty voice of pure sex and need.

Hunter's climax skipped all warning stages and burst out of him with wild abandon. He roared with ecstasy, never stopping his brutal rhythm into her once, his hands gripping the sheets, puncturing holes in them. He didn't stop. He couldn't. He knew he wasn't through with her and wouldn't be for a long while yet. He thrust through the wet river of his own semen inside of her, glorying in the sensation. It just seemed to incite the predator inside of him all the more.

Tatyana found herself abruptly on her belly, a massive male body following her down and taking her hard and fast from behind. She lost all control of herself, her body bursting into spasm and a ripping orgasm that was teased higher and higher by the rough fingers that sought her clit out from between her body and the bed. She had asked for this, and the conqueror was in complete control. He made her come, but he did it almost purely for his own pleasure . . . or so he thought. He grunted with satisfaction as she squeezed around him in a fist of blissful muscles. Then he braced his hands and drove into her again and again until she burst like thousands of bubbles.

The truth was, even though he threw back his head and greedily basked in the sensations burning in and out of his body, it wasn't all about physical satisfaction. He wouldn't feel half so good if he hadn't been fulfilling his inner desire to fulfill hers. But now, with both halves of his self merged and set free inside of her thrust by wicked thrust, he was learning the awesome chasm of difference between himself and his brother. If at any time she had cried out with genuine pain, hurt, or denial, he would have heeded it. She believed that. Because as bad as this beast was, it came attached to the man of deep conscience. She even tested the theory.

"Ow!"

The shout of pain made Hunter freeze. Tatyana reached back and pushed at him and he backed up onto his knees as she rolled over.

"Angel, what—?"

"Charley horse," she giggled, hooking an ankle up on his shoulder and beckoning him back to her body with eager fingers and a caress over her breast. "Don't stop now, honey. You are on a hot streak."

Hunter grabbed her ankle and grinned, dropping her knee into the crook of his elbow instead. At her raised brow he said, "It's better for your leg."

"So long as you don't lose that amazing intensity, I don't care if you put my ankles behind my ears."

"We'll try that later, after the charley horse eases." Hunter moved over her and into her once again, making her gasp and moan with lusty relief. He joined her, the urgent need to ride her coming over him as if he had never been interrupted. Except this time, his thrusts were deep and determined, a slower more focused cadence that made her go utterly mindless with reaction. Her back arched, her body reaching to meet his, and Hunter felt his entire spine rushing with heat as the visual stimulus of her reactions to him burned through him.

"Oh baby, you are on fire," he gasped as he reached for her mouth with blind need for her taste. "I feel you burning around me. Like wet flames . . ."

Tatyana clutched at his sweating skin, her fingers sliding to and fro over him in time with the surges of his body. "I'm ready to come again," she moaned, "I need you . . . wild and hard. I need you and your beast, Hunter."

Hunter nodded, but he would have agreed to anything at that point. He took her instruction to heart, however. His mouth dropped to her breast and his teeth plucked roughly at her. He shifted so his every inward thrust ran over her widely exposed clit for a good minute before finally hitting into her so hard that the smack of their flesh echoed into the room.

"Oh God," she moaned in a high-pitched warning.

"You need to say something to me," he ground out between panting breaths. "Or I'm going to stop."

"What?! No! Oh God, don't stop!"

Hunter grinned evilly as he caught up her other leg, lifting her ass up off the bed and realigning himself into her. He rode her until she started gasping out chains of pleasured noises, obviously coming on a quick crest. Then he stopped, dead still inside of her, fighting for breath as she keened out in dismay. He was burning with the desire to ejaculate, his own release right on the brink of going beyond his control. It was her enthusiasm and vocal cries of ecstasy that did it to him.

"You've been in my mind all of this time, haven't you?" he asked, shaking sweat out of his eyes as he punctuated the query by sawing into her like a bow drifting over the strings on a violin, creating perfect notes.

"Yes!" she cried, her head jerking back restlessly.

"Then tell me what this is all about. What are you doing?" he demanded of her.

"Make me come first," she begged him, "and then I'll tell you how much I love you. Please! Later!"

Hunter had never loved a woman before. Nor had he come even close to it. So, he had never really experienced why people thought that feelings of love were among the most powerful psychological aphrodisiacs around. Not until her declaration clicked over every pleasure neuron housed in his body. Only his roaring realization of how lost his heart was to her kept him from ruining her brimming release. He would barely remember what happened next, except to say it was the closest he had ever come to blacking out from an orgasm. He had lousy rhythm, gritted his teeth through the whole thing, and saw black blobs floating before his eyes as he came into her.

Tatyana didn't need much finesse in any event. She felt his recognition of his feelings for her racing through his mind and felt how it lit the fuse of his release. The knowledge allowed just the act of him pressing inside of her to pour himself out to ignite her body. She lit up like a blazing marquee, dazzling and announcing its news to all comers. She was in love, and he was, too.

Hunter released her aching legs and gathered her up

against his slick body, hugging her tightly as he maneuvered them into comfort onto the pillows and under a sheet and comforter.

"I'm anticipating the cooldown after heat like that," he said, still breathing and speaking raggedly. "We'll be freezing our asses off in another sixty seconds."

"And he's thoughtful, too. Will miracles never cease?"

"I was just thinking the same thing about you," he said as he reached to kiss her against her temple. "Am I going to find out what's wrong with you someday soon? You have your head on eerily straight for someone so young. Where's the downside?"

"Hmm. Where's your optimism?" she countered. "I do have that temper, though," she reminded him. "And I'm stubborn. I can be sneaky. Willful. Domineering. Oh, and . . . I get horrible PMS."

"Good to know," he said. "So, which of those thought it would be fun to flirt with something really damn dangerous just now?" He frowned as he thought about it a little more now that he was calmer. "You don't understand . . ."

"I understand better than anyone. When you seal off this room to protect my mind, that leaves only my head and yours open for occupation and random or specific eavesdropping. I've gotten to know you pretty well recently. I definitely know how your mind works. Frankly, I'm shocked that you would mistake any part of yourself as being like your brother. I don't care about all that genetics crap and the history of your blood relations," she said before he could argue, waving his objections off with an impatient hand. "And I want you to know I'm highly insulted that you think my children will turn out to be little monsters. Especially in this kind of environment. It's an insult to me and to your kids to expect bad things from them without ever giving them a chance. Children can sense those things. How do you think they will feel if they realize their father expects them to be perverse and evil right out of the gate?"

"I think it's ridiculous to dismiss ten generations of warlocks, as well," he retorted sharply. "If you get careless they will give in to that darkness they could be born with."

"Oh. You mean like you just did? You lost yourself to that side of yourself, yet I'm still here to tell the tale. And it's a really cool story, if you ask me. But I'm post-orgasmic, so I could be biased."

Hunter sat up suddenly over her, looking down on her with a dark frown. "This isn't a joke," he said gravely. "What you did was dangerous. Don't you get it? There's a killer inside of me."

"Don't you get it," she shot back, "there's one inside of me, too! Or did you forget who killed your bastard of a brother?"

"I take joy in what I do, damn it!" he barked sharply. "I just took pleasure in treating you like . . . like . . ."

"Please!" she scoffed. "You couldn't treat me like your brother did if you tried! You haven't got the capacity to be that sick and twisted! A rough lover doesn't make a rapist, Hunter. And exactly what part of all of that made you think I wasn't enjoying myself? The screams of pleasure? The begging for more? Maybe it was the ripping orgasms."

She punctuated her sarcasm with a popping slap on his shoulder, making him smirk in spite of himself.

"Was that supposed to hurt?" he asked.

"No. It's supposed to . . . oh, shut up. Jeez. The worst thing I have to fear from you is your obnoxious maleness, and frankly, growing up with seven brothers, you don't scare me one damn bit."

"I can see that." He chuckled softly, reaching to brush back her hair. "I just don't want to hurt you."

"Well, I'm sorry to say it's bound to happen. Look at Dimitre and Annali. They just had a really painful misunderstanding, but they got through it. They survived. I want to believe that you and I are more than strong enough to survive, too. I love you so much already, Hunter, after only so little time. All I can think of is how much I will come to love you if we have a lifetime together. But you have to trust not only me, but yourself. This isn't ten years ago. You know what you are and aren't responsible for. What you are and are not capable of. Yes, you made mistakes, but they are human errors, and they are forgivable. If they weren't, do you think the people in this house would ever have craved your return as much as they did? Is it really that hard to accept that people love you—mistakes, genetics, assassin, and all?"

Hunter knew she was right. There was no longer any reason to doubt how this household felt about him. Even Asher had come to forgive him enough to entrust him with a visit from his sister Amber. Amber herself had never blamed him as much as he had blamed himself. He was hard on himself for good reasons, he thought. Not because he enjoyed self-flagellation, but because it was so important to himself to keep on the proper path. He never wanted to see within himself the evil he saw in his brothers.

"You don't have the capacity, Hunter. You never did," she said vehemently, reaching to wind her arms around his neck and pulling him down to her warm body and warmer kiss. "You take joy in your killing because you know you've just saved the lives of untold numbers of innocent people. You know you are freeing captive familiars. You take joy because you know what you are doing is good and it thrills you! And you think I wouldn't want a man like that to be the father and guide for my children?" She kissed him again, making his heart race with that same joy he felt after a victory as Sentinel.

He drew back, looking down into her jade eyes as they blazed with love and faith in him.

"Did I tell you that I love you?" he asked softly.

"Not in so many words . . . out loud," she said with a light laugh.

"Did I tell you I've never been in love before, Tatyana?"

The seriousness of his tone and statement made a visible impact on her. She could only swallow audibly and shake her head. "I figure," he said softly, "I was just waiting for you to wake that up inside of me, just like you were waiting for me to wake your magic inside of you. I'd say that's a hell of a trade."

"I'll let you know if I agree, after the brain hemorrhaging stops."

"It will. You've already gotten stronger; you just didn't notice it yet. You are going to be a hell of a witch one day, angel."

"I hope to be. I'm glad I'll have you to guide and teach me. I trust you. Not just with me, but with my brother's life, too. With the life of my future niece or nephew. With the lives of our future children, as well as the raising of them."

Hunter exhaled, slow and steady, staring down at her. "I am going to marry you and be the father of our babies one day," he both warned and promised her. "I'll be happy to give us time to learn each other even better, but that is always going to be my goal."

"I promise you," she said with a teary laugh, "I have no problem with that idea at all!"

Epilogue

"Did he get down on one knee and everything?"

"Of course," she laughed. "And he looked very handsome doing it, too. I could barely speak."

Asher grinned and tucked a hand behind his head, shifting in his infirmary bed with only a little discomfort, a marked improvement from a week earlier. "That must have been rough on him. He's very private and hates to draw attention to himself."

Annali snorted at that. "Usually, but this time he wanted to enlist every human being in a ten-mile radius to help him. I swear, there wasn't a soul in that restaurant who wasn't aware of what was going to happen . . . except for me! I didn't know whether to hit him or hug him, I was so flustered!"

"Well, I'm glad you got over that enough to say yes," he chuckled, reaching to squeeze the fingers of her left hand, making the new diamond on it sparkle with fabulous brilliance. Asher's smile faded a little, his brown eyes turning a bit more serious. "How's our Grace doing? Any improvement?"

"It's going to take time. A lot of time. Gracie never pictured herself being a victim before. She's always been a survivor, always struggled and fought tooth and nail, but she never experienced a defeat like this. She doesn't know yet that it wasn't her fault or failure that made it happen. She won't accept help or even affection from anyone . . . except for Hunter. All of my hope for Grace lies with Hunter." Annali smiled with a little flash of recollection. "He saved me physically the night he destroyed Evan, but during the year afterward, he was the one who truly saved my mind and my soul. Ryce too, of course, but Hunter . . . well, it's hard to explain."

"No, hon, I was there. I saw it from the outside. It's not the same, I know, but I saw what he did for you. I'm glad he's here for her. For all of us."

"Including you?" she asked.

"Yes." He looked at her sheepishly. "I've come to regret a lot of what happened after Amber died. Mostly thanks to Amber herself. She refused to come to me for two years, did you know that?"

"No! I didn't! You always said that Amber blamed Hunter for her death and told you so every night. You even said it to Hunter before he left. Asher! What a terrible thing for you to do! He believed you!"

"That's probably why I did it," he said regretfully. "I knew he would. I was so angry back then and I felt so victorious when he left. Until I realized Amber was furious with me for doing it. Even then, it took me two years before I started having even a single regret about my behavior. It wasn't until she felt that break in my anger that she finally came to me. It took a long time before I truly understood everything clearly, but Hunter had been gone for six years or more by then."

"But you started searching for him," Annali said.

"Yeah, but he was way off the grid. No credit, no banks. No medical records. No coven that I could find. I even asked Ryce to call him home, but he refused."

"He had made a promise. But it was good you did. It let Ryce know you were ready. Ryce couldn't have made that scry for Hunter any sooner or any later than he did. It was meant to be this way. Without knowing Dimitre as we all did, we wouldn't have acted so definitively to bring Tatyana over. Besides, Hunter has found something very precious in her that I don't think he ever expected to deserve in his life."

"A sentiment I'm partly to blame for, I'm afraid."

"Perhaps. But in the end even Hunter realized you were not the interpreter of what really happened that day. Only he could realize the truth of it and come to accept it based on fact and not emotional blackmail."

"Yeah. We had a pretty long talk about it when I first woke up from this."

"I heard you called him to you. I figured this was what would be discussed." She squeezed his hand in return. "I'm glad there is an understanding between you two now."

"I told him I was sorry for what happened to Tatyana. It was like a nightmare, Annie. I was watching myself, feeling my body respond to something that absolutely horrified my soul, and there wasn't a thing I could do about it. When Hunter literally showed up in the nick of time, I swear I wanted to kiss him."

Annali nodded. "I'm sure you did. But even if he hadn't, what happened wouldn't have been your fault. No more than it was Gracie's. You were a victim, too, don't forget. He held you prisoner for nearly five days."

"Yeah, well, he only beat the hell out of me the first day. Then sent a couple of Healers to fix me up when I guess he realized I could be useful. He messed with my head a lot. Did a few other things," he said dismissively. "Nothing I can't handle. Luckily the spell took up two days and no one could come near me while it was being cast. So actually, he didn't have much time to screw around with me."

"I know his type," she said grimly. "It only takes a few hours for them to screw around with you." She studied his expression carefully as she said, "We have an empath in this house now. A wild-card Mentalist whose powers aren't under her control. If you are hiding anything, Asher McBride, she might find it."

"She might. And she might not," he said with a dismissive shrug. "Look, the worst of it was in that room upstairs. I am so glad she doesn't see me as her attacker. I couldn't bear her looking at me and thinking . . . thinking of me doing that to her. Especially now she's coming to live with us. And facing Dimitre would have been a nightmare."

"Well, making like Greg Louganis out of the window has earned you everyone's forgiveness. We all know it wasn't really you. The blame and anger were focused solely on Braen, and he is dead now."

"How are all those familiars doing? Ryce said there were over two dozen."

"Two dozen salvageable. There were more that were . . . beyond repair. Ryce has placed them in institutions. There's nothing else we can do for them. Modern medicine and therapies might help, but . . . well, we know better, I guess."

"Yeah, we do." Asher reached up to touch her face when she turned it down to hide her emotion. "But twenty-four souls saved is a powerful number."

"Barely saved," she edited him. "We have our work cut out for us trying to heal this group. Oddly enough, Tatyana has been a big help. She also suggested it might be good therapy to get Grace involved. I don't think she realizes it, but there's a bit of a psychologist inside of that girl. She sees things and understands egos very well."

"Good. She'll need it if she's hooked up with Hunter."

"Ash," she scolded with a laugh. "Oh! Did you get to thank Amber for me?" As she said it, her hand rested instinctively over her lower belly. "If Dimitre hadn't told me I was pregnant, I would have pitched a fit and demanded I go with them to Pennsylvania. It was a horrible fight, I'm told. Everyone came back injured. I shudder to imagine . . ." And she did exactly that, her slender frame shaking sharply with her thoughts.

"I did thank her. She's tickled to death for you, you know."

"So am I," she said, her eyes lit with pleasure. "I never would have guessed my entire life could change so quickly."

"I never would have guessed you wouldn't use a condom," he snickered.

"Oh, hush!" She scolded him with a swat as she blushed a deep scarlet. "I know it sounds terrible, but Dimitre said that, for the first time in his life, it never once occurred to him. He's completely baffled and still trying to figure it out. I think . . . well, I suppose I think that the Goddess works in very intriguing ways."

"Hon, that is the most enormous understatement of the year." Asher grinned. "But I want to know if She's ever going to work something my way. Oh! Or better yet, my vote is for Ryce. I would love to see him fall apart over a woman."

"Not bloody likely," Ryce spoke up from the doorway of the infirmary. "I've got my hands full enough with this household stuffed with untried witches. I think adding Dimitre and Tatyana to our coven is enough for one year. I'll stick with my little Latina from town who only wants me for my body."

"Men!" Annali huffed.

"This is what happens when you get too much testosterone gathered together in one place," Tatyana announced as she marched into the room. "Greetings, witchlings. I come bearing good tidings." She nudged Ryce out of her way and brought Kaia forward. "Or good Kaia, in this case."

"This infirmary isn't big enough for the traffic flow in here ever since you woke up, Asher McBride," Kaia announced. "So I'm kicking you out."

"Yes!" Asher shouted.

"But it's bed rest for you still," Kaia stipulated.

"Yes, but it will be my bed, in my room. Unless you've given it away to some foundling witch, Ryce?"

"No. All of the familiars are housed above the pool in the servants' quarters. Your rooms are novice free. Kaia's been stretched thin, though, so we're all on our own for healing. Except for Annali's endless supply of healing teas," he stipulated. "I've got two dozen witches who swear by it."

"Two dozen rather talented witches," Tatyana remarked. "They all seem eager to use their new talents helping out around the house."

"I did the same thing," Annali remarked. "For me, it was the gardens. But since it's so cold out, they are forced to express themselves indoors."

"Not necessarily. Hunter has at least three of them out riding as we speak. I think he is trying to console himself after learning the horrifying news that his city girl has never been near a live horse in her life, never mind knowing how to ride one."

Ryce groaned as if he were in pain when Tatyana said that, and she pointed to him and said, "See! That's the exact reaction he had. 'Cept, he went a bit paler."

"That's because Hunter has an actual tan. Ryce is that lovely British white," Asher teased.

"You know, I've gotten nothing but abuse since I arrived. I think I'm going to take my leave before it gets much worse." Ryce waved and left despite their group protest.

The High Priest of Willow Coven walked down the hall with a grin toying at his lips. He was incredibly happy. Not only was his family finally back together, but it was growing. At the moment, exponentially. However, the new witches would leave within a few months to make their own way in the world. Some would succeed, some would fail, and he could already see that some would end up facing white justice one day. Still, every last one of them deserved a chance, and if there were ever a time where he could influence that outcome, it would be while he had them within his coven, surrounded by the mature witches he was so proud of.

What gave him the most joy? Annali. Annali and Dimitre's impending offspring. The birth of their baby was a dream come true for him. The first of a new generation born to his family of witches.

He couldn't possibly want anything more.

If you loved HUNTER,
then keep reading for a preview of

DANGEROUS
by Jacquelyn Frank!

"You could get any number of people to guard you," he said at last, studying her stoic features very carefully. "There are some fine firms out there. Why did you pick NHK in specific, Ms. Candler?"

"Devon," she persisted gently. Then more directly, "I prefer your . . . umm . . . style."

"And what style is that?" Liam asked, a thrill of anticipation shooting down the back of his neck as he realized there was potentially a lot more going on here than the average babysitting job.

Devon stopped and looked at him. She suddenly kneeled before him in a graceful sweep of silk, her knees settling between the toes of his boots and her hands resting lightly on his knees. Their eyes locked with an instant sense of intimacy, and he held himself very still as he tried to decide how to react.

"You dislike my being this close. It makes you uncomfortable. If I close the distance, the discomfort increases . . ." She demonstrated her point by sliding her hands up his thighs and leaning her body toward his.

For Liam, it was as if he'd forgotten how to breathe. Or move. It was as good as having her kneeling naked in front of him, an image he had no trouble conjuring in his active mind. She'd been hot-wiring his senses from the minute she'd entered the room, and now she was about to drive the car right off the showroom floor. He felt her ribs sliding against his inner thighs, the soft weight of her breasts a torturous brush over the material of his blacks. Devon's scent flooded up and over him with a hint of orange citrus and some unidentifiable spice that blended so deliciously with the smell of warm, sexual woman. On the back of that scent came heat. It was a body warmth that, as she leaned even closer, penetrated in fast furious waves over his thighs, groin, and belly; methodically seeking its way up his chest. Completely out of his control, Nash's body responded to her lure, hot blood pulsing low into his hips until he was hardening in answer.

Discomfited, Liam reacted by dropping the folder on the floor and grabbing her shoulders tightly.

"Defense," she said quickly to make her meaning. "You've stopped me from doing what you don't want me to do. But this is basic physics. You have to continually expend effort to keep me where I am. The threat stays, your energy is uselessly spent keeping me constantly at bay, and this doesn't change. Not until one day when you weaken, or when you aren't paying attention . . ." She marked her line of reasoning by sliding her unimpeded hands all the way up the insides of his thighs until her fingertips flirted just shy of discovering her effect on him. "One day something gets by you and you're victimized. There's only one thing you can do to stop it. Only one thing, or you must face the inevitable." Her hands twitched and he felt the brush of stroking fingers along the rigid length of his fly.

Liam exploded off the couch, hauling her up and shoving her backward. All he wanted in that instant was to get her as far away from him as he could reasonably manage before . . . well, *before.* He wasn't expecting her to stumble back awkwardly, landing hard on her bottom on the floor.

"Are you out of your goddamn mind?" he bellowed as he marched to tower over her, knowing that at his height and in the peak of fury he was beyond imposing. He told himself he didn't give a damn, as his hands rolled into mighty fists. He fought not only his temper but an agonizing pulse of blatant sexual arousal. *What in hell was she thinking?*

"Offense," she gasped out, her expression folding into a taut tension. "Don't you see?" she panted softly. "Offense is the only true defense, otherwise you'll always be fighting to protect yourself."